SWORD

of

APOLLO

SWORD

— of —

APOLLO

Book III of the Warrior Trilogy

NOBLE SMITH

WITHDRAWN

Thomas Dunne Books ⚏ St. Martin's Press New York

THOMAS DUNNE BOOKS.
An imprint of St. Martin's Press.

SWORD OF APOLLO. Copyright © 2015 by Noble Smith. All rights reserved. Printed in the United States of America. For information, address St. Martin's Press, 175 Fifth Avenue, New York, N.Y. 10010.

www.thomasdunnebooks.com
www.stmartins.com

Maps by Cameron MacLeod Jones

Library of Congress Cataloging-in-Publication Data

Smith, Noble Mason, 1968–
    Sword of Apollo : a novel / Noble Smith. — First edition.
        p. cm.
    ISBN 978-1-250-02559-3 (hardcover)
    ISBN 978-1-250-02644-6 (e-book)
1. Soldiers—Fiction.   2. Sparta (Extinct city)—Fiction.   3. Athens (Greece)—Fiction.   I. Title.
    PS3569.M537837S96   2015
    813'.54—dc23

                                                          2015017125

Our books may be purchased in bulk for promotional, educational, or business use. Please contact your local bookseller or the Macmillan Corporate and Premium Sales Department at (800) 221-7945, extension 5442, or by e-mail at MacmillanSpecialMarkets@macmillan.com.

First Edition: December 2015

10 9 8 7 6 5 4 3 2 1

For my uncles: Robert Barton Smith and Richard Noble Smith

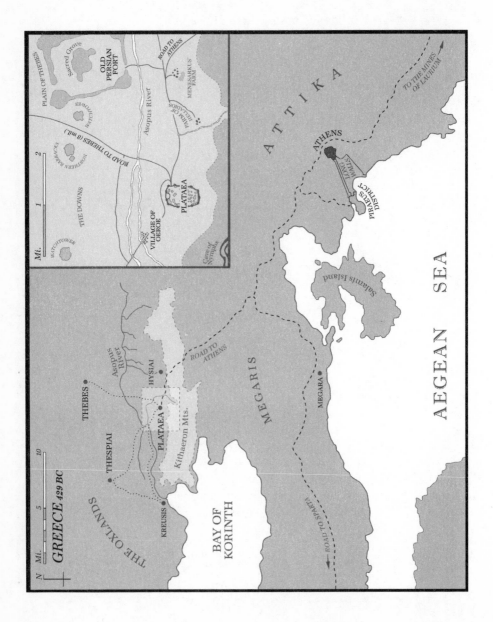

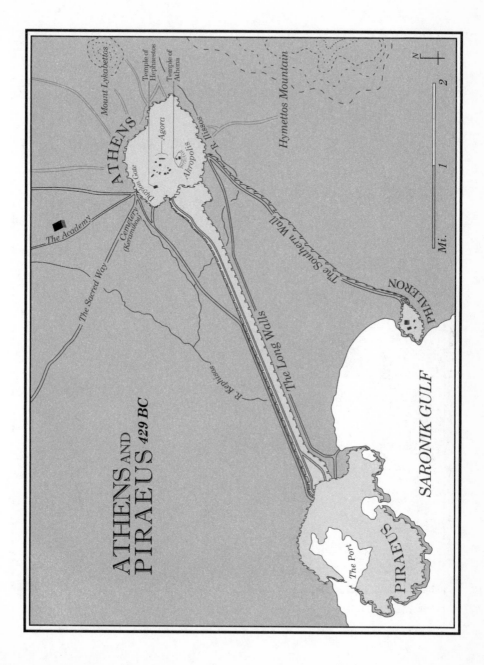

ATHENS AND
PIRAEUS 429 BC

ATHENS

Mount Lykabettos

Temple of
Hephaestos

Temple of
Athena

Agora

Akropolis

R. Ilissos

Hymettos Mountain

Dipylon Gate

Cemetery
(Keramikos)

The Academy

The Sacred Way

R. Kephisos

The Long Walls

The Southern Wall

PHALERON

SARONIK GULF

PIRAEUS

The Port

N

Mi.   1   2

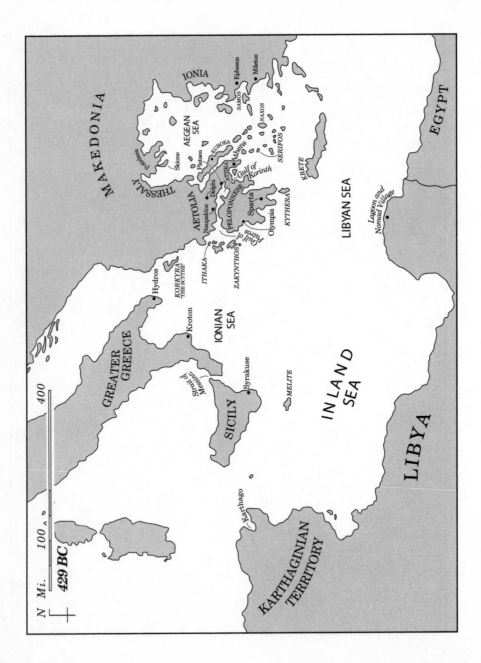

N Mi.

100

400

429 BC

MAKEDONIA

THESSALY

IONIA

AEGEAN SEA

SAMOS

NAXOS

SERIFOS

Ephesus

Miletus

EUBOEA

Athens

ATTIKA

Gulf of Korinth

Plataea

Skione

Poteidaia

AETOLIA

Naupaktos

Delphi

PELOPONNESE

Sparta

Olympia

Gulf of Patras

KYTHERA

KRETE

LIBYAN SEA

Lagoon and Nomad Village

EGYPT

KORKYRA
"THE SCYTHE"

Hydros

ITHAKA

ZAKYNTHOS

GREATER GREECE

Kroton

IONIAN SEA

MELITE

INLAND SEA

SICILY

Strait of Messina

Syrakuse

Karthago

KARTHAGINIAN TERRITORY

LIBYA

To carry on, trusting in what hope he has—*that* is courage in a man.

—Euripides of Athens

PART I

———— ◆ ————

"The failed sneak attack on the city-state of Plataea was like a lightning strike that kindles a raging fire on a parched mountainside. The great war between Athens and Sparta had begun. The Spartans invaded Attika, and the Athenians hid behind their high-walled citadel, refusing to meet the enemy on land in the field of battle, content to control the seas with their vast fleet of ships. For two and a half years the Spartan hoplites and their allies ravaged the Athenian territory, burning homes, cutting vines, trampling crops. During that time they left Plataea and the Oxlands alone. But then, quite suddenly, the enemy's policy changed. Once again the servants of the dual kings of Sparta turned their rapacious eyes toward the rich plains of the Oxlands, and the proud citadel that had brazenly defied them. . . ."

—Papyrus fragment from the "Lost History" of
the Peloponnesian War by the "Exiled Scribe"

The Oxlands. Month of Damatrios
(September), 429 BC.

ONE

———◆———

An angry bull and a fearless young man faced each other with their eyes locked.

They stood on a treeless hill under the noonday sun, a gentle wind whispering through the dried thistles and tall brown grasses. The bull's tail swished menacingly against its muscled haunches, swatting the flies dancing on its hide. It snorted violently through gaping nostrils: a fierce sound that resonated from deep inside its great head—a warning to stay away. The beast was enormous. The biggest in the Oxlands. The biggest anybody had ever known.

But the young man didn't flinch. He stared unblinkingly at the bull, keeping his sturdy legs planted. His name was Nikias of Plataea, and he had trained since childhood in the fighting technique called the pankration—a skill that taught a warrior to stay alive in the savage press of a phalanx battle. His brutal training had made him strong and agile.

But most of all it had made him brave.

He continued to stand his ground, even though he knew the beast carried ten times his weight. Even though the bull had gored five men to death in its ten-year-reign as King of the Bulls.

"Steady," Nikias whispered, cocking his head slowly to the left. He'd suffered a terrible beating some time ago that had broken his nose and an eye socket. The wounds had healed, but his features on the left side were slightly misshapen—as though a skilled sculptor had carved a handsome face on one half of a marble head before handing the chisel and hammer to an untrained apprentice to finish the work. His nose, once straight and proud, was now crooked, and the eye on the left side was set in a perpetual squint.

The bull let forth an indignant bellow and Nikias repeated his command—"Steady." He ignored the stinging sweat dripping down his forehead and into his eyes. He lowered his rugged face and gritted his teeth. He would not back down. "Zeus Olympian," he prayed under his breath, "watch over me now . . ."

The bull snorted and took a threatening step forward. And still Nikias did not flinch.

"Young master," came a boy's nervous voice from the other side of the hill—from behind the bull. "What should I do?"

Keeping his gaze fixed on the bull's bulging and red-veined eyes, Nikias replied in a calm but carrying voice, "Bring her, Mula! Quick!"

The bull rumbled in its throat and pawed the ground—its flanks rippling as it tensed for the charge. Nikias fought the urge to run like a hare. He could almost feel the horns spearing through his guts, spilling his life into the dust.

"Mula?" he called out with mounting urgency. "I said *now*!"

There came the dull ringing of a cowbell and the bull snapped its head toward the sound with a frightening speed for such a massive creature, letting forth an excited bray.

The woolly pated head of a twelve-year-old lad appeared over the rise. He clambered up the hill, pulling hard on a rope that was attached to a sleek white cow straining to be free, the bronze bell on the animal's neck clanging with every step.

The bull reacted as though it had been struck by a god's magic. It glanced at Nikias one last time, let forth a prodigious sneeze, and then sauntered over to the cow. Before the gangly boy and the cow had even come to a stop on the top of the hill, the bull mounted the cow, plunging into it with awkward abandon.

Nikias wiped away the sweat dripping into his eyes and let forth a sigh. That had been close.

"What should I do?" asked Mula, cringing as the ravished cow mooed loudly in his ear.

"We let Asterion have his way for a while," said Nikias with a grin, and took the rope from Mula's hand.

Asterion the bull had bolted from his pen at their farm in the middle of the night. And it had taken Nikias and Mula several hours to track the bull down across the rolling grasslands of the Oxlands—the lazy cow in tow. The sleek female, Nikias had learned over the years, was the only way of luring the wandering bull back to the farm. Once the bull had planted his seed, he would become as docile as a tamed dog, at least for a while, and follow them home, clinging to the cow's side and nuzzling her like a drunken lover.

But they were four miles from their farm and close to enemy Theban territory. And Nikias had left in such a rush that he'd forgotten to bring his Sargatian lasso: a whip that Mula's father—a man skillful with leatherwork—had woven for him from the whole skin of an ox. It was a vicious weapon that could rip the flesh from a man's bones, but it was useless against Asterion. The slightest tap from a leather thong on the bull's rump sent the animal into the murderous rage of the Minotaur. But the whip was quite useful against the hides of Thebans.

"We should go," said Mula nervously.

Nikias made a low sound in his throat that meant, "Stop pestering."

The hill on which they stood was in the no-man's-land between Plataea and Thebes, near the hallowed site of the final battle of the Persian Wars where, fifty years ago, the allied Greek forces had crushed half a million Persians and a small contingent from Thebes. The Thebans had been the only Greek city-state to offer earth and water to each of the two Persian kings who had tried—and failed—to conquer Greece. Hundreds of thousands of Persians had perished here . . . the ground was still littered with their sun-bleached bones. And Nikias's grandfather Menesarkus, only sixteen at the time, had won renown as a hero of that famous battle, leading the first charge alongside the Spartan allies against the vast earthen stronghold called the Persian Fort. There he had captured Mula's father, Saeed, who had been a groom for a ruthless Persian lord. After the war Menesarkus had gone on to become a famous Olympic pankrator and then a respected general, and Mula's father had served Nikias's family faithfully all those years. Now Menesarkus was the Arkon of Plataea—the elected leader of their independent city-state.

And Nikias's grandfather loved Asterion like a favorite dog.

"We're a couple of fat geese sitting on a log," muttered Mula.

Nikias didn't respond even though he knew the boy was right. This was not a safe place. And the bull was making a din that would wake the dead. It pumped wildly, bellowing with each thrust, as long trails of saliva dripped from its maw.

"Patience," said Nikias. "He's almost done."

Nikias peered north toward Thebes, but the rolling hills and trees hid the enemy's walls. He turned and looked in the opposite direction, scanning the gently sloping foothills of the Kithaeron Mountains to where his family's farm stood near an ancient olive grove surrounded by vineyards. All that he could make out was a thread-thin stream of smoke wafting from the chimney of the house. His pregnant wife, Kallisto, and their twin girls were there now, and he pictured the three of them in the kitchen—Kallisto at her loom and the girls crawling at her feet, playing with the weights tied to the ends of the dangling yarn.

The house had been burned to the ground two and a half years earlier when the Thebans launched a sneak attack on his farm as well as the citadel of Plataea—an attack in which Nikias's mother and most of his friends were slaughtered. But the Plataeans in the countryside rallied their forces and came to the aid of their brethren trapped in the city, defeating the enemy in a great battle at the gates of Plataea, where Nikias helped lead the forces to victory. Two weeks later the Plataeans went on to trounce a small army of Spartans—allies of the Thebans—who'd come to the Oxlands hard on the heels of the Theban attack. Five hundred full-blooded Spartans were captured where they'd made camp at the old Persian Fort.

Years ago, in the wars against the barbarian invaders, the Spartans had been allies of Plataea and Athens. But over the decades enmity had grown between the Athenians and Spartans—the two great powers of Greece. They were like a pair of wolves fighting over the carcass of a deer, each with sharp teeth clenched into the hide of the prize, neither one willing to unlock its bloody jaws. The Athenians were the masters of the seas and controlled the islands, keeping their army safe behind the walls of their vast citadel. But even though the Spartans lacked a powerful navy, they were a dominant force on land, and no Greek army dared to meet them in pitched battle.

But the small Spartan expeditionary force that had ventured into Plataean territory two and a half years ago had been filled with hubris. They did not expect the Plataeans to venture from their high-walled citadel and launch a bold attack on the Spartan encampment, and the enemy was surprised and overwhelmed.

Nikias had not taken part in the defeat of those Spartans, however. He'd been recovering from wounds he'd suffered at the hands of a Theban spy named Eurymakus, a man who'd captured Nikias on his way back from a foolhardy journey to Athens to hire mercenaries. A man who had tortured him to the threshold of death. . . .

He glanced down at his right hand—a hand with only four fingers. The littlest one, his signet ring finger, had been cut off where it had joined to the hand so that his signet and the bloody finger could be delivered to his grandfather to let him know that his heir had been taken prisoner. The skin at the nub of the severed digit was still pink and tender. He wondered if it would ever heal.

Eurymakus had broken Nikias back then—hung him by his ankles from the rafters of a dark undercroft like a piece of meat in a butcher's shop. The enemy had wrecked his body and toyed with his mind . . . hollowed him out like an ox horn that's been carved clean of its pith. And then the Theban had handed him over to the Spartans, who had in turn exchanged Nikias for a Spartan of royal blood. That warrior, though a few years older than Nikias, was his look-alike. And for good reason. He and Prince Arkilokus were first cousins—grandsons of Menesarkus of Plataea, who had traveled to Sparta after the Persian defeat as a guest-friend of the royal family. While there the young Plataean hero had been unwittingly selected for the Spartan "wise breeding" program—seduced by a female royal who harvested his champion's seed. . . .

"Young master?" asked Mula, shaking his arm. "Shouldn't we go?"

"Do you want to try and pull Asterion away from his task?"

"No, but—"

"Then shut up, little brother," said Nikias, and slapped Mula on the back.

Mula frowned and dropped his head submissively.

Nikias's gaze traveled up the forested mountainside of the Kithaerons to the peak where the ridgeline resembled the withers of a swaybacked horse. That was where the Cave of Nymphs lay—the place where he and Kallisto had first made love. His eyes passed down to the citadel of Plataea at the foot of the mountain. The city's mighty twenty-foot-high walls, interspersed with square guard towers every hundred and fifty feet, stood like a stout armored hoplite waiting for battle.

The Thebans had not breached those walls on the night of the sneak attack. Instead the gates had been opened by one of its own citizens—the traitor Nauklydes, a Plataean magistrate who had been bought by the spy Eurymakus . . . bought with Persian gold. Nauklydes had forged a secret alliance with the Thebans and Spartans. But they had been defeated, and Nauklydes had been tried and convicted of treason and given the dreaded tunic of stones as his punishment—buried up to his chest in the marketplace and stoned to death by the citizens he had tried to destroy. His bones had been cast outside the boundaries of Plataea to rot in the open: a horrible desecration of a man's flesh that was certain to cause Nauklydes's shade an everlasting torment. For surely the vengeful Furies pursued his spirit now and forever in that other world.

After their defeat, the Thebans had laid low behind their walls, licking their wounds. And the Spartans, fearing reprisal against their elite warriors being held as prisoners in Plataea, had turned their wrath against Plataea's closest ally—Athens—burning homes and trampling crops in the region of Attika while half a million Athenians and their slaves dwelled in safety behind the walls of their immense citadel.

For thirty months neither Theban nor Spartan had attempted to attack Plataea again. The Plataeans in the countryside had sown and harvested, working together to build up a storehouse of supplies in the citadel. And Nikias and his grandfather, with the help of their neighbors, had rebuilt their house, but only after Nikias had recovered from Eurymakus's torture. It had taken months to regain enough strength to hold an adze to hew a beam, or to lift heavy stones to put up a wall. But the making of that house—rebuilding it from the ground up—had slowly helped him regain his soul.

The Spartan prisoners held in Plataea had been released in small groups, a few every month to stave off a full-scale Spartan invasion—to buy the city-state precious time to prepare for a siege. But now there were only a handful of the Spartans still held as prisoners inside the citadel. Time was running out for peace in the Oxlands. Everyone in Plataea knew that this lull between two violent storms was about to end.

Mula cleared his throat loudly. "I heard something."

Nikias cocked his ear, but the noise of the bull and cow drowned out all sound. Then he felt the ground suddenly tremble beneath his feet and a rider charged up the hill, reining in his mount a few strides away, staring at Nikias and Mula and the copulating beasts with a mystified expression.

Nikias and Mula returned the stranger's astonished gaze.

"Odd place to practice animal husbandry," the horseman announced nonchalantly, resting his javelin under the crook of one arm. His dark hair fell in ringlets to his shoulders, and the spirals of his beard and mustache cascaded down his face like the curls of an ancient kouros statue. At his hip was a long sword in a scabbard embellished with precious stones, and on his head was a golden cap. His clothes were outlandish: red silk pants and a colorful padded tunic woven with silver and gold thread worn over golden scale armor.

"Breeding on the top of a hill," the rider continued. "And yet this ghastly place *is* called the Oxlands," he added to himself, flexing the bejeweled fingers on his right hand. It took Nikias a few moments to realize that the man was speaking in Persian, a language that Nikias had learned in his youth from Mula's father. This strange horseman was almost two thousand miles from the capital of Artaxerxes's empire.

"I said: odd place for animals to mate," the rider repeated, this time in heavily accented Greek. He looked back and forth at Nikias and Mula, and then rolled eyes that were painted round the edges with black lines. To Nikias he looked ridiculous—like an overdressed Persian warrior from a play he had seen years ago, or a ghost from the past.

"Imbeciles," the Persian muttered under his breath; then, turning in his saddle, he shouted behind him in his own tongue, "I'm up here, you laggards!"

The ground thundered and six armed horsemen crested the hill, coming to a halt next to the Persian rider. Nikias planted his feet, fighting against the overpowering urge to run, for these newcomers were Median cavalrymen—skilled warriors and vassals of the Persians.

"Zeus's balls," hissed Mula out of the corner of his mouth.

The riders, like the Persian, wore trousers and padded coats, but their outfits were plain and unembellished. They had long mustaches that trailed down past their chins, and they were armed with swords, bows, and short spears. Nikias had fought one of their kind before—a servant of the spy Eurymakus. And he had barely escaped from that duel with his life.

Nikias grabbed Mula by the arm to keep him from bolting. If the boy tried to run, the Medians would merely ride him down and slay him.

The horsemen glared at him with their killers' eyes and Nikias raised his hands in the sign of submission. Two of the Medians reached for their bows and quickly nocked arrows while the other four walked their horses slowly toward Nikias and Mula as the bull shuddered and roared one last time in triumph.

TWO

———◆———

"Cut off his head and now it's mine, gild it with gold and fill it with wine!"

Kolax sang his favorite drinking song at the top of his voice as he raced down the rocky pine-covered slopes of the Kithaeron Mountains on his nimble-footed black steed. He was dressed in the leather trousers of a Skythian warrior, and wore the skin of a lion as a cloak—the head of the snarling beast covering his head like a hat. Unlike the Greeks, who rode bareback, he used a saddle.

As the trees thinned near the edge of the forest, Kolax could see the valley of the Oxlands stretching out below. He caught a glimpse of Nikias's farm where the foothills met the floor of the valley. The house was surrounded by vineyards—the neat rows of vines were lush with bright green leaves. These grain-eating Greeks were miserable archers and even worse horsemen, Kolax mused, but they could make a bowl of wine to please Dionysus himself. Soon Kolax would be at the farm and drinking some of that wine with his best friend, Mula. He could already taste it now! Uncut. Thick and purple. Like earth blood.

He glanced down at his drinking cup where it was attached to his belt. The gilded bowl shone in the afternoon sun as it bounced on his hip. He'd made this cup from the skull of a Dog Raider he had killed on a raid in Megaria, on the other side of the mountain. Dog Raiders were the Megarian hill marauders who wore helms covered with the hides of wild dogs, and they peeled the skin off their still-living victims to send a warning to any who would challenge them.

But Kolax wasn't afraid of Dog Raiders. Although he had just turned fourteen, there were already twenty-three notches on his bow—each one the shade of a Dog Raider he'd sent to the underworld. But his proudest kill was not a man. It was the lion that had foolishly stalked him in the forest. Stupid cat. He had killed the beast with a perfectly aimed poison-laced arrow, and then turned its hide into this wonderful cape!

"My drinking cup, my drinking cup! Raise it to the ceiling—raise it up, up, up!"

He was in a happy mood, for he had been sent by his father—the commander of the Plataean mountain fortress called the Three Heads—to deliver a message to Arkon Menesarkus at the citadel. Kolax relished the chance to be free of the confines of the small fortress that guarded the high pass and the road to Athens. By Zeus's hairy bunghole, that place was a bore! All day long standing guard duty on the top of the wall, on the lookout for Spartan invaders creeping amongst the stones and trees—invaders who never came.

Kolax slowed his horse, Pegasos, as they came to a switchback trail, then cut across it to a big field of grass and tall weeds where hundreds of goats grazed. He started galloping again, racing past a pair of startled shepherds. Two big sheepdogs took off after him, barking crazily as they gave chase. Kolax glanced over his shoulder and laughed at the dogs.

"Stupid hounds!" he shouted, and his lion's-head hood fell off to reveal his long copper-red hair flowing freely from his loosened topknot. "You'll never catch Pegasos!"

He dug his heels into his mount's sides and the sleek animal surged ahead, leaving the dogs in the dust. Kolax breathed in the warm air through his nostrils and relished the scents of grass and wild herbs. He loved the Oxlands. He wanted to stay in this place forever. It was now his home.

But his long journey from the grasslands of Skythia to this place had been a strange one. When Kolax was six years old his father went away from their homeland to Athens, enlisting as one of the Skythian guards of the citadel—fierce archers who policed Athens and guarded its walls. For Skythian bowmen were famous throughout the world for their speed and accuracy: a warrior from the grasslands could shoot an arrow for every three heartbeats. Kolax was raised by his uncle, riding and hunting on the plains of his homeland, always dreaming of one day joining his beloved papa in Athens. But then the good king of Skythia was murdered and the hated Nuri chieftain called the Snow Dog seized the Grass Throne. Kolax's tribe of Bindis were slaughtered, and he was captured by the enemy Nuri and sold into slavery. He ended up in Plataea, purchased by a curious inventor named Chusor who wanted Kolax to teach him the secret method of making the deadly Skythian poison.

And then the Thebans invaded Plataea, and during the chaos of the sneak attack, Kolax had fallen in with Nikias's slave, Mula. Together they escaped from the citadel and had had many wonderful adventures that night, killing Thebans and ultimately fighting alongside Nikias in the great Battle at the

Gates. Afterward Kolax traveled with Nikias to the strange city of Athens. Nikias went there hoping to find mercenaries to bring back to the Oxlands to help defend Plataea from a coming Spartan siege. Kolax came along in hopes of finding his papa—the great warrior Osyrus.

Kolax did indeed find his father. And when Osyrus learned that the Snow Dog had taken the throne of Skythia, he abandoned Athens—a place crawling with enemy Nuri—and rode north with a score of loyal men to take up service with the Plataeans and earn gold. The fortress of the Three Heads was given to Osyrus to command after he and his warriors had helped rout the Spartan army, who were occupying the old Persian Fort.

The sound of men's voices jolted Kolax from his thoughts. He trotted through an olive grove where farmers were beating the trees with sticks to make immature olives fall to the ground, singing a song to Athena, the creator of the first olive tree. The workers waved at Kolax as he passed and eventually he rode through the grove and came to vineyards laden with grapes. The air buzzed with wasps.

Kolax pulled back gently on the reins and Pegasos came to a stop by one of the rows. The Skythian stared at the wasps with fascination. These insects had been bad this year—the worst in anyone's memory. At least, that's what the Plataeans had told him. The wasps killed off many of the farmers' bees—laid siege to their hives, picking off the bees one by one—and stole their larvae for food. They made Kolax think of Spartans.

He leaned over and snatched a wasp from the air with a lightning-fast movement, shaking it in his fist, letting it sting him a few times before crushing it. Then he grabbed a cluster of grapes from the vine and kept riding toward the farmyard, eating the sweet fruit and spitting out the seeds. He glanced at the little red welts on his palm, savoring the fiery pain that was now throbbing in his veins—the insect's poison. How many wasps would it take to kill him? A thousand? Ten thousand?

Pegasos ambled into the farmyard and headed for the stables. There were several men in the yard fixing a broken plow, and they looked up at Kolax and nodded—they'd seen him there many times before. They were freemen from the citadel who were helping to work Menesarkus's land. All of the Arkon's slaves had been butchered during the Theban sneak attack. Everyone in the city had been pulling together over the last two and a half years to store up supplies in the event of a Spartan siege. Kolax would welcome such an exciting event and the chance to kill more Red Cloaks!

He slid off his horse's back and led him to the stables, putting him in a stall next to Nikias's horse, Photine, who whinnied a greeting to the familiar horse.

"Here is your old friend," said Kolax to Photine. "Don't give him any more of your love bites," he warned, shaking one of his fingers.

Kolax saw Nikias's Sargatian lasso hanging on a peg on the wall. The braided leather whip resembled a coiled snake, and Kolax regarded it for some time, wondering why he was suddenly filled with a sense of foreboding. He grabbed a bucket and headed to the well for some water for Pegasos, passing the pitch house—the place where pine sap was turned into resin for torches. The powerful smell hit his nostrils and he breathed in the heady scent.

Under the protected shade of a storage shed nearby he saw the two infant girls—the beautiful black-haired daughters of Nikias and Kallisto—crawling in the straw, playing with some tortoises that Kolax had found up on the mountain a few months ago and brought as presents. Nikias's sister, Phile, sat on the ground, spinning wool and weeping softly. When she saw him she looked embarrassed and turned away.

"Why do you shed tears, Phile?" Kolax asked, walking over to the shed. He knelt down and held out his thumbs for one of the girls—he could never tell which was which—and the child grabbed them, swinging from his arms and laughing.

"What are you doing here?" Phile asked faintly.

"My f-father—" stuttered Kolax. "He . . . let me leave the fort. I've come for one of our writing lessons."

"Maybe later," said Phile, wiping away her tears from her big dark eyes. "Kallisto is sick and needs peace. And Grandmother is at the market in the citadel. So I'm watching the girls."

"Where is your brother?" Kolax asked. "And Mula?"

"I don't know," said Phile, staring numbly at girls. "They went to get the bull an hour ago."

"Asterion escaped again?" asked Kolax, shaking his head with disdain. Poor Nikias. Such a knucklebrain when it came to animals. He'd told him how to make a proper Skythian enclosure for such a powerful bull. But did Nikias listen? No.

He put the lion's head over his own and crawled around, snarling comically, until one of the girls started to laugh but the other began to cry.

Kolax's stomach growled loudly and Phile smiled out of the corner of her mouth.

"Go into the kitchen," she said. "You'll find something to eat."

Kolax left Phile with her thoughts and walked somberly to the house. He knew why she was sad. She'd been in love with a young man—Kallisto's brother, Theron by name. But the unlucky young man died of an illness last year.

He'd come from a cursed family, though. Their father had been in league with the traitor Nauklydes, and three of his brethren had died—one way or another—on the night of the sneak attack.

He entered the house calling out a greeting and made his way to the kitchen. He was surprised to find Kallisto by the bread oven, kneading dough, her face pale and sweaty, dark circles under her eyes. Normally he found her to be a strong, good-looking woman with her thick black hair and prominent nose. But today she looked haggard and weak, save her fetching muscular arms that rippled as she worked the dough.

"What are you doing?" asked Kolax. "Phile said you were ill."

"Someone has to make the bread," she replied. She stepped back to reveal her swollen belly. The baby would come soon. Kolax hoped it would be a boy, for Nikias's sake. Such a disaster if a man were to sire three girls and no sons.

Kallisto made a strange face and breathed through her nose.

"You're not going to have the baby now, are you?" he asked, horrified.

She smiled and shook her head. "A big kick," she said. "Hard."

"He's a boy," said Kolax with a knowing grin. He quickly took off his gear—his lidded quiver, bow, knives, and leaf-bladed sword—and leaned it against the wall. "Let me do that," he said, helping Kallisto to a bench by the window. He took the bread and started to knead it expertly, breaking off balls and flattening them. Phile had taught him how to make bread last year after he had proclaimed that the job did not seem like such a difficult task. Phile was always complaining about making bread. Kolax had been wrong—it was indeed a very hard task—but he had persisted until he could bake a perfect round loaf.

While he worked he told Kallisto about the goings-on at the fort, how many Dog Raiders he had killed, and other adventures, like his slaying of the lion. But she did not seem too interested, and after a while he stopped talking. Something wasn't right. He could feel it in his gut. He got her some water from a big jar and made her drink it all, sitting by her side. Kolax's mother had died giving birth to his sister, and even though she had been under the grass now for seven years, he still missed her. He did not want Kallisto to join her.

When he was done with the bread, he put his weapons back on and wandered into the yard. He stood for a while watching the men, who were still mending the plow. They were having trouble fitting one of the iron pieces together with the other. Kolax was glad that he didn't have to plow a field. What a miserable way to spend one's life.

He strolled down to the place where Asterion the bull was kept. He saw the broken fence—the place where the animal had broken through the rails. He found the prints of Nikias and Mula in the mud and followed them through the tall sodden grass. A fat snake with orange and black rings slithered in front of him, and Kolax jumped on it, picking it up and staring into its beady black eyes.

"Poor thing," he said. "Your poison is weak. You can't even kill a mouse."

He flung the snake into the grass, then followed the tracks of Nikias and Mula as the indentations in the grass turned and headed north. He stopped and looked back toward the busy farm. He could make out the shape of Phile sitting under the eaves of the shed. Should he go back to her? Maybe she would feel like giving him his lesson now. Not only had she taught him to read, but she had also taught him to write.

Just then a crow flew overhead, cawing loudly. It was headed in the same direction that Nikias and Mula had gone. The crow seemed to be calling to Kolax. But what was it saying?

THREE

Sweat poured down Nikias's face and a fat fly landed on his forehead. However, he dared not move to brush it aside. Four glinting speartips hovered inches from his face.

But the Median riders regarded him with little concern. He was nothing more to them than a useless farmer. Their eyes were fixed on their master expectantly, waiting for him to give them an order.

The princely Persian had been lost in thought for several minutes. "This must be the place," he said distractedly, astride his mount and looking about the hilltop with the uncertain squint of a nearsighted man. He was at least thirty years of age, Nikias reckoned, and he was small and wiry compared to most Greek men.

"This *must* be the battlefield where my ancestor fell," declared the Persian. He closed his eyes and said a quick prayer under his breath—a prayer, Nikias recognized, to the Persian's deity Ahura Mazda. When he was done he dismounted and tossed his spear to one of his riders, then bent down and dug around in the tall dry grass as if he were searching for something that he had lost. "I've heard you can still find arrows," he said. "And even bones."

Nikias's mind raced. The Persians were Theban allies. They would kill him and Mula if they knew they were Plataean. He had to get away with the boy. But even if he and Mula managed to bolt past the spear-wielding horsemen, they could not outrun the riders—or their arrows. And they were four miles from the citadel of Plataea. If only he could get on the Persian's horse, which stood so tantalizingly close. The animal looked fast. He could outride the Medians and head for the borderland watchtower a mile away . . . but he would have to leave

little Mula behind. He glanced at the boy, who was looking at him with terrified eyes.

"Zeus guide me," he said to himself, for he was frozen with uncertainty.

The Persian wrenched something from the grass and held it close to his eyes:
it was a bronze spearhead, green with age. "That's not a Persian design," he said
under his breath, and tossed it aside. "But which way is Thebes?" he muttered,
standing up. "Damn this ugly country." He reached around and pulled a wineskin off his back and took a long draft. "Where is that stupid Tanagraean guide
with the runny arse?" he asked the riders.

"He could not stop shitting, Anusiya," replied one of the Median bodyguards.
"He stopped a league back. He said this is dangerous country and begged you
not to ride ahead. But he was inconvenienced."

The Persian laughed and spit some wine in the direction of Nikias and
Mula. "Dangerous?" he said with a sneer, pointing a crooked finger at the bull
and the cow. The bull had finished his efforts and was gently nibbling the cow's
neck. "Are you afraid of love-making beasts?"

"No, Anusiya," said the Median, avoiding the Persian's haughty gaze and
staring hard at Nikias.

"Are you afraid of a skinny slave boy and a naked farmer?"

"No, Anusiya."

Nikias knew enough Persian to understand the foreigners' words. This well-
dressed Persian was an *anusiya*: an elite warrior. And he'd ridden into the Oxlands with a guide from Tanagra—a Theban ally twenty miles to the east of
that citadel. The place where Nikias had been held captive and tortured by
Eurymakus.

This Persian, he realized, had gotten lost on the last leg of his journey to Thebes. He'd left his guide and gone looking for the famous battleground from the
Persian Wars like some sort of sheep-stuffing tourist!

Nikias noticed that the Persian carried a leather satchel on his back: a messenger's pouch. He must be an envoy. If only he could get his hands on that bag.
What secrets lay within? The Persians had backed the venomous Eurymakus—
the Theban assassin who had launched the sneak attack on Thebes. And the
current Spartan war against Athens—the endless raids into Athenian territory
to burn homes and fields—was rumored to be financed with Persian gold.

The Persian's eyes alighted on Nikias and he started, as if coming out of a
deep trance. He ordered his men to drop their spears, strode over to Nikias, and
stopped with his face a few inches away. "You've taken some beatings about the
head," he declared. "Handsome, in a brutish Greek way." He looked at Mula

and bent down, inspecting the boy's looks like a patron at a boy brothel, putting his hand under Mula's chin and raising his face to his own. "Pretty child, though," he said.

The Persian crossed his arms on his chest and stared at Nikias and Mula in a lazy, self-satisfied manner. Then he glanced over his shoulder and said to the Medians, "I'll take the boy and you can share the big farm lad, though I doubt he'll be quite as easy to manage."

Nikias saw Mula's eyes grow even wider with fear and he moved his head from side to side, mouthing the word "no."

Four of the Medians dismounted and the Persian envoy started to untie the drawstring of his pants. Nikias tensed, readying himself to strike.

"Thebes is that way!" blurted Mula in Persian, pointing in the direction of Plataea. "We are Theban. We can show you the way over the river and through the forest. Over the stone bridge that spans the Asopus!"

"So you speak my tongue?" said the Persian, peering in the direction that Mula pointed. "Good, very good. You'll lead us there when we're done."

"The boy—he is right," said Nikias in halting Persian, bobbing his head deferentially. "Follow us now, Anusiya. We take you to Thebes."

"Come with us," said Mula. "We show the way to the bridge. Very dangerous spot here. Plataean scouts come, maybe."

"No good for making like the bull with us now," said Nikias, affecting a dumb laugh.

The Persian envoy looked Nikias up and down. He scratched his beard and squinted toward Plataea with his obviously defective eyes.

"Anusiya," said one of the Medians. "We should wait here for the guide."

"Silence!" erupted the Persian, holding up his right hand imperiously. He put his face close to Nikias's again and asked abruptly, "What is your age?"

"I have twenty years and six months," answered Nikias.

"Have you been in battle? I've been admiring the many scars on your body." The Persian put his hand on a scar that ran across Nikias's left pectoral and held it there, then looked up into Nikias's eyes.

Nikias glanced down at the Persian's hand on his chest and saw that his nails were painted with gold. "Yes, Lord," he said. "I have been to war against the Plataean sheep-stuffers. I kill many Plataeans."

"Can you fight the pankration?" observed the Persian. "I hear this region is famous for breeding pankrators."

"Oh, no," said Nikias sheepishly. "I only punch my grandfather's cows when they disobey."

"Ha!" said the Persian. "I like you, lad. I hope that you will come and visit me when I'm ensconced at my residence in Thebes. I will buy you a pretty tunic and a belt."

"I would be honored," said Nikias, affecting a demure tone. "And happy to show my thanks in other ways."

The Persian put his hand on Nikias's shoulder and nodded his head. "A well-built lad. I like this one," he added, as if speaking to an invisible peer standing by his side. "If this is what Thebans are made of, I'm going to like living in this country for a while."

He patted Nikias on the cheek, then turned and walked briskly to his horse, mounting it with agility. Once he was seated and his scabbard and the various pouches and bags upon his person were arranged just so, he gestured with a flick of his wrist at Nikias. "Lead the way."

Nikias pulled on the cow's rope and started walking quickly down the hill with Mula at his heels. The bull snorted and lurched forward, sidling up to the female and rubbing his nose on her neck, keeping pace.

"Don't say anything else," Nikias whispered to Mula, taking a sidelong glance at the Persian and his bodyguard riding close behind. "We're going to walk these goat-rapers right up to the gates of Plataea."

"Yes, young master," said Mula, and stifled a giggle.

"Quick thinking back there," said Nikias.

"Thank you," replied Mula, beaming.

Nikias stole another glance over his shoulder—the Medians had fanned out behind and were looking about warily as they rode. But the Persian trotted off to the side, seemingly oblivious to any danger, picking something from between his front teeth with a gilded finger.

When he was young Nikias had been told that Persian boys were taught only three things: riding, shooting, and telling the truth. Fortunately, he mused, they had not been given lessons in reading maps as well. "The hubris of the Persians," thought Nikias, "is unbounded." Had they learned nothing from their crushing defeats in Greece? At one time the Persians had controlled all of the Greek city-states in Ionia, but then those people rebelled, incurring the wrath of the Persian kings. But the Persians had lost all of their Greek vassal states, and their invasions of Attika and the Oxlands had utterly failed.

"Have you ever heard of Arshaka the Eye Snatcher?" queried the Persian, catching Nikias's eye and trotting up beside him.

"Of course," replied Nikias. "A famous pankrator who died here during the big war. He was killed by Menesarkus of Plataea."

"The Bull of Plataea," said the Persian with a mocking tone. "I heard he cheated in his bout with the great Arshaka," he added with disdain. "A tiny blade hidden in his fist. He slit the artery in Arshaka's neck."

Nikias bristled. This was a lie. He had heard the true story of the fight many times from his grandfather, sitting by the hearth in their farmhouse during the rainy season. Fifty years ago Menesarkus had been sixteen years old and an Olympic fighter in training. He'd been chosen by the Greeks to fight the Persian Arshaka in a combat of heroes to precede the commencement of the battle: a fight to the death. Menesarkus had not been chosen for his abilities as a fighter, however. Rather, he had been selected as a sacrificial offering to Ares—the god of war—and a means to put fire in the blood of the Greeks. Nobody had expected the sparsely bearded lad to actually defeat the terrifying Arshaka.

"The story that I heard," said Nikias, "was that Menesarkus surprised Arshaka by breaking his knee, and then put him in the Morpheus hold."

"What is the Morpheus hold?" asked the Persian, with an indifferent air.

Nikias smiled. "Morpheus is the god of sleep. The pankrator wraps his arm around his opponent's throat and cuts off the blood to his brain. If he holds him long enough, then he sleeps forever."

"We call that move 'Azi,'" explained the Persian. "The Snake."

"A better name, Anusiya," said Nikias with deference.

"Too bad this Menesarkus is dead."

"He yet lives," replied Nikias.

"In truth?" asked the Persian, impressed. "He must be ancient."

"The men of the Oxlands live long. A citizen of Plataea or Thebes must bear a shield until they are in their seventies. That is the law."

"Hardy men. When Plataea has fallen, I will send Menesarkus back to Persia as a gift for Artaxerxes. He can fight for the king's amusement until he is dead. Or perhaps the king will skin him alive and bury him in a pit of insects." He made a clicking sound with his tongue against his teeth and grinned. "That's the sound the bugs make as they nip at the flesh. There are worse ways to die, though. I've also seen men forced to eat themselves alive, starting with their own cocks and then—"

"Then we are to invade Plataea again?" asked Nikias, mustering a false tone of enthusiasm. "Does the great Artaxerxes send men to aid Thebes in our war?"

The Persian smiled and patted his dispatch bag. "I bring important words. And sometimes words are much more powerful than men and swords."

They walked for a quarter of a mile without incident. But as they approached the stone bridge spanning the swiftly flowing Asopus River, Nikias heard a distant voice calling out anxiously from behind:

"You're going the wrong way!"

Nikias snapped his head around and saw a horseman galloping toward them, waving one hand wildly, calling out in Greek.

"Come back!"

"What's this fool of a Tanagraean about?" asked the Persian, turning his horse around. The Medians turned their horses, too, with their backs away from Nikias and the bridge.

"Give me your dagger," Nikias commanded Mula in a harsh whisper. Mula always wore a thin blade on his belt—a gift that Nikias had given him. It was a weapon that had been crafted by a clever smith named Chusor who had once lived in Plataea. Mula slipped him the dagger and Nikias held it behind his back. "Now run, boy. Run all the way back to the city gates. Don't stop."

Mula nodded obediently, but the anguished look on his face said that he did not want to leave.

"Now," hissed Nikias.

FOUR

———◆———

Mula dashed over the bridge and sprinted across the ground as fast as a hound, vanishing from sight in the tall grass. Nikias looked back toward the approaching Tanagraean rider, who was almost on them.

Nikias's grandfather had told him when he was a boy never to be captured by the enemy. "Slit the artery in your neck," he'd said. "Death will come swiftly." He clutched the dagger and felt that vein throbbing in his neck.

"Come on, girl," he said to the cow. He quickly turned her around—with the enraptured bull still glued to her side—so that both animals now faced the Persian and his riders. He dropped the rope and slunk back so that he stood next to Asterion's rump. The flies buzzed round the bull's arse, and he swished his tail with irritation.

The Tanagraean guide charged up to the other riders and slid awkwardly off his horse. He shot a glance at the bridge and scowled at Nikias. The man's face was ashen and covered with sweat, and even from fifty paces away Nikias could see that the Tanagraean was very ill. Nikias recognized him at once. He'd met him at the gates of Tanagra two and a half years ago: a guardsman with sly eyes who'd recalled how Nikias had fought his brother in a pankration tournament and broken his arm. Sly Eyes shambled over to the Persian and bowed clumsily.

"Anusiya," said Sly Eyes. "Forgive me. I had to stop. My bowels . . . I am not well. But you are going the wrong way. That man there is a Plataean"—he pointed at Nikias with a trembling finger. "He is leading you to the enemy citadel."

The Persian turned and squinted at Nikias with astonishment. "A what? A *Plataean*, you say?"

The Medians turned their horses back to face Nikias. Two of them drew their swords while the others adjusted their spears.

"His name is Nikias," said Sly Eyes. "Heir to the Arkon of Plataea. We must bring him back to Thebes. Which is that way," he added, shooting his arm northward with an exaggerated expression. "There's a Theban guard tower a mile from here."

Nikias gripped the dagger. The flies swarming on Asterion's back buzzed in his ear, and the bull's tail swished gently across his face.

"I'm not going to *bring* him anywhere," the Persian said slowly, his face twisting with rage. "I'm going to cut him open and hang him by his own guts here and now. Take him!" he shouted at the Medians.

The riders charged, weapons lowered for the kill.

Nikias plunged the dagger into the thick hide of Asterion's haunch. The animal reacted to the stabbing pain as though he had been struck by a lightning bolt. He bellowed and sprang forward with his head lowered. He gored the lead rider's horse in the chest and lifted it off its front legs with a single motion, such was the strength of that beast when powered by a red rage. The horse and rider flipped over in a backward somersault, crashing into another rider.

The other horses reared and neighed with terror.

But Asterion did not stop. He plunged ahead, spearing one of the fallen riders through the head, his horn passing through the warrior's skull with the ease of a sharp skewer passing through a piece of cheese. Without hesitating, he attacked another horse, plunging his horns deep into the animal's side, sending the rider tumbling. The bull shook himself loose and charged another, breaking the horse's forelegs as though they were nothing more than dry sticks.

An arrow struck Asterion in the neck. But this did not slow his progress. He roared with an unearthly sound and ran at the Median who'd just shot him, bowling over the warrior's horse before he could unleash a second arrow. The moment the Median hit the ground, the bull impaled the fallen rider on his bloody horns, flipping him into the air like a clay doll.

Nikias watched in awe at this killing storm he had unleashed. It was like a whirlwind made of muscle and horn. Three of the Medians were down. The three remaining horsemen did their best to stay out of the bull's way, trying to spear the beast. But Asterion was faster than a cat, bucking and leaping, kicking out with his back legs and twisting his gigantic head this way and that. He leapt upon the back of a horse as though to rape it, slamming his terrible horns through the rider's back and out the other side of his torso.

"Do something!" the Persian cried to the Tanagraean. His frightened horse danced in a circle on the outskirts of the melee. He threw his spear at the bull, but his aim was poor and made worse by his rearing horse, and his weapon passed through the breast of one of his own men, killing him.

"Anusiya!" yelled Sly Eyes. He had remounted in the confusion and had ridden an arrow shot away. "Come this way!"

The bull flipped another horse onto its back as Nikias ran past. He sprinted straight for the Persian, leaping up and knocking the warrior off his horse. Nikias landed hard on top of him, slamming his forehead onto the Persian's nose with the force of a hammer blow. The Persian gasped and clutched his face, blood spurting through his hands. Nikias kicked him in the side, then rolled the stunned and gasping Persian onto his stomach. He grabbed the warrior's left ankle and sliced clean through the tendon. The Persian let forth an animal shriek and squirmed to free himself.

"Stay!" ordered Nikias, his voice harsh and full of command. He was no longer playing the deferential farmer—he was a hardened warrior, a reaper of men. "Stay, or I'll cut your other tendon and you'll never walk again." He stood over the Persian, brandishing the bloody dagger.

He looked to the right. He saw the Persian's horse bolting across the grass, hard on the heels of the Tanagraean now riding toward Thebes. Sly Eyes held a hunting horn to his lips and blew forth a call as he rode. The sound continued to blare even after he had crested a hill and disappeared over the other side.

Nikias snapped his head toward the bridge. He saw dead horses and men on the ground. A horse with two broken legs was struggling to roll over. Another fallen Median had managed to stay on his mount, but he had taken flight, galloping along the river with the rampaging bull pounding the turf behind him. Only one Median was still moving: a warrior on his knees amongst the carnage of horses and men, clutching a wound to his abdomen, looking about with a dazed expression.

Suddenly the Persian envoy rolled onto his back, reaching for his sword, but Nikias bent over and grabbed his arm before he could pull the sword out of the scabbard, cutting through the muscle of his biceps. The Persian shrieked and clutched his arm.

"Stay!" yelled Nikias. He seized the Persian's sword and held the gleaming blade inches from the man's eyes. "Or the next stroke of this blade will blind you!"

The Persian squeezed his eyes shut and babbled, "I am an envoy of King Artaxerxes!"

"Quit talking," Nikias said with disdain, and marched toward the pile of dead men and horses, sword in one hand, dagger in the other. The Median who was still alive got to his feet and drew his sword, clutching his stomach with one hand. He spat a mouthful of blood.

Nikias flung the dagger with a snap of his wrist. The blade flashed in the space between them, and then the startled Median clutched at the handle protruding from his chest. Nikias lunged forward, swinging the sword from low to high, and half of the Median's face and skull, from jaw to brow, popped off like a section of melon. The warrior stared at Nikias with his remaining eye, standing perfectly still, his brains exposed to the sun. Nikias's second stroke sent the rest of the Median's head flying into the dust.

FIVE

———◆———

Nikias breathed hard, the blood pounding in his ears. The horse with the broken legs was still trying to roll over. Nikias put the wounded animal out of its misery. Then he checked all the warriors sprawled on the grass, making sure they were dead. The bull had done his work. Only one of the Medians yet breathed, so Nikias stabbed him through the heart with the sword. His grisly work done, he strode back to the Persian. The envoy had managed to stand up on his good leg and was hopping away in the direction the Tanagraean had gone. Nikias smashed him in the back of the head with the handle of his sword and the Persian fell to the ground, unconscious.

Nikias went to work stripping him of all his gear and clothes—the golden helm, his plate armor, his gold bracelets, and even his beaded slippers. All of these riches he tossed aside, leaving only the man's rings, until the Persian lay naked on the grass.

Grabbing the leather envoy pouch, Nikias slung it around his own neck. Then he knelt down and hoisted the man onto his shoulders and started jogging. He headed over the stone bridge. After a mile his legs started to ache, but he did not slow down. He was still three miles from the citadel. He had to get the Persian to Plataea so that his grandfather could question him and read the contents of the message.

His legs and back quickly started aching along with his legs. His body dripped with sweat. He thought of the terrible fate that awaited this Persian in Plataea. Nikias had endured the pain and terror of torture, and he did not wish that cruel destiny on any man—not even an enemy. But the lives of his people were at stake. If the Spartans and Thebans captured Plataea, every man left alive would be executed, and all of the women and children taken into slavery. The thought of his wife and their two daughters—and their unborn child as well!—turned into thralls and sex slaves filled him with a burning hatred that drove his legs onward despite the shooting pains in his back.

"Keep moving," he told himself.

He thought of his failed quest to Athens that he'd set out on after the defeat of the Thebans. He'd gone to raise an army of mercenaries to help defend Plataea from the Spartans, bearing the gold that had been given to the traitor Nauklydes. He'd lost the gold in Athens, but he'd fallen in love with a young hetaera—a courtesan of Athens—and had made love with her, betraying Kallisto.

How strange the mind of a man, he mused. Even now, carrying this heavy burden, running from death, his thoughts fled helplessly back to that night in the temple of Aphrodite where he had made love with the ravishing Helena. . . .

A crow raced overhead, croaking loudly. Nikias glanced up and thought he saw a flash of white on the bird's tail feathers, but he was not certain. That strange bird seemed to follow him everywhere—a messenger of Apollo. It was the same crow that men in Plataea said landed on the corpse of Nauklydes after he had been given his tunic of stones.

"Hera's jugs!" he cursed as one of his knees buckled. He'd stepped in a depression—the opening to a rabbit hole. But he pressed on.

He remembered a game that he and his best friend Demetrios used to play when they were younger. They would take turns picking up a young bull to see who could carry it on his shoulders the farthest around the walls of the citadel. Nikias, in all of his attempts over the years, had only made it halfway round the circuit. But Demetrios—probably the strongest lad in the Oxlands—toted the docile bull around the entire two and a half miles, cheered on by the men in each guard tower, spewing his guts from exhaustion but refusing to give up.

Nikias wondered if Demetrios was still alive. His father, Nauklydes, had sent him off to Syrakuse several years ago to live with a wealthy and powerful general called the Tyrant. Nauklydes must have known, even back then, that he was going to betray Plataea to the enemy, and so he had sent his heir to a city-state that was an ally of Sparta. Would Demetrios ever return home? If so, he would find that his sister and father were dead and that his family name was now poisonous to Plataean tongues.

He heard a sound that he'd been dreading: horse hooves trampling the ground behind him, coming from the direction of Thebes. The sun burst through a rent in the clouds, illuminating his place on the hilltop as if Zeus were shining a lantern on him from above.

He turned and saw a patrol of cavalry a quarter of a mile away, led by the

Tanagraean guide. He counted five riders in a close pack bearing down on him, spears lowered. Thebans. There was nowhere to hide. Mustering all of his strength, he headed for a little hillock where a stand of ancient and gnarled olive trees grew. That's where he would make his last stand. When he got to the top, he let the Persian slip from his shoulders and arched his aching back. Then he drew his sword and crouched low, waiting for the moving wall of death, trying to catch his breath.

He thought of Kallisto and the girls. He wondered if she had a boy in her womb. Did it really matter? He would have loved another daughter just the same. . . .

"Young master!"

He caught sight of Mula clinging to the upper branches of the tree nearby.

"Mula!" spat Nikias in wrath. "Why didn't you go to the farm? Stupid boy! There's no reason you should die here as well! Run!"

"Master!" said Mula. "Lie down. Lie down on the grass."

The riders were at the foot of the hill. The horses lowered their heads and climbed the slope. The spearheads of the Theban riders sparkled in the sun. He could see their faces now—Thebans wearing open-faced helms revealing their long beards. They carried notched shields of the Oxlands bearing the letter theta.

"Get down!" screamed Mula.

Nikias saw something rustling in the tall grass next to him. At first he thought it was a snake. Then he saw the snarling face of a lion and he started. The creature spoke to him in a harsh voice, "Get down, you mare-milking fool!"

Nikias dropped to the ground, flat on his belly as the Theban horsemen crested the hill.

The lion figure sprang from the grass. A hail of arrows sang with the thump of his bowstrings. The Thebans screamed and fell from their mounts, writhing on the grass as the poison coursed through their veins.

The Tanagraean had fallen off his mount in the confusion and tumbled down the hill, screaming in terror. Kolax shot him through the back of the head the moment he lurched to his feet, and Sly Eyes fell forward onto the grass, twitching in his death throes.

Kolax poked Nikias with the end of his recurved bow.

"You can get up now," he said. "Good thing I decided to follow your trail from the farm."

"I ran into Kolax," said Mula, swinging down from the tree and running to the Theban horses, which were milling about nervously, and gathering up their reins.

Nikias stood on shaky legs and smiled at the barbarian lad.

"Thank Zeus," he said.

"Don't thank *him*," said Kolax, pointing at the sky. "Thank *me*. I'm the one who killed these Thebans." He pulled out his dagger and went to work slitting the throats of the enemy warriors to make sure they were dead. "What would you do without me?" he muttered. "Saved you yet again."

"Don't kill that one!" ordered Nikias, for Kolax was about to dispatch the Persian envoy. "He's a present for my grandfather."

"Can I have one of his pretty finger jewels?" asked Kolax. He pulled off one of the rings before Nikias could reply, then dashed down the hill to the Tanagraen, kneeling by him and plucking the arrow from the dead man's skull. But Kolax reeled instantly, his face screwed up in disgust. "This one stinks!" he proclaimed, and spit on the ground as if ejecting poison from his mouth. "He shit himself when he died. He reeks of sickness."

"Are you killing him or wiping his arse?" asked Mula.

"Ha, ha!" laughed Kolax, standing up and holding his belly. "Good one, Mula."

"Come here and help me with this man," said Nikias.

They heaved the unconscious prisoner onto a horse, laying him sideways with his midsection across the horse's back. They worked fast, tying his wrists to his ankles under the horse's belly so that the Persian was strapped to the animal like a load of baggage. Then Nikias, Mula, and Kolax mounted the other three captured horses and galloped swiftly toward the citadel of Plataea.

SIX

———◆———

A strangled cry broke from Menesarkus's lips as he lay facedown and naked on the stone floor of a darkened chamber. At the same time he kicked out—a great jerking thrust of his leg that struck a wooden armor stand looming in the corner of the room, bearing his bronze armor and helm. The tree and its burden toppled, crashing to the floor with an enormous clatter that echoed in the small room. The light from a single lamp cast a gleam on the Bull of Plataea's bronze helm where it wobbled on its side on the floor; it seemed to throb like a living thing in the flickering glow.

A moment later a frantic knock sounded on the chamber's door.

"Arkon! Are you well?"

Menesarkus pulled off of his wife, Eudoxia, where she lay unclothed and sprawled on his robe beneath him, her long hair splayed out behind her like silver wings. He remained on hands and knees for a moment, panting from exertion, staring down at her, enraptured by her beauty, stunned into speechlessness by the power of his orgasm. Even though Eudoxia was approaching her seventh decade of life, the constant labor on the farm had kept her body svelte. Her breasts, though certainly much longer by her own admission, had remained comely. And her face, in his opinion, had become more and more alluring with every season since they had first met, so many decades ago.

He still burned for her.

"Arkon? Are you well?"

"I am well, damn you," said Menesarkus gruffly. "Go away," he added. "I merely tripped and knocked something over."

They were in his private and windowless chamber in the government offices in the citadel of Plataea. There was only one door into the room, and Menesarkus had made sure to bar it before they had started their love play. Menesarkus slept at his house in the citadel to be close to the government offices, while Eudoxia stayed on the farm, managing all of its many affairs. For two years and more they had been sleeping apart. And they hated it.

The door ring on the other side of the portal made a scraping sound.

"Go away, Hesiod!" he yelled at his secretary. He could picture the young man outside the door, with his ear pressed to the wood, a concerned expression on his meddling face.

"If you're certain, Arkon . . ."

"As certain as a punch in the face. Now leave!"

After he heard Hesiod's departing footsteps, he sighed and cast his big body down next to Eudoxia, floating . . . floating . . .

She propped herself on one elbow and ran a slender hand over Menesarkus's hairy barrel chest, smiling at him with her dark eyes full of mischief.

"After fifty years you still destroy me," he said, staring at her with one eye. He scratched his black beard, which was streaked with white stripes, and let forth a great yawn that split his wide and handsome face. His jaw crunched loudly as he closed his mouth—the result of one of his old pankration injuries.

"I think you dented your armor," said Eudoxia, smiling.

"You dented my *balls*," he replied.

"Oh, you are still such a foulmouthed boy!"

"You love it when I talk like that," he said with a grin. "You probably thought about all the dirty things I would say on your way from the farm. And you! Sneaking off to meet me here in the citadel like a teenage girl! Did you tell Kallisto and Phile that you had to come to the market again? Or did you tell them the truth—that you were hunting for Bull meat!"

She cuffed him on the side of the head. "You're the one who taught me to be a sneak," she said, laughing girlishly.

"Remember when you stole away from your father's house?" he asked, his eyes shining. "A few nights before the battle with the Persians . . . I propped you up in the bough of that one tree that had been split and blackened by lightning. And I fell on my knees, blind with lust, and pledged to worship forever at the altar of your honeyed loins. I swore to kill every Persian in the Oxlands so that I could come back to your side."

Eudoxia put her mouth close to his ear and said, "I died a hundred times that day, wondering if you would return to the citadel. And when I saw you walk back through the gates . . . my heart swelled and I thought it might burst from joy."

"I couldn't wait to shower you with Persian gold," he said with a laugh.

She covered his mouth with her own, kissing him hungrily, then got on top of him. "I wasn't done yet," she said, and pressed her heavy breasts against him. "When you kicked over your armor, I was almost to the top of the mountain."

"Tell me what you want me to do," he replied obediently. "I'm strong enough to carry you to the peak."

"Is your spear still unbending?" she asked, reaching down. "Ah, just like a teenage boy in more ways than one."

When she was satisfied they lay side by side, staring at the ceiling, which was lit by the orange glow of the lamp, and watching a wall lizard stalking a fly. They had been making love like this during the day often over the last year, and these lusty assignations had helped keep Menesarkus from going mad from the day-to-day toil of running Plataea. Most of his day was spent poring over documents, recording the amount of food and supplies that were being stocked away in the citadel: jars filled with olive oil; casks of smoked meat; skins filled with wine; arrows; swords; helms; herbs for medicine. It was mind-numbing. Especially with Hesiod always by his side. The young man had lost his arm fighting the Thebans. No longer fit for battle, he had been assigned to assist Menesarkus in all his duties. But he was long-winded and overly attentive, and drove Menesarkus mad.

"What are you mumbling?" Eudoxia asked.

"Eh?" he said.

"Are you already back to your accounts? You're rattling off numbers."

Menesarkus covered his eyes with his forearm. "We've got enough food to keep all twenty thousand of us fed for ten months or so during a siege," he said. "That's not enough time."

"But the Spartan prisoners—"

"There are only a score of them left," he cut in. "Twenty more to buy us time. A few months at most. The Spartans are due to send another emissary demanding that we break off our alliance with Athens. And then I'll have to let the final prisoners go to stave off invasion for a little while longer. I'll keep Draco the Skull till the very end, though."

He thought of the Spartan general, who'd been his prisoner in Plataea for the last two and a half years—a desiccated, noseless warrior whom Menesarkus first met during the Persian War. They had fought side by side against the Persians at the battle of Plataea fifty years before, storming the Persian Fort together. Later Menesarkus went to Sparta as a guest-friend of one of the Spartan dual kings as a reward for his heroics in battle. There he fought Draco in a pankration contest to honor those who had died against the Persian invaders. Draco, a wily fighter, tried to rip off Menasarkus's testicles, but Menesarkus responded by biting off the Spartan's nose. There were no rules in the Spartan version of the pankration. The Spartans fought dirty. And that was the only way to beat them.

"Have you heard lately from General Perikles?" she asked.

Menesarkus nodded and cracked the knuckles of his rough and callused hands. "I had a messenger pigeon yesterday. The same news as always: the Athenians cannot spare any men. But Perikles welcomes any and even all Plataeans to come and stay behind the walls of Athens."

"It's a long and dangerous road to travel with children," said Eudoxia, and stared into space with a haunted look.

He got up and poured them a bowl of wine, and they sat on the floor with their backs to the cool wall, sharing sips, relishing this time to be completely alone together. They played a game of pebbles, and Eudoxia captured all of Menesarkus's pieces off the wooden game board, giggling with every triumphant move.

"Oh, I give up!" he said, shoving the board aside.

"The great general is defeated by a woman," declared Eudoxia.

"Most men are outstrategized by women," said Menesarkus. "Nikias likes to think that he wooed Kallisto, but it was the other way around."

"She is a fine wife," said Eudoxia. "A hard worker. A good mother."

"I did not say otherwise. But she is cleverer than he. Just as you are cleverer than me."

"I am worried about her," said Eudoxia.

"Why?"

"She is spotting. I'm afraid she might lose this child. She is in the eighth month. She conceived too soon after the twins were born. Not more than two months passed before she became pregnant again."

"Kallisto is fertile and strong," said Menesarkus, and quickly added, "Not that you were weak, my darling," for he suddenly recalled that Eudoxia had bled like this before she had lost her second pregnancy. One son she'd born him— the striking Aristo, a poet and sprinter who was killed fifteen years ago in a pointless battle against the Thebans. Aristo never was a warrior. And he never was lucky. But somehow he fathered the brave and fortunate Nikias. Menesarkus had had no idea how much he loved his grandson until that day Nikias returned to Plataea a broken man after being tortured by Eurymakus the Theban.

He realized that Eudoxia had risen and put on her dress and was now gathering her hair—tresses that stretched to her shapely calves. He stood up and braided it for her, and she handed him a golden hair clip she always wore at the end of the braid. It was a prize he'd taken from a Persian princeling he'd slain at the Persian Fort. His first wedding gift to her. She had just turned sixteen, only a few months older than he.

"I wished that I could have given you more children," she said at last. "And I don't begrudge you the child that you made while in Sparta, for I know you have suffered greatly since that secret was revealed to me."

Menesarkus grunted. He thought back to that night in the palace of the kings in Lakonia when that irresistible royal had sauntered into his bedchamber wearing one of those alluring Spartan dresses with the hem that rode far, far above the knees . . . an athletic girl—a female wrestler of twenty-three—with shorn straw-colored hair and one plump bosom hanging out of her gown, giving her the appearance of a wild Amazon woman who'd cut off one of her breasts to facilitate shooting an arrow. The Spartan elders wished to steal his seed, thus bringing Menesarkus's skills into their bloodlines, but the young pankrator gave it as freely as a rutting bull. Two years and six months ago, when the Spartans sent their expeditionary force to the Oxlands, Menesarkus's Spartan grandson, Prince Arkilokus, was amongst the warriors. Injured during a riding accident, Arkilokus was captured and kept as a prisoner in Plataea, and later exchanged for Nikias after he had been taken by the enemy.

Menesarkus turned Eudoxia around and put his hand gently to her cheek. "I love you, Eudoxia," he said. "All of my victories on the battlefield and the pankration arena would have been meaningless without you to share them."

She smiled and kissed his hand. Then she looked deep into his eyes and frowned, saying, "I've wanted to tell you something—"

But her words were cut off by a forceful pounding on the door.

"Hesiod!" shouted Menesarkus. "Go away!"

"It's me—Nikias!" came a familiar voice from the other side. "Grandfather! Quickly. Open up!"

SEVEN

Menesarkus limped to the door, slid back the bar, and opened the portal.

"Hera's jugs, boy! What happened?" he asked when he saw Nikias standing there. "You're covered in blood!"

Eudoxia gasped and rushed to him, crying, "Grandson, what have you done?"

"I'm fine," said Nikias. "I was chasing old Asterion and . . ." he trailed off as he noticed his grandmother's disheveled appearance and his grandfather's nakedness. He smiled wryly and said to his grandmother, "I need to steal Grandfather from you."

"Is Asterion hurt?" asked Menesarkus with a stricken voice.

"He yet lives," said Nikias. "But he is running free over the Oxlands."

Menesarkus scowled. "That bull is worth many talents of silver for his seed alone. What happened?"

"I've found something far more valuable," replied Nikias. "A Persian prisoner. And I don't have time to explain. Linos is interrogating him now."

Hesiod pushed his way into the chamber and grabbed Menesarkus's robe from the floor, throwing it over his master's bare shoulders. Then he stooped and grabbed Menesarkus's foot and lifted it off the ground, causing the old pankrator to hop on one foot and lunge for the wall to keep from falling.

"Idiot!" barked Menesarkus. "My bad knee!"

"Sorry, Arkon!" exclaimed Hesiod, slapping a sandal to Menesarkus's foot. "Not a moment to be lost."

Nikias led a limping Menesarkus down the hallway and into the first open courtyard. A group of ten guards stood in a semicircle around the naked Persian, who was weeping as he knelt on the pavers. His hands were tied behind his back and blood seeped from the wounds on his biceps and ankle tendon where Nikias had cut him. He had pissed himself, and his urine was mingled with the blood in a little pool at his feet.

An aged man with a white beard knelt by his side, speaking to the prisoner in Persian in a low voice. This was Linos—a spy who had returned to Plataea after many years, and had quickly become one of Menesarkus's closest confidants. The prisoner nodded and wept even harder and spoke quickly—words that Nikias could not hear.

Zoticus, the senior general of Plataea and the leader of the cavalry, paced behind the Persian, staring down his beaklike nose at the prisoner and prodding him now and again with the butt end of his riding whip, causing the Persian to shake violently each time he did it. Kolax—a favorite of Zoticus because of the lad's skills as a horseman and archer—stood next to the general, laughing and chewing on a piece of dried meat.

After a few more minutes of questioning, Linos touched the Persian on the shoulder with a conciliatory gesture, then got up and approached Menesarkus. Zoticus knelt by the Persian and said something in his ear, and the prisoner let out a terrified yelp.

"What is going on, Linos?" asked Menesarkus. "What have you learned? Is this man truly a Persian?"

"Your grandson," said Linos, glancing at Nikias, "has made a remarkable discovery." He gestured for Nikias and Menesarkus to follow him to the corner of the courtyard, out of hearing distance of the guards and the prisoner. Hesiod came with them, standing dutifully by Menesarkus's side.

"The man claims he is an emissary who got lost on his way to Thebes," Linos explained. "Apparently, Nikias killed all of his troop of Median guards and captured him."

Menesarkus's jaw dropped and he looked at Nikias, who responded with a modest shrug. "It wasn't a troop," said Nikias. "There were only six Medians. And that Persian is as blind as a gopher. Here is his dispatch bag," he added, and took the leather bag from his shoulder, handing it to Linos, who immediately opened the flap and riffled through the contents.

"What were you saying to the Persian just now?" asked Menesarkus.

"I was telling him," replied Linos, not looking up, "that he will be treated with the deference accorded to someone of his rank. And I thanked him for offering to reveal the code to decipher his documents. In all my years I have never met a more timid creature so willing to give up information. He is terrified of torture."

"That's strange," said Nikias. "He enjoyed telling me about all the men he'd had the pleasure of seeing tormented in his king's torture chambers."

"The greatest tyrant often possesses a fawn's heart," answered Linos.

"I don't understand," said Menesarkus. "Why was a Persian emissary on his way to Thebes?"

"He is the servant of a man called the City-Killer," said Linos. "A siege master who has been advising the Spartans for the last few years."

"Have you heard of this City-Killer?" asked Nikias.

"Oh, yes," said Linos. "I have seen the aftermath of his destructive genius in eastern Ionia. He has never failed to conquer a citadel, because if he does so, he will be forced to eat all of his children and grandchildren over a great and excruciating span of time."

"Quite the incentive," said Menesarkus.

"But why was he on his way to Thebes?" said Nikias.

"The City-Killer is to make his base of operations there," replied Linos.

"Base of operations for what?" asked Hesiod, piping in.

Linos ignored Hesiod's question as he rooted for something in the bag and held it aloft—a cylindrical object with carvings on it. "Very useful," he said. "A Persian cylinder seal." He glanced at Hesiod and said, "In answer to your question: the base of operations for the siege of Plataea. That cowering creature just informed me that there are more than fifty thousand hoplites and slaves marching across the Isthmus of Korinth as we speak, on their way here. They will be here in five days, when they will be joined by another ten thousand from Megaria and Korinth."

Nikias stared in amazement at Linos, then turned to his grandfather, whose face was twisted in a mocking smile.

"That's impossible," said Menesarkus. "That would be the entire force that Sparta could muster. Their entire army of Spartiates and Helot slaves, as well as warriors from vassal city-states." He chewed on this information for a while before waving his hand, saying, "That Persian is inflating the numbers."

"I don't think he is lying," said Linos. "But I will know more after I have deciphered all of these documents in this bag . . . and tortured him, of course," he added in an apathetic tone. "He says the Spartans are going to build a wall around the entire citadel to prevent reinforcements or supplies and starve us out—part of the City-Killer's advice."

"A wall?" asked Nikias. "Around the entire citadel? That's impossible. It would take ten years to make a wall of stone—"

A trumpet blared from the wall and all of the men in the courtyard swiveled their heads in unison toward the sound. Three short blasts followed by a longer note. Then repeated.

"The warning call from the mountain lookouts," said Linos, staring in the direction of the mountain with his piercing eyes, as though he could peer straight through stone.

EIGHT

———— • ————

Nikias dashed out of the courtyard and into the street with Hesiod hard on his heels. They ran past the black marble Assembly Hall and into the open area of the agora where crowds of curious people milled about, wondering what was happening. When they got to the gate, the guards had already shut the two ten-foot-tall wood-and-iron-bound doors set into the eastern wall.

"What's going on?" Nikias yelled at the men standing on the guard tower, for he saw a crowd of warriors sprinting along the parapet wall in the direction of the southern section of the wall.

"Watchmen on the mountain!" a guard called down. "They sounded the alarm!"

While the guards hurried to obey, Nikias heard a shout behind him and turned to see Zoticus charging across the agora on his horse from the direction of the stables, followed by a score of riders, including Kolax.

"Open the gates!" bellowed Zoticus. "Open the gates!"

Nikias headed straight for the door to the guard tower flanking the right side of the gates and scrambled up the stairs to the level that led to the parapet wall. He ran along the walkway, passing through six guard towers on his half-mile-long sprint to the southernmost section of wall—the place that afforded the best view of the mountain. He entered the seventh tower and bounded up the stairs. When he came out onto the roof it was crowded with guardsmen armed with bows, all of them standing at the battlements, peering up toward the mountain. Nikias pushed between two of the men and leaned on one of the gaps in the stones. Below he saw Zoticus and his cavalry charging up the hill that stretched toward the mountain.

"What's going on?" asked Nikias. His best friend, Leo, wearing the armor of a tower guard, stood nearby. "What's happening?"

"Enemy," said Leo. And after giving Nikias a quick glance he said, "What happened to you? Kill someone?"

"Long story," replied Nikias, scanning the forested hillside. "Where are they?"

"Near the top of the mountain," said Leo, pointing. "Watchmen on the peaks sounded the first alarm. They've almost made it back down. Look!"

Nikias saw two Plataean horsemen, riding at breakneck speed, emerging from the spot near the foothills where the dense forest thinned to a few pines. They had been stationed on the peaks of the mountain, standing guard as an early warning against invasion. Far above them, coming over the ridgeline of the mountain, was a file of men marching methodically into the trees and then disappearing amongst the canopy on their way down into the valley. Nikias thought he caught a flash of red, but from this great distance he couldn't be sure if his eyes weren't playing tricks on him.

He watched expectantly as Zoticus and his small band of cavalry met up with the Plataean watchmen, then escorted them back to the citadel.

"Those enemy hoplites up there must have come directly from the fortress of Aigosthena in Megaria," said Hesiod, breathless. He had finally caught up to Nikias and was red-faced from exertion. "Otherwise the Skythians at the fortress of the Three Heads would have alerted us if the enemy had marched through that pass."

"Unless the Three Heads is already under attack," said Nikias despondently.

Nikias and the other watchers on the tower stood for an hour in almost complete silence, hypnotized by the seemingly never-ending line of men coming down the mountainside. After a while the invaders started to emerge from the woods—red-cloaked warriors, clad in armor and helms, who assembled silently on the treeless hillside above the citadel in a field of tall grass and spiked thistle, far beyond bowshot. During that time General Zoticus returned to the area in front of the wall after rounding up all his riders, this time in full force: four hundred men—every cavalryman in the citadel. The horses stood in four orderly groups, but the animals shifted nervously and swished their tails.

Between the Spartans and the walls of Plataea stood three large grass-covered mounds. These were the Graves of the Heroes—mass burial pits where the allied Greek dead killed in the Battle of Plataea had been buried with honor fifty years ago.

The southern wall now bristled with men—a thousand warriors with bows and spears. Nikias looked over at the tower to his left: there stood Menesarkus and Linos. They were speaking to the two watchmen who'd been stationed on the mountaintop, questioning them, no doubt, about what they'd seen of the enemy's movements.

Nikias's gaze wandered down to the citadel and Artisans' Lane below and the empty blacksmith shop that had once belonged to his friend, Chusor. The sign that hung outside the building—an old shield painted with a picture of the crippled god Hephaestos—squeaked on its rusted chains as it blew in the wind. Chusor, a foreigner who had set up shop in Plataea when Nikias was sixteen, had become one of Nikias's best friends. The man had saved him on the night of the sneak attack, rescuing him from a band of Theban warriors who had caught Nikias and his friends unawares in the street below. The smith was an ingenious inventor who had created something he called the "sticking fire," and had used it to burn down the Theban barricade that the enemy had set up in front of the gates—the wooden wall that trapped the Plataeans in their own citadel.

But Chusor had departed Plataea soon after the Theban attack and had not returned. Nikias wondered if he was still alive. He wished the inventor were here now. If it was true that this siege master—the City-Killer—was coming to Plataea, they could use a man like Chusor to help outwit the wily and deadly Persian. . . .

"I only count two thousand or so Spartan hoplites assembled on the hill," said Leo, interrupting Nikias's thoughts.

"That's better than sixty thousand," said Hesiod.

"What are you talking about, Hes?" asked Leo.

"Hesiod is talking out his arse," said Nikias, shooting Hesiod an exasperated look. Hesiod needed to learn to keep his mouth shut. Starting rumors of a massive invasion force would only lead to panic. Hesiod, catching sight of Nikias's black look, flushed and turned away.

"There's no way we could attack them," said Leo. "Not with them on the high ground."

"We would need twice those numbers to face a Spartan shield wall," said Nikias glumly. "Even with our cavalry. And Plataea can only muster twenty-five hundred armored hoplites. And half of those men are in the countryside now, on their farms."

He looked up and down the wall. All of the towers and parapets on this side of the citadel were now crowded with warriors armed with spears and bows. He looked back at the tower where his grandfather and Linos stood. They had stopped questioning the two riders and were staring at the Spartans with stony faces.

"Will they attack today?" asked Hesiod.

"They haven't brought any siege weapons," said Nikias. "They would be mad to attempt an attack."

"Then why are they here?"

"I have no idea," replied Nikias.

It was two hours after zenith—an hour since the horns had been sounded along the wall—when all of the Spartans who had come over the top of the mountain were finally lined up in several squares of tightly packed phalanxes.

And then, disconcertingly, the light started to fade from the sky. At first Nikias thought it was just a cloud passing over the sun. Then he glanced up and drew in his breath at the startling sight: the moon had taken a notch out of the sun.

"An eclipse!" shouted a voice on the wall.

The cry was taken up by many more. Men pointed and cried out in fear. Women shrieked from all over the citadel. Even the Spartans became unhinged and started shifting about, craning their necks to catch a glimpse of the ominous event. Nikias saw a warrior with a tall horsehair crest march up and down the Spartan ranks, screaming at the red-cloaked warriors in fury as the sky continued to darken and the stars that had been hidden by the blue cloak of the sky started to shine brighter and brighter.

"Do not look at the sun!" bellowed Menesarkus. "Do you hear me? It will blind you! Do not look at the eclipse! Avert your eyes, you idiots!"

Leo shielded his gaze obediently, but Nikias flicked a glance at the sun: the moon had almost completely covered it—there was still a crescent of glowing light at the top. He forced his eyes away and stared at the Spartans. The enemy had formed up ranks and were now staring straight ahead at the walls of Plataea.

"What does it mean?" asked Leo with a horrified whisper.

"Nothing good," said Hesiod tersely.

"This is what it must look like in Hades," said Nikias, gazing about at the darkened world that had been drained of color and life. He gazed at the faces of his friends and the other men standing on the tower. They all looked stricken . . . horrified. And afraid. Thankfully this terrible and unsettling shift in world lasted only a few minutes. The moon quickly passed across the sun and light returned to the earth. Nikias watched in awe as the transition from night to day happened before his eyes. The men on the tower exhaled as one.

After a long silence a Spartan warrior stepped forward from the rows of hoplites and approached the wall. Out of the corner of his eye Nikias saw his grandfather raise his hand in greeting.

"Here!" called Menesarkus. "Herald, come to me!"

The Spartan walked straight up to the tower where Menesarkus stood. He stopped at the base and tipped his head back to peer to the top of the forty-foot-tall square turret.

"Peace!" called out the Spartan herald. "And greetings to Menesarkus of the Nemean tribe, hero of the Persian War, winner of the Funeral Game of Leonidas, Olympic champion, Arkon of Plataea, and former guest-friend of the royal houses of Sparta!"

"Peace!" spoke Menesarkus with a booming voice. "I am Menesarkus. Old friends are welcome in the Oxlands, but I would remind you of the oath that your forefathers made after the Persian Wars when they vowed never to invade Plataea, such was the honor accorded to my city for the glory we shared in the defeat of Xerxes the Persian!"

"I have come from my king, Arkidamos the Second, regent of the Eurypontid tribe," said the herald, "to summon you to a meeting at the Graves of the Heroes!"

Menesarkus did not reply for a long moment, and Nikias saw him peering intently at the assemblage of Spartan hoplites.

"You mean that King Arkidamos is here now?" Menesarkus asked at length, and in a surprised tone.

"The king asks that you come alone and unarmed," stated the Spartan herald flatly.

"One of the kings of Sparta?" asked Leo. "Is out there? Stuff my arse!"

"He's joking, right?" whispered Hesiod. "They don't expect our leader to just walk out—"

"Quiet," said Nikias. He stared at his grandfather, trying to read his face, but he was too far away to see his expression.

Menesarkus turned and said something to Linos, then leaned over the parapet and called down, "Yes! Of course! I will come! I am honored to meet with him!" Then he turned and headed for the opening that led to the lower levels of the tower.

Nikias bolted to the tower stairs, flying down the steps until he came to the archway that led to the wall parapet, then dashed across the bulwark to the other tower just as his grandfather emerged onto the walkway.

"Grandfather!" Nikias blurted out. "What are you doing? You're not going down there, are you? Not after that sign from Apollo!"

"A Spartan king has come to parlay with me," replied Menesarkus. "He cannot enter into the citadel with Sparta engaged in open war with our Athenian allies. And so we must meet on open ground. The Graves of the Heroes will do nicely. The Spartans did not cause the eclipse. The gods are angry. With whom they are angry, however, is anyone's guess."

"What if the Spartans try to kill you or take you prisoner?" said Nikias desperately.

"They would be fools," said Menesarkus. "We keep twenty of their warriors as well as General Draco as hostages. If they kill me, they will never see their brothers alive again. Their hostages are worth far more to them than my old bones."

"But you cut off his nephew's finger!"

"*Great*-nephew," replied Menesarkus archly. "By his elder half sister's daughter, and thus not in direct line to the throne. Still a potential heir, however. Many accidents befall Spartan kings. King Leonidas died fighting the Persians at the Gates of Fire, we must remember. And now the Spartan Agiad king is in exile under suspicion of taking bribes from the Athenians."

Nikias put his hands on his grandfather's shoulders and looked hard into his eyes. "This is madness! Don't go!"

Menesarkus stared back intently and put one of his big hands on the back of Nikias's neck. "Calm yourself, my boy," he said with a faint smile. "The Spartans may not play by the same rules as us, but they are not as treacherous as Thebans, either." He smiled cynically. "That Spartan herald was very polite, was he not? Now go back to the tower and watch. You might learn something."

He kissed Nikias on the cheek and headed down the stairs that led directly to the street below the wall. Nikias watched him as he made his way through the crowds of people in the direction of the Gates of Pausanius; then Menasarkus vanished around a corner that led to the agora and was lost from sight.

NINE

———————◆———————

Nikias walked back up the tower stairs with heavy legs and took his place back amongst his friends, who were staring silently over the parapet. After a time Menesarkus appeared on the path below the wall that ran along the outside of the southern bastions. He walked slowly, leaning on his staff. To Nikias he seemed very small and frail . . . he looked like a doddering old man going on a stroll, rather than the powerful bull of a warrior who could still beat Nikias in a pankration bout.

"We'll have a good view from up here," said a voice from behind.

Nikias turned and saw Linos standing behind him.

"I told him not to go," said Nikias. "The eclipse . . ." he trailed off, not knowing what to say.

"I advised him the same," said Linos. "I begged him to send me instead, but he refused, of course. The eclipse has filled me with apprehension as well."

Nikias's heart raced as Menesarkus made his way between the rows of Plataean horsemen, then started climbing the gentle slope toward the Spartan lines alone. A tall warrior stepped from the Spartan ranks and removed his sword, handing it to the herald. Then he gave him his helm as well, and strode down the hill toward Menesarkus, scattering small birds that hid in the tall grass. The three large earthen mounds lay between them. Every year Plataea held a festival in honor of these dead: Plataean, Athenian, Spartan. This was hallowed ground for both the Plataeans and Spartans.

All of the Plataeans on the wall stood in utter silence. The only sound was the whistling wind and the distant clamor of some crows bickering with a flock of gulls near the cemetery outside the western wall of the citadel.

"What's the Arkon doing?" asked Hesiod, for Menesarkus had stopped near one of the grave mounds and was staring down at the ground, pushing something with the butt end of his staff.

"I don't know," said Nikias. "Maybe there's a snake in the grass."

Menesarkus glanced back toward the tower as if he could hear Nikias speaking, then turned and continued on his way toward the Spartan king, who had already come to a stop midway between the Spartan and Plataean burial mounds, which lay side by side. Nikias could make out the regent's face from this distance. He was a little younger than his grandfather and had long grayish brown hair and a thick beard of the same color.

The Arkon and the king spoke for a few minutes. During that time Menesarkus nodded his head and spoke little. At one point in the conversation Arkidamos made a sweeping gesture that encompassed the whole of the mountain looming behind them.

"Satyrs' pricks!" cursed Leo. "What is he saying?"

Nikias glanced at Linos, who raised his bushy gray eyebrows as if to say, "I don't have any idea."

The two leaders conversed for a few minutes longer. And then, without warning, their conversation ended abruptly. Menesarkus and the king simply nodded to each other, then turned and walked in opposite directions—the Spartan striding to his hoplites, Menesarkus limping back toward the Plataean cavalry.

"That's all?" asked Leo.

"Spartans are not known for being verbose," said Linos dryly.

When Menesarkus got to his horsemen he paused by General Zoticus and spoke to him quietly. The general nodded, then called up to the tower, "Bring the Spartan prisoners. All but Draco."

In a little while the prisoners appeared on the path below the wall: a score of lean and naked men with shaved heads. They marched in file on stiff legs, squinting in the sunlight. They had been kept in cramped, dark quarters, and their long hair had been cut to rid them of lice. They were led by their jailers—forty or so strong and grim-faced Plataeans who had guarded the Spartans day and night since they had been captured. The Spartans had not been treated cruelly: there had been no beatings or torture. But they had not been allowed freedom of movement, and their rations had been less than they were used to. And so they were in a weakened condition.

Menesarkus went up to the Spartan prisoners in turn and shook their hands. Each of the Spartans looked him in the eye and nodded. And then the Arkon of Plataea released them from their bondage, saying:

"Go in peace."

The Spartans walked slowly up the hill, between the burial mounds, and thence rejoined their brothers on the hill. When they got to their king they lined up in a row, bowing in unison. At a word from Arkidamos, twenty men in the front rows of the Spartan lines took off their cloaks and gave one to each naked prisoner, who clasped it around his neck. Then the freed men fell in with the ranks, blending into the sea of red.

King Arkidamos took one last look at Menesarkus, then marched past his men and headed up the goat path that led into the forest. Then the Spartans started to break from the phalanx in an orderly manner, following their king and vanishing into the trees.

TEN

———◆———

Nikias, Linos, and Hesiod found Menesarkus standing alone with his back to the southern wall, leaning on his staff, watching as the last of the Spartans departed the field. Zoticus and the four hundred horsemen had spread out and moved a little farther up the hill, away from the citadel—ready to ride to action if the Spartans returned. But the enemy was gone . . . at least for now.

"What did the king say to you?" asked Linos.

Menesarkus ignored his question and asked, "What is the bare minimum number of warriors it would take to man the walls of Plataea? To hold off a sustained siege—a siege meant to starve a city into submission."

"What does—"

"How many?" cut in Menesarkus. "We've spoken of this before but you always dither about the number. Tell me, Linos."

Linos peered up at the twenty-foot-high limestone wall rising behind Menesarkus. "Six hundred warriors," said Linos. "Two hundred standing watch on eight-hour-long watches."

"And how long could those men last with the supplies that we have now?"

"Almost three years," said Hesiod, chiming in.

Linos nodded. "Young Hesiod has been paying attention during our tallies."

"Three years," repeated Menesarkus. "Yes. Those were my calculations as well."

"What did the king say, Grandfather?" asked Nikias, bursting out with impatience. "Did he threaten to besiege Plataea?"

Menesarkus smiled out of the corner of his mouth and said, "On the contrary. He said nothing about a siege. He asked to *borrow* our citadel." He patted the rough stone wall behind him and grinned.

Nikias gave a nervous laugh. His grandfather did not say funny things very often. And this seemed a strange moment to make a joke.

Linos seemed to agree with him, for he scowled and said, "This is no time for jests, Arkon."

"I'm not jesting," said Menesarkus, a serious look in his eyes. "Those were his very words. 'We wish to borrow Plataea.' King Arkidamos told me that he knew that it was impossible for us to break our alliance with Athens, so he asked if Sparta might simply *occupy* Plataea until they have defeated the Athenians. We move out, they move in, they wage war and conquer all of Greece, and then we simply come back like returning swallows. He even offered to pay us rent."

"Rent?" laughed Linos. "Absurd!"

"Is he insane?" asked Nikias.

"All Spartans are mad in their own way," said Menesarkus. "But this one was completely lucid. He believes that this plan is a solution to both of our problems. There is a stipulation, however: we must abandon the city *completely*. We cannot leave any warriors behind to man the walls. And if any of our people try to make their way to Athens while Plataea's walls are still manned by our men, then the Spartans and their allies will set upon our women and children in the open country and slaughter them."

"How much time did he give us to abandon the citadel?" asked Linos.

"A week," said Menesarkus. "He said that the eclipse was Apollo's way of warning us."

"It's an absurd proposal," said Linos. "The Athenians would never give refuge to our people if we just abandoned the strongest city-state in Greece outside of Athens and gave it to their greatest enemy. Where does he expect us to go?"

"The Spartan king did not offer any counsel on accommodations," replied Menesarkus sharply. "He expects us to leave the citadel. Where we go afterward is of no concern to him." He paused and chewed on his lower lip contemplatively. "The eclipse fills me with great foreboding," he said at last. "Something horrible is going to happen."

"But did the king threaten a siege if we did not comply with the terms?" asked Nikias.

"I told you," said Menesarkus testily, "he avoided the subject altogether. And that is what worries me. I think that the Persian prisoner was telling the truth about the size of the army that the Spartans will bring to the Oxlands. That was no invasion force up on the hill," he said, pointing his staff at the place where the two thousand Spartan hoplites had stood just a few minutes ago. "Those warriors were merely the king's royal guard. Arkidamos came to try and stop a costly siege—quite possibly of his own accord, in contradiction to the orders of his ephors. And so he offered us this unusual way out of our dilemma. Technically we would not be betraying Athens, because we would not be fighting for the Spartans."

"It's a path that we cannot possibly take," said Linos.

"Of course not," replied Menesarkus. "The Spartans may break their oaths as it suits them, but we may not. Our alliance with Athens is carved in stone. If we hand over our citadel to them, we will never get it back. We will be a people without a city. Vagabonds on the road. Exiles."

"So what did you tell him?" asked Nikias.

"I said that we would consider his proposition," said Menesarkus. "And I gave him our remaining Spartan prisoners as a show of good faith. General Draco, as you could see, was not amongst the released men. He I will keep to the bitter end, along with that Persian messenger."

"One week," said Linos under his breath.

"Yes," said Menesarkus. "We have one week to get the aged, the women, and the children, and those not fit to defend Plataea to the safety of Athens. Eighteen thousand people."

In his mind's eye Nikias saw his pregnant wife and their two little girls, his sister, and grandmother, walking to Athens: a hard journey that would take at least three days on foot with so many people carrying their baggage. The Plataeans would have to take all the supplies that they could hold, for they couldn't show up empty-handed in Athens, a city already bursting with refugees from the countryside.

His stomach sank and he was overwhelmed by a feeling of dread. Anyone who fled to Athens would have to go over the mountain pass, then down the other side of the range and through Athenian lands that were now occupied by Spartan and Megarian raiding parties. The Plataeans could easily be caught out in the open and slaughtered like animals. The walls of the citadel looming up behind them seemed so high . . . so strong. To make their families leave such a powerful stronghold and put them in that kind of danger seemed like folly.

"But if he said nothing about a siege, Grandfather," Nikias said at last, breaking the dreary silence, "if the king made no threats, then we might just be jumping out of our skins for no good reason. Subjecting our people to attack on the road. It could be a trick to expose us."

"Do you remember what the Persian said to Linos?" asked Menesarkus. "About the Spartans making a wall around Plataea?"

Nikias nodded.

"When King Arkidamos and I were speaking just now," Menesarkus continued, "he asked me to see the logic of his proposition. His plan, he told me, was so simple a child might understand it. 'You can't see the forest because there are so many trees in front of you,' he said to me, and then he waved his hand at the forest on the mountainside."

Nikias recalled seeing the Spartan king make that gesture. "What does that—"

Suddenly and violently Menesarkus slammed his staff into the earth. "The king's thoughts were bent on the thousands of trees covering our mountain," he said. "The trees that he had just passed through. Zeus let me see into my enemy's mind at that moment. His plan was revealed to me! They're going to cut down the forest and use the trees to build their own wall around our citadel. A wall of stone would take years to erect. But"—he pointed to his staff—"a wall of trees, with enough men laboring night and day, could be put up in a matter of weeks. They would have us trapped, like badgers in a hole. The Spartans are patient. They would be willing to wait over a year until our citizens were feeding on rats and then . . . worse."

Linos cursed under his breath. Hesiod's eyes got bigger as he evidently contemplated Menesarkus's words. They all knew what Menesarkus meant. Citizens of cities under siege had been known to eat human flesh to stay alive. Nikias looked around, imagining a wall of timber surrounding Plataea, cutting it off from all help . . . his people feeding on the corpses of the dead.

"Six hundred Plataean warriors will stay behind," said Menesarkus suddenly. "The rest will go to Athens to protect our people: all of the women, children, and aged."

"But they'll be massacred on the road," said Nikias.

Menesarkus looked at Nikias and his eyes narrowed. "We'll create a diversion."

"Impossible," said Nikias with exasperation. "We can't hide our people in a . . ." He fought for words. ". . . in a magical mist."

"We would need Zeus himself to cover us with a cloak as big as the sky," added Linos bitterly.

"Yes," said Menesarkus, his eyes flashing with sudden insight. "That's it. A gigantic cloak. We need to create our own eclipse of the sun. And then General Zoticus and the cavalry—and you, Nikias—will help lead our people to Athens under its protection."

Nikias shook his head, utterly perplexed. "What are you saying? You can't make an eclipse!"

"Apollo has sent us a message," said Menesarkus. "It is always wise to obey the gods."

ELEVEN

This was not the first time that Chusor the smith had been as drunk as a satyr at dawn, and he reckoned it would not be the last. But this morning, with the ship bucking on the waves, and the overpowering scent of fried squid congealed in a bowl next to the sleeping alcove filling his nostrils, he wished that he had not been so self-indulgent last night. The eclipse that had occurred yesterday had filled him with dread.

But his lover, Zana, refused to drink alone. She was a stern mistress as well as the captain of their trireme—the *Spear of Thetis*. And despite the ominous eclipse, they had had a victory to celebrate: the capture of two Phoenician merchant ships laden with wheat. Those ships, now manned by some of the *Spear's* own crewmen, sailed close behind them. The convoy was on its way to an island where the crew of the marauding ship had its stronghold—the place where their families lived in safety while they pillaged the seas. After a day of rest and the restocking of food and water they would take the grain another sixty miles to the port of Piraeus.

The Athenians, who were trapped behind the walls of their citadel while the Spartans ravaged their lands, needed a constant supply of provisions to feed their people. Because of the ingeniousness of the Long Walls—the six-mile-long barricaded roadway that led from the walled port of Piraeus all the way to Athens—the Athenians were not about to starve inside their citadel. They ruled the seas with their fleet of three hundred triremes, and could ship in supplies from their island empire or faraway Egypt. But they still relied on marauders like the *Spear* to disrupt enemy shipping. And Zana's ship had been given a license by

General Perikles himself to capture any vessel that was not an ally of the Delian League, from the Inland Sea to the shores of Ionia.

After the grain was delivered the crew of the *Spear* would fill their pouches with more Athenian owls—shining silver coins made from the ore of the fabled mines of Laureion. But right now Chusor could give a fig about spoils. He pushed the bowl of squid away, then leaned over and puked violently into a bucket. Groaning miserably, he lay back down on the wool-stuffed mattress in the tiny cabin he shared with Zana—the only private cabin on the ship—listening to the heavy snoring of the naked woman sprawled next to him. Outside the shut door he could hear the wooden poles of the rowers squeaking in the oarlocks, and the rhythmic beat of the drummer keeping time. He couldn't decide which of the noises was more grating: the oars, the drum, or Zana's snoring.

She murmured sleepily and reached out, groping between his legs. But he pushed her hand aside.

"What's wrong with your prick?" said Zana lazily.

"I have to spill some water," he said.

Zana had the sexual appetites of a man. Which was perfectly fine with Chusor, for she was built like an Amazon, with big firm breasts and legs that seemed to go on forever. She could do things in bed that no other woman he'd lain with knew how to do. Her face was not beautiful, but it was not unlovely, either. She resembled a stern temple goddess—handsome rather than pretty. But she also possessed many bad habits. She was insanely jealous. She was murderous and rapacious. And she was as haughty as a Persian satrap.

Excellent qualities, he had to admit, for a captain of a pirate ship. She was, in fact, the exiled daughter of a deposed Phoenician ruler. She had been raised in a palace and had been taught to rule sternly and without mercy. Chusor was the one man who had managed to tame her.

But only just.

The satrap of Lydia, a Persian upon whose ships the *Spear* often preyed, had offered a bounty for this ship that would have made any man as rich as Kroesus, were he to win it. For the bounty was the weight of Chusor himself in the coins of Lydia: shining yellow electrum stamped with the head of a snarling lion.

And Chusor was no small man.

"The Egyptian" was what the people of Plataea had called him. He was a half-African, half-Phoenician giant, with a head of woolly untamed hair and a thick black beard. Not too long ago he had been as muscular as an Olympic athlete, with bulging biceps and pectorals as big as serving plates. That was when he'd been a blacksmith in the citadel of Plataea, hammering iron and bronze all day long to forge armor and weapons and other inventions. That's where he had befriended young Nikias.

But the luxury and indolence of a marauder's life at sea had made Chusor bloated. Eyes that once shone with intelligence were now glassy. A jaw that used to be lean and strong had turned into a double chin covered with a tousled beard. And his stomach, once rippled and defined, was now a flabby paunch.

Last week his friend Diokles told him that he was as fat as a pig. Fat! He'd never been called that word in his life until the stocky yet absurdly muscled Diokles—a runaway Spartan slave—hurled the insult at him. And if any man on the ship other than Diokles the Helot had insulted him that way, he would have ripped off his head. But Diokles was one of his oldest and most trusted friends.

"And sadly," Chusor mused, "he's right about my present condition."

He heaved himself to a sitting position and reached for a wineskin, draining the last drops from the leather bag, swishing it in his mouth, then spitting it into a bowl. The image on the bottom of the bowl showed an Amazon woman wearing a giant phallus and taking a muscular man from behind. Zana had had the bowl painted especially for Chusor as a gift. It was her own design. Was the picture a symbol of their relationship?

He glanced at something in the corner of the room—an empty cage hanging by a hook, banging against the hull with the rocking motion of the ship. The cage used to hold a messenger pigeon—a pretty bird that Chusor had kept as a pet for years. But the animal had flown off one day and never returned. A very bad omen.

He got up, stumbled to the door, and flung it open, ducking under the low sill and stepping awkwardly down the ladder to the floor of the hold. He stared blearily along the long gangway that ran from bow to aft between the three decks—one hundred and seventeen feet long. Rowers—twenty-seven on either side in single file—stared back at him with dull, glassy eyes: the long, staring look of men lost in the ceaseless rhythm of the oars. These were the men of the bottom deck. Their oar holes were so close to the waterline that the openings had to be covered with oiled leather sleeves to keep the ocean from flooding the ship—tight-fitting covers that, from the outside, resembled sagging pricks. Thus veteran mariners called the hold rowers "foreskins." This was the worst deck in the ship—sweat, piss, and occasionally even vomit from the men above leaked down on them through the planks. It was the hottest part of the boat, too, and if the trireme got rammed during a battle and the ship was swamped, the hold rowers were most likely to be drowned first.

The hold rowers sat with their faces practically in the arses of the oarsmen of the middle deck; these were called the thwart rowers and were of equal number on either side. And above them, seated on outriggers that jutted from the top of the boat, were the stool rowers, the elite men of the topmost deck—thirty-one to each side. The top deck was the most preferable place to be on a trireme, and only the strongest and most veteran oarsmen had the honor of keeping those positions, for the air was better up there, and you weren't covered in anyone's sweat or piss or vomit but your own.

One hundred and seventy rowers, along with a helmsman, a shipwright, a boy drummer, the captain, and the exhorter—the man who encouraged the men at their seemingly endless labor. Zana had given Chusor the title of prow officer, which was a meaningless rank but suited Chusor just fine, for he could wander freely about the ship, "prow-ling about," as he jokingly said.

All told, there were one hundred and seventy-five men and one woman on board the *Spear*—a small army of cutthroats and adventurers. They had already made a fortune in pay, such was the combined luck and skill of the *Spear*. Chusor had used his share to buy land on the small island where the marauders made their outpost. There, in that little haven, protected by the walls of a small but sturdy stronghold, his most important treasure lived, safe from the dangerous world: a coltish fourteen-year-old girl, his slender beloved, the only child he'd made with the courtesan Sophia—beautiful Sophia, dead and gone forever. He had not known of the girl's existence until two and a half years ago, when Nikias returned from his ill-starred journey to Athens with the news. And when he had learned that Melitta was living in the household of an evil man, he immediately went to Athens and took her, saving her from a life of indignity.

It was strange having a full-grown child, however. Especially one who gave him as much trouble as Melitta. He reckoned he knew how Zeus must have felt when, upon suffering a splitting headache, Athena emerged fully developed from a crack in his forehead.

He caught sight of his friend Diokles. He sat in the thwart row on the left side, pulling hard with his huge arms, squinting at Chusor with a disapproving look on his flat-featured face. Diokles was skilled enough to row in the top deck, but he liked being in the middle of the ship, hidden behind the wall of the boat; the sight of the sea unnerved him, for a soothsayer who used to be a member of their crew prophesied that Diokles would drown one day.

Chusor and Diokles had been mates on Zana's first vessel years ago, but they bolted from her ship after growing tired of Zana's caprices and the murderous life of a marauder. The friends had traveled to Plataea in the hopes of finding an ancient treasure that was rumored to be buried beneath the citadel. After years of searching, they had found the legendary trove—a tomb from the days of

Homer's heroes filled with gold, statues, and precious gems. With the threat of war looming in the Oxlands, they had rejoined Zana and used most of the treasure to buy the *Spear of Thetis*—a warship built in an Athenian shipyard that Chusor, along with the ship's carpenter, had modified along Chusor's designs.

These changes had made the *Spear* a terror on the seas. On the topmost deck—the battle deck, as it was called—they had built a railing, which most triremes lacked. This was a foolish omission, in Chusor's opinion. Shields could be attached to this balustrade to create a wall for warriors to use for cover when the *Spear* was forced to fight hull to hull with an enemy. At the prow was a detachable bronze ram of his own design. And mounted on the prow and aft were giant bolt shooters. A bolt shooter resembled a heavy bow set on its side, mounted on a swiveling wooden base. Turning a crank pulled the taut string back and locked it in place. The bolt shooters launched three-foot-long arrows, forged of solid iron, with such force that the projectiles could pierce the side of an enemy ship.

The *Spear* also carried Chusor's deadliest creation—the secret to the marauders' success on the seas. The thing sat in a special compartment at the prow, separated from the rest of the hold by a sealed bulkhead. Inside was an odd-looking contraption: a huge bronze container sealed by a stopper, with pipes connecting it to a great bellows attached to the floor. Coiled on the floor around it, like a fat black snake, was a long watertight tube crafted from skins and sealed with pitch. The chamber reeked of naptha—a flammable oil—and no man was allowed to enter the chamber, save Chusor and Diokles.

"The Kiss of Hephaestos"—that's what men called it, after the god of fire.

And hidden in a secret compartment under a false part of the hold was the last of the treasure: a gold cup, some rings and necklaces, and an exquisitely carved head of solid gold, about the size of a pomegranate, with the name Apollo inscribed at the base. These Chusor had saved so that one day he could return them to Nikias and the rightful heirs of Plataea. But when would that day ever come?

"You should take a turn at an oar!" called out a short and wiry man with squinting eyes who was standing in front of the bulkhead. He spoke cheerfully in Phoenician—the language in which he and Chusor usually conversed. This foreigner was named Ji, and he came from a far-off eastern land, a place of mighty warring kingdoms—so he said—where he had begun training in the arts of hand-to-hand combat as soon as he could walk. He was one of the longest-standing members of Zana's crew. His good-natured smile and pleasant demeanor always unsettled Chusor, for he knew these were merely an act: Ji was one of the deadliest killers he had ever met. He served as the ship's exhorter, the man who encouraged the rowers and also kept them in line. But the crew of cutthroats didn't need much motivation, and so Ji's duties on the boat were, like Chusor's, largely pretense. Ji's chief duties were protecting Zana and, when need be, the killing of men.

Ji left his post and stepped lithely across the things stowed in the hold—the bags of grain, masts, sails, and rigging—and came to a stop a few feet from Chusor, grinning up at him with his wide upper jaw of uniform teeth.

"I'm not feeling up to it," said Chusor.

"It would do you good. You could use one of Zana's silk pillows for your fat arse."

Diokles let forth a barking laugh and he and Ji exchanged a knowing look.

Chusor smiled wryly. "An oarsman is only as good as his arse," as the old saying in Athens went. So the men were careful to protect their posteriors by buying the finest padded leather cushions they could get their hands on. But Chusor hated rowing. When he'd first joined Zana's crew years before, he'd been forced to plow the sea with an oar, and it had been misery. The effort hadn't been the hardest part. It was the spectacular boredom that had nearly destroyed him.

It always amazed him that such wild and freedom-loving men could have the discipline to pull the oars for eight hours at a stretch. They always made Chusor think of the automatons who served Hephaestos, god of smiths, in his magic castle.

Ji gestured toward Diokles. "I'm sure Diokles would give up his place."

"I can fart longer than he can pull an oar!" called out Diokles.

Some of the oarsmen within earshot laughed heartily, but others turned their eyes away from Chusor, not wanting to incur his anger. He was the captain's man, and they were afraid of him.

Chusor scowled at Diokles. Then he clambered up the stairs to the battle deck, grumbling under his breath. For an instant he wished he were back inside Plataea, surrounded by the enemy. He wondered what Nikias was doing now. He wished that he could make an invention that would send thoughts across the sky. But what would he say to his friend now? "I stole your city's treasure . . . and I have grown fat."

TWELVE

Chusor stood on the deck at the stern of the *Spear*, pissing with the wind, sending a stream of urine soaring off the aft in a great arc that reached all the way to the water fifteen feet below. The two captured cargo ships, their sails unfurled in the strong breeze, followed in the *Spear*'s wake. He felt a sudden urge to dive into the sea and just swim until he either drowned or was washed up on the shore of some little island. He felt like Odysseus taken captive by Kalypso—only instead of being a prisoner on a witch's island, he was trapped on this stinking ship, screwing in that stuffy little cabin night and day. The thought made him queasy again.

His life in Plataea had been so much more fulfilling. There he had made things rather than destroyed, and he had gained the respect of his friends because of his skills rather than his deviousness. Menesarkus had assigned him to be the master of walls as a reward for his services during the sneak attack on the citadel, and had even offered to grant him citizenship if he stayed in Plataea and helped devise ways to repel a Spartan siege. Chusor had been born a slave in Athens, and the notion of citizenship had held the lure of a siren's song. But he had betrayed the people of Plataea, and his friend Nikias, by stealing the treasure from beneath their city, and had bolted from danger, abandoning his friends and giving up forever the opportunity to become a citizen of a city-state.

He looked down at his protruding gut and was filled with self-loathing. How had he come to this wretched state? The other night he had dreamt that he possessed the magical ring of Gyges—a golden ring that made the wearer invisible. When he put on the ring, however, it only made his prick disappear. A disconcerting dream. He almost wished that their old shipmate Barka the eunuch was here. Barka was a soothsayer who had enjoyed interpreting Chusor's dreams for him . . . usually casting a pall with his gloomy predictions. Annoyingly, the eunuch's prophecies often came true. But Barka was on the island of Sicily now, living at the palace of a wealthy man who was so powerful in the shaky democracy of Syrakuse that people called him the Tyrant.

Just then he heard a strange sound carrying on the wind. At first he thought it was a seabird. But there were no gulls in the sky.

"What was that sound?" asked the helmsman, Agrios, who sat nearby on his throne-like seat affixed to the top deck at the aft of the boat. The gray-bearded man—the oldest and most valued member of the crew—craned his neck to peer down the length of the deck and around the upswept prow at the other end of the long ship.

Chusor walked swiftly along the left side of the upper deck until he came to the bow, jumping down onto the little sloping foredeck. He leaned around the wooden bow-like piece jutting from the prow and saw a two-decked galley a quarter of a mile away. Even from this distance he could see that the boat was in disarray. Its main sail was rigged but askew, and the lines were tangled. A few men stood at the side railings, waving their arms frantically.

Chusor turned and shouted down into the hold, "Ji! Come here!"

Ji scrambled up the ladder.

"Ship," said Chusor. "It's Greek."

"A trap?" asked Ji.

"I don't see any other vessels. And none of its oars are at the ports. It's just drifting."

Ji shouted directions to Agrios, who turned the *Spear* slightly to intercept the other boat. As they got closer Chusor saw objects floating around the ship, as though the crew had jettisoned everything on board because of a leak in the hull. But there was no sign that the ship was swamped—it sat high in the water.

Zana appeared at Chusor's side. She had thrown on a man's tunic and strapped her sword around her waist.

"What's floating around that ship?" she asked.

"I don't—"

Chusor stopped midsentence. His eyes grew wide with horror as he realized what he was looking at. Corpses in the water. And there were sharks moving round and round the ship, and they paused now and then to tear on human flesh.

The men on the deck of the other vessel pushed another lifeless body over the edge to join the floating throng of death.

"What in the name of Astarte are they doing?" asked Zana, horrified.

Chusor shook his head. He realized there must be seventy or more bodies in the water. Nearly the entire crew of the bireme.

When the ship was close enough to hail, Zana cupped a hand to her mouth and shouted, "Who are you?"

A man on the ship called back, "We need help! A sickness swept through the decks. It happened so fast. Nearly all of our slaves are dead. We don't have enough to man the oars. We're stranded. Please, help us!" he begged.

"He's a Korinthian," said Chusor. "I can tell by his accent."

"I know," said Zana.

Ji ordered the oarsmen to stop rowing and the *Spear* came slowly to a stop almost parallel with the other boat on the open water.

"What kind of sickness?" Chusor called back.

"I don't know," said the man. "A terrible fever, followed by . . ." The wind came up hard, drowning out his words.

"What did he say?" asked Zana.

"Black bile from the nose," said Chusor. "I couldn't hear the rest."

Ji said, "'An unquenchable thirst' were his words."

Zana shook her head violently. "We can't bring them on board. I've never heard of a sickness killing that many men so fast."

"We must leave them," agreed Ji. "Their ship is cursed. The eclipse."

Zana glanced at Ji. "Put us back on course for Serifo."

Ji nodded and shouted a command to Agrios.

"What's that?" asked Zana, pointing at the Korinthian galley.

A man was squirming through one of the lowest oar holes near the water-line. He had torn away the protective oiled leather cover that prevented water from getting in through the round opening, and had greased his skin with oarlock tallow to make himself slippery enough to squeeze through the small hole—a hole that didn't seem big enough for such a broad-shouldered man. It looked as though the Korinthian ship were giving birth. The man dropped into the water and pushed aside corpses, lashing out at a shark that got in his way. He started swimming desperately toward the *Spear*, a hundred feet away.

"He's mad!" declared Zana.

The mariners on the top deck of the Korinthian ship spotted the swimmer and reached for weapons, throwing spears and shooting arrows that whizzed past his head, but the man dove under the water and vanished from sight.

"Where did he go?" asked Zana.

"Maybe a shark got him," said Ji.

The swimmer didn't come up for such a long time that Chusor thought he was most likely drowned or taken by one of the giant rapacious fish. But suddenly the man burst from the water right next to the *Spear*, gasping for air and clawing at the hull.

"Let me on board!" he screamed in Greek. "Let me on board! I'm not sick! I didn't have the fever! Help me! I'm Athenian! My friends will pay you a great reward—"

He tried to grab onto one of the poles sticking out from the lowest level, but an oarsman jerked it hard, cracking the escaped slave on the side of the head. He fell back and slumped down with his face in the water.

Chusor didn't hesitate. He jumped over the side. The plunge into the cold water was a shock. But he swam quickly to the escaped slave, grabbing him around the chest from behind and pulling the man's head up, treading water with his powerful legs.

"What are you doing?" Zana screamed down at him, her face twisted in wrath.

"I'm not going to let an Athenian drown," Chusor yelled back. "If he didn't catch the fever that killed the others, then he has been blessed by the gods."

An arrow slammed into the hull above Chusor's head. Zana reached down and grabbed a bow, nocked an arrow, and sent it flying at the enemy ship. One of the Korinthian archers fell over the side with an arrow in his neck, and the others scattered.

Zana glared down at Chusor, shouting, "I should leave you both in the sea."

"So be it!" Chusor spat back, choking on a mouthful of water.

"Bring them on board," Zana said to Ji. "But Chusor and the other are to stay on the top deck until we get to the island." Then she stormed off in the direction of her cabin.

Ji called for help and mariners ran up to the rail—led by Diokles—and lowered down a rope, quickly pulling Chusor and the Athenian to the upper deck. Then Ji barked out commands to the men at the benches and Agrios at the helm. The *Spear*'s oars dipped into the water and the ship started moving quickly away from the stranded Korinthian vessel.

Chusor knelt by the Athenian. The man's back was covered with hundreds of scars—years of whip marks. He had obviously suffered many abuses while a prisoner of the Korinthians, but he was attractive and well built. The skin on his shoulders was scraped raw where he had squeezed through the oar hole. Suddenly he coughed and spat up water, then rolled onto his side and glanced up at the curious mariners staring down at him.

"Are you a . . . friend or foe of Athens?" the stranger asked with ragged breaths.

Diokles offered him a wineskin and he drank from it greedily.

"We have a license to raid for the Athenians," said Diokles. "But we are no man's servant."

"Thank . . . the gods," the stranger replied. He got slowly to his knees. "I need a knife," he said.

Diokles looked at Chusor and he nodded back. Diokles slipped a boat knife from his belt and gave it, handle first, to the stranger. The man clutched the knife, and held out his left hand where the letter *K* had been tattooed between his thumb and pointer finger. With a quick stroke he sliced off a hunk of skin, removing the flesh with the tattoo; it landed on the deck with a sickening slap. The man made a fist and raised it at the other ship, which was now far behind them. "Die!" he screamed. "I have escaped from your prison! I am your slave no more! The eclipse foretold your doom! Go to Poseidon's house and join all of my brothers who died by your hands!"

He turned and stared at Chusor, breathing hard. His shoulders slumped and he started to sob, covering his face with his hands. Blood trickled down his arm and dripped onto the deck. He dropped the knife.

"Who are you?" asked Diokles, reaching down and taking his blade.

"My name is Phoenix."

Chusor said, "Welcome aboard the *Spear of Thetis*, Phoenix the Athenian."

THIRTEEN

———◆———

It was midnight and Nikias sat in a chair holding his sleeping daughter Agathe on his lap, cradling her in his arms, singing in a quiet voice to lull her back to sleep. Her heavy eyelids sagged, but she was trying desperately to stay awake. She was a fighter, Nikias mused, just like her father. She battled Morpheus every night. But the god of sleep always won.

"How come a sculptor has never made a statue of a man holding his child?" Kallisto asked from the other side of the darkened bedchamber. Her voice was somber and distant.

Nikias peered across the dim lamplit room. His wife sat propped up in bed nursing their other daughter, Penelope. Kallisto looked so lovely now, with her long black hair unloosed from its braid and pouring over her shoulders. The single oil lamp cast the room in a pale glow that made Kallisto's striking face appear to be carved from marble. She lovingly stroked the top of Penelope's head, and Nikias felt a pressure in his throat . . . as though the vast love he felt for his little family was swelling his heart and leaving no more room in his breast.

He said, "Men only carve what they see as important—warriors and ath-letes, gods and monsters. And sometimes horses," he added wryly, and stood up very carefully, rocking the child as he walked to the shuttered window. He stepped on something hard and a sharp pain shot through his heel. He cursed under his breath. Looking down, he saw a wooden doll sprawled on the floor, and he pushed it aside with his foot in annoyance. He went to the window and opened the shutter, peering down into the courtyard below where a torch burned in a sconce, illuminating his grandmother and sister as they knelt by some travel bags—checking over everything that they would need for the long journey to Athens.

Kallisto switched Penelope to her other breast. "This one needs so much more milk." She spoke out loud, but she was talking to herself. After a pause she asked, "What would you carve a statue of, husband?"

"I prefer statues of goddesses," said Nikias. "So I would sculpt you."

Kallisto frowned and sniffed, a sign that she was not in the mood for honeyed words. "I don't want to go to Athens," she said flatly.

"We must," Nikias replied.

"I'm afraid."

"Grandmother said—"

"She lied to you," said Kallisto with abrupt ferocity, causing Penelope to start. Kallisto made a shushing sound and rocked Penelope for a little while, soothing her back to complacency, then said in a softer voice, "She said that to make you feel better. I fear that if I am forced to travel tonight I will lose the child. The bleeding is getting heavier."

"You will ride in a covered cart with the girls," said Nikias. "I've padded it with blankets and pillows. Don't worry. Artemis loves you. She will protect you and the baby."

Kallisto shook her head. "But you are worried. I heard you praying to *Zeus*, not Artemis. You know how dangerous it will be for us to cross the mountains. Four days on the road to Athens. We might be attacked. The girls—"

"We can't stay here," insisted Nikias. "Imagine you and the girls and the baby behind the walls of Plataea when it's surrounded by the enemy. The siege might last years."

"I would rather die at home than on the road to Athens," said Kallisto.

"And what of our children?" asked Nikias. "Where would you rather have them die?" The moment the words had left his mouth he regretted saying them, for Kallisto's eyes welled with tears and she stifled a sob. Nikias looked at Agathe—the child who had been named after his beloved mother. She was sound asleep, so he set her down in her little bed and went to Kallisto's side and knelt. "I'm sorry," he said, taking her hand and kissing it. "I'm sorry for what I said. But we don't have any choice."

Kallisto turned her face away as tears rolled down her cheeks. "What will we do when we get to Athens?" she asked. "How will we survive?"

"The women can weave," said Nikias. "And the men and I will join the triremes and fight for Athens."

"Weaving and rowing," said Kallisto. "While Plataea stands alone."

"Enough warriors will remain behind to protect the walls," said Nikias.

"You wish you were staying, don't you?" she said.

"Grandfather has entrusted me with helping to bring everyone safely to Athens. I would not let my family make the journey without me." But it killed him to be leaving his grandfather and friends behind, Leo and Hesiod among them.

"The eclipse has filled me with fear," she said. "The gods are angry."

"At whom?"

"Nobody ever knows," replied Kallisto. "And that's why men always stumble their way blindly to their dooms."

He leaned forward and kissed Penelope on the forehead and Kallisto put her cheek on the back of his head. They stayed like that for a long time, just breathing. The redolent scent of Penelope's hair mingled with the natural perfume of Kallisto's body was intoxicating. He would be astonished if the air of Elysium was more fragrant than this.

"When my grandfather was walking to the Graves of the Heroes to speak to the Spartan king," said Nikias, "he told me that he saw a sign: there was a dead fox in the grass. It had no wound. It had just died. Very strange."

"What does it mean?"

"You know the old story of the Spartan boy? The one who held a stolen fox under his cloak and let it eat his guts, rather than admit he had taken it?"

"Yes, of course."

"The dead fox in the grass stands for the Spartans. And the gods were letting my grandfather know that they could be defeated, no matter how cunning they might be."

Kallisto shrugged with one shoulder. Evidently she was not impressed with the story of the dead fox, but his grandfather's story had filled Nikias with hope.

"Young master?"

It was Mula, standing in the doorway.

"You must go and join the others," said Kallisto. "We'll see you when you return from the mountain."

Nikias stared into Kallisto's eyes for a long time and she gazed back intently. Then he kissed her on the lips and left the room.

A slender Persian man waited at the bottom of the stairs, holding a lamp. His gaunt yet regal face wore an austere look. This was Mula's father, Saeed. The Persian had only been nine years old at the time he was captured by Menesarkus at the Battle of Plataea—a prince's groom who had spent his miserable life up until then mistreated by his vicious master. Menesarkus beheaded the prince and Saeed fell at the Greek warrior's feet, weeping and begging for his life. Nikias's grandfather, splattered with the blood and guts of the men he had destroyed that day, ruffled Saeed's hair and smiled at him in a kindly way, saying

"You my prize now" in broken Persian. At least, that's the story Saeed had told Nikias since he was a little boy, for Saeed had helped raised Nikias, teaching him how to ride as well as to wield the Sargatian lasso. He was more like an uncle than a family servant. And he had saved Nikias's life at the Battle of the Gates against the Thebans.

"Come, Nik," said Saeed. He led Nikias into the biggest room, where he had laid out all of the family's weaponry. "The bows have all been strung, the strings are waxed," he said. "Each of the women will carry one on the journey. There are twenty arrows in each quiver," he added, gesturing at a pile of arrow cases.

"Good," said Nikias. His sister, his grandmother, and Kallisto, like most of the women in Plataea, were better archers than the men, learning from childhood to shoot and participating in the sacred festival of Artemis every year—a day when the women hunted in the fields and forests alone and the men stayed home with the children.

Saeed said, "I sent all the armor and shields to the citadel with the men who came to collect the last of the supplies today."

"They got all of the pitch?"

"All except one jar. I will use it to burn down the house after we have departed."

"Make certain there is nothing left," said Nikias. He regretted destroying the house they had so recently built. But they couldn't leave any habitations in the countryside standing. The Spartan invaders would have to make their own shelters in the Oxlands, and not occupy Plataean homes like birds that steal nests.

He regretted having to leave behind his cherished gear—a breastplate, greaves, and helm that had been made by Chusor—but they were too heavy to bring on the journey to Athens. He was glad that one of the warriors who stayed behind would be able to make use of it. "Let Pelops have my armor," he said, naming a warrior who would remain in the citadel. "He's almost my size."

Saeed nodded. The Persian slave would be staying behind as well, along with Mula. Saeed would never leave his master Menesarkus's side, and thus his young son would stay with him as well, despite the danger. He reached down and picked up a sword belt with a scabbard and fastened it around Nikias's waist. Then he tied on Nikias's Sargatian lasso in a breakaway knot.

Nikias pulled the sword from the sheath and looked keenly at the blade in the lamplight. It was the weapon that Chusor had found in a tomb beneath the citadel, and it was engraved with words in an ancient tongue signifying that it was the Sword of Apollo. It had been wrought of some mysterious combination of metals and was extremely sharp. And it had remained in perfect condition for hundreds of years, wrapped in oiled skins, even though the handle and pommel had rotted away. Chusor had replaced these parts and had given the sword to Nikias after he had been released by the Spartans. The pommel was made of bronze with the inscription "Of Plataea" scored into it.

Suddenly a scream pierced the night.

Nikias, his heart pounding, flew through door and into the courtyard. His sister stood with her hands to her gasping mouth, while Eudoxia was holding a broom nearby. She had pinned something underneath it—a long, fat, squirming thing.

"Snake," said Eudoxia

"Step aside," said Nikias. "I'll cut it in half."

"No," said Eudoxia. "Look."

Nikias grabbed the burning torch from the wall sconce and held it down low. The snake had something sticking from its mouth—two little yellow legs and talons.

"It swallowed a baby owl," said Mula, horrified.

"This is bad," said Saeed.

"Spike and hammer," ordered Eudoxia.

Saeed darted out of the courtyard. Mula bent down and grabbed the snake behind the head and picked it up, letting its tail dangle. It was almost as long as the boy was tall—with black and orange rings. And it was fat.

"Nikias!"

He looked up to where Kallisto stood at the window. "What happened?" she asked in a harsh whisper.

"Nothing," said Nikias. "Don't worry. It's just a snake. My sister got scared. Go back to bed."

But it wasn't just a snake. It was a snake that had swallowed an animal sacred to Athena. It was a terrible omen. A foreboding of death and disaster. Saeed quickly returned and gave a hammer and a spike to Eudoxia.

"Take it to the door," she commanded, uttering a prayer to Hestia, goddess of hearth and home.

Mula dashed out of the courtyard with the snake and everyone followed him through the house to the front portal. Nikias opened the door and they all stepped onto the threshold, then he shut the door behind them.

"Hold the creature to the door," said Eudoxia.

Mula did as he was told, and Eudoxia put the spike in the middle of the snake and nailed it to the wood with two firm blows. The creature writhed wildly but did not release the owl, thrashing against the door like a worm on a hook, its body slapping against the planks, drumming out a dull and chaotic beat, as though a persistent visitor stood knocking gently at the door and would not go away. Blood and guts oozed from the hole made by the spike.

"Nikias," said Saeed. "You must get back to the city. The men will be leaving for the mountain soon. Take Mula with you in case the Arkon needs to send us a message."

Nikias pried his eyes away from the sickening yet mesmerizing sight of the snake.

"Be ready to depart at dawn," said Nikias. He went to the stable and found Photine, then took her into the yard and mounted. Mula came running up and Nikias reached down, lifting him up so he sat in front. Then he kicked the horse and galloped down to the road that led to the citadel, staring at the dark walls of the city looming ahead, but all that he could see was the image of the writhing snake that was burned onto his brain.

FOURTEEN

———◆———

At three hours after midnight the gates of Plataea opened silently—the great hinges on both doors had been greased so that they would not make a sound. A throng of warriors—five hundred strong—stood bunched together at the entrance to the citadel, staring silently into the darkness outside the walls. None of the men wore armor or helms, only tunics and sandals. They all had large amphoras affixed to their backs with leather strapping. And each had a leaf-bladed sword on his hip.

Without a word they exited the citadel, moving along the outside of the wall to the southern section of the barricade. Once they got to this point they separated into smaller groups of four to ten and headed up the slope toward the great mountain that stood frowning above the valley. After the last man had departed through the gates, the tall wooden doors swung shut from the inside and were barred. Less than a minute had passed for this sortie to exit the citadel.

Nikias, Leo, Kolax, and another young warrior named Baklydes walked together through the field of thistles to the south of the citadel toward the Graves of the Heroes—the same place where Menesarkus and the Spartan king had met the day before. The moon had set long ago, and the sky was covered by a high lid of wispy clouds, blocking out some of the starlight. Nikias glanced to his right and saw another group nearby. He gave a slight wave and the leader waved back. Beyond this company of men Nikias could just make out a few more groups heading west. There were no goats or shepherds or their dogs in the fields. All of them had been brought into the citadel earlier that day. The men with their strange burdens were the only ones moving in the night.

"These things are heavy," whispered Kolax, adjusting the straps of his jar.

"Shhh," hissed Leo. "I'm counting out the time."

"No talking," said Baklydes. He was Hesiod's much less talkative older brother.

Nikias came to a shelf of rocks and clambered up, coming out onto a narrow goat path that led straight into the forest. He paused and peered into the gloom of the trees, listening for any sound. The Spartans might have scouts positioned near the citadel, or Dog Raider spies could be lurking in the shadows, so they had to be cautious. He looked at Leo and saw his lips moving as he counted.

"You are all like Prometheus tonight," his grandfather had told the men when he addressed them in the agora just before their departure. "Bringers of fire."

Nikias hefted the bulky jar into a more comfortable position, then started walking up the path. The only sound was the whisper of their sandals on the gravel of the path, and the occasional hoot of an owl. Soon they were walking amongst gnarled oak and olive trees; he breathed in the air, which was rich with those scents. A deep sadness washed over him. The forest on the mountainside—a sacred refuge of the goddess Artemis—was ancient and famous throughout Greece. The god Dionysus and his followers used to walk these hills. And the baby Oedipus, doomed from birth to slay his father and marry his mother, had been left by a shepherd to die on the mountaintop. The summit itself, though, was the most sacred spot of all. And this was where they were headed.

"But all of this must be destroyed," he thought morosely. The people of Plataea had been given no other choice. Tonight they would burn the forest to the ground to keep the Spartans from using the trees against them.

"Did you hear that?" asked Kolax. He stopped and whirled, nocking an arrow to his bow and pointing it down the path behind them.

Nikias peered into the dark and saw a shape moving there. "Don't shoot," he commanded.

But Kolax had already dropped his bow and was smiling. "Mula," he said. "I know his footsteps."

Sure enough, the boy scampered up the trail and stopped in front of them, breathing hard.

"What are you doing here?" Nikias growled.

"I wasn't going to be left behind," said Mula. "I snuck out with the other men when the gates were opened."

Kolax laughed and cuffed Mula on the side of the head. "Good one," he said with admiration. "I didn't even see you."

"Your father is going to have the skin off your arse when we get back," said Nikias.

"I don't care," said Mula. "I'm not going to stay in the city with the women and babies."

Nikias turned to Leo. "How much time has passed?"

Leo held up ten fingers then five more.

"Keep moving," said Nikias.

They continued their quick ascent, following the trail that had been worn by countless goats and shepherds, deep into the heart of the pine forest. At one point a large buck bounded across the trail right in front of Nikias—one of its antlers brushed against his chest—causing his heart to leap in his breast, for his first thought was that it was a lion. But the only other sign of life that he saw was the occasional tortoise feasting on the leaves of weeds that lined the path, or startled hares and lizards darting in the undergrowth.

Nikias pushed on, breathing hard, heedless of the stabbing in his calves. His group had been selected for their speed. Nikias, Leo, and Baklydes were three of the fastest mountain climbers in the city. And Kolax was strong despite his wiry frame. Even little Mula was keeping up with them. But every step of the way Nikias expected an enemy arrow to come flying from the dark.

"Thirty minutes," whispered Leo behind him.

They had made good time and were almost to the top of the mountain. Nikias could see the glow of the moon rising from behind the trees on the summit, twenty feet above. He found a place where stairs had been graven in the rock and climbed quickly all the way to the top, the wind growing stronger with every step.

He emerged into a small clearing lit by starlight. Here the pines had been cut down hundreds of years ago to make a gathering place. He stood for a moment, catching his breath, looking about anxiously, squinting into the wind that whipped around the summit.

In the center of the clearing was a heap of dead branches—a jumble as big as a house. A wooden effigy stood atop the pile. It was the figure of a smiling young woman draped in real clothing. The painted face grinned down at him in the moonlight, its dress undulating in the wind, causing it to look very much alive.

An old legend said that Zeus's wife, Hera, had become angry with the god and had run away to the island of Euboea. Zeus asked King Kithaeron of Plataea to help him mend his marriage, and the wise king ordered a statue carved of a beautiful woman and placed it on the summit of the mountain. Then King Kithaeron told Hera that Zeus was going to marry a fetching Plataean maiden, and the worried Hera came flying to the mountain to stop the nuptials. When she saw that the bride was made of wood, she laughed and forgave her husband, and Zeus set the statue on fire with a bolt of lightning.

A statue of a maiden was burned every seven years during a spring festival. But the bonfire would be coming early this year.

Nikias glanced at the statues of Zeus, Hera, and King Kithaeron standing sentinel on the right side of the clearing. These statues were also made of wood and attired in clothes. They had been here for untold years, smiling enigmatically, cracked and weathered by wind and sun and rain.

He walked around to the other side of the pyre and gazed down the southern slope of the mountain toward Megaria. The wind whipped into his face, blowing hard from that direction. Perfect conditions to fan the flames and send the fire spreading back down the mountain and toward the Oxlands.

When Nikias came back around, the others stood waiting for him in front of the pyre. He slipped his arms from the leather straps and removed his burden, setting the clay jar on the flat pavers. The others did the same. Then Nikias removed the wax plug from the mouth of each jar and the pungent reek of pine resin punched him in the nostrils. Kolax, kneeling at his side, laughed softly.

"This is going to be fun," said the barbarian. He reached into his pouch and pulled out a handful of white powder. This was the stuff that Chusor had taught the men of Plataea to make: crushed gypsum mixed with limestone and bat guano. A powder that caused fires to burn with an unstoppable ferocity.

"Don't use the powder until the fire is already raging," Nikias told him.

"I know, I know," muttered Kolax, thrusting his hand back into his pouch.

"Now spread the pitch on the driest trees," said Nikias, hefting his jar.

They went to work pouring out the highly flammable liquid. Nikias dumped most of his over the branches beneath the effigy, then dripped the remains of the syrupy substance in a line across the stone floor to some dry shrubs at the edge of the clearing.

Out of the corner of his eye he saw something standing in the black shadow of the statue of King Kithaeron: a cloaked and hooded figure of a man, as still as stone. Had somebody brought another wooden effigy to the summit? Nikias wondered. He stared for several seconds, but the thing did not move.

He walked slowly toward it, drawn by the eerie apparition. As he got closer he noticed that the figure's hand gripped a thick branch.

"Die!" The figure lunged at him with the makeshift club, swinging for his face, and Nikias swept up with the empty jar, using it as a shield, smashing it into the attacker's arm.

"Eye snatcher!" shouted the man, staggering toward the pile of branches and clutching his wounded arm. "Cursed of Zeus—eater of shades!"

Nikias stepped back, wide-eyed, clutching the rim of the broken jar. The stranger threw back his hood and stared at Nikias with a single bulging eye.

His gaunt face was covered with a ragged beard. His long hair was greasy and lank. The man sucked in his breath, then let forth a bloodcurdling scream that echoed down the mountainside, the tendons in his neck bulging.

Nikias's companions rushed to his side, staring in wonder at the shrieking man.

"The mad seer!" said Kolax, and uttered an oath in Skythian.

"Make him shut up!" said Leo. "You could hear him screaming in Plataea!"

"We can't kill him," said Kolax, dropping his bow. "He's holy."

The Theban pointed a finger at Nikias. "You!" he cried. "Honor taker! Nothing for you, Plataean, but death! Death to your unborn!" He let forth another hair-raising cry.

Nikias stood frozen by this nightmare figure. He had grappled with the young warrior in the streets of Plataea on the night of the sneak attack and had gouged the man's eyeball from his skull, digging his thumb deep into the enemy's brain. And then, on that fateful eve that Nikias had departed the Oxlands for Athens, he had run into the Theban near the Cave of Nymphs. The madman had cursed him then, just like now. The sight of him filled Nikias with loathing . . . and terror.

"Stop screaming!" commanded Baklydes. He stepped forward and punched the Theban on the side of the head, and the madman stumbled and fell down but continued to cry out.

Leo darted forward and grappled with the man, putting him into a headlock and dragging him to the edge of the summit, then hurled him over the southern edge. The Theban tumbled like a stone before coming to a stop against a toppled tree.

"We must light the fire!" said Baklydes, turning to the others. "Quickly!"

Nikias passed a hand over his face, stunned into inaction by this terrible omen he had just witnessed. Why had the Theban come here, of all places? On this night? And how did he know that Nikias had an unborn child? His skin prickled and the world seemed askew, as if in a nightmare.

"Who has the firestone?" asked Leo.

Nikias checked his pouch and found that it was empty. He had somehow forgotten to put one of the spark-making stones in his pouch. "It's not there," he said, his heart sinking even further.

"Oh, come, now!" exclaimed Kolax. "What a sheep-stuffer! Lucky for us I can start a fire with my bow, but it will take a long time in this wind."

"Don't worry!" said Mula. "I brought a firestone." He held forth a hunk of the glimmering rock and it glinted in the dim starlight.

"Good work, Mula!" said Leo, patting him on the back.

"Yes," said Nikias with relief. "Good job—"

His words were cut short by a menacing noise: horses' hooves and the shouts of men.

"Riders!" said Kolax, pointing to the west.

Through the trees Nikias saw a line of torches approaching fast along the ridgeline. At least twenty horsemen. They must have been stationed near the summit and been alerted by the screams of the mad Theban. The sight of them roused him to action. He grabbed the firestone from Mula's hand and drew his blade, kneeling on the ground by the pile of branches. He struck the sword against the stone and sparks flew, but the pitch didn't ignite. The wind was too strong.

The horsemen were coming fast.

"Run!" Nikias yelled at his friends. "I'll stay!"

"Stuff that!" replied Leo, and squatted next to Nikias, shielding him from the wind. Baklydes and Mula joined him, putting their backs to the gusts. Only Kolax ran away, scrambling up some rocks and disappearing into the shadows of the trees.

Nikias struck the stone frantically and a shower of sparks leapt from it. But still the pitch would not ignite.

"Move closer!" he said.

They pushed themselves together, making a wall against the gusts.

The pitch caught fire and started to smolder, and then burst into flames that shot up underneath them, scorching their legs. Mula cried out and they all leapt back onto the stones of the altar. Two horsemen, fast riders who had outpaced their cohorts, broke through a gap in the trees, charging toward the Plataeans with their javelins raised. They were Dog Raiders and wore open-faced helms covered in the hides of spotted dogs. They wielded short javelins—the bronze spearheads gleamed like death in the cold light of the stars.

Baklydes and Leo jumped to their feet, drawing their swords. The horsemen were ten feet away when the men convulsed and fell from their mounts—one shot through the neck, the other in the thigh—and lay writhing on the ground. Their horses careened across the clearing and into the woods beyond. Kolax's high-pitched Skythian screech sounded from the rocks above. Leo and Baklydes fell on the poisoned men, hacking their heads from their necks.

But more were coming.

The pitch fire had spread fast along the ground to the shrubs and the other trees on the edge of the sacred space—everywhere that had been drenched with resin. Nikias reached into his pouch and threw a fistful of white powder on the flames and they roared ten feet high. Dog Raider horses screamed and halted on the other side of this wall of fire. Leo and Baklydes flung their powder onto the growing inferno, and the orange flames leapt even higher.

An arrow whistled past Nikias's head like a hummingbird. He touched his temple and felt blood. Through the flames he saw the face of a Dog Raider with a black forked beard, staring back at him with surprise and hatred. Nikias recognized the man! He'd fought him before, on the road to Athens—a Dog Raider commander. Fork-Beard shouted a command to his men and the horsemen checked their mounts, turned, and headed back into the forest. Nikias knew where they were headed: they were going to go around the other side of the summit and cut them off.

From the direction of Plataea came the distant blaring of the war trumpets. The spotters on the walls of the citadel had seen the fire, and the signal had been sounded to let the other men know it was time to kindle their own flames across the mountainside.

"Run!" shouted Nikias to his companions. He sprinted across the summit to the other side, flying down the rocky slope on the southern side of the mountain—away from the Oxlands and into enemy territory.

FIFTEEN

From where he stood on the Eagle's Turret—the highest tower on the southern wall of Plataea—Menesarkus could see the flames on the peak of Mount Kithaeron: a tongue of fire licking the sky. "Good work, my lad," he said to himself. A second later the shattering noise of the trumpets erupted all along the wall. The sound was so deafening, he reckoned as he glanced at the score of trumpeters spread out across the bastion, that the noise must be heard all the way to Thebes.

He looked back toward the mountain peak. The flames on the pyre had spread quickly, and white smoke billowed toward the full moon that rose above the summit like a shining shield.

"Stop the signal!" he bellowed. "Stop!"

The trumpets ceased.

He stood awhile longer, waiting silently until he saw more fires begin to glow lower down the slope, spreading in a thin line all the way across the dark face of the mountain from east to west about a quarter of a mile from the summit. Nikias and his companions would have had more than enough time to retreat from their position down the slope and get beyond the next level of fire. The conflagration on the summit already burned fiercely, fanned by the increasing wind, and it rose higher than any pyre that Menesarkus had ever seen.

"What will you think of *that*, Arkidamos?" he said under his breath. He imagined the Spartan king on the other side of the mountain, staring up at the fire and wondering what was happening.

The fire on the summit had grown stronger and was moving downward toward the first line of flames. Soon the mountain would be covered with a forest fire greater than any living Plataean had ever seen, creating a cloak of smoke that would hide the exodus of Plataea. It was a trick worthy of the wily Odysseus.

Menesarkus turned away from the parapet and made his way slowly down the four flights of stairs to the ground level. He had to lean on the wall of the tower with every step, for his right knee gave him considerable pain—he could feel the bone rubbing on bone. Chusor had offered to make Menesarkus a brace, but he had turned down the clever smith out of vanity. He regretted that decision right now.

When he got to the street he found it nearly deserted. Doors of houses were flung open as if people had fled in great haste, and there was refuse and cast-aside furniture littering the ground. Down the lane he could see families hustling along, bearing heavy burdens—the belongings they deemed necessary for the journey to Athens. These stragglers were supposed to have assembled in the agora an hour ago, but they must have lingered in their homes until the sound of the war trumpets had caused them to bolt like frightened hares.

He watched as a middle-aged man tried to pull a heavy wooden chest through a doorway, but it would not fit. The man cursed the gods as he pulled with all his might, until finally the leather handle broke and he fell backward, sprawled on his arse on the street, screaming in pain and clutching his lower back.

"What are you doing?" Menesarkus asked, his voice dripping with scorn.

"What does it look like, you sheep-stuffing idiot?" said the man. He struggled to his feet, turning on Menesarkus with a glare; but when he saw that it was the Arkon who had spoken to him, he dropped his eyes and stammered, "I—Arkon, forgive me—I didn't know it was you."

"What is in that chest that is so important, Telemakos?" Menesarkus asked with a kinder tone. He had known Telemakos his entire life, watching him grow from a thoughtful child to a stalwart warrior and a skilled artisan—a painter of vases. Telemakos had painted the funeral jar image of Menesarkus's only son, Aristo, after he had died in battle against the Thebans sixteen years ago. And Telemakos had so skillfully painted the likeness of his late son that his work looked as though the figure on the vase was actually thinking and breathing.

Telemakos scratched his thick beard with a long, delicate finger and said, "The box is full of my samples, Arkon. I packed the very best of my craft in there, along with my tools. I need them if I am to find work in Athens. My back is not strong enough to join a trireme—I have a bad spine. An old injury."

"It was at the second siege of Sardis," said Menesarkus, laughing. "You thought I had forgotten? That great Median warrior knocked you off the scaling ladder and you landed on a rock that went right up your arsehole. How you did howl!" He thought back to the siege in Lydia—an expedition financed by Athens that Plataea had joined years after the defeat of the Persian invaders. The ostensible goal had been to retake city-states in Ionian Greece that were still under the control of King Artaxerxes—son of Xerxes the Invader. Sardis had come under siege several times over the decades, but it had never been taken. That changed during the siege that Menesarkus, a young general at the time, had helped lead. Freedom for Ionian Greeks had been the rallying cry, but it had really been an excuse to pillage and slaughter Persian satrapies.

Telemakos replied proudly, "But I got right back up and scaled that ladder again. And I killed that Median with his own club."

"That you did," said Menesarkus. He recalled the fury with which the Greeks had slain the people who had defended Sardis . . . and the terrible aftermath in which they had raped the women and slaughtered the men. A cold hand seemed to clutch his heart as he thought of the Spartans breaking through the walls of Plataea. . . .

The faint smell of wood smoke filled his nostrils, and he recalled the hideous stench of burning human flesh from the blazing homes of Sardis. He gazed into space for a long while, then started when he realized that Telemakos was prying apart the door frame, trying to make it wider so that he could get his crate through the opening.

"Leave it, friend," said Menesarkus. "You must come with me to the agora now. I can smell the smoke from the forest fire. Soon our people will have to travel under its protective mantle. You are a craftsman, and your name is already known in Athens. A man of your reputation need not burden himself with a box of samples, nor even tools of his trade. You will be like a great warrior who shows up at a battle naked and unarmed. Men will know your worth and provide you with gear. So leave anything behind that might encumber you on this desperate journey. Bring only your sword, bow and quiver, and a little food, and leave everything else behind. Your home and its belongings will be safe as long as we hold the walls, and I promise you we will not give them up to the enemy."

Telemakos dropped his chin to his chest and began to weep. Then he nodded his head submissively. He pushed the crate back inside the house, then shut the door and headed toward the agora.

Menesarkus took a shortcut through the center of the citadel and wended his way back to the house where he slept when he was away from the farm. He needed to get some wine and food before he faced the crowd in the agora—

before he gave them a final speech and sent them on their way into peril and exile.

When he got to the house he saw a mule cart out front—the cart from the farm. He knew in that instant that something was wrong. The women were supposed to wait at the farm and join the exodus as it passed on the road going east. Why had they brought the cart back to the city?

Saeed dashed from the front door of the house and started running in the opposite way from him, evidently on some urgent errand in the direction of the agora.

"Where are you going?" Menesarkus called.

Saeed stopped abruptly and ran back to him. "It's Kallisto," he said. "She's bleeding worse now. My mistress said that we had to bring her to the citadel. She cannot make the journey to Athens."

Menesarkus found Eudoxia and Kallisto in one of the upstairs bedchambers. Kallisto lay on her side, taking quick short breaths, eyes half closed. Her forehead was beaded with sweat. Eudoxia sat by her side, stirring something in a bowl. She looked up as he entered and shook her head of silver hair slightly—a familiar look that said, "Do not say anything rash, husband."

"Is she unwell?" asked Menesarkus.

"Kallisto is staying in Plataea," said Eudoxia firmly. "Otherwise she will lose the child for certain. And perhaps her own life as well. I am staying with her," she added, even more forcefully. "The two of us would only slow down the travelers. We're staying and there is nothing to argue about." She spooned some of the potion into Kallisto's mouth, who swallowed it with a great effort.

Menesarkus lowered himself into a chair in the corner of the room, brooding silently. He knew that Eudoxia was right—Kallisto could not make the journey to Athens in this condition. But he dreaded the thought of his wife and Kallisto trapped inside the walls of the citadel during a siege, like rats in a box. They might starve to death before it was over. Or worse . . . if the Spartans defeated Plataea and overran the walls, then the women would be raped without mercy—defiled with such violence that their bodies would be ruined forever. And Kallisto's baby, if it was still alive, would have its brains dashed out against the walls in front of its own mother's eyes. Eudoxia would live the rest of her short and miserable life as the lowest kind of laboring slave, and Kallisto would spend the rest of hers on her back in a brothel.

It was too horrible to imagine.

If only they could go with the others! What god had brought this evil upon his family? Upon his unborn great-grandchild? Plataea was so vulnerable now.

But the walls of Athens were unassailable. *That* mighty stronghold—a city that could fit almost all of Plataea in its agora—was a refuge from war that he had hoped would protect all of those whom he loved. His head felt heavy all of a sudden, as though it were filled with lead. He wanted to roar with rage and punch the wall out of frustration.

"But where are the twins?" he asked abruptly.

"They are still at the farm with Phile," said Eudoxia. "They will go to Athens."

"And Nikias," said Kallisto, speaking for the first time, her voice barely audible. "Nikias will protect them. But you cannot let him know I am here. Otherwise he will stay by my side. He is foolish that way. He loves me more than our children."

Menesarkus left the chamber and went downstairs to the kitchen, where he forced himself to eat some bread, cheese, and a handful of olives. He didn't have to give his speech until dawn. He washed down his food with two cups of uncut wine. Then he became drowsy and sat by the fire, drifting in and out of a fitful slumber. He dreamt that he was on the rooftop of the farm on the night of the Theban invasion, when Eurymakus had trapped everyone in the house and set it on fire. In the dream Eurymakus knelt before him, cradling the body of his brother Damos—the fighter that Menesarkus had killed in the pankration championship. "Murderer," said Eurymakus, and then he pulled apart his dead brother's jaws and a writhing mass of black smoke issued from his gaping maw. The smoke turned into worms, beetles, and maggots that gushed forth, filling the room with a murky and churning chaos, like a ship swamped with bilgewater. . . .

He awoke with a cry. A cock crowed in the distance. The room reeked of smoke.

Hesiod entered, breathing hard, his eyes red with tears. "Arkon," he said in a funereal tone. "The fire starters have returned from the mountain and have assembled with the citizens. Zoticus and his cavalry wait outside the walls to lead them. Dawn approaches. The smoke is heavy and covers the entire valley. Our people only wait on your command to depart for Athens."

"And what will I say to my people?" thought Menesarkus. "What words of wisdom can I impart upon them before they head off to Athens? Before they leave their homes, perhaps forever?"

"Arkon . . ." began Hesiod, then stopped and dropped his head, wiping away tears.

"Why do you weep?" asked Menesarkus. He realized, with a sinking in his guts, that Hesiod was not crying because of the stinging smoke. "Is Kallisto dead?"

Hesiod frowned. "Kallisto? No. It's Nikias. He did not return from the summit. Neither did my brother or Leo or the barbarian boy. It's been two hours and more since they lit their fire."

Menesarkus felt as if a hand clutched his throat. He forced himself to swallow and practically gagged on his spit. He cleared his throat and said, "Hand me my staff. I must send our brothers and sisters into hateful exile with what well-meaning words I can muster."

SIXTEEN

"Leave me to die," moaned Baklydes. "Just leave me to die."

"We're not going to leave you," said Nikias in a voice raspy from smoke.

"And you're not going to die," added Leo, and cleared his throat, spitting onto the ground. "You've got a broken ankle, not a gut wound. So quit crying."

Baklydes had an arm draped over Nikias's shoulder and the other around Leo as they helped him hop across the rocky escarpment on the southern slope of Mount Kithaeron. It was an hour after dawn and the air was thick with haze. The sun appeared as a dull glowing disk behind the veil of smoke, reminding Nikias of a silver coin that had been rubbed smooth of all its features.

Baklydes had broken his ankle in their wild flight down from the summit, stepping into a small depression a mile from the top and snapping the bone. The three took refuge in a gully surrounded by a thick pine forest, hiding out from the Dog Raiders who had been swarming about on this side of the mountain. But after the wind shifted from the northwest with the coming of the sun, smoke wafted down the southern slopes, blanketing the forest in a choking vapor, and the Dog Raiders vanished, most likely riding back to their fortress. And so the three companions set out for their destination as fast as they could manage.

"Do you think everyone from the citadel has made it to the Three Heads by now?" asked Leo.

"They should have," said Nikias. He thought of Kallisto and his little girls riding in the cart and prayed that the journey over the pass from the Oxlands had gone well.

"How far are we from the fort, do you reckon?" asked Baklydes.

"A couple of miles by the flight of a crow," said Nikias. "But it's hard to tell in this smoke."

"Look," said Leo. "A stream."

Nikias and Leo lowered Baklydes by the edge of the stream, then all three plunged their faces into the water, washing the grime from their eyes and gulping water down their parched throats.

"I've never tasted any water better," said Baklydes.

"It's probably filled with goat piss," said Leo.

"I don't care."

"What do you think happened to Kolax and Mula?" Leo asked, rubbing his eyes with such force it looked as though he might dig them from his skull.

"I don't know," said Nikias. "They're both fast runners. And Kolax can take care of himself." The last he'd seen, they were being chased down the mountain back toward Plataea by at least twenty Dog Raiders. If they'd made it to the second line of fire, they might have found other Plataeans to help them, but he didn't hold out too much hope. Poor Mula. He seemed to be born under an unlucky star. He hoped the little boy hadn't been captured alive. He shuddered to think of what the Dog Raiders would do to him.

"Why do you think there were so many Dog Raiders on the mountain?" asked Baklydes. He pulled some broken barley cakes from his pack and offered them to the others. Leo took one and ate it greedily, but Nikias declined.

"I'm starving," said Leo, his mouth full of food.

Nikias splashed his face with some water, then said, "I think that Spartan king has brought the Dog Raiders into his service. They were probably just on patrol, guarding against a sneak attack from us on the Spartan camp. Arkidamos is no fool. He knows that my grandfather is wily and capable of anything."

Leo raised both hands in the air. "And he would be right. Look at what the Arkon has brought about. He's like Zeus the Storm Bringer."

"Zeus the Smoke Bringer, more like it," said Baklydes, shoving the cake into his mouth.

They laughed hard at this lame joke. More laughter than was justified by Baklydes's attempt at wit. But they were exhausted and had been on edge for hours. Baklydes lifted up his tunic and sent a stream of urine into the gurgling water.

"What are you three doing here?" a voice demanded from the other side of the stream, and they stopped laughing abruptly. An old man stood on the opposite bank, leaning on a staff and squinting at them. He wore a ragged robe and his beard and hair were greasy.

"Hermit," said Leo under his breath.

"Peace, father," said Nikias, getting to his feet.

"Would you like a barley cake?" offered Baklydes.

"I'm not your father, you Megarian goat-rapers," said the old man with a sneer. "And this is a sacred stream. Stop that! And stuff your cake up your arses!"

"I can't," said Baklydes, turning his jet of urine away from the water.

Leo got up and whispered in Nikias's ear, "He thinks we're Megarian."

Nikias chewed on this for a moment, watching the old man as he stood scowling at Baklydes. Megarian territory was several miles south of here, across the mountains. This was Dog Raider territory. Why would there be Megarians here? And then it hit him: there must be a Megarian force nearby. "Stranger," said Nikias in a cajoling tone, "we got separated from the others in the smoke. Could you tell me where they are?"

"Just follow the stream," said the old man. "They're camped in the flats."

"Peace," said Nikias.

The old man gave him a black look, then headed up the escarpment and disappeared into the smoke.

"You two stay here," said Nikias. "I'm going to go down and have a look."

"I'm coming with you," said Leo.

"You need to stay with Baklydes," said Nikias. "He's helpless without you."

"I'm not helpless," said Baklydes.

"What are you going to do?" asked Nikias. "Piss on the enemy?"

"I have my sling," said Baklydes, holding up a leather thong.

"Give me that," said Nikias, snatching the thong from Baklydes.

"Well, if you're going to take that, then here's my bag of shots," said Baklydes as he removed a bulging pouch from his belt. "Those shots were made by Chusor and they cost me an amphora of wine. The *good* stuff, mind you."

Nikias strapped the pouch to his belt and took out one of the egg-shaped lead shots, slipping it into the sling. Chusor's shots were the best in Plataea: hurled by a skilled peltast, one could blast a hole through a man's face and out the back of his skull from thirty feet away. And Nikias was an expert with the sling.

"If I'm not back in half an hour, make for the Three Heads," he said to Leo.

"How are we supposed to do that?" asked Leo. "I can't carry Baklydes on my back."

"You'll find a way," said Nikias.

He followed the stream down the hill. He could only see a few feet in front of his face because of the smoke, so he stared at the ground, walking carefully so as not to injure himself on the uneven terrain. He didn't want to end up helpless like Baklydes. That would be a death sentence here in enemy territory. After a mile he heard noises in the distance—the unmistakable din of an encampment . . . a large force of men, by the sound of it. He heard occasional good-natured shouts, the neighing of horses, the clank of arms and armor.

He kept walking, and then the shape of a prostrate dog tied to a tree materialized before him out of the smoke. The dog was the saddest creature that Nikias had ever seen. It was a dirty white Molossian hunting hound that had been starved nearly to death, for all its ribs showed and its face was gaunt like an old man's. It looked up at Nikias with sad eyes and beat its skinny tail against the ground.

"Hello, boy," said Nikias in a soft high voice, and the dog's tail pounded the ground even harder.

The figure of a warrior stepped from the smoke and the man started when he saw Nikias. He drew his sword and made to shout, but his mouth was so stuffed with food that all that he could utter was a muffled cry.

"Don't shit yourself," said Nikias, affecting a Megarian accent and laughing in a friendly way. "I was just scouting in the hills for the general and got lost. Where did you get that bread? I'm starving."

The Megarian warrior smiled with relief and put his sword back in its sheath. He chewed his food, then swallowed in a great gulp. "What did you see? Any sign of Plataeans?"

"No," said Nikias. "Nothing but this accursed smoke."

"They say we'll move on the fort despite the smoke," said the Megarian, sitting next to the dog with a grunt. He was a heavily built man in his thirties with small, wide-set eyes and a bushy brown beard. The dog craned its neck forward, sniffing at the bread in the man's hand. The Megarian gave the dog an evil look and slapped it on the side of the head—a severe cuff that made the dog yelp pitifully.

"The worst watchdog in the camp," said the Megarian. "I suppose he didn't make a sound when you approached the outskirts."

Nikias grinned and shook his head. "You should sell him to the Dog Raiders so they can make a hat from his hide."

"I might," said the Megarian, then paused and bit another hunk of bread, chewing with his mouth open. "But I can't abide those filthy marauders. If we hadn't formed a truce with them for this attack on the Three Heads, I'd be happy to gut every Dog Raider in these hills." He glanced at the dog, which was still staring hopefully at the bread in his hand. "You're not going to get a piece of this," he said with a cruel smile, then looked at Nikias and grinned. "Nestor says he's going to slit this dog's belly and watch him eat his own guts tonight after we've seized the fort. We're going to take bets—see how long it takes before he chews himself to death."

"Sounds like fun," said Nikias. Then he got on his haunches and asked in a conspiratorial tone, "Aren't you afraid of the Skythian archers who guard the Three Heads?"

"Afraid?" asked the Megarian. "Of course I'm afraid of those barbarians with their poisoned arrows. But there will be three thousand of us Megarians taking part in this attack. And there are only a score or so of Skythians manning the walls. Nestor just told me that the Spartans are sending along five hundred of their men and another two thousand Helot slaves with scaling ladders. The Thebans are going to block the pass in the Oxlands on the other side to prevent the Skythians from riding back to Plataea. The Skythians won't be expecting us to hit them so hard. Especially not in this smoke. The fort must be taken before the Spartan siege of Plataea begins."

"Yes," agreed Nikias. "If Plataea is to be cut off once and for all from any relief from Attika, then the Three Heads must fall."

"Well," said the man, "we'll know in a couple of hours. We're moving out soon."

"I'll be glad to start fighting," said Nikias. "Instead of just sneaking around."

The Megarian nodded and handed Nikias a piece of his bread. "I don't think I know you. What's your name."

"Nikias."

"Where are you from, Nikias?" asked the Megarian, a hint of suspicion clouding his face.

Nikias, who had been so smooth with his answers up until this point, went utterly blank. It was as though he had been running nimbly down a flight of steps, only to miss the last one and fall flat on his face. He couldn't think of the name of a village in Megaria, and so he simply stared back with a stupid smiled fixed on his lips.

The Megarian shifted uncomfortably. His arm twitched and his hand started moving ever so slowly for his sword handle.

"Look, it's Nestor," said Nikias, flicking his eyes to a spot over the warrior's head.

The Megarian turned his head slightly to look, and that was all that Nikias needed. He lunged forward, smashing the man in the nose with his right fist—a punch landed with such ferocity that the Megarian's face burst in a spray of blood and he toppled backward, stunned but not unconscious. Nikias leapt on him like a lion, punching him in the throat, then shoving a lead shot into the man's gasping maw. He wrapped the leather thong around his neck, choking the life out of him. The Megarian struggled for several minutes, kicking his feet, gurgling deep in his throat. But Nikias was too strong and would not let go, and soon the man's legs stopped moving.

Nikias looked at the dog. It stared back with an excited and approving look.

Nikias got to his feet, breathing hard through his nose. He stepped toward the dog, holding his hand toward its nose, but the animal started to growl. At first Nikias thought the dog was afraid of him and was going to bite, but then he heard heavy footsteps coming from behind. A man approached. Someone whom the dog hated. Nikias took out a shot from his pouch and slipped it in his sling, then turned and saw another Megarian emerging from the smoke. This one was a tall warrior—much taller than the man that Nikias had just slain. He wore a breastplate and greaves, and held his helm under one arm. He stopped dead ten paces away and glanced at the corpse on the ground, then back at Nikias with a baffled expression.

"You must be Nestor," said Nikias pleasantly, snapping his arm and hurling the shot from the sling. The Megarian's left eye exploded, sending blood and brains out the back of his head. The warrior stood for a second as rigid as a plank, then his knees buckled and he fell face forward upon the ground.

Nikias pulled out his dagger and went to the dog, quickly slicing through the rope that held it to the tree; then he took the rope in hand and started walking back in the direction of the stream. The dog got to his feet with an effort and followed him dutifully on shaky legs, his tail wagging happily.

"What in Hades is that?" asked Baklydes as Nikias clambered up to the spot where they waited by the stream.

"Looks like the god of death's own hound," said Leo, raising his eyebrows.

The panting dog smiled at Leo and Baklydes, then raised one leg and dribbled into the stream.

"Don't let that old man see you," Baklydes said to the dog. "He'll give you a piece of his mind."

"I took the dog from the Megarians," said Nikias. "At their camp. He hates them as much as we do."

"How many are there?"

"Near to six thousand," said Nikias. "Megarians, Spartans, Helots, and Dog Raiders. And they're going to attack the Three Heads." He briefly told them the tale of his encounter with the Megarian and what he had learned from him.

"Stuff my arse," said Leo when Nikias was finished. "How did they know about everyone leaving Plataea and marching across the pass?"

"I don't think they do know," said Nikias. "It's merely a coincidence. The Spartan king must have ordered this combined attack on the fort just in case we tried to get our people out without giving up the citadel."

"But he's too late," said Baklydes, smiling broadly. "Everyone will be at the Three Heads by now and on their way south."

"They're not too late for anything," snapped Nikias. "Don't you see? This army will catch our women and children on the road and slaughter them."

"They can go inside the fort," said Baklydes.

"The fort can only hold a few thousand people," said Leo. "And they'd be crammed in there like olives in a jar."

Nikias handed Baklydes the sling and shots. "I'm sorry, old friend. We have to leave you here. We'll come back for you if we can."

Baklydes nodded his head, trying to look plucky. "I know," he said. "Run fast."

"We'll leave you the dog," said Nikias, tossing him the rope.

"Thank the gods!" said Baklydes with an acerbic laugh. He picked up the rope and the dog looked at him over his shoulder with a doubtful expression. "What's his name?"

"Nestor."

"That's a stupid name for a dog," said Baklydes.

Nikias and Leo took off at a run. Leo went out front—he was a faster long distance runner than Nikias. They could barely see the disk of the sun behind the clouds, but they could judge which direction to go. When they were half a mile away from the stream, Nikias heard a sound of something approaching from behind. He grabbed the handle of his knife and shot a glance over his shoulder. Nestor the dog appeared from the smoke, tongue hanging from his mouth, legs pumping with joyful abandon as he raced toward his new master.

SEVENTEEN

———————◆———————

Mula and Kolax had squeezed themselves so far into a crevice in the Cave of Nymphs that they were like two maggots up a sheep's arse. At least, that's what Kolax kept saying over and over again in a choking voice. They had been holed up in the place for what seemed like an eternity—crammed tightly into the rocky niche at the back of the cave—and yet smoke continued to billow into the mouth of the cavern from the raging inferno blazing across the mountainside, illuminating even the back of the chamber in a red glow.

The cave had hidden them from the enemy horsemen who had chased them down from the summit, but the smoke from the forest fire had nearly killed them. Holding their tunics over their mouths had filtered out some of the poisonous vapor, but Kolax felt as though his lungs and sinuses were stuffed with charcoal.

"I'll never eat smoked meat ever again," he croaked, and lifted the decapitated head of the pursuing Dog Raider he had slain outside the cave entrance. He put it to his lips, letting the blood from the dead man's neck trickle onto his tongue. The liquid oozed down his parched throat and brought a little relief to the burning in his esophagus. "Want some?" he asked.

Mula shoved aside the proffered head and rasped, "For the last time, no! I don't want to drink a man's blood."

"In Skythia we always drink the blood of our enemies," said Kolax.

"We are not in Skythia," replied Mula in a tone that the Skythian boy found irritatingly prim.

"I know," replied Kolax in a singsong voice that he knew Mula hated. "We're up a sheep's arse. We're up a sheep's arse. We're up—"

"Leave, then!"

"I'll wait until the fire has died down."

"Then shut up," snapped Mula, and punched Kolax in the arm.

"Ow!" said Kolax, and punched him back.

"Quit it!"

"You started it!"

After a long silence in which Kolax slurped some more blood, Mula said, "My father is going to kill me. I lost the young master." He reached into his pouch and pulled out one of the firestones, staring at it morosely.

"You didn't lose Nikias," said Kolax, snatching the sparkling stone from his hand. "He ran the wrong way. Lucky for you I yanked you in the right direction."

"I didn't want to go with you," said Mula. "I wanted to follow the young master. What if he's dead?"

"Then you would be dead too," said Kolax. "But your young master is harder to kill than a tick," he added with admiration.

"A tick?"

"Yes. You squeeze and squeeze a little tick between your Titan-sized fingers with all your might and what happens? Nothing. You stop your squeezing and that bastard of a tick just crawls away, saying, 'Eat shit.' That's Nikias." He tossed the firestone into the air and caught it. "We don't use these things in Skythia," he said. "But I can start a fire using my bow, a stick, and a flat piece of wood. You just rub the—"

"Nikias is not a tick," interrupted Mula. "He's like a hero from a story."

"A hero who's always getting his balls between hammer and tongs," said Kolax with a derisive laugh. "No disrespect to your young master, of course. The sky god seems to love and bless him. But I can't tell you how many times I've had to save his Plataean arse. Remember when I revived him with my magic griffin's blood and—"

"My poor father will be so worried," cut in Mula, holding his head in his hands. "He told me that the eclipse meant something bad was going to happen."

"When the moon covers the sun, it's a good sign," said Kolax. "It means that something wonderful will occur. At least, that's what my father always told me."

"You don't know anything," said Mula petulantly.

"Let's do my lesson," said Kolax. "To pass the time." Mula had been teaching him to speak proper Persian over the last year. "How do you say, 'I've found myself up a sheep's arsehole'?"

Grudgingly Mula taught him how to say this, and several other sayings that Kolax thought might be useful were he ever to travel to the Persian Empire, including, "Where are the chariot races today?" and, "How much for your fine horse's semen?" before they both fell into a grim silence.

Kolax thought of Phile and the Plataeans who were going to Athens. They must have departed the citadel hours ago and would soon be passing close to the fortress that guarded the pass. Would his papa worry when he saw that Kolax wasn't amongst the exiled Plataeans? He thought of his horse Pegasos and wondered if Saeed had remembered to feed him and give him water. Would he have left Pegasos at the farm, or taken him to Athens?

And what about Nikias? Even though he had spoken to Mula in a light-hearted tone about him just now, Kolax was actually worried about his friend. The gods would only save a favored man from death so many times before they grew irritated and cried, "Enough! Let this Nikias's shade join the other unlucky fools in Hades!"

Mula dropped his head onto Kolax's shoulder and fell into a fitful sleep. Kolax wrapped his arm around him to get into a more comfortable position. It felt nice to clasp like this with his friend. He put his cheek against Mula's soft and curly hair. Kolax's dead mama had had soft and curly hair like that too. And he used to sit clasped with his mama just like this in their round tent. He wondered if, after he died, his mama's shade would meet him on the Great Field and hold him in her arms again. Or would she say, "You're too big to hug now, my son! You're a man now!"

He hoped not. That would be a gut blow.

He adjusted the pouch he wore around his neck so that it was no longer digging into his side. It was filled to the top with the flammable white powder—he had not been able to spread any of it on the summit before the Dog Raiders had come. It was useless now. He reached for his quiver where it was strapped to his belt and opened the lid. There was only one arrow left. He had used all of the others shooting Dog Raiders as he and Mula scrambled down the summit. He must have killed at least ten of them before the rest turned back, fleeing from his wrath and the raging fire. One of them, however, managed to follow them all the way to the cave. Kolax used his long knife on that one. It was a good fight, one that Kolax nearly lost. But that made it all the sweeter when he sent the man's shade to the underworld. He stared at the warrior's head with its face frozen in an expression of surprised agony.

"Not so fierce now," he said in a mocking voice.

He tossed the head onto the cave floor, where it landed with a dull thud. Then he snuggled up close to Mula and fell asleep with a smile on his face.

He awoke several hours later, startled by a noise that sounded like a muffled cry. He looked about in a daze. Had he been dreaming? His tongue was so dry, it felt as if it had been glued to the roof of his mouth. He realized, with alarm, that Mula was no longer next to him. Where had he gone? Most likely to see what the fire had done to the forest.

He squeezed himself out of the crevice and made his way stealthily to the mouth of the cave, thirty feet away.

"There you are!" he said with relief when he saw Mula standing at the opening. The boy, leaning at an odd angle, faced away from him. White smoke still wafted in the air outside the cavern, but it was less thick now. Kolax could discern the shapes of blackened trees through the vapor. How many hours had they been asleep? "Don't stand in the open like that," he said. "Come back here. It's not safe yet and—"

He stopped abruptly as a gust of wind caused the smoke to clear, for he saw that Mula's hands were tied behind his back and there was a noose around his neck. The rope stretched tautly upward like the straight line of a spider's web and disappeared from view above the mouth of the cave. Something pulled on the rope and Mula rose up a few inches so that he stood on his tiptoes. He pivoted around, ever so slowly, until Kolax saw his terrified face. There was a gag in his mouth. His nose was bleeding. And his eyes were open wide in terror.

"Come out, Skythian!" said a harsh voice with the accent of a Dog Raider. "Can you hear me in there, you red-haired barbarian mongrel?"

Kolax shrank back and crouched down against the wall of the cave, peering into the vapor, trying to see the enemy. And then he remembered, with a pang of shame, that in their haste to escape the fire he had left the headless body of the Dog Raider at the cave entrance instead of pulling it inside. The Dog Raiders must have come back after the fire had died down and found the corpse of their brother.

"How could I have made such a blunder?" he asked himself.

"Come out of your hole," called the Dog Raider, "or my man on the cliff above pulls the rope and your little friend hangs!"

"How many are out there?" Kolax asked Mula in a whisper.

Mula made a gurgling sound.

"Blink once for less than ten, twice for more," said Kolax.

Mula blinked rapidly.

"That many?" asked Kolax. "Stuff my arse. Why did you leave the cave, you idiot?"

Tears poured from Mula's eyes.

"There's no escape!" shouted the Dog Raider. "Come out now!"

The rope went up a little more so that Mula was balanced on one toe. Piss dribbled down his leg.

Kolax thought fast. If they were both captured by Dog Raiders, they would be arse raped until they were practically dead and then skinned alive. Or worse. There was only one option: kill Mula and himself with the poisoned arrow. They could die together and go visit his mama. He could bring her the pretty fire-stone as a gift. But then a terrible thought struck him: Could Mula's shade go with him to the Great Field of the Skythians? Or would he, the son of a Persian, have to go to some different region of the afterlife? He had never thought of this before. . . .

"Come out!" barked the Dog Raider.

The rope yanked upward and Mula's body jerked off the ground, his feet kicking the air in desperation.

Kolax clutched the fire stone in his hand, snarling in his throat in frustration. Then an idea came to him like an explosion in his brain.

He put the shaft of his arrow between his teeth, slung his bow over one shoulder, leapt up, and yanked on the rope holding Mula—yanked downward with all his might. A surprised cry came from the cliff above, and Mula dropped to the ground, followed by the Dog Raider who had been holding the rope. The warrior landed on his back next to the boys, cracking his head on the stones.

"There he is!"

Kolax turned in the direction of the blackened trees. He saw a gang of black-clad warriors charging from the smoke.

The Skythian did not hesitate. He grabbed his pouch, opened the flap, and thrust it forward, hurling the white powder into the air. It hung in the air like a cloud of milled flour. In a blindingly fast motion he tossed up the firestone into the midst of this cloud, fit his arrow to bow, and let fly the arrow—a perfectly aimed shot that struck the firestone, causing a spark.

The powder ignited instantaneously, bursting to life with an explosion of light and searing heat, and the throng of attacking Dog Raiders who were beneath it caught fire like torches, screaming in agony as their hair and faces melted.

Kolax grabbed the rope around Mula's neck and pulled him to his feet. "Run!" he yelled. He pulled Mula forward, darting through the burning and screaming men. And then—

A mad scramble. Leaping over smoldering logs. Arrows whistling past their heads. Mula fell several times, but every time Kolax pulled him to his feet by the rope, urging him on, running blindly through the gray smoke, but always going down, pulled by the force of Gaia—Mother Earth—toward the valley below the mountain.

But still they heard footsteps behind—a relentless trampling that followed them through the choking vapor. Kolax reached for the small knife he kept strapped to his thigh. As they ran he sliced through the rope binding Mula's hands, then cut the noose to unburden him.

"Keep going!" he ordered. "Don't stop! I'll be right behind you!"

Mula did not argue. He bolted down the hill, jumped over a smoldering log, and disappeared from sight. Kolax stopped and crouched low. The footsteps were closer. He clutched the dagger in one hand, blade downward, baring his teeth like a dog. A shape burst through the smoke—a huge buck with a singed and blackened hide. It stared at him, wild-eyed. Kolax tried to step aside but it ran straight at him, lowered its antlers, and flipped him up in the air, then let forth a mad bray and kept on running.

He lay on his back, staring at the white smoke and the charred shapes of the ruined trees above. He couldn't move. He couldn't breathe. The antler felt like it had punctured his lung. What bad luck! After a while he heard footsteps, then an evil face with a forked beard came into view, staring down at him, smirking. Kolax had seen him before—on the road to Athens when he saved Nikias from a band of Dog Raiders, slaying them all with his poisoned arrows. This marauder was the one who'd gotten away.

"Finally," gloated Fork-Beard. "After thirty months of hunting for you. You can't imagine what we're going to do to you, Skythian boy." He raised a club and swung it down, and all went black before Kolax's eyes.

EIGHTEEN

———◆———

Nikias's throat burned as he ran across the rocky ground. The smoke was so thick that he couldn't see more than ten paces ahead. Nestor ran by his side, the dog's long tongue lolling from his mouth and a happy gleam in his intelligent eyes.

Nikias's ankle hurt with every step—he'd twisted it in a hare's hole near the start of this mad dash. Despite the pain he continued to move his legs as fast as they would go, staring at the ground in front of him, constantly on the lookout for more pitfalls. He couldn't afford to break his ankle as Baklydes had done.

He and Leo had parted ways half a mile back. Leo had gone up the hillside, following a little gully in the direction of the Three Heads with the purpose of warning the Skythian archers of the coming attack. But Nikias was on his way to the valley at the bottom of the pass. He had to find his wife and children and warn the others that an army was on its way.

He reckoned he had gone another mile when he heard horses and the creaking of wooden wheels up ahead. He slowed down and cupped a hand to his mouth.

"It's Nikias!" he cried. "Someone answer me!"

"Nikias!" cried a Plataean voice. "Over here."

Nikias loped in the direction of the voice and an ox-pulled wagon and the figures of men and women materialized before him. He saw the smiling face of Myron the sandal maker standing next to his wife and several other members of his extended family. Nikias came to a stop in front of him, leaning over with his palms on his thighs, gasping for breath.

"Here's some water, lad," said Myron, holding a skin to his mouth. "Where have you been? You didn't come down from the mountain with the others."

Nikias greedily sucked down some water. "Where's everybody else?" he asked, ignoring Myron's question. He could see wheel ruts beneath his feet. They were on the road. But where were the others? He made a cup with his hand and put some water in it and Nestor lapped it up, gazing at him with humanlike gratitude.

"We're at the end of the line," said Myron. "I had a problem with my wheel and—"

Nikias gripped his shoulder. "You're going to have to move faster, Myron," he cut in. "The enemy is coming."

Myron turned his red eyes in the direction Nikias had come and touched the handle of the sword on his belt. He glanced at his grandchildren sitting in the wagon and asked, "Who?"

"Megarians," said Nikias. "And Dog Raiders. Hurry up, now!" He took off running again, guided by the ancient ruts that had been carved by centuries of cart wheels wearing away the limestone road. Soon he came upon more stragglers and called out, "Hurry! You must join the others!" as he ran past. After another mile the road became thick with people and animals and Nestor started barking excitedly.

"Where's Zoticus?" Nikias called out. "Where's General Zoticus? I must find him!"

Nikias pushed his way through the crowd to the center of the slowly moving throng, smiling with relief when he caught sight of Saeed astride his black gelding up ahead. Nikias's white mare Photine and Kolax's horse Pegasos walked by his side with Saeed holding their reins. The farm cart was directly behind the horses, pulled by two oxen. In the back of the cart, sitting amongst the heaps of baggage and supplies, was the huddled shape of a woman with a shawl over her head. She cradled two sleeping girls in her arms.

"Thank Zeus," said Nikias under his breath, and forced himself not to call out to Kallisto and the girls.

The oxen were led by thirteen-year-old brothers named Ajax and Teleos. Their father had been killed by Thebans at the Battle at the Gates, and their despondent mother committed suicide some months after. Chusor took them on as apprentices for a time, but after he departed the citadel the boys came under the guardianship of Menesarkus's family. They were troublesome boys. Chusor had called them "ape-like," but Nikias had never seen one of those animals to know whether or not the comparison was apt. He was glad that Saeed had put the boys to good use.

"Saeed!" Nikias called out as he ran up to the group with the dog by his side.

Saeed slid off his mount and embraced him.

"Where's Mula?" Saeed asked anxiously. "Did he sneak away to the mountain with you?"

"Yes," said Nikias.

"I knew it!" said Teleos to his brother. "The lucky fool."

"I'm the one who guessed first!" replied Ajax petulantly. "I said Mula had gone to the mountain, but nobody believed me."

"Shut up, you bloody sheep-stuffer!"

"Piss hole!"

The brothers started to tussle and the oxen came to an abrupt stop. Nestor jumped on them playfully, snapping his jaws and pawing at them.

"Keep the cart moving," yelled Nikias, "or I'll whip you both!"

The boys stopped fighting, cowed by his ferocity, and stared straight ahead, pulling on the oxen to make them start moving again. The dog looked ashamed and put his tail between his legs.

Nikias turned to Saeed and said, "Mula was alive the last time I saw him. I don't know any more, old friend. And I haven't time to explain what happened. I must find Zoticus. There's no time to lose." He put his mouth close to Saeed's ear. "The enemy is coming—an army of six thousand men."

Saeed cursed in Persian. "Zoticus is not here," he said. "He and the cavalry have gone on ahead to scout out the road to Athens."

Nikias flushed with indignation. "He left everyone behind? He's supposed to be protecting the women and children."

"He did not expect the enemy to come from the west. We made it over the pass without any problems. He was most concerned about the road south toward Eleusis."

Nikias glanced into the cart and realized, with shock, that Phile was the one huddled there with the girls and not Kallisto, for his sister had slipped off the shawl from around her face and was staring back at him with a worried look.

"Where's Kallisto?" Nikias blurted out, craning his neck to peer around the other side of the cart, searching for his wife amongst the many faces of the refugees. "Why isn't she riding? And where's Grandmother?"

"Kallisto had to stay in Plataea," said Phile. "She started to cramp and bleed. The baby would have died if she had come."

The world seemed to tilt before Nikias's eyes. He had to suppress a wild urge to take off running back in the direction of Plataea. "How bad?" he asked.

"Grandmother is with her," Phile said.

He gazed at the sleepy faces of his daughters in the cart, blinking at him from the folds of the scarves wrapped around their faces to protect them from the smoke. One of the girls started cry, "Mama!" and the other began to wail. Phile held her closer and made a shushing sound.

"Auntie is with you," said Nikias in a quiet voice, walking beside the cart. "Don't worry, daughters."

He took Saeed by the arm and led him off the road away from the others, but they continued moving, keeping pace with the wagon.

"What should we do?" asked Nikias.

Saeed chewed on his lip. "Close to six thousand men, you say?"

"Armored hoplites," said Nikias. "And five hundred Spartans amongst them."

Saeed cursed again. "Those of us at the front of the line could make a run for it," he said at length. "The enemy would fall upon the stragglers. Some of us might make it."

"The enemy controls all of Attika!" replied Nikias. "These Megarians and Dog Raiders will follow us all the way to the gates of Athens."

"We can't let them fall upon us when we're spread out on the road," said Saeed. "That would be the worst thing that could happen. That would be a slaughter. And we're too far past the Three Heads to retreat back there."

"That wouldn't do any good," said Nikias. "Everyone can't fit inside the fortress. And we can't go back to Plataea. There's a Theban army waiting on the other side of the pass by now." He crossed his arms on his chest and ground his teeth with indignation. How had things fallen apart like this? The plan had been so beautiful. The smoke had worked perfectly. It was simply bad luck that the Megarians had been planning this attack on the Three Heads. The Plataeans had tried to escape from the Oxlands one day too late. He thought of Kallisto back in the citadel. He wondered if she was still alive or if she had already hemorrhaged and died. The thought brought him low.

The dog, Nestor, barked excitedly. Teleos and Ajax were feeding him hunks of meat, and the hound gobbled them happily, dancing around and wagging his tail, which made the boys laugh.

"What happened to Mula?" Saeed asked.

"We were attacked on the summit," said Nikias. "Dog Raiders surprised us. Mula fled with Kolax."

Saeed said, "He was with Kolax? Thank the Great God! Then there is hope for my son. Kolax is wily. And he loves Mula like a brother. He will protect him. That barbarian is the best archer I have ever seen."

Nikias stopped dead. "Our women can shoot better than the men," he said in a preoccupied voice, and glanced at his sister, who was now singing to the girls.

Saeed was puzzled. "What are you talking about, Nikias?"

"The Tower of Theseus," said Nikias, naming the ancient and abandoned watchtower that stood a bowshot off the road, two miles south of the Three Heads. "We should be close."

"It's just up ahead, I reckon," replied Saeed.

"We must gather everyone there!" said Nikias as he ran over to Photine and mounted. "Come on, Saeed!"

"Where are you going?" asked Phile anxiously. "You're not leaving again, are you?"

"Let me come with you!" said Teleos.

"And me!" said Ajax.

"Both of you stay with the oxen," said Nikias firmly. "You have an important duty." He caught Phile's gaze. "Is your bow strung, Sister?"

"Yes, but—"

"I'll be back soon," Nikias interrupted. Photine tossed her head as Saeed mounted his own steed. "You go north and round up the stragglers. I'm going to the front of the line to start leading everyone to the tower."

Saeed nodded. They wheeled their horses about and charged down the side of the road in opposite directions, the dog chasing rowdily after Photine.

NINETEEN

"The Skythians are gone, Commander!"

Prince Arkilokus the Spartan stood on the narrow and rocky path leading to the fortress of the Three Heads, shaking his helmeted head in consternation. "How long?" he asked his subordinate—a winsome, narrow-hipped, and broad-shouldered youth by the name of Hippios.

"No more than two hours. At least by the looks of the embers of their fires. They left them burning in their haste to depart."

Arkilokus stared at the twenty-foot-tall bastions that appeared and reappeared before his eyes like a phantom fortress in the smoky haze. The gray limestone-block walls were thick with scaling ladders. His army had waited outside the walls for over an hour before venturing to attack, only to make this mystifying and anticlimactic discovery. The Megarian warriors who'd climbed the ladders stood languidly on the tops of the battlements, more than one of them pissing over the edge. Above the nearest guard tower Arkilokus could just make out the circle of the sun shining dimly behind the forest fire's smoke.

He looked over his shoulder at the thousands of men milling about in disarray on the slope behind him—the force of Megarians and Dog Raiders that King Arkidamos had cobbled together for this raid. The prince's own five hundred Spartiates stood off to the side in a neat phalanx, as still as statues, their faces glistening with sweat from their fast march up the steep hill to the small plateau where the fortress stood, guarding the entrance to the pass. His men were full-blooded Spartiates and not this other rabble.

"The king will be happy," said Hippios, and suppressed a cough.

Arkilokus took off his helm to reveal his head of sandy-colored hair and grim but handsome face. The smoke had blackened the area around his gray eyes and mouth where his skin had been exposed by the mask's horizontal and vertical slits. "Yes," he replied distantly. The king, Arkilokus's great-uncle, would indeed be pleased with how easily this had all come about. The Three Heads was an important piece of territory in the coming siege against the Plataeans. With the fort taken, the citizens of that city would be trapped in the Oxlands with no hope of escape over the mountains. But there was a nagging voice in the prince's head telling him that something was wrong. "How had the Skythians been warned?" he wondered aloud. And thought to himself, "And where have the barbarians gone?"

He started moving with his stiff-legged gait, a jerking walk that was the result of an injury he had suffered in a fall from a horse outside the walls of Plataea more than two years ago—a fall that had resulted in his capture by the enemy. For a time he had been paralyzed from the neck down. At first he'd thought that he would never walk again, but then the sensation in his limbs returned. He was kept in Menesarkus's own house and tended by the women of his family. Including the ravishing teenager, Kallisto. He was released after a brief imprisonment . . . traded for Nikias—the Plataean whom Arkilokus resembled as though he were an older brother.

"My *cousin*," he mused, and rubbed the stump of his missing ring finger on his right hand—the finger Menesarkus had cut off when he threatened to kill him when the exchange with Nikias started to go bad. Now he and the Plataean not only shared their looks: they both had the same mutilated sword hands. A warrior with a missing digit or even a limb was given great respect because that man had given his flesh for Sparta. But a Spartan baby that was born with the tiniest flaw would be thrown off a cliff after birth: no defects were tolerated in Spartan newborns.

"A paradox fit for an Athenian philosopher," Arkilokus mused.

He moved through the open doorway of the fort's only gate and entered the inner courtyard. There were the remains of smoldering fires here and there, and heaps of garbage. Some of the Megarians who had scaled the walls were picking through the debris left behind by the barbarians, searching for prizes. The place stank.

"Skythians," muttered Hippios with disdain.

"We'll leave five hundred Megarians to man the fort," said Arkilokus. "All of their archers will remain here."

"The Dog Raiders will protest," said Hippios. "I've heard them grumbling about who would take control once the Three Heads was captured."

Arkilokus smiled wryly. "Do you think I care what a pack of whining mountain marauders have to say?"

"No, my prince."

Arkilokus put his hand on Hippios's shoulder and smiled. "We captured a fortress," he said. "It doesn't matter if the enemy was not here to defend it. This is a good day. We'll celebrate tonight, you and I, when we're back at the king's camp." He thought back to the night before in his private campaign tent and the extremely satisfying bout of love play with the acrobatic and enthusiastic Hippios. Perhaps this evening he would invite that dashing Korinthian emissary he had met at the king's feast to join them.

"Don't touch that!" warned Arkilokus, for Hippios was reaching for a sword sticking from a pile of arms and armor that the Skythians had left behind. Hippios withdrew his hand as if it had been stung.

"Skythians leave poisoned traps," said Arkilokus. "Now, I'm going to take a walk around the walls. Find the Megarian commander and tell him to choose his men who will remain behind."

He exited the fortress and made a circuit around the outside of the walls. The bastions were well made—a knifepoint wouldn't fit between any of the well-cut rectangular blocks. He stood on the southernmost promontory of the little plateau on which the fortress sat, gazing in the direction of Athens, which lay over the rugged hills beyond, twenty miles or more as the raven flew—but the landscape was completely obscured by the smoke. The forest fire had died down on the mountains, but not before burning down nearly the entire northern slope, and part of the southern side as well. Because of the prevailing wind, the forest near the Three Heads had been spared.

He wondered why Menesarkus had set the fire. The obvious answer was so that the king's army could not use the timber to construct siege towers or a countervailing wall. The forest fire was a clever albeit destructive plan. Now they would have to haul trees from the southern side of the mountain—a great labor that would take much longer than had been planned. But that was what Helot slaves were for.

If the girl Kallisto survived the coming siege, he mused, he was going to take her back to Sparta as his own prize—like Akilles and the beauty Briseis. She would make an excellent breeder for him, for she was as fine a specimen of womanhood as he had ever seen. She would produce good children.

He walked down the steep slope, lost in thought, and found himself on the roadway. He spotted something lying there and froze. Was it a body? He drew his sword and approached it warily, then smiled when he realized that it was just a sack. He poked it with his sword's tip, cutting it open, and some things spilled out: a child's clothing and a clay doll. He picked through the bag and found other things—a mirror, a brush, and some sandals.

He made his way down the road a few hundred paces, scrutinizing the ground. When his army had crossed the road earlier, they rushed across it in great haste. But now he noticed signs that made his heart start beating faster. There were animal droppings, and other things—a crust of fresh bread. And cart wheel ruts dug into the side of the road, as if a huge number of people had passed this way—a throng that marched right past the base of the Three Heads several hours ago in the direction of Athens.

The skin on his neck prickled with excitement.

And then . . . an agonized scream erupted from the fort.

"Hades's hot prick!" he barked, thinking that the Dog Raiders had started fighting with the Megarian warriors. He sprinted back up the hill, around the wall, and to the gate, pushing his way through the crowd of men milling about the entrance to the fortress. Then he saw a sight that made his blood run cold, for lying on the ground, squirming spasmodically, was Hippios. The young warrior stared back at Arkilokus with terrified eyes—eyes that wept blood.

"Hippios!" he cried.

"He stepped in a hole," said the Megarian commander standing over him. "And then started to scream."

One of the Dog Raiders knelt by the hole in question. "Old trick," he said indifferently. "The hole is covered with straw. And a poisoned arrowhead embedded at the bottom to pierce through the sandal."

Hippios raised his hand beseechingly at Arkilokus and let forth an animal shriek with his tongue sticking from his red lips. His body convulsed violently and his jaws snapped together, biting off the tip of his own tongue.

Arkilokus knew there was no cure for the poison of the Skythians. Hippios would die only after his body had drained itself of blood through every orifice. He reached for his sword handle, fumbling for the hilt. When he found it, he clutched it firmly with his four remaining fingers and drew it, stepping forward and slicing clean through Hippios's neck with a powerful stroke.

The prince focused on his duties to prevent himself from going mad with rage. First he sent a Spartiate messenger on horseback to the king's camp at Aigosthena with news of the capture of the Three Heads along with a message: that he believed the Plataeans were on the march toward Athens. He didn't dare suggest that the king send horseman to head off the Plataeans in Attika. He would never presume to make suggestions to a monarch. He hoped, however, that the canny king would issue just such an order. After the messenger departed, he ordered four of his men to bear Hippios's remains back to the camp—warriors who bore the head and body on the fallen man's shield. Finally, he commanded the hundred Dog Raiders—the only mounted men in this small army other than his Spartiate and Megarian messengers—to ride down the road, scout out the situation and then report back.

Arkilokus stood mutely on the promontory, staring morosely into the haze, thinking about poor Hippios and waiting for the Dog Raiders to return with their report. He had killed many men in his life, but none that he had loved. What a terrible twist to befall the beautiful and strong young warrior. He imagined the hateful old hags—the Fates—cackling with glee as they guided Hippios's feet to that Skythian trap. The moment he had seen the eclipse he'd known that it would bring about some personal disaster. With every passing minute his heart became more inflamed with anger. An hour went by, but the Dog Raiders did not come back.

"They must have bolted for home," said the Megarian commander as he strode toward him.

"The scum!" said Arkilokus, and cursed.

"They were angered that they were not given the fort," said the Megarian, and went into a coughing fit.

"They'll regret their actions," said Arkilokus, rubbing the nub of his amputated digit with the fingers of his other hand.

The time for standing and waiting was over. He didn't care how long it would take him to find the Plataeans. He would chase them to the Dipylon Gates on foot if he had to. How far could his men run in full armor? Arkilokus had entered the armored footrace several times, but that distance was only half a mile. Without armor he'd run fifty miles or more at one stretch. His Spartiates, who'd been raised in herds from childhood, had each run a hundred miles without stopping on many occasions.

He mustered the men—both Spartan and Megarian—and ordered them to remove their armor. "Sword and sandals!" he shouted, stripping off his own equipment. Soon the air was filled with the din of clinking bronze.

They marched down to the road, then lined up in phalanxes. Then Arkilokus went out front and started running. He did not feel stiff or awkward. His feet felt as though they had grown wings. He reckoned they had gone four miles when he caught sight of many carts and wagons blocking the road, as if their owners had abandoned them in great haste and fled. The wind had shifted and the smoke was starting to clear. He could see five hundred feet in every direction now.

Suddenly a white horse leapt from a thick olive grove and reared in front of him. A skinny dog bounded after it and, catching sight of Arkilokus, started barking fiercely.

Arkilokus recognized the rider at once.

"Nikias!" he screamed. "Nikias!"

Nikias glared back at him with a look of surprise mingled with fury, then kicked the horse and rode toward a crumbling tower an arrow shot away, followed by the dog.

"Run!" Arkilokus cried to his men. "Follow the rider!"

He sprinted. Sword in hand. Screaming. Flying across the rocky landscape with his Spartiates behind him. The Megarians followed, screaming with bloodlust as they charged.

Nikias was just up ahead. He reined in his horse in front of a line of standing figures and dismounted, then slapped the horse on the flank and the animal bolted, running toward the tower. Nikias stood with his sword raised, smiling fiercely.

Arkilokus realized that all of the people standing behind his Plataean cousin were women. Thousands of women lined up like warriors in a phalanx! Where were the men? He almost regretted the slaughter that was about to take place. He glanced up at the tower and saw someone standing on top of the broken crown—a man with a horn held to his lips.

And then Nikias dropped his sword in a sweeping motion and cried out "Now!" and the women in the front of the line pulled back their robes and knelt in unison—a graceful, dance-like motion. They each held something in their outstretched hands. Staffs? Spindles? Arkilokus blinked and the next instant something struck him in the thigh. His leg buckled and he fell flat on his face. The air buzzed as if a thousand insects had all taken flight. Men fell all around him. The ones who did not fall stopped dead and crouched low, instinctively covering their chests and stomachs with their arms, for none of them had shields or armor.

The man in the tower blasted the horn.

Out of the haze from the left and the right sides came the thumping of more bowstrings and the screams of arrows. Spartan and Megarian warriors dropped like wheat mowed down by a scythe. The horn sounded again and a thousand more arrows flew from the bows of the women. A Spartan fell dead at Arkilokus's feet with two arrows in his face—one through each eye!

And then the terrible horn sounded thrice in a row. The noise was followed by a thundering din that shook the earth—the unmistakable sound of horses. Cavalry charging from behind. Now they were under attack from all sides!

Chaos followed. And a whirl of blood and screams and death. Bodies crashing into each other. Heads and arms flying. At one point Arkilokus saw Nikias running at him, but then the Plataean was cut off by a wall of Spartiates who sacrificed themselves to save their prince. Arkilokus did not know how he came to be standing on the road with less than a hundred of his warriors. Had an hour passed? A day? Or had it been mere seconds? Most of the men who'd dragged him from the field were wounded. One was missing a hand, the other an arm.

"Prince Arkilokus, can you run?" asked one of them—a warrior whose chin had been sliced clean off his face.

Arkilokus nodded with a sharp jerk. They formed up a retreating mass with him in the center, heading back up the road toward the Three Heads. The surviving Megarians—a thousand or so—were retreating west, chased by a mass of Plataean horsemen, three hundred or more strong, who speared them in the backs as they ran toward the olive grove, hemmed in by the line of carts blocking the road to the south.

Arkilokus had never seen such a rout. The world did not seem real. It was like living in a nightmare. "Keep moving," said the voice in his head.

"The Megarians are drawing the enemy riders away from us," said one of his men.

"Keep moving!" Arkilokus shouted. He ran fast despite the pain in his leg. He saw Nikias's face in his mind's eye, smiling smugly. The Plataean had lured them into that killing ground. His people had blocked off the road with the carts to funnel the Spartans and Megarians toward the tower where thousands of archers—mostly women—had been waiting. And the Plataean cavalry had been hiding in the olive grove on the other side of the roadway the whole time, ready to crush Arkilokus and his army from behind.

"You underestimated him," said a mocking voice in Arkilokus's head. "You should have heeded the warning of the eclipse."

They'd run at least a mile when a pack of horsemen charged out of nowhere, shooting as they rode. Spartans screamed and dropped to the ground, writhing in throes of anguish.

"Skythians!" yelled Arkilokus.

He looked up. The smoke had cleared enough to reveal the fortress of the Three Heads on the hill. Now he had his answer to what had happened to the Skythians. They had not run away. They had only been hiding in the foothills nearby . . . waiting like wolves.

One of Arkilokus's men put a horn to his lips and gave a great blast. Then an arrow sliced through his cheeks—through one side and out the other—silencing the horn.

The barbarians whittled them down, riding round the pack of warriors, always shooting from a distance, taunting them, pointing to the fresh Dog Raider heads they wore tied around their waists.

By the time Arkilokus and his men made it to the slope below the fortress, there were only ten or so of his warriors left alive. All seemed lost. The Skythians were closing in for the final kill. But then a host of Megarian archers sprinted down the road, shouting as they came, and loosed a hail of arrows at the Skythians to drive them away. But the barbarians were already galloping down the southern road, jeering and whooping as they went.

"We heard the horn!" said one of the Megarians, stooping by Arkilokus's side. "What happened?"

Arkilokus lay down on the road, gasping for air. He couldn't talk. He couldn't catch his breath. He looked at the arrow in his right leg, then realized that he had another shaft stuck through the biceps of his left arm. Thank the gods it wasn't a Skythian arrow, or he would already be dead. He touched his face—it was slippery with blood and sweat. There was a gash on his forehead. A deep one. He rolled over and vomited.

"What happened?" a Megarian archer asked again.

"Ni . . . Ni," wheezed Arkilokus after he'd stopped heaving. "Nikias . . ." was all that he could force himself to say.

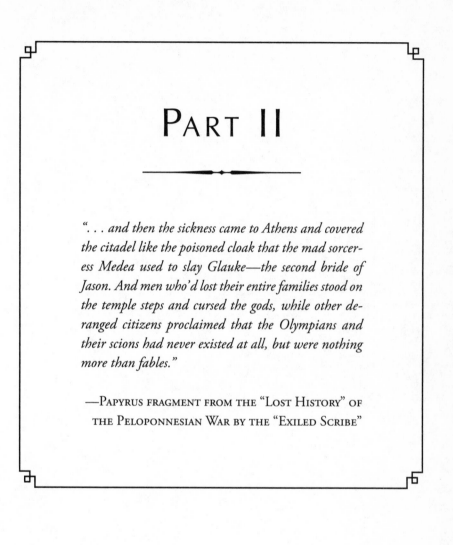

PART II

"... and then the sickness came to Athens and covered the citadel like the poisoned cloak that the mad sorceress Medea used to slay Glauke—the second bride of Jason. And men who'd lost their entire families stood on the temple steps and cursed the gods, while other deranged citizens proclaimed that the Olympians and their scions had never existed at all, but were nothing more than fables."

—PAPYRUS FRAGMENT FROM THE "LOST HISTORY" OF THE PELOPONNESIAN WAR BY THE "EXILED SCRIBE"

ONE

———————— ◆ ————————

The *Spear of Thetis* cut through choppy blue and white-capped waves with its shining copper ram at the prow, cruising toward the walled harbor entrance of the port of Piraeus a mile away. Every man was at the trireme's benches, and the one hundred and seventy oars dug into the water, then swept back in unison like the limbs of a strange and many-legged water insect. The two captured merchant vessels followed in the *Spear*'s wake.

Chusor stood on the top deck next to Agrios the helmsman on his throne-like seat, gazing at the familiar sight of the sturdy walls and towers of the great Athenian port. The entrance to the first harbor was a narrow gap in a seawall guarded by two stout towers on either side. If there were a threat of invasion by sea, a giant chain could be linked between these two towers, and triremes would be anchored to this chain, creating an impenetrable floating wall. But no enemy had attempted to enter the harbor since the days of the Persian Wars.

Chusor liked it up here on the open deck with Agrios as his only companion, where the constant annoying drone of the oar drums was drowned out by the wind. Agrios hardly ever spoke, which suited Chusor. He could lose himself in his thoughts while he gazed at the sea. His mind drifted back to his brief visit with his daughter, Melitta, on Serifos. She was a tough girl who liked to wear a boy's tunic and keep her hair short. The rough island life suited her.

In Athens she had lived in the household of her elder half sister who had been a hetaera—a high-class prostitute. But Melitta didn't miss anything about the urbane life in the citadel. She craved adventure more than anything, and he knew that she had inherited that quality from him. Despite dressing and acting like a boy, there was no denying her extreme beauty. The islanders said that she favored him in her looks, but they had never known her mother—the hetaera Sophia . . . the most beautiful woman Chusor had ever known. And he saw Sophia's eyes staring back at him whenever he looked at his daughter.

The voyage from Serifos had passed without incident. The sea had been the calmest in recent memory, but as soon as they had caught sight of the island of Salamis the wind started to blow hard from the northwest, and the three ships began to buck on the waves. Chusor could see a thick haze of smoke obscuring the mountains in the direction of the Oxlands beyond. And there were numerous trails of dark smoke emanating from the city of Piraeus and even more from Athens, like thin tufts of black goat hair pulled from a spindle.

They approached the walled isthmus of Piraeus, cruising past the tomb of Themistokles, which stood on a rocky point outside the bastions. Themistokles—the great admiral who had defeated the Persian navy at Salamis in the last war—had died far from home after being ostracized by his own people. But then he had been honored by the Athenians after his death.

"A hero one day, a goat the next," muttered Agrios.

"That must be a big forest fire," said Chusor, pointing his chin toward the mountains to the northwest. They were in a wide channel now, heading toward the harbor of Kantharos. To get to this harbor the *Spear* and the two grain ships would have to pass between a narrow gap in a breakwater. The breakwater itself was capped by walls that connected to the bastions of Piraeus on the right, and the walls of the outer city to the left side of the channel. On either side of the entrance were sturdy guard towers.

"A big fire," repeated Agrios. "But what are those strange dark streams of smoke coming from Piraeus and Athens?"

"Odd," said Chusor. He squinted into the wind.

"Odd indeed," said Agrios under his breath.

"What's this?" asked Chusor abruptly.

A small sailing vessel, no more than thirty feet long, shot from the narrow gap in the breakwater, its sails bellying on the strong wind. It headed straight toward the *Spear* and then turned suddenly and awkwardly, nearly capsizing as it hit the choppy sea outside the protection of the harbor. Screams emanated from the boat and Chusor caught a glimpse of many people crammed inside the open hold—women and children and even some animals and many belongings stuffed into sacks.

"Lubbers," said Agrios with disdain.

The sailboat's crew worked frantically to get the ship in order, pulling on the rigging and fixing a boom that had come undone from the mainsail, which had deflated like an empty sheep's bladder. The sail caught the wind again, puffed out, and the vessel jumped forward like a kicked horse just as the galley came parallel to it. A man at the tiller of the sailboat cupped his hand to his mouth and shouted something at the *Spear* as they went by, but Chusor could barely hear him over the wind.

"What did he shout?" asked Agrios, cocking his head to one side as if to catch a lingering voice on the wind.

"All that I heard was something about 'the pyres,'" said Chusor, and he felt a chill despite the warm afternoon.

Agrios expertly guided the *Spear* toward the gap in the breakwater. The towers on either side were usually bristling with Skythian archers, but there were only a few Athenian archers up there today. No Skythians in sight. They were a bowshot away from the bastions when Zana climbed the stairs at the opposite end of the deck, along with Ji. Zana looked disheveled and debauched.

"Better late than never," Chusor muttered.

"Stop oars!" Ji called to the lower decks, and the *Spear* slowed down, gliding toward the entrance to the harbor. Agrios made little adjustments with the tiller handles to prevent the trireme from turning in the strange eddies swirling here.

"What ship are you?" a guard on the left tower shouted down.

"The *Spear of Thetis* and two captured vessels," said Zana. "Bearing grain."

"Enter the harbor! Go to the grain docks at the Emporion." The guard said something to a man at his side and he blew thrice on a horn to signal the arrival of the ships.

"Oars, pull!" cried Ji.

The *Spear* cruised through the breakwater gap and into Kantharos harbor.

"Gods!" exclaimed Agrios, "where are all the boats?"

Chusor looked around. Usually this area of the harbor was teeming with triremes and other ships. But it was strangely empty. And there was a foul reek in the air. There was only one small galley approaching quickly, and this vessel—like the sailing ship—was filled to the upper edges with people and their goods. The oarsmen were rowing frantically.

"I think we should turn around," said Chusor. "Something strange is happening."

Agrios glanced over his shoulder and said, "Too late for that."

Chusor turned and saw that the Athenians were already at work setting up the great chain to block the gap between the towers, pulling it across in a boat made for this purpose. Zana had seen this, too, and she walked clumsily across the deck toward Chusor and Agrios, snapping at them, "What are they doing? Why are they putting up the chain?"

"Well, *I* didn't tell them to do it," said Chusor. "Your guess is as good as mine."

They watched as the small Athenian galley approached the breakwater towers and came to a clumsy stop, crashing into the rocks at the base of the tower on the right and breaking some of its oars.

"We have your silver!" said a man on the deck of the galley, his voice carrying across the still water of the harbor.

One of the guards leaned over and called down, "You're late! And the price has doubled!"

"They're bribing the guards to leave the harbor," said Zana, aghast.

"So it would seem," said Chusor.

"What is going on?"

"We'll find out soon enough," said Agrios.

"We should go back now," said Zana.

"And pay the guards with grain?" said Chusor. "We need to unload our shipment, take our payment, and then try our luck with those guards."

"Chusor is right," said Agrios. "We have only enough silver on hand to give the men their shore coins."

Zana chewed on a nail nervously.

They soon arrived at the docks on the eastern shore of the harbor. The place was deserted.

"I don't hear any hammers or chisels," said Chusor.

The frames of ten or so vessels could be seen like the skeletons of giant animals in the shadows of the outbuildings and boat sheds. Usually this cove was bursting with activity, for this was where the triremes were built or mended, and it was never without the noise of hammer and chisel on wood, except on great holidays or the funeral processions of important men. Chusor, who had spent his first twenty years in Athens—most of that time around the docks and shipyards—had never seen it so desolate.

They glided up to the long dock where grain ships unloaded their cargoes. But there was nobody there to greet them: no port officials or even slaves to unload the grain. Crewmen from the *Spear* and the merchant vessels jumped out and tied the ships to the dock. Zana stood looking around with a confused and owlish expression. Finally she said, "I'm going to my cabin. Bring me any news."

She hastily made her way down the stairs.

"I'm going to go find my brother," said Agrios as he locked the tiller handles in place. "He lives in northern Piraeus, near the gates to the Legs," he added, using the local slang for the Long Walls. Then he dashed across the deck and leapt nimbly to the dock, sprinting toward the sheds on his bandy legs.

Chusor went below decks. The oarsmen were all stretching their limbs and rubbing their muscles after the long pull. The men were happily talking about all of the wonderful things they were going to do in Athens, most involving women or dancing boys and wine. The noise of their voices in the cramped space was deafening.

"Give us some owls!" the men demanded from him. Athenian coins were all stamped with the image of an owl on one side.

"Hold up," said Chusor as he pushed his way to the center of the ship, where he found Phoenix standing by one of the big water jugs, splashing his face. The Athenian had sat on an oar bench for the entire voyage and his chiseled torso glistened with sweat. Diokles stood next to him. The two had become friends over the past three days. Phoenix had quickly regained his strength and seemed like a new man, unrecognizable from the half-drowned escapee whom they had dragged on board, and he was smiling happily.

"I never would have made it home without you," he said to Chusor.

"Don't thank me yet," Chusor replied.

Diokles took one look at Chusor's grim face and asked, "What's wrong?"

Chusor lowered his voice for their ears alone. "There's something terribly wrong in Athens." He briefly told them what had transpired on their arrival— the ship frantically leaving Piraeus, the strange smoke, and the lack of activity at the docks.

The color drained from Phoenix's face as Chusor spoke, and the mariner looked full of dread. "Come with me to the city," he said. "We'll find out what's going on."

"I can't," Chusor replied. "I have a price on my head here. I'm a wanted man in Athens. I must stay with the ships."

"I'll go with Phoenix," Diokles said.

Chusor put his hand on Diokles's wrist. "Find Ezekiel," he whispered.

Diokles nodded, then he and Phoenix stole from the trireme amidst the chaos of the cheerful crew. Chusor gave each of the mariners a small advance on their pay and the oarsmen slowly dispersed from the vessel, leaving only Ji and a skeleton crew. Chusor peered out one of the oar holes, watching as the last of the men disappeared into the streets leading from the docks.

"Chusor!" Zana called out from the cabin with a high-handed tone. "Come to me!"

Chusor sighed and tossed the empty money pouch on the deck. Then he went obediently to the cabin to perform his duties.

TWO

———————◆———————

Nikias and Leo stood over the corpse of General Zoticus, the leader of the Plataean cavalry. Other horsemen jostled into them, crowding around to get a better look at the body of their fallen leader.

Zoticus lay on his back with open eyes, his hawkish gray-bearded face peering skyward. He had been wounded in the chaos of the battle—cut across the back of the thigh by an enemy javelin, but despite this injury he had fought valiantly, leading the rout of the enemy and chasing them for several miles before turning back. It was only after returning to the Tower of Theseus with his men that he fainted and fell from his horse. He died minutes later.

Nikias had seen this uncanny thing happen before: warriors who'd suffered a mortal blow fought with fury, only to collapse and die the moment that the day had been won. His grandfather had explained the phenomenon as the ikor of the gods—the magical blood that flowed through a warrior's veins in the heat of battle.

"He's smiling," said one of the riders with solemnity.

"A great victory," said another.

Less than a score of Plataeans had perished during the battle, while thousands of the enemy lay dead upon the field in front of the tower. Unarmored and unshielded men were no match for well-aimed arrows—arrows that the skilled women archers rained down like a hailstorm from three sides. Nikias could not believe how foolish the enemy had been to rush headlong into the trap that he and Zoticus hastily devised after Nikias had found the Plataean cavalry returning from their scouting expedition.

Nikias only wished that Arkilokus had been killed or captured. He'd looked for his cousin's body amongst the dead but had not found it. The most important thing, however, was that the road to Athens was now clear, and his daughters, sister, and all of the other Plataeans were safe.

At least for a while.

"We must build a pyre for him and the other dead," said a deep voice.

Nikias turned and saw a tall, broad-shouldered man with a black beard and a scar running from his left eye to his chin. This was Sarpedon, Zoticus's second-in-command.

Sarpedon sent men to search for dry wood, then opened a pouch on his belt and poured a handful of silver Plataean coins onto the ground. He knelt down and picked up a single coin, placing it in Zoticus's open palm, curling his dead fingers over it. This was payment for Kiron the Ferryman to take his shade over the river Styx.

"Here comes another Plataean hero," chanted all of the warriors in unison.

Before Sarpedon moved on to the next body to place a coin, he glanced up at Nikias. "Get everyone back on the road," he ordered. "We leave as soon as the funeral fires are lit."

Nikias nodded and pushed his way through the circle of men, followed by Leo.

"The Skythians want to talk to you," said Leo.

Nikias looked over to where the Skythians sat apart from everyone else astride their stock-still horses. They all wore their long hair in topknots like Kolax, and their bare arms were covered in tattoos. He spotted Osyrus, Kolax's evil-looking father, staring back at him. He strode over to the Skythians with Leo at his side and raised his hand in greeting.

"Nikias," said Osyrus in halting Greek. "To Plataea we return now."

"Very dangerous," said Nikias. "Thebans control the other side of the pass."

"Athens is shut to us," replied Osyrus. "The only Skythians in Athens now are the enemies of our tribe."

"Please tell my grandfather what happened here," said Nikias. "Tell him the Sword of Apollo will return to Plataea with help. He will understand what I mean." "The Sword of Apollo" was the code that he and his grandfather had chosen to use in case Nikias had to send a message.

"The Arkon will learn," said Osyrus.

"Kolax became separated from us on the mountain and—"

"Leo already told us what happened to my son," interrupted Osyrus gruffly. "When he came to the fort to warn us."

"We did not see Kolax captured by the Dog Raiders," said Nikias.

"But my heart tells me he is in great danger," replied Osyrus. "Good-bye.

May Papaeus guide you to the city of the Athenians." He turned his horse and rode off, followed by his men, galloping up the road back toward the Three Heads. Then they left the road and vanished into the ancient olive grove.

"What do you think will happen to them?" asked Leo.

"I don't know," said Nikias. "They're like a swift-riding plague bringing death. If only we had another thousand of them we'd win this war."

Nikias walked over to where Saeed and Phile sat in the wagon. Saeed's face and tunic were splattered with enemy blood, and Phile's hands trembled uncontrollably as she tried to take a drink of wine from a skin. The girls lay asleep on a pile of clothes. Nestor, utterly worn-out from the day's events, lay curled up on the ground with his head on Teleos's lap. Ajax was using the dog's bony haunch as a pillow.

"Where did you get this dog?" asked Teleos.

"I stole him from a Megarian," said Nikias.

"Can we name him?" asked Ajax. "He's the best dog ever."

"He's got a name," said Nikias. "It's Nestor."

"That's a stupid name for a dog," said Teleos. "We were thinking Hellhound. We love him."

"He's Nestor," said Nikias impatiently. "We're heading out. We need to get everyone back on the road." Teleos jumped to his feet and the tired dog groaned.

Saeed shot a concerned look at Phile. "Your sister—"

"I'm fine," Phile said, and smiled wanly. She held up a hand to show that it was shaking. "Only I can't control my hands."

Nikias leaned over and kissed her on the cheek. "Your hands did not tremble when you shot that bow," he said. "That's all that matters."

She dropped her eyes and bowed her head. Then took her brother's hand quickly in her own and kissed it. "Thank you," she said in a choking voice.

Nikias, Leo, and Saeed went up and down the line of refugees on horseback, calling for everyone to get back on the road. Within an hour the men, women, and children of Plataea were on the march again, with Sarpedon at the lead and the rest of the cavalry spread out all along the line. Nikias, Leo, and Saeed were at the rear, riding behind the carts.

It was slow going with so many thousands of women, children, and elderly. Every time a cart wheel broke, Nikias encouraged the owner to leave the thing behind; but the men were stubborn and couldn't bear to give up their belongings, so Nikias found all of the smiths and woodworkers and organized them into crews to make quick repairs. He made Teleos and Ajax his runners, and they dashed about with the loyal dog, Nestor the Hellhound, who had decided that the boys were much more amiable companions than Nikias . . . and much more likely to supply him with food.

The land they walked through had been ravaged by repeated Spartan attacks over the last year. The farms and villages that they passed had been burned—all that was left were the charred remains of beams and blackened roof tiles or the stone threshing floors that had sprouted weeds between the cracks. Fields had been cut and trampled last spring by the enemy before the wheat could ripen, and the vines that would now be laden with grapes had all been hacked off near the ground. Only the sacred olive groves had been left untouched, and the branches were laden with unharvested fruit. They marched until the sun began to set and made camp in a fallow field, huddled together with all of the warriors standing guard in a great ring about the women, children, and old men.

"Our exhausted warriors make our walls," said Leo, making a play on the old Spartan saying, for in the far-off country of Lakonia they had no walls around their citadels, such was the Spartan confidence in their military prowess. Leo's joke was quickly taken up by all the men, and could be heard uttered—followed by sharp laughter—throughout the long night.

Nikias sat with his back to a wheel on his family's cart, so spent from the last two days he could hardly move. Saeed stood nearby, staring back toward Kithaeron Mountain with his arms crossed. Nikias knew that he was thinking about his son. Teleos and Ajax were sound asleep, curled up with Nestor like three huge pups. Every once in a while Nikias heard one of his daughters call out in despair for their mama. Not only did they miss their mother's touch, they were still nursing. The resourceful Phile had found a young woman who had given birth to a stillborn child a week before, and the teenager willingly took to feeding the girls to ease her swollen and painful breasts. She was in the cart with the twins, and Nikias could hear her speaking sweet words to the girls through a voice filled with tears.

Phile came around from the other side of the cart where she had been kneading bread for the morning's breakfast and sat next to him. "You can't sleep?" she asked.

"I won't sleep until we're inside the walls of Athens," he replied.

There was a long silence and then Phile said, "I was so scared when the attack came that I pissed myself, Brother."

Nikias grinned. "Grandfather shit himself before they faced the Persians during the Great War."

"He did?" asked Phile.

"Old Linos the bard told me. He was standing right behind him in the phalanx."

She paused, then asked hopefully, "Did you ever shit yourself, Brother?"

"No," said Nikias. "But I spent my childhood fighting Grandfather in the arena. Nothing in life seems terrifying after facing him," he joked.

"I suppose not."

Nikias took Phile's hand and held it tightly. "Are you worried about Athens?" he asked.

"Of course. I've never even been there. But I've heard so many stories. Will we be scorned?"

"It won't be bad. Athens is beautiful. The most beautiful city on earth. Wait until you see the statue of Athena on the Akropolis."

"But will they accept us there?"

"They will. Perikles will force them to accept us. And he rules Athens."

Nikias wrapped his arm around Phile's shoulder and she put her head on his arm and exhaled. He was suddenly overcome with love for his younger sister. He had fought with her his entire life and had always resented her. But now he was so thankful that he had her by his side—so grateful that she was here to watch out for his girls. He thought about Kallisto and wondered if she was still alive.

"Don't fret about Kallisto," said Phile, guessing what he was thinking. "Grandmother is with her. She has helped bring many children into this world."

"All I can do now is pray," said Nikias.

"I love her, too, you know?" said Phile. "I loved her even before you. She is like my sister. And I was jealous when I thought that you had stolen some of that love. But then I came to realize that Kallisto's love is boundless—for me, and you and the girls."

Nikias turned his face away. He didn't want his sister to see the tears coursing down his cheeks. After a while Phile went back into the cart to sleep next to the girls and Nikias fell into a dreary and fitful sleep, full of bad dreams. He was awakened by the growling of Nestor.

"Who's there?" asked Nikias, sitting up with a start, for he saw the large shape of a man looming over him.

"Get up," said Sarpedon with a surly voice. "I need you. Bring your sword."

Nikias strapped on his weapons, then followed Sarpedon through the labyrinth of sleeping bodies to the area where the horses were tethered. Photine stood apart from the others, champing on some grass.

"What's going on?" asked Nikias.

"I'm sending out scouts in every direction to look for the enemy," said Sarpedon. "You're one of my best riders. And you're lucky. Head west for two hours after the rising of the sun, and then report back."

THREE

Nikias and the other ten chosen riders waited until the first glow of the sun above the mountains in the east, then went off on their missions. Photine was happy to be running free and trotted across the Attik plains. But all that Nikias discovered on his journey was more ravaged countryside: burned homes and fields and the occasional corpse rotting in the sun—the bodies of Megarians and Korinthian pillagers who had no doubt been killed by Athenian cavalry sorties. He rode for ten miles, then headed back to camp. A fresh scout was waiting to take his place and headed off in the same direction.

Each morning for the next three days Nikias headed off on this mission, only to find the same thing—a desolate landscape and no sign of the enemy. And each day the refugees managed to travel about fifteen miles before stopping for the night to allow the many stragglers to catch up.

On the fourth morning after the battle at the Tower of Theseus, Nikias awoke before dawn from a nightmare. He had dreamed that his best friend from childhood, Demetrios, stood by the tree that held the golden fleece, encouraging Nikias to reach up and seize it. But when Nikias tried to grasp the magical treasure, the tree came to life and attacked him. It was a recurring dream that always filled him with foreboding. He had first experienced the vision when he was tortured by Eurymakus the Theban, hung upside down from the rafters of an undercroft in the city-state of Tanagra and beaten mercilessly.

Now, as he rode across the barren fields, lost in grim musings, he wondered what had happened to Demetrios. His friend—more like a brother than a mere gymnasium companion—had been sent off by his father to Syrakuse, years before the Theban sneak attack, ostensibly to study at the house of a wealthy general on that island. Demetrios had had the bad luck to be born the heir of Nauklydes, the traitor who had opened the gates of Plataea to the enemy. Nauklydes, a prominent magistrate and Menesarkus's protégé, had made a secret alliance with the Thebans and their Spartan overlords. He'd been promised that he would be given control of Plataea after it was taken. But once he opened the gates he was betrayed by the enemy, and his daughter was raped and killed before his eyes.

After the invaders had been defeated, Nikias uncovered information that Nauklydes had been the traitor. He helped bring him to justice, and the man who had once been a hero of his citadel was convicted of treason and given the tunic of stones: buried up to his waist in the agora and stoned to death.

Nikias still couldn't comprehend how a man as principled as Nauklydes could have betrayed his own people. Was it out of fear of the Spartans and their designs on Plataea? Or simply an insatiable lust for power and wealth? Nauklydes had sent Demetrios to Syrakuse to get him out of the way—so that his beloved son would be safe from the threat of Spartan invaders. But Syrakuse, as it turned out, was a puppet of the Spartans. Nauklydes was like a foolish shepherd who'd sent his sheep to live amongst the wolves.

Was Demetrios still alive? It wasn't likely. The Spartans had certainly ordered the Syrakusans to murder Demetrios after they had been assured of Nauklydes's complicity in the sneak attack. If they hadn't slain him, then the Syrakusans would have thrown Demetrios into the notorious Prison Pits of that city-state: deep marble quarries where men toiled until they died. Or so the rumors told of that awful place. Demetrios was strong . . . even stronger than Nikias. But his friend wouldn't last more than a few months in the Prison Pits, let alone the more than two years since Demetrios's father had been betrayed by the wily foes of Plataea.

"Why do you keep coming to me in my dreams, Demetrios?" Nikias asked aloud. "Eh, brother?"

He looked around, startled from his dark thoughts by the sudden realization that he recognized his surroundings. He was at the farm of his friend Konon—about fifteen miles from Athens. He thought back to the day he stumbled onto this farm, delirious from a blow he'd taken in a fight with Dog Raiders. Konon's kindly family took him in and nursed him back to health.

The place, which had been prosperous and lovely back then, was now utterly destroyed. All that was left were the footings of the buildings, scattered roof tiles, and the house's chimney. He went past what had been a fine fig orchard, but the trees had all been chopped down. The sight of the place made him depressed and he quickly departed, heading up a little hill that looked over the plains.

When he got to the top he saw something flashing in the distance. He peered across the plains and beheld an unmistakable sight: spearheads held high, catching the light of the sun on their gleaming bronze points. A great army of horsemen was riding straight at him, less than two miles away, six hundred or more.

"Hera's jugs!" he cursed, then wheeled Photine around and kicked her hard, riding back toward the abandoned farm. It would take him half an hour to get back to the refugees on the road, he reckoned, if he pushed Photine as fast as she would go. There would be time to warn them. But the majority of the refugees would still be a few miles or so from Athens by the time the Spartan cavalry arrived. They would be caught in the open fields and massacred within sight of the walls. He let forth a furious scream of frustration.

"Nikias!" cried an astonished voice.

Nikias snapped his head around. Standing amongst the ruins of the farm was a young man waving frantically with one arm—his other arm was only a stump, having been cut off at the elbow.

"Konon!"

Nikias checked Photine and trotted over to his friend. The one-armed Athenian, a stolid farmer with a plain but ingenuous face, looked pale and emaciated since the last time Nikias had seen him.

"It *is* you!" said Konon, smiling back with a similar disbelief. "You just disappeared from the city that night! I thought you were dead!"

"I had to leave quickly," said Nikias. "I didn't have any way to get word to you. What are you doing here?"

"I could ask the same."

"I'm helping to lead refugees from Plataea," explained Nikias. "We've come to the safety of Athens until the Spartans are defeated. Perikles told us to come. I was just scouting for the enemy."

Konon's face fell. "Nikias. This is a black time to come to Athens for safety."

"What do you mean? Because of raiding parties? Or have the Spartans started to besiege Athens?"

"No," said Konon. "Something worse." He held up a blackened pot. "We buried some coins under the doorsill. I came to get them so I could buy medicine."

"Medicine? For what?"

"The contagion," Konon replied flatly. "My father—do you remember him? He's dead. So is my grandfather. And my brother's wife. My grandmother clings to life."

Nikias's heart sank. "What is this contagion?" he asked, horrified.

"It's bad. A burning fever that strikes you down, stabbings in the guts and eyes, and a black vomit. So many have died already. Once you get within a few miles of Athens you'll see the funeral pyres. They're burning hundreds today. It might be thousands tomorrow. We're running out of wood."

Nikias shook his head in disbelief. This could not be happening. An army of Spartan horsemen was advancing across the plains, and the only refuge for his people was a city infected by some terrible plague. They hadn't brought any medicine to remedy what Konon had just described. The only things they carried in the cart were opium and hemp for pain, honey to sterilize wounds, and a powerful emetic made from narcissus flowers. He knew all this because he had helped Saeed carefully pack the jars the day before they left the farm.

"It was the eclipse," was all that he could think of to say.

"The illness started weeks before the eclipse," said Konon.

"It was a warning," said Nikias. "We should have stayed in Plataea. But now we have no choice. Do you have a horse?"

"Just my old mule," said Konon. "Everyone's animals were transported to the island of Euboea for safekeeping over a year ago."

Nikias pictured the long island of Euboea in his mind's eye. It was separated from the mainland by a narrow channel that had powerful shifting currents. He had passed through this channel years ago on an ill-fated trireme commanded by his cousin Phoenix. But their ship had been attacked by Korinthian raiders and Nikias jumped overboard, swimming to shore. He never knew what had become of Phoenix and the others.

"Why doesn't Perikles send all the people in Athens to Euboea?" he asked.

"He said it would be a sign of weakness to abandon the citadel," explained Konon. "The only people allowed on Euboea are some warriors and shepherds to guard the flocks."

Nikias took a deep breath, then exhaled quickly. "Ride your mule back to Athenes as fast as you can," he said. "An army of Spartans is heading this way. I have to go now, old friend. I have to warn my people."

"We're living in a little cave near the Temple of Hephaestos!" Konon called out as Nikias galloped away.

"I'll find you in Athens!" Nikias yelled over his shoulder.

FOUR

"We must charge straight at them," said Sarpedon. "It's the only chance for our people to make it to the walls of Athens."

Sarpedon was surrounded by a semicircle of his men with Nikias standing before him, still breathing hard from the fast ride from Konon's farm. They were six miles from the city. He could see the walls and the smoke from funeral pyres. He could see the Temple of Athena shining in the sun, and Mount Hymettos looming behind it. They were so close now. But death waited for them on both sides of the walls of Athens. Nikias was not the only one who was thinking this.

"We should head to the Piraeus District," said one of the Plataean cavalrymen. "Hire ships to take us to Euboea."

"I agree!" said another. "Euboea is a big island. And it's close to Athens."

"If this contagion is spreading throughout the city," said Sarpedon, "the Athenians will ship out their own people first."

"Sarpedon is right," said Nikias. "It would take the entire fleet to transport us all to Euboea."

"We could swim there!" said another man. "It's not far."

"The currents are deadly," said Nikias, shaking his head. "It's impossible."

"Then what do we do?" asked another rider.

"We sacrifice ourselves so that our families can have a chance," said Sarpedon. "A contagion won't kill everyone. But the Spartans surely will." He scanned the eyes of his men with a steely resolve. "Understand?" The men nodded grimly. "We mount up now and cut them off before they reach the road."

Nikias said, "I need a spear and a shield."

"You're not coming with us," said Sarpedon. "You're to lead our people to the Dipylon." He was referring to the great two-gated entrance on the north-western wall.

"But—"

Sarpedon grabbed Nikias's biceps. "If you disobey me now, I'll cut off your balls!" he hissed. "Now do your duty and look after our people." His eyes softened for a moment and he added in a voice for Nikias's ears alone: "Look after my wife and daughter if I don't come back. Understand?"

Nikias nodded.

He watched the men ride off, throwing up a dusty haze as they went. How many of them would survive? Not one might make it to Athens alive. He mounted Photine and headed up the road, looking for Saeed. His family's cart was in the middle of the throng. The twins, sitting in the back of the cart with Phile's arms wrapped around them, looked at him blankly as he came up. Saeed walked alongside the lead ox. Ajax and Teleos were nowhere in sight.

"Where did Sarpedon take the cavalry?" asked Saeed.

"Just a precaution," lied Nikias. There were many other families nearby, looking at him expectantly. They'd all seen the cavalry ride away. The Plataean riders would be slaughtered. Nikias knew that in his gut. And then the Spartans would keep coming, like a moving wall of reapers, cutting down men and women and children.

"We must go faster," urged Nikias in a carrying voice. "Just a little further now."

"Brother," whispered Phile, "what are those strange smoke fires in the citadel?"

"Not now," said Nikias, his stomach churning with anxiety. How long would it take the contagion to strike down his sister and children? How many of them would live? Did they have any medicine strong enough to thwart a terrible illness that could bring even a big warrior like Konon's father to his knees?

And then an idea hit him like a clap to the head. The Spartans feared contagion more than any foe. At least, that's what his grandfather had told him once.

"Phile!" he blurted. "Where are the medicines?"

"Are you sick?" she asked, rummaging behind her for a wooden box and opening it.

"The emetic!" said Nikias. "Quickly! Give it to me." He took the small bottle from her hand. "And a lump of charcoal. And a small wineskin."

"What are you—"

He seized the proffered charcoal and wineskin, then turned to Saeed. "Ride up the line to the front," he commanded. "Tell everyone to go as fast as they can. I'll be back." He turned Photine and shot away from the road, back in the direction that the cavalry had taken—to the west.

"Where are you going, Brother?!" cried Phile. But he did not look back. He shoved the charcoal into his mouth and chewed until his jaws ached, washing it down with the wine. He quickly caught up to the cavalry, for they had stopped a few miles from the road, waiting for the advancing mass of Spartan cavalry. He rode straight up to Sarpedon, who cried out in anger when he caught sight of him.

"Sheep-stuffing fool! I ordered you—"

"Stay here, Sarpedon!" shouted Nikias, his voice full of authority and strength. "Don't follow me! If I die, then I die. But if I succeed, then you all will live." He uncorked the bottle of emetic and forced himself to swallow the bitter liquid.

"Are you mad?" asked Sarpedon. "What are you doing?"

Nikias threw the little clay jar on the ground, then quickly unstrapped his scabbard and tossed it to Sarpedon, who caught it. Then, without explaining himself, he bolted away from the cavalry. He glanced back over his shoulder but nobody had attempted to follow him. Sarpedon sat on his horse, openmouthed, stunned into silence by Nikias's strange actions.

Nikias rode hard, straight at the heart of the enemy cavalry—a seemingly endless mass of horses and men and armor gleaming in the sun. He felt a churning and bubbling in his stomach and forced himself to concentrate. Scouts out in front saw him and turned their horses to intercept him. He raised one hand, palm up.

"Peace!" he shouted, coming to a halt. "Peace! I need to speak to your general! I'm unarmed! I have important news!"

The Spartans surrounded him on all sides, boxing him in with their horses, then directed him toward their cavalry. The enemy horsemen had come to a stop evidently to rest their horses before their charge against the Plataeans. The scouts brought Nikias to the center of the cavalry, where a gray-haired warrior was getting his armor strapped on. Nikias recognized the man at once—he was King Arkidamos himself. Standing next to him was a tall man with an intelligent face who was dressed like a Korinthian cavalryman.

The scouts came to a stop and pulled Nikias from Photine's back, grabbing him by either arm and escorting him to within ten paces of their king. Then they forced him to his knees.

"What is this?" asked the king, perplexed. "Who are you?"

"I'm Nikias of Plataea," replied Nikias. "I am Menesarkus's grandson."

The king's face did not show any emotion—neither surprise nor concern. Nikias felt his stomach turn, and his face broke out in a cold sweat. The king took a step forward but Nikias held up his hands. "Stand back, Your Majesty!" he warned. "I'm sick."

"Sick?" asked the king with a slightly perplexed tone. "What do you mean?"

"The contagion," said Nikias.

The Spartan scouts holding on to his arms let go almost immediately and stepped back. The king recoiled as well.

"What are you doing here?" asked Arkidamos.

"I've come to warn you," said Nikias, "and in doing so save my people from your army. If you attack us, you will catch this illness."

The Korinthian stepped forward and bowed his head deferentially to the Spartan royal. "King Arkidamos," he said, "this Plataean is lying. He doesn't appear to have a fever. There is nothing wrong with him."

"I'm not lying," said Nikias. "Look at the smoke rising from Athens. Thousands have died in the citadel already."

The king turned his gaze toward Athens and squinted.

"An Athenian ruse, as I told you already," said the Korinthian. "This Plataean is crafty, I'll give him that. He knows their exhausted cavalry will be overwhelmed."

Nikias started to panic. Why wasn't the emetic working? He felt perfectly well—his stomach had even stopped churning. He looked around desperately, like an animal caught in a box. Hundreds of Spartan warriors stared at him impassively.

"Let me take Menesarkus's heir back to the fort," said the Korinthian. "He will make a valuable prisoner in our negotiations with the Plataean Arkon."

But the Spartan king appeared not entirely certain what to do. He looked Nikias up and down, then asked, "What are the symptoms of this illness?"

"A stabbing in the eyes and stomach," said Nikias. "And a black vomit." He stopped speaking and tried to will himself to throw up, but nothing would happen. "It's the eclipse. It was a warning."

"And *you* have this illness now?" asked the Korinthian with a sly voice. He strode up to Nikias and stopped a few paces in front of him. "You look perfectly well to me. Scared, perhaps, but not sick." The wry expression on his face reminded Nikias of a pedantic teacher who'd caught a student in a lie.

"He was brave to come here," said the Korinthian in a booming voice. "But he knows we stand to kill or capture most of his people before they reach the walls of Athens. Do you have children, Nikias of Plataea?" He leaned forward and said in a whisper, "Perhaps I'll take them for my own slaves. And your woman too."

Nikias grit his teeth, trembling with rage. He had failed. And he'd thrown his life away for nothing. At least he could take this smug Korinthian down before the Spartans killed him. All he had to do was smash his palm into the man's face, driving the nasal bone into his brain. He tensed his legs for the attack. But then a strange feeling overcame him and he gasped. "Gods," he blurted, for suddenly it felt as if his stomach had swelled to thrice its size . . . like he was about to give birth to his own guts from his mouth. He put his palms on the ground and spewed forth a dark vomit—a black bile that sprayed the Korinthian's feet.

The man let forth a startled cry and jumped backward, and everyone within ten feet of Nikias edged back. The king stared with horror at the dark mess Nikias had made, and the charcoal-black slime trailing down his chin. Nikias heaved again and his body shook violently.

"The Plataean isn't clever enough to do *that*," said the king. "He can't conjure the black bile from his guts on a whim." He quickly mounted his horse and shouted to his men, "Back to the camp! The Plataeans and Athenians are infected with contagion." And, turning to the Korinthian, he said, "Don't come back with us, Andros. You might have his sickness now. Once you are back at the Megarian camp, send a messenger to me."

"But the Plataean," said Andros the Korinthian. "Shouldn't we kill him?"

"Leave him to his fate," ordered the king in a solemn tone. "I will not slay a man dying of the contagion. It would bring us bad luck."

Nikias could not stop vomiting. He retched over and over again until his eyes were streaming tears. He saw the Korinthian—the one the king had called Andros—wipe the vomit from his feet with a rag, a look of disgust mingled with hatred in his dark eyes. Then he threw the rag at Nikias and stalked away.

Nikias watched as all the Spartans mounted up and rode away. Finally he lay on his side, breathing shallowly as the waves of nausea receded, listening to the ground tremble with the sound of pounding hooves.

He was alone in the field. The sun burned his cheek. He drifted into that comfortable state of profound relief that comes after vomiting. He watched as a trail of ants carried grass seeds in a line—an orderly line of workers. After a while he felt the rumble of horses coming from the direction of Athens. He forced himself to get to his knees. When he could finally look up, he saw Sarpedon and two other horsemen riding toward him.

"What happened?" asked Sarpedon. He leapt from his horse and rushed to Nikias's side. His face wore a rare smile—a grin so wide it looked like it might split his face. "We saw the Spartans ride away! All of them! What did you do?"

Nikias wiped his mouth on the sleeve of his tunic and said, "I scared them off."

———

The gates were shut when Nikias and the cavalry arrived at the northwestern walls of Athens. The Plataean refugees were still a mile behind them on the road, spread out in a broken line of exhausted travelers.

Acrid smoke from the funeral fires filled the air around the walls with a sickening stench. Up on the high walls Nikias could make out the figures of a few archers, but the bastions seemed undermanned since he had been here last. Back then the ramparts had been thick with watchmen.

"I am Sarpedon of Plataea, and we seek entrance to the citadel!" called out the cavalry captain. There came no reply from the walls. But one of the archers turned to a companion and the man vanished from sight, apparently sent on some errand. They waited for half an hour on their fidgeting horses until the first refugees started to crowd around them, wondering what was going on.

Sarpedon was growing red-faced and agitated. "This is absurd," he grumbled.

Nikias saw Phile and Saeed arrive, and they gazed back at him expectantly. He smiled and gave them a little wave.

"Who speaks for the Plataeans?" called down a weary yet officious voice from the wall.

Nikias saw a pale and sweaty man leaning over the parapet wall.

"I, Sarpedon, son of—"

"Athens is infected with a sickness," snapped the Athenian, mopping his face with a rag. "Tens of thousands are dead. More are dying. The gates are shut. Go back to Plataea for your own good."

Sarpedon turned to Nikias with an outraged and bewildered expression. "Is he joking?"

Nikias thought of the terrible omen at the farm—the snake swallowing the baby owl. "Tell him that Perikles sent a message to my grandfather four days ago," he said, "offering us refuge from the Spartan invaders."

Sarpedon called out, "Perikles sent word to our Arkon, Menesarkus—"

"Perikles is dead," said the man on wall. "He died this morning. General Kleon rules Athens until the Assembly can meet. The gates are shut." He turned abruptly and vanished from view, leaving the stunned Plataeans in total silence, staring up at the wall looming above them like the face of a frowning cliff.

FIVE

———◆———

"There's the slow way to kill him and the fun way," said the big Dog Raider standing in front of Kolax with his hands on his hips and an evil glint in his eye. "Skinning takes the longest, but the four-chop is more entertaining."

The horseman's companion, a shorter and younger warrior with greasy black hair and a patchy beard, shrugged with indifference. "Both are fine with me," he replied. "I'm just looking forward to listening to him scream."

Kolax, bound with ropes to an olive tree, stared back at the Dog Raiders with wide-eyed horror. He would have screamed but his mouth was gagged.

"Ah," said the first Dog Raider with a thoughtful look, scratching his brown beard. "For screaming there's nothin' better than a red-hot poker up the arse."

"Why not start with that, then move on to skinning and then the four-chop to finish up?"

"The four-chop! No!" Kolax tried to shout, but his words came out as an unintelligible garble. He felt something hot and wet spray out his arse and groaned with mortification. He'd never shit himself before. At least, not in front of anyone.

"So be it," said the Dog Raider. "I'll get the others. Sun will be setting soon. Best to do this in daylight."

As soon as the two men strode off into the bustling Dog Raider camp to find their companions, Kolax started squirming against the ropes that bound him to the olive tree with his legs spread wide and his arms trussed behind him, his back to the trunk. His wrists and ankles were raw and bleeding, but the blood wasn't enough to lubricate his bindings. He bit into the rope in his mouth, screaming in the back of his throat in frustration.

It had been ten hours or so since he was captured near the Cave of Nymphs by the fork-bearded Dog Raider. He and the other marauders brought him over the Kithaeron Mountains into Megaria and to the outskirts of the sprawling Spartan camp where they had bivouacked for the night. Fork-Beard, the snarling piece of filth, then went off to find someone called "the Korinthian" to question Kolax, but he had been gone for hours, and now the Dog Raiders at the camp had decided to put an end to Kolax.

He called upon the sky god Papaeus to save him. He didn't want to die with a hot poker up his arse! Or skinned alive! And then finished off with the four-chop—to have all four limbs hacked off at once so that you wriggled like a maggot while the Dog Raiders laughed and made bets to see how long you lived before you bled out. This was a mortifying way to die, Kolax knew from firsthand experience, having helped four-chop several captured Dog Raiders with his Skythian kin. There was nothing funnier than watching an armless and legless man wriggling in the dirt, cursing and crying. Unless that armless and legless man was you.

"Oh, Great Sky God," he said to himself in Skythian, "if you save me from this terrible death that is far beneath a warrior of my stature, I promise to cut off my topknot and burn it on your altar, and even give you my foreskin, and any number of other things. Please, please save me!"

He peered at the Dog Raiders. There was a crowd of them now, gathered around the cooking fire. They pointed at him, laughing. One of them was heating a poker over the coals!

He squeezed his eyes shut to block out the sight.

Where was that gods-forsaken Fork-Beard? Kolax had gathered from Dog Raider conversations he overheard while tied to the tree that the man Fork-Beard had gone searching for—the one named Andros—was an important Korinthian spy who always paid the Dog Raiders well for information about Plataea. Kolax was ready to tell this spy any number of lies about the Plataeans to keep himself alive. He would even offer to lead the enemy through the secret tunnels beneath the walls of the citadel, if only to buy himself some time to escape. . . .

He felt a hard slap on his cheek and opened his eyes to see Fork-Beard standing in front of him! Oh, sweet relief! He could have kissed the man.

"Wake up," said Fork-Beard gruffly. "Time to die."

Kolax stared at him dumbly. Where was the Korinthian spy? He thrashed against the tree. The group of Dog Raiders left the fire and came toward him. The one with the greasy black hair held the poker, and it glowed red.

"Where's Andros?" asked one of the Dog Raiders.

"Couldn't find him," replied Fork-Beard. "He didn't return with the Spartans who'd gone to attack the Plataeans."

"Was there a battle?"

"No," replied Fork-Beard. "There's a sickness in Athens. And a Plataean emissary came to the Spartans. He was suffering from the sickness—a fever and black vomit. He said that the Plataeans are infected as well."

"Gods," uttered the man with the poker. "We should go back to the mountains. I don't want to be anywhere near a contagion."

"Me neither," said another with undisguised fear.

"That's why we're not taking this little monster back to Kyros," said Fork-Beard, indicating Kolax with a jerk of his thumb. "We leave his corpse here. And we're buggering out of the Spartan camp tonight."

Kolax's eyes passed from man to man with a look of hatred. He hoped that each and every one of these Dog Raiders got this sickness and died puking up his own guts. The young man with the poker caught his gaze and thrust forth his lower jaw.

"I'll burn those evil eyes from your skull," he said, then stuck the hot iron into Kolax's shoulder. The flesh made a hissing sound. At first there was no pain, then a searing white light exploded in Kolax's brain and he shrieked in fury and agony.

The Dog Raiders laughed. This was good sport.

Kolax breathed hard through his nose, glaring at the man with the brand. The Dog Raider was laughing so hard that tears were rolling down his cheeks. "Wait until I put this up his arse!" he declared to the others, and did a little excited dance.

"Cut him off so we can bend him over," said Fork-Beard. "Let's do this."

One of the Dog Raiders pulled out a long knife and went to work on the ropes.

The instant Kolax's bindings were cut he swooned to the ground, as if he had no more strength left in him. He lay on his belly with his arms hidden beneath him, quickly wrapping the cut ends of the ropes around his hands. Two Dog Raiders bent over to grab him, but Kolax leapt up like a cat and grabbed the hot poker by the glowing end—his hands protected by the rope—and wrenched it from the young Dog Raider's grasp. He swung it, striking the nearest Dog Raider in the head, then flipped it over and plunged the hot end through the eye of the one who'd burned him. The Dog Raider howled and staggered backward on wobbly legs. Before the skewered man hit the ground, Kolax scrambled up the tree like a squirrel. He crouched in the topmost bough, twenty feet off the ground, and yanked the gag from his mouth.

"Come on up, you cistern-arsed mother cunnies!" he shouted. Through the foliage he could see the man he'd got with the poker writhing on the ground and gurgling like a madman. The thing must have gone into his brain and melted it, considered Kolax with satisfaction. The Skythian gave a mocking laugh that infuriated the Dog Raiders. One of them shot an arrow into the tree, but it missed Kolax and stuck into the limb directly in front of his face. He yanked the arrow from the wood and smiled—now he had a weapon! "You can suck my spear, you garlic-eating sons of whores!"

More Dog Raiders shot arrows into the tree, but the limbs were gnarled and thick and shielded Kolax. He leapt from branch to branch, laughing and taunting the enemy for their poor aim. When one of the men hazarded to stand underneath him, craning his face upward, Kolax flung his arrow down like a dart, skewering the Dog Raider through the mouth. He stumbled away from the tree, choking to death on the arrow.

"Ha!" barked Kolax. "Chew on that!"

"The little Skythian viper!" yelled one of the Dog Raiders.

"Bring wood!" ordered Fork-Beard. "We'll burn down the tree!"

Kolax curled up in the crotch of the highest branch and made himself very small. How long would it take them to start a fire? How many more minutes did he have to live? At least he had killed two of them. He'd have one more story to tell in the next life. He gazed into the distance toward the Spartan camp and the thousands of men and slaves milling about. He saw a troop of horsemen riding this way from the south. Could it be his father and the others in disguise? His heart swelled with hope. He stood up to his full height and waved frantically.

"Papa!" he called. "Papa!"

An arrow whizzed past his head from the ground below and he ducked back down, making himself small again. Smoke filled his eyes and he glanced down to see a fire burning at the base of the tree. He coughed and covered his face with his hand. He waited expectantly for the riders to approach. He would know soon enough if they were Skythian. But his hopes were dashed when he heard a Greek voice call out, "What's going on here?"

"Ah! Andros," said the voice of Fork-Beard with a deferential tone. "I came to find you earlier. We have a Skythian boy—a prisoner for you to interrogate."

"Where is this prisoner?"

"Up the tree," replied Fork-Beard.

"A curious place to keep a prisoner."

"He escaped."

"And killed two of your men, I see."

Kolax squinted through the smoke and tried to see this new arrival. This man Andros's voice was so familiar. He could see his silhouette in the smoke below, staring up into the tree.

"You're going to be burned alive," said Andros in a friendly voice. "Why don't you come down and talk."

"I'll come down!" said Kolax. "I'll tell you everything you want to know about the Plataeans. Just get me away from these Dog Raider cunts."

Andros's laugh was caustic. "What could you possibly know about Plataea?" he asked.

"I have lived with them for these many moons," replied Kolax desperately. "I know all their secrets. The underground tunnels—everything! I could draw you a map of the citadel."

The smoke was thick now. The flames at the base of the tree crackled. He could feel the heat on the soles of his feet.

"Come down," said Andros.

Kolax knew that if he stayed in the tree he would die—the Dog Raiders would eventually catch him and kill him. He would rather die at the hands of a Korinthian than one of the dirty mountain marauders. "I'm coming," he said, but he did not move.

"If you try to run," said Andros in a cold and menacing tone, "my men will catch you. And then you'll wish the Dog Raiders had kept you."

For a moment Kolax thought of dropping into the flames and letting himself be burned alive. At least he would be choosing his own way to die. But while there was life, there was hope of escape. With a heavy heart he slowly inched down the top of the tree, then swung out on a limb over the flames and dropped to the ground in front of Andros. The Korinthian held a long dagger, ready to strike.

Kolax stared into the man's familiar face and his jaw dropped. He was transported back to the events in Athens two and a half years ago when he'd gone to the citadel with Nikias to recruit mercenaries to come back to Plataea. He became separated from his friend and met a wandering bard atop the Akropolis—a man who spoke fluent Skythian and who took Kolax under his wing. They became fast friends, smoking hemp together. And later, after Andros mysteriously vanished from the streets, Kolax hunted throughout the entire city until he found him: tied to a rack in the courtyard of the city jail and nearly flayed alive. The man told Kolax that he'd been mistaken for a spy, and so Kolax acted on impulse, risking his life to cut his bindings and help him to escape, saving him from more torture and a certain death.

Now, under the branches of the burning olive tree, with the acrid smell of

smoke in the air, surrounded on all sides by Dog Raiders and Korinthian warriors, the man stared back at Kolax with an equally dumbfounded expression.

"You?" Andros whispered, mystified.

So Andros really was a spy, Kolax suddenly realized. And he was a Korinthian, in league with the Spartans. An enemy of Plataea . . .

Kolax didn't hesitate. He flung himself into the man's arms, hugging him
tightly, crying out, "Andros! My friend!"

"What is this?" asked Fork-Beard with astonishment, stepping toward them
with his sword drawn. "Do you know this filthy Skythian boy?"

Andros was silent, and Kolax tensed, squeezing his eyes shut with apprehension, waiting with dread for the feel of cold iron plunging into his spine. But
Andros put a hand on the back of Kolax's head and held him tightly to his breast.

"You idiots!" Andros barked. "You've captured one of my best spies. What
have you done to him?" He leaned down and put his mouth to Kolax's ear and
said very quickly, "Play along, lad, and you'll make it out of this camp alive."

Kolax nodded vigorously.

"*Your* spy?" said Fork-Beard.

The Dog Raiders started to grumble. There was a large crowd of them now
standing around the olive tree—fifty or more—and they'd surrounded Andros's
Korinthian horsemen, blocking their way to the Spartan camp.

"This is my slave Kolax," said Andros. "I purchased him in Skythia when he
was very small and trained him." He spoke rapidly in Skythian, telling Kolax
to look submissive and kneel at his feet. Kolax instantly obeyed.

"This little barbarian," said Fork-Beard with mounting fury, "has killed
dozens of my kin. We've been hunting for him high and low in the Kithaeron
Mountains and caught him in Plataean territory."

"Which is where he should have been left to fulfill his duties," said Andros
angrily. "You've made a pig's breakfast of my plans. And you're lucky I don't
report you to the king's whisperers. Who do you think gave us the information
about the Skythian archers at the Three Heads? Kolax was placed inside Plataea
and has been feeding me vital intelligence. Come, Kolax."

Andros made to go but Fork-Beard grabbed him by the arm and glared at him
with a look of frustrated wonder. "What you tell me is hard cock to swallow."

"Take cock in mouth and swallow, then," replied Andros under his breath.
"For swallow you must. I am expected back at King Arkidamos's camp. If you
try to thwart me or take my slave from me, you'll all be slaughtered. This olive
tree that you're burning happens to be sacred, by the way. One of the Megarian
priests in the king's entourage told me this whole grove is blessed." But Fork-
Beard did not release his grip on Andros's arm.

The Dog Raiders within earshot grumbled angrily, but they quickly kicked the burning branches away from the tree. A sacred olive was never to be violated. Kolax remained kneeling, his heart pounding in his ears. Just then a trumpet sounded nearby. A body of Spartan warriors, on their way back from the fortress of the Three Heads, was coming toward the Dog Raider camp. Fork-Beard shot a hunted look toward the Spartans.

"Take your hand off me," Andros said in a low voice, "or I'll cut it from your arm."

The moment the Dog Raider let go, Andros grabbed Kolax by the neck, pulled him to his feet, and led him to his horse. He mounted and Kolax leapt up behind him, hugging his back. The Dog Raiders parted as Andros and his men galloped away from the Dog Raider camp.

"I told you that I would repay my life debt to you someday," Andros said. "Did I not?"

"Debt paid," replied Kolax with a sigh. He looked back over his shoulder and made an obscene gesture at the confounded marauders standing in front of the smoking olive tree. Soon the Dog Raiders disappeared behind the cloud of dust thrown up by the Korinthian horses. "Where are we going?" asked Kolax. "We're heading south."

"To Korinth," came the terse reply. "And don't try to escape from us, young Skythian. You're *my* prisoner now."

SIX

———————◆———————

"Zeus help us," said Phile, her teeth chattering. "It must have snowed a foot up in the mountains last night."

Nikias rolled over in the cart where he lay next to his sleeping daughters and sat up with a start. How long had he been asleep? He looked around with blurry and itching eyes, the reek of campfires thick in the air. He remembered where they were—an abandoned village ten miles north of Athens. He looked around at the thousand or so Plataeans rising from their makeshift beds and tending to their bodily needs. The dawn was curiously quiet, however, for the number of people and animals crammed so close together. Everyone seemed to be in shock—numbed by the strange journey they had been on since abandoning Plataea and the Oxlands.

The last day came back to Nikias in a crazy rush—the battle with the Spartans and his cousin Arkilokus at the old tower, the frantic journey from there on the road to Athens, Nikias's desperate ruse to trick the Spartan king, and the snub at the gates of the citadel. His teeth were still gritty from the charcoal he had swallowed, and his legs ached from so much riding. For, after being denied entrance to Athens, Nikias had headed north toward Mount Parnes leading a fraction of the Plataeans who had fled the Oxlands.

The other seventeen thousand Plataeans had elected to make camp in the cemetery outside the walls of Athens. They were either too exhausted or too terrified of the unknown to continue. Sarpedon had told Nikias that the Athenians must eventually let them into the citadel. But Nikias had argued that until Kleon deigned to open the gates to the refugees, they would be vulnerable to attack from Megarian and Spartan raiders. And even if the Plataeans were allowed inside Athens, they would then be risking infection. Sarpedon said that Nikias was right, but he wasn't going to force his people to keep moving. They would take their chances there. But he appointed Nikias the leader of the group that wanted to go to the mountains north of Athens, and sent him on his way with his blessing, giving him a small contingent of cavalry—twenty riders.

"How many more miles until we get to the mountains?" asked Phile.

"Ten or so," said Nikias, getting down from the cart and relieving himself. "There's thick forest cover there. Many places to hide. And there are Athenian watchtowers every few miles. We can make our camp near one of these. The Spartans won't go that far north. They have no reason to." He had been in the Parnes range after the Athenian ship he was on was attacked near Marathon; he escaped and ended up in a cove near the eastern foothills of the mountains. He walked over the range to the city-state of Tanagra, aided along the way by some Athenians in one of the guard towers that lined the road to their northern allies. It was a heavily wooded and sometimes treacherous range with isolated yet defensible positions—the perfect place for a bunch of Plataean vagabonds to hide out until the war was over. A war, Nikias reckoned, that could not last more than a few years.

"What will we do for food?" asked Phile.

"We brought enough grain to last several months," said Nikias. "And we can all hunt." He peered toward the rising mound of Mount Parnes, covered with trees and dusted with snow along the summit from a freakish late-season storm that had blown in during the night. Even though Nikias was still furious that his people had not been allowed entrance into Athens, he was also relieved. Fear of the Spartans had driven them blindly toward the citadel. And even after learning that Perikles and thousands of others were dead, it at first seemed better to risk disease than to face Spartan iron. But he quickly realized that going to the mountains was a much better option.

"We must get out of here," he had said to anyone who would listen. "This is a sign from Apollo. The Parnes range will be our fortress." Some listened to him, but most turned away in morbid silence.

"I am happy to hunt," said Phile proudly, interrupting his thoughts. "Artemis came to me in a dream and told me that I would provide for my family with my bow."

"You'll have to," said Nikias.

The girls started to stir and Phile tended to them. Nikias watched as his sister spoke to the girls with loving words and gently roused them from sleep, kissing them on their cheeks. She was a warrior *and* a surrogate mother . . . a strange duality that was encompassed in the goddess Athena—a duality that Nikias reckoned most men could never truly comprehend.

He looked around for Saeed. The Persian and his horse were gone, and Nikias was seized by a sudden fear that Saeed had ridden back to the Oxlands to find his son, Mula. Would his grandfather's faithful slave have deserted them?

"Have you seen Saeed?" he asked Phile.

"He was gone when I awoke," she replied.

Nikias caught sight of Ajax and Teleos exiting derelict house bearing long planks. "What are you doing?" he called to them.

"Scavenging," Teleos called back.

"We tore up these floorboards," said Ajax. "To make a shelter."

Nikias looked around and realized that other Plataeans were doing the same—taking every piece of wood that they could from the homes in the abandoned village and loading them on their wagons. When Ajax and Teleos got to the cart with their burdens Nikias said, "Good work. Get as much as you can. We're moving out soon."

He found his mare, Photine, eating grass with the cavalry horses. For once she let him take her reins without shying away. He mounted and rode around the outskirts of the camp, then found hoofprints leading north and followed them for a ways. Soon he saw a rider coming toward him and knew it was Saeed.

"Where did you go?" Nikias asked as he rode up.

"Scouting," replied Saeed.

"Find anything?"

"Follow me," he said, and turned his horse in the direction from which he had come.

Nikias rode beside him for half a mile. They went around a bend in the road and came suddenly upon a tall square guard tower. This one was nearly identical to the tower near the Three Heads, but unlike that crumbling fortification this one was perfectly intact and well maintained. But it didn't seem to be occupied. No soldiers could be seen on the battlements. But there was a strange-looking mound piled at the base of the wall. And something big dangling from one of the upper openings.

"What—" he began to say, then stopped himself. He realized what he was looking at on the ground: a pile of corpses left to rot in the sun. As they got closer he counted at least seven bodies. They were sprawled in strange attitudes, arms and legs in disarray, some of them upside down. "What happened?" he asked.

"The sickness," said Saeed. "The men must have died one by one. The living dropped the dead from the upper stories to clear the putrid corpses from the death chamber. There is the last man in the tower," he observed, pointing at the dead body hanging from the third-level opening, as if he had pushed one of his brothers from the room with his last bit of strength and then expired. The sound of buzzing flies was like the drone of bees.

"There should have been at least twenty men in this tower," observed Nikias.

"The ones who did not become ill most likely fled back to Athens," said Saeed.

"How do you know?"

"I inspected the tower. The door on the other side is wide-open. And there are tracks heading from there south. They left in great haste."

"Gods," said Nikias with abhorrence. This sickness was so powerful. How did the men in the tower catch it, being so isolated from Athens? Had a messenger from Athens come and unwittingly infected them? Or was the illness borne upon the very winds? The thought made him shudder. "We'll take our people far around this place."

"Going to the mountains was a good idea," said Saeed. "Athens will soon be a city of shades."

It took another day to make it to the higher hills, and then they camped for the night. Nikias went around relentlessly, checking on people, looking for signs of illness, but nobody showed any symptoms.

The next day they took a steep and bumpy roadway leading up, and were soon amongst a dense forest of pine and fir. They met no one on the road, nor did they see any signs of wildlife. Not even rabbits. But the rattling of woodpeckers filled the forest, echoing like the sound of taut drums. Ajax, Teleos, and Nestor the dog slipped off into the woods and came back triumphantly bearing two plump grouse, and that night they feasted around their little campfire on the first meat they'd had since leaving Plataea. The refugees slept on the steep hillside, spread out along the stony road.

"Are we going all the way to the top?" asked Phile. "There's so much snow."

"The snow will melt," said Nikias. "And we're not going to the summit of Mount Parnes itself," he added, pointing to the snowy summit rising to the northwest. "We'll stay in the foothills."

When they got to the rocky and treeless top of one of the lower mountains the snow had indeed started to melt, but that did not stop the people from taking pleasure in the few inches of snow that remained. Teleos and Ajax organized the older children into a phalanx of snowball fighters and made an assault on Nikias and the cavalry. Nikias and the other men leapt from their horses and joined in the fun, scooping up snow and flinging balls, happy to forget the evils of the last several days. Nikias was in such a good mood, he didn't even mind when Teleos hit him smack in the face with an ice ball, but he chased the boy and shoved a handful of snow down his loincloth in retribution.

Later, when they crested the hill, the Plataeans saw an awesome sight: the humps of mountains stretching north into the distance, tree covered and silent, empty of human habitation . . . a haven built by the gods.

It took Nikias and Saeed a while to find the ancient pathway that connected all of the mountain forts. A few hundred feet from the crest of the hill the snow disappeared and the pathway, which had been hidden on the top of the mountain, reappeared as though by magic. They followed it for another two miles until they came to the first Athenian mountain fortress—a squat square building, twenty feet high with battlements, standing on a flat piece of ground. This place, like the tower in the foothills, appeared to be deserted, but there were no corpses lying about. Evidently the guards had forsaken the stronghold before anyone had taken ill.

The place was surrounded by a wall. Nikias, Saeed, and three other men clambered over it and dropped down into a large courtyard with a well. It was a big space that could hold all of the Plataeans if absolutely necessary. They investigated the tower but found nobody inside. It had been completely abandoned—save the storeroom, which held several hundred bags of wheat and over twenty amphoras full of wine, and a few others with honey.

"Treasure," said Saeed.

Nikias nodded. "We'll keep this place safe until the Athenians return," he said with a wry smile. "And we'll build our camp around the walls. Plenty of firewood at hand, and we can all crowd into the tower behind the walls in case of attack."

They spent the next few days breaking down the carts and using them and the wood taken from the Athenian village to build shelters on the outside of the wall. There were many stones at hand and they were able to use these to start constructing another wall around their habitations. There was a palpable air of cooperation and goodwill amongst the Plataeans. They were so relieved to be away from the Spartans and the pestilence in Athens that there was no complaining—only hard work and good cheer. Hunting parties made up of the best archers, including Phile and many other women, went on expeditions in the woods, and started providing meat on the very first day of their arrival at the fort. Phile killed a great buck, and Nikias praised her for her skill. After a week they had built a Plataea in miniature—at least, that was how Nikias referred to it. Everyone knew their place in the order of things, and nobody lacked for food or clothing because all was shared.

"This is how it must have been in the olden days when our people first came to the Oxlands and started the habitations of Plataea," Nikias observed to his sister while they stood at the forest's edge, watching everyone hard at work around the fort. They had gone for a walk with the girls and Nestor, but the dog had disappeared, no doubt hunting on the trail of some animal. Nestor had filled out over the last couple of days and no longer looked like a walking skeleton.

Both Nikias and Phile had their bows on their backs but had not found anything to shoot. "This is how our democracy began," Nikias continued. "Just a few thousand people, working together. The first law must have been, 'Share.'"

"I wonder what is happening back home," Phile said.

Nikias wondered the same thing. Had the Spartans attacked yet? Had Kallisto given birth to their child . . . and, if so, were they both alive? And what had become of General Sarpedon and the others who had stayed behind in the Athenian cemetery?

"I miss Grandfather and Grandmother," said Phile dreamily, then asked abruptly, "Where are the twins?"

"There," said Nikias with a laugh. The girls had wandered down the path and into the forest. "They're getting so fast," he said.

"It's like a god put wings on their feet," said Phile.

They both started moving in the direction of the girls when a light brown shape leapt from the undergrowth toward the twins. The instant Nikias saw that sleek, muscular blur, he knew that it was a lion, and he screamed and started running toward the girls even though he knew he would never get to them in time. A white shape bounded from the other side of the path, barreled between the girls, and slammed into the lion, snarling and snapping its great jaws.

It was Nestor. The big dog was nearly the same size as the enormous cat. The animals—ancient enemies that had been pitted against each other for a thousand years or more—rolled on the earth, fighting and throwing up sticks and forest debris while the girls, ignorant of the danger, stood a few feet away, watching in bemused silence.

Nikias grabbed them in his arms, scooping them up and bearing them away. And then the lion was running away with Nestor chasing after it, barking madly.

A bowstring thumped and an arrow flew, striking the lion in the ribs, but the cat kept running. Phile nocked another arrow to her string but could not get off a clear shot.

"Nestor!" Nikias called to the dog, but the animal did not heed him, and vanished along with the lion into the dense trees. Phile and Nikias each took one of the girls and ran back to fort. The girls were laughing, completely unaware that death had stalked them so closely, but Nikias and Phile were both ashen and shaking.

Nikias, Leo, Ajax, Teleos, and four others took spears and mounted up, following Nestor's trail through the forest. They found the dog a mile away, his jaws locked onto the dead lion's neck, struggling vainly to drag his heavy prize back in the direction of the fort. Nikias leapt from his horse and ran to the dog, hugging his big neck and heaping praise upon him. Nestor smiled at him, wagging his tail and licking Nikias with his blood-covered tongue, then barked happily when he saw Ajax and Teleos.

"Phile's a fine shot," said Leo, who had dismounted and was kneeling by the lion's side. He pulled the shaft from the ribs with an effort. "It must have pierced its vitals. Otherwise I don't think the dog could have killed it."

"I don't care," proclaimed Nikias. "This dog has earned his keep for the rest of his life."

"We told you he was the best dog in Greece," said Teleos.

"The king of dogs," put in Ajax.

That night all of the citizens who were of age met in the courtyard and discussed what should be done next. Nikias volunteered to go back to Athens and find out what was happening there, and this was determined to be the best course of action. The eldest amongst them was elected the temporary leader of the outpost, and the next morning at dawn Nikias kissed his daughters and sister, patted Nestor on the head, and then departed the camp with Leo, moving down the narrow path that led to Athens.

SEVEN

———◆———

Chusor awoke from a long, dark dream—a terrifying and claustrophobic dream that seemed to have lasted for eternity. In the nightmare he'd been imprisoned in the honeycomb—a place in the Prison Pits of Syrakuse where men were put headfirst in tiny grave-like cells, like pupae in a beehive, and left to rot. Most went mad first. Mad maggots squirming in their own filth.

But then he was magically released from this heinous prison and was floating through a black mist toward a gray light, carried on the wings of some helpful daemon—the ghost of Ikarus? Zephyros—the west wind? He was set free, and his body was suddenly as light as pig's bladder filled with air. . . .

He opened his lids and saw the familiar wall of the ship's cabin before his blurry eyes. How long had he been asleep? And where was Zana? He tried to say her name, but his tongue was so dry that it had stuck to the roof of his mouth. He opened his jaw with great effort and rolled onto his back. It felt as if his skin were as heavy as iron. At the end of his dream just now he had felt so light, but now it took all his strength merely to raise his eyes and peer at the ceiling. What was happening? Was he drunk? Drugged?

"He's awake," said a gruff voice. A Helot's accent.

"Thank the gods!" exclaimed another man in the room—this one with a Plataean accent. "I told you he would come back. Didn't I tell you all?"

"That you did, Leo," replied a third—this one with an Athenian accent. "Diokles, go find the doctor."

Chusor strained to look in the direction of the voices, but he could not move a muscle, for he was overcome by a debilitating fatigue. "What's . . . happen . . .

happening?" he rasped, struggling to sit up, but he barely shifted more than a few inches.

Phoenix appeared by his side and lifted Chusor to a sitting position. "Bring the wine, Leo," he ordered.

A moment later Leo was next to Chusor, holding a bowl to his lips. "So that's who had spoken," thought Chusor. "The Plataean accent. But why is Leo here on the ship?" He took a sip of wine and it trickled down his aching and parched throat and made him think of a rivulet of water washing over hot coals. He tried to speak again and started choking.

"Don't talk," said Leo. "You've been unconscious for a long time. Do you understand, Chusor, old friend?"

Chusor closed his eyes and leaned against Phoenix's strong arms, drifting for a time, relishing the taste of the wine in his mouth. Leo's words seemed to echo in his head. He thought he had asked, "How long?" but when no reply came, he realized that he had asked the question in his mind but not out loud.

"How long have I been unconscious?" he asked.

"Almost two weeks," said Phoenix. "The day after we arrived at the port."

"Did I fall?" asked Chusor. "Hit my head?"

"Then you don't remember anything?" asked Leo. "Do you know where you are now?"

"I was in Syrakuse," said Chusor wearily. He heard the sound of footsteps entering the room, then a gaunt and bearded face with a crooked nose appeared close to his own. The homely man's breath reeked of wine. Chusor could not remember his name and it vexed him.

"Where were you?" asked this newcomer.

"I was in the honeycomb," continued Chusor. "I was dying in my own filth. Going mad. The Tyrant put me there. Don't you remember?"

The bearded man pried open Chusor's lids and stared at his eyes through a piece of magnifying crystal. "Many of the victims experience amnesia that wipes out their memories," he said to the others in a phlegmatic tone. "Some even lose years of memories. The fever can cause brain damage. Chusor might not be the man we knew," he added. "I warned you all."

Chusor smiled with relief as the man's name suddenly came to him. "No, I'm not brain damaged, Ezekiel. No one could ever forget the reek of your breath."

Ezekiel gave a surprised but hopeful smile. "Who am I?" he asked.

"You're a Jew," said Chusor. "And a Persian. A curious combination."

"Good, good," said Ezekiel, breaking into a smile. "And where are we?"

"The *Spear*," replied Chusor with growing confidence. His head had begun to clear, as though a bright sun were slowly burning off a mist in his mind.

"And do you remember what happened to you?"

Chusor forced himself to think—to fight the overpowering urge to drift back into sleep. He remembered coming into the port of Piraeus. And paying off the men. And making love with Zana. The next morning a few men came back to the ship feeling ill. And then, sometime later that day, he experienced a feeling of profound melancholy, the likes of which he had never before experienced. A strange sense of doom, as if nothing in the world was any good, and never would be. As though the sun were black and gave no heat. The gut cramps followed soon after. He crawled into bed and promptly soiled himself. Zana was so kind. So unlike her usual haughty self. She cleaned him and comforted him. But then she departed on some errand. She said she was going to search for Ezekiel.

"The sickness raced through the men of the *Spear* like fire," said Phoenix. "Half of the oarsmen are dead."

"Where is Zana?" Chusor asked. He saw Phoenix and Diokles exchange a brief look and instantly knew what had happened. His heart dropped to his stomach and his eyes instantly welled up with tears. "How—how long has she been dead?"

"She went quickly," said Diokles, shielding his eyes with his hand—a Helot sign of grief. "She got sick soon after you and her shade left the next morning."

"I could not save her," said Ezekiel with a sigh. "I haven't been able to save *anyone*, for that matter. I gave you drugs to ease the agony of your fever, thinking that you would die like all the others. But you slipped into a state of unconsciousness and here you have lain for all this time. You would have died for certain if Diokles hadn't spooned water into your mouth now and then. He sat by your side every day and night."

Chusor looked at Diokles, who smiled back.

"Thank you," said Chusor.

Diokles grunted in response.

"Weren't you afraid of getting the illness?" asked Chusor.

"We Helots already have this sickness," replied Diokles. "I almost die from it when I was a boy. It cannot hurt me now, I reckon. And besides, where else can we go? Not enough men on the crew to leave Athens now."

Chusor turned to Leo and asked, "What are you doing in Athens? And where is Nikias? Is he alive?"

"It's a long story," said Leo. "Nikias is alive, but he's in jail here in Athens."

"In jail?" asked Chusor. "For what?"

"Inciting the youth of Athens to mutiny against the government," said Leo, raising his eyebrows. "At least, that's the official charge. He was just trying to find men willing to go back to Plataea with him to help withstand the siege."

"Is the city under siege?"

"I don't know. We don't know anything. We only just brought the citizens of Plataea to Athens two weeks ago and—"

"Chusor must be allowed to rest," interrupted Ezekiel. "His face is pale. He can barely keep his eyes open."

"If the sickness couldn't kill me, I can certainly withstand one of Leo's tales," replied Chusor. "I must know what has taken place."

They helped him drink more wine and propped him up in the bed with pillows. Then Leo told him the entire tale of their flight from Plataea—from the kindling of the great forest fire on Mount Kithaeron to the journey to the Parnes range and the discovery of the abandoned fort. An hour it took in the telling, and by the time he started in on the return journey to Athens, Chusor begged for something to eat. Ezekiel had already been preparing a bowl of chicken and lentil soup, and Chusor, voracious after two weeks without food, devoured it. He did not know it but he had lost more than forty pounds. Neither Diokles nor Ezekiel, who had known him for many years, had ever seen him so thin.

"It only took Nik and me a day to ride back to Athens from the Parnes foot-hills," Leo said, continuing on with his tale after this brief break. "We arrived at the Athenian cemetery at sunset and searched amongst the tombs for the Plataean refugees, but there was nobody there. We went to the Double Gates and called up to the guards. They told us that our people had been allowed entrance to Athens a few days after we had gone to Mount Parnes. An army of Megarians and Dog Raiders had returned to Attika, you see, and the Athenians—seeing this new terror—had relented and opened the gates. Thank the gods our people didn't have to fight a battle with their backs to the walls. Nikias and I were both relieved but scared for our own skins. We could see campfires in the distance and reckoned they were Dog Raiders. And the Athenian guards told us that we couldn't come into the citadel until morning. So we camped in the tombs with a band of seasoned prostitutes who had fled the city because of the sickness and were taking their chances outside the walls. And trust me when I tell you that we neither slept nor took pleasure that entire night."

Leo paused to take a drink from his own cup. The lad had always annoyed Chusor with his loquaciousness during the years that he had served as his apprentice at the smithy in Plataea, but now the blacksmith was grateful for his ability to properly tell a tale.

"So, the next morning?" prompted Chusor.

"They let us in the gates and told us where to find everyone," said Leo. "The Plataeans were camped in the territory between the Long Walls. We went straight there and discovered . . ." Here the young man stopped for a moment and took a slow deep breath. "We discovered that the sickness had spread quickly amongst our people. Many had died. Perhaps five thousand or more. Nikias and I wandered through the camp, dazed by the number of cold funeral pyres as well as bodies waiting to be burned. They have run out of wood, you see. They've started breaking old ships for the fuel. Nikias wanted to find Sarpedon—to tell him to lead the survivors up into the mountains around Mount Parnes. But Sarpedon was one of the first to die, along with his entire family. Nikias wondered if it had been a mistake to leave Plataea. We fled a danger and ran straight into another. They say at least fifty thousand people in Athens have died so far."

"The gods are cruel," said Chusor.

Ezekiel, who had been silent this whole time, added wearily, "My own god tries the human spirit as well. There was a man named Job that I will tell you about someday. This sickness—this *miasma*, we doctors call it—is not caused by the gods, however. It is simply a disease that is transmitted from person to person. It first appeared in Piraeus, so my guess is that it came on one of the grain ships. I charted its progress from there passing through the citadel—the most deaths occurring where people are crowded together."

"So what happened to Nikias?" asked Chusor. "Why was he arrested?"

"We left the Plataean camp between the Long Walls and went into Athens," said Leo. "Nik wanted to find Ezekiel, and he kept talking about a woman—Helena is her name. He hoped to find out whether or not she was still alive. But she was not in her home and nobody had seen her for years and Nikias got very depressed—more depressed than I've ever seen him. Then we ran into one of Nikias's friends, a one-armed Athenian farmer name Konon. But Nikias became suddenly and violently ill. He had contracted the sickness, you see. Konon helped me get him back to the Plataean camp before Nik finally collapsed."

"How did he fare?" asked Chusor.

"He was sick for a few days," said Leo, raising his eyebrows and shaking his head with amazement. "And then it passed and he was fine. He is blessed."

"The sickness is curious that way," said Ezekiel. "Some it slays with the power of an axe stroke. Others it merely plays with like a cat who, batting about a mouse, grows bored and finally lets it go free. And for some lucky people the illness does not affect at all."

"Like me," said Leo. "I have yet to get the sickness." He looked at Chusor and gave a wan smile. "Your friend Barka, the soothsayer, told me once that I would die a happy old man."

"Barka's predictions usually come true," said Chusor.

"Anyway, that's when Nikias's cousin found us," said Leo, and he gestured at Phoenix where he now sat on the window ledge, staring into the distance with a thoughtful look.

"Nikias's cousin?" asked Chusor, bewildered.

"Our mothers were sisters," said Phoenix. "Did you not know that Nikias was half Athenian?"

"I did know," said Chusor. "But it is strange that the gods put you in our path out on the sea."

"Strange indeed," said Phoenix. "It was I who captained the ship that was taking Nikias back to Plataea two and a half years ago when we were attacked by Korinthians. Nikias escaped and did not know that I was still alive, and I, for my part, thought that *he* had perished on the sea. I went to the Plataean camp as soon as I heard that the Oxlanders had come to the citadel. And I can tell you that when Nikias and I came face-to-face"—here he paused to compose himself—"it was like each of us was seeing the other's shade." He smiled and wiped a tear from the corner of his eye.

"So how did he end up in jail?" asked Chusor. "Fighting, no doubt," he added under his breath.

"Actually," said Leo, "it was from *talking.*"

"He got it in his head to raise an army of young warriors to aid Plataea," said Phoenix. "The young men of Athens who are bristling at a chance to fight the Spartans—the ones who are furious that they are trapped behind these high walls while their enemies pillage their countryside. They gather in the agora every day and make trouble. Nikias went to the agora and called on anyone who would join him. He gave a stirring speech—told them that death in battle was far preferable to wasting away from disease or starvation. The gods value our deaths in battle over the Spartans' deaths, he told them, because we come from a democracy and thus value life and freedom more than the enemy."

"Nonsense," muttered Ezekiel.

"The young men ate it up," said Phoenix. "Nikias said that the Plataeans had money. Enough to buy ships and outfit them for a voyage around the Peloponnese. But they needed volunteers to man the ships and go to the port of Kreusis on the Gulf of Korinth. He promised them a war. He promised them blood. Then the police came and arrested him and his friend Konon, but Leo and I got away."

"Kreusis?" asked Ezekiel. "Where is this port? I have never heard of it."

"Eight miles from Plataea," said Leo. "It's one of our strongholds—still manned by our warriors, at least when we left Plataea. From there it's an easy walk through an olive-tree-filled valley to the citadel. The Spartans would never expect a relief force coming from Kreusis."

"But why would Perikles lock up Nikias?" asked Chusor. "I thought he had taken a liking to the lad when he was here before. Surely a young man expressing his warlike intentions against a hated enemy was not breaking any Athenian laws."

"Perikles," replied Phoenix flatly, "my leader . . . my teacher . . . he is dead. Kleon, his bitter rival, rules Athens now. Nikias killed one of Kleon's henchmen when he was here last. And Kleon thinks that Nikias had something to do with this hetaera Helena disappearing from Athens—a woman for whom Kleon had some strong claim."

"Nikias didn't have anything to do with *that*," said Chusor. "*I* did. And Kleon hates me more than Nikias, for he is my bitter enemy and the reason that I was forced to flee Athens a decade ago."

"Well, it matters not," said Phoenix morosely. "Kleon is the enemy of us all, it seems. And he will not be persuaded by any means to free Nikias. He'll let him rot in jail. Perikles's allies are either dead or in exile. There is nothing left for me in this city anymore. I might as well have died with my brothers when we were attacked by the Korinthians on the sea. Athens is a city of shades. I have nothing . . ." he trailed off, staring out the window.

"Where is Ji?" asked Chusor suddenly. "Don't tell me that he is dead as well."

"Ji bought a fishing boat and sailed away," said Diokles. "He said that he had seen this sickness before and he was not going to take his chances."

Chusor mulled on this information for a while. He wished the stalwart fighter were still here, but he was glad that the man had escaped from the disease. "May Poseidon guide him," he said.

"What are we going to do?" Leo asked the room.

Everyone was silent for a long time. Even though Chusor felt piteously weak, his mind was clear. Nikias's idea to raise an army and take the sea road to the Gulf of Korinth was actually quite sound. Any intelligent and able-bodied young man would gladly escape this city of death for a chance to kill Spartans.

"Let us leave Chusor," said Ezekiel. "We are taxing him. Come, come." He tried to usher out Diokles and Leo but they sat unmoving.

"What are you thinking?" said Diokles, who had also been watching Chusor intently.

Chusor swung his shaky legs over the edge of the bed and planted his feet on the floor. "We've broken into sturdier buildings than a flimsy Athenian jail," he said with a forced laugh.

Ezekiel reached for the wine. "I was afraid you were going to say that," he said miserably.

EIGHT

"You're dead, Nikias of Plataea," said a voice oozing with triumph. "You're a dead man."

"Hera's jugs!" bellowed Nikias.

The small cell echoed with Nikias's wrathful cry as he swept his hand across the grid scratched in the floor, scattering the small stones that served as markers in the game of pebbles. Konon laughed and clapped his hand against his thigh as the winner of the game, a slender Athenian teenager named Aristophanes, pulled a face at Nikias.

"Are all Plataeans such poor losers?" Aristophanes asked Konon.

"I wouldn't know," said Konon, grinning. "I've only met the one."

Nikias sat fuming with his arms on his chest, shaking his head. "Ten games in a row, that makes it."

"Eleven," said Aristophanes, "but who's counting?"

"How are you so lucky at this game?" asked Nikias, who had always fancied himself a good pebbles player.

"It's not luck," came the smug reply. "It's all skill."

"Gods, when are they going to let us out of this place?" asked Nikias with frustration. They had been in the cell for two days. In that time they had not been questioned. Nor had they been given any food. Only foul-tasting water. The place reeked of their own waste.

"Just be glad the Skythian guards buggered out of the city," said Aristophanes. "If they were still in charge of the jail, they would have whipped the three of us for laughs."

The Skythians, Nikias had discovered after arriving in Athens, had fled at the first sign of the plague in their own ranks. A Skythian warrior feared dying of illness more than anything else—they believed that their shades would be putrid for eternity, just like their diseased corpses. And so they had absconded from the citadel—down to the last man—and hired two grain ships to take them to the island of Euboea. Without their ruthless police force to keep order, Athens had plummeted into a state of chaos.

"Want to play another?" asked Aristophanes.

"No, thanks," said Nikias.

"I'll play," said Konon.

Nikias leaned against the wall and watched the two play, studying the young Athenian closely to see if he was cheating. But he couldn't detect any sleight of hand from the actor—a man he had met on his last trip to Athens. He had been at the symposium at Helena's house, and Nikias learned that Aristophanes was famous in Athens for playing women on the stage. He had a slender but muscular build, and wore his hair very long. Nikias liked him, despite the fact that he kept beating him at pebbles. Aristophanes had been thrown into the cell with him and Konon the night they were arrested. Aristophanes had been caught "liberating" an amphora of wine from a shop. Nobody went to the theatre anymore—everyone who had not contracted the illness was afraid of crowds. So actors were starving. Aristophanes's older friend, the playwright Euripides, had fled to his cave on the island of Salamis. And Aristophanes had said that he wished he were there with him now.

It was just like that playwright to hide in a cave while disaster befell his city, Nikias mused with disgust. He had no use for writers like Euripides, whose characters talked incessantly but did not take action. Or when they did finally act, it was always to do the wrong thing, like blind oneself or kill a friend by mistake. Were men really that foolish? Were the gods truly that cruel? Perhaps they were. And the thought brought him low.

" 'He who learns must suffer,' " Nikias quoted drearily.

"Ah, Aeskylos," said Aristophanes. "Now, there was a playwright. I wish I could have met him."

"You did," said Nikias, surprised. "He was at Helena's symposium."

"Ha! That old man?" said Aristophanes with a smirk. "He was just one of Helena's pets—a crazy dotard who liked to call himself Aeskylos. The real *playwright* Aeskylos has been dead for twenty years and more."

Nikias scoffed. Was everything in Athens an illusion?

"I think I've got you!" said Konon.

"You think?" replied Aristophanes with a shifty look. "Watch out."

Nikias went to the door and peered through the iron grille at the top of the portal, staring down the empty hallway. He wondered where the guards had all gone. They had yet to see a single jailer since Aristophanes had been brought to the cell the night before. Perhaps they were sick, or hiding in their rooms. He reckoned that he should be content that he wasn't getting beaten right now by one of Kleon's thugs. Kleon had been Perikles's archrival in Athens, and had even tried and failed to get Perikles ostracized. Two and a half years ago Kleon's henchmen had caught Nikias meeting with the Athenian spy Timarkos—one of Perikles's whisperers—and given him a fierce beating before he escaped in a mad dash through the Piraeus. Where were his thugs now? Perhaps Kleon himself was sick. If Perikles had died—Perikles, blessed by the gods!—then no man was safe in Athens.

"Sorry, Konon," said Aristophanes. "Your city has fallen. I win."

"What?" shouted Konon with a startled cry. "Gods! You are a shifty fellow," he added with a good-natured laugh.

Nikias sat down again and the room became silent. The sun was setting—Nikias could see Hesperos, the evening star, glinting like a tiny jewel in the small high window of the chamber. Konon curled up on the floor and shut his eyes. Soon he was snoring. Nikias felt sorry for the Athenian farmer. He had lost nearly his entire family to the sickness.

"How did he lose his arm?" Aristophanes asked. "Do you know?"

"Yes," replied Nikias. "It got caught in the mechanism of an olive mill when he was a boy."

"Poor wretch," said Aristophanes. "Actors like me will never welcome his kind in a theatre."

"Why is that?" asked Nikias.

"He can't clap," said Aristophanes with an ironic laugh.

"He'll never be a hoplite," said Nikias ruefully. "He can't hold a shield."

"I have never been in battle," said Aristophanes.

"Doesn't seem like you ever will—not with all of Athens hiding behind these walls."

"We should march on Sparta and infect them," said Aristophanes. "We don't need swords to kill them. We can just shit and breathe on them."

Nikias laughed despite himself. He thought of vomiting the black stuff onto the Korinthian's feet and the look of horror on the man's face. "Might not be such a bad idea," he said.

"I heard about your speech at the agora," said Aristophanes. "My friends couldn't stop talking about it. They were ready to risk exile and run off with you to Plataea. Many of them have stopped believing in the gods, you know. People say they were all invented."

"And what do *you* believe?"

"I think men believe in gods when things are going either splendidly or horribly. Anything in between and we have no use for them."

Nikias didn't agree with Aristophanes's jaundiced view. He had always believed in the gods. In good times, bad times, and in between. The notion that they had been made up by men—like characters in a play—seemed inconceivable. What mind could have created Zeus and Hera, Dionysus and Athena, from its imagination?

"How did you hope to get back to Plataea with an army?" asked Aristophanes. "Logistically, I mean."

"We brought silver with us from Plataea," said Nikias. "All of the wealth left in our citadel. Our general, Zoticus, had planned on purchasing several vessels and loading them with grain and any willing volunteers, then going to the port of Kreusis near Plataea. But Zoticus is dead—killed by the Spartans on our way here. And the man who took his place—General Sarpedon—died of the sickness. I took it upon myself to make something happen."

"Where is this silver?" asked Aristophanes.

"Distributed amongst the elders in the Plataean camp," replied Nikias. "They will give me whatever I ask for. They trust me as the Arkon's grandson. But I seem to have let them all down again." He chewed on his lips pensively, staring at the floor.

"Do you remember the night of the symposium?" asked Aristophanes.

"How could I forget?" said Nikias.

"The beauteous hetaera Helena naked and painted gold," said Aristophanes, waving his hand in front of his face as if conjuring her life before his eyes. "Like a living and breathing Athena, come down from the Akropolis temple to bewitch us all."

"No woman can compare to her," said Nikias, and instantly felt guilty. Kallisto's dignified face flashed before his eyes. If the two women were standing side by side, whom would he pick to spend the rest of his life with? The mother of his children? Or the gorgeous concubine who had bewitched him like Kirke the witch had done with poor Odysseus?

"Where could she be now?" asked Aristophanes. "Where could she have gone?"

"I don't know," said Nikias. "I went to her house. Her neighbors told me she's been gone for years."

"She left the city about a month after you did," said Aristophanes. "Both her and her little pert slave girl. The dark-skinned one."

"Melitta," said Nikias.

"Yes. That was her name."

"Kleon, they say, was in a rage to rival Zeus," said Aristophanes, stroking a finger across his cheek in a contemplative manner. "Helena was his favorite, you see. And she just vanished, like a conjuror's trick. The henchmen who had been guarding her house were found with their throats slit from ear to ear."

"Really?" asked Nikias. "That is how it happened?" He smiled inwardly. Only Chusor and his pirate crew could have pulled off something like that. He was suddenly filled with hope that Helena and the girl Melitta—Chusor's own child whom he had conceived with Helena's mother—had escaped and were now safe, far from the citadel.

"Then you didn't know?" asked Aristophanes with a piercing look.

"I knew nothing," said Nikias. "I already told you: I went to her home when I first got here. To try and find her."

"But surely you have some idea. You were her lover."

"How did you know that?" asked Nikias coldly.

"I mean—I meant—" Aristophanes broke off and shrugged. "I just assumed."

Nikias turned away from Aristophanes and stared into space. "I made love with her. I was never her lover."

"Then you don't know where Chusor took her?"

Nikias stared at his right hand—the hand with his missing little finger. The flesh where the finger met the hand was smooth and pink, and sometimes it itched fiercely. Men would do terrible things to other men to get what they wanted. They would maim, kill, and betray. And spy. He thought of Aristophanes's sly looks—the pointed questions about Helena and the crafty way the actor had gotten him to divulge the location of the Plataean silver that was to be used to purchase ships and grain. . . .

Nikias shot out his hand with the speed of a striking snake and grabbed Aristophanes around the throat. The actor's eyes bugged out of his head and he kicked like a frightened rabbit, striking Konon in the stomach, who awoke with a cry. "What's—hey! Nikias! What are you doing?"

Nikias leaned close to Aristophanes's terrified face. "I never told you about my friend Chusor," he said with a low voice. "I never mentioned him to anyone in Athens except the spy Timarkos. You're one of Kleon's men. It wasn't a coincidence that you were thrown into this cell."

"I—I had to," said Aristophanes in a choking voice.

Nikias let Aristophanes go and stood up quickly, breathing hard.

Aristophanes clutched his throat and gagged. Tears poured from his eyes as he took a ragged gasp. "He'll . . . he'll stop at nothing to find her," he said at last. "His man said he would cut off my prick and make me eat it if I didn't do his bidding."

"You sneak!" exclaimed Konon, glaring at Aristophanes. His ingenuous face wore a grimace of disgust. "And I thought Nikias was being a poor sport just now."

"I'm sorry," said Aristophanes, on his knees like a supplicant. "Don't hurt me."

"I'm not going to hurt you," said Nikias icily, going to the portal and slamming it with his palm so hard that the door rattled as if it might burst from its hinges.

"I've got to get out of here," he said. "Let us out of here!" he yelled.

There was no answer to his shout, and he slammed the door again before turning back to Aristophanes. "Were you working for Kleon that night? At the symposium?"

"No," said Aristophanes. "Not when I came. But by the time I left they had convinced me to spy for them. Fear is a great persuader."

All of a sudden from outside the window came the sound of shouting in the lane running past the jail.

"What's going on?" asked Konon.

"Help me get up to the window," Nikias said.

Konon stood beneath the small window and planted his legs, then Nikias got on his back and peered into the street. It was dark now and he saw burning torches coming toward the jail. There was a crowd of at least a hundred men, and they were shouting something.

"What are they saying?" asked Konon.

Nikias realized, with a cold thrill, that the crowd was shouting his name as they marched: "Nikias! Nikias!" He got down off Konon's shoulders and looked around the chamber with a hunted expression.

"They're shouting your name," said Aristophanes.

"Who are they?" Konon asked Aristophanes.

"How am I to know?" came the nearly frenzied reply.

"Kleon's men?" said Nikias.

"Why?"

"Maybe they've come to string me up in the agora and stone me."

"Gods!" uttered Konon.

The noise got louder and louder. They could hear the men assembling directly on the other side of the wall. The shouting became more savage. "Get him out!" voices started calling amidst the chanting of Nikias's name. "Pull down the wall!"

Something rattled on the bars of the window: a grappling hook attached to a heavy rope. The rope went taut and the bars vanished in a cloud of dust, along with a section of wall. Sledgehammers pounded on the stones. Nikias's heart throbbed in his breast. He backed away from the outside wall and shouted at Aristophanes and Konon to do the same.

"When the wall comes down, both of you make a break for it," Nikias said.

"Watch out!" screamed Aristophanes as a huge section of the wall exploded and toppled inwards, strewing rubble at their feet.

Nikias clenched his fists, ready to spring.

A head shot through the opening—a dark face with eyes peering into the gloom of the cell.

"Diokles!" shouted Nikias.

"Hello, Nikias," said Diokles, grinning. "Time to go now."

NINE

———◆———

It was an army of young Athenian men who marched toward the agora—more than two hundred bearing cudgels and old shields torn from the walls of temples or taken from their fathers' dusty storerooms. Nikias had lost sight of Konon and Aristophanes in the crush. They'd disappeared amongst the throng of drunken revelers. Diokles had vanished as well, but not before telling Nikias that Chusor was waiting for him at the docks and would see him soon.

Most of the Athenians were screaming their heads off as they marched down the street from the jail, bearing Nikias on their shoulders. But a few started singing a song in full-throated voices, and the others soon took up the words:

"*To Plataea—Plataea! To set our brothers free!*
To Plataea—Plataea! To save democracy!"

The shuttered windows of houses opened briefly as they passed, then slammed closed again. Nobody wanted to deal with this kind of intoxicated rabble. Nobody had the energy anymore. Best to let the young men have their fun. In the morning the streets would be covered in their puke and blood, and then everything would be quiet for a while.

Nikias was filled with a curious sense of elation mingled with unease. He was grateful that these Athenians had got him out of jail and that they were willing, at least for this exciting moment, to defy their families and leaders and head out on a dangerous journey—a journey from which they might never return. But how long would they stay loyal to such a cause? The voyage around the Peloponnese was treacherous enough. But that was nothing compared to what waited in store for them in the Oxlands. And none of these young men, Nikias reckoned, had ever been in battle—let alone faced a dreaded Spartan phalanx. Would Nikias be able to lead them all the way back home? Would they listen to him? How was he to find ships? Who would be the captains? Nikias knew nothing about the sea, except that he was one of the most worthless mariners in all of Greece—the last voyage he'd made he'd been sick as a dog for two days running.

"Nikias!"

He caught sight of Konon a few paces away, jostled by the crowd and trying to get his attention. "I have to find my grandmother, tell her that I'm coming with you!" he shouted above the din.

Nikias cupped his hands to his mouth. "You don't have to come, Konon!"

"I wouldn't miss it for the world!" Konon shouted back, smiling with a kind of overwrought glee; then he turned and blended into the crowd.

The mob headed across the agora toward the Temple of Hephaestos where it sat on a little hill. They were joined by others who had been waiting in the shadows—evidently this was the place they had agreed to congregate after freeing Nikias from the jail. The ones who had been toting him along set Nikias down on his feet.

"To the temple steps!" they cried. "He's waiting!"

Nikias climbed the stone path that led to the temple, wondering who could be waiting for him there. There was another group of men standing on the steps—broad-shouldered mariners bearing torches and long oars. One of these sailors stepped forth and Nikias shouted, "Phoenix!" He rushed forward, embracing his cousin in a bear hug.

"Cousin," said Phoenix. "It seems like I'm always saving your skin."

"So this was *your* doing!"

"You lit the flame with your speech the other day."

"So what happens next?"

"Watch and listen."

The crowd gathered in front of the small temple, shoulder to shoulder, and after everyone was assembled, Phoenix held up his hand for silence. The voices became subdued and Phoenix looked from man to man for a time, as though taking stock of each of their characters.

"You have waited long enough, young warriors of Athens!" exclaimed Phoenix. "For years you have been forced to hide behind the walls of our city. But now is the time to show your worth! Now is an opportunity for heroism! The great admiral Phormion is already on his way to the fortress of Naupaktos in the northwest with a fleet of twenty triremes."

Nikias had never been to Naupaktos, but he knew that from there it was only a few days' pull across the Gulf of Korinth to the Plataean-held port of

Kreusis. And from there he could run to the citadel of Plataea in less than an hour!

"Many of you know that he departed a month ago," continued Phoenix, "sent by Perikles to disrupt enemy shipping in the Gulf of Korinth. More ships were supposed to join him to bolster his forces, but Kleon has failed to make good on that promise. And so Athenian warships sit rotting in the sheds, and our brave brothers stand idle on the shores, dying of disease. Listen to me! There are five triremes ready to depart for Naupaktos tonight, commanded by veteran mariners! But we need strong backs and even stronger hearts to help pull the oars! Who will come with us? Who will take the sea road tonight and help fight the enemy?"

There was a murmur from the crowd. Some were smiling, while others looked unsure.

"You're actually leaving *tonight*?" asked a slender beardless lad near the front row.

"Yes, tonight!" said Phoenix. "Within the hour! Did you think this adventure tonight was nothing more than a lark? We seek only those who fear not death! Only those who crave glory. The rest . . . you can stay behind and gather firewood for the dead."

There was a long silence. The young men stared back with eyes shining in the torchlight. Many wore startled expressions. Some looked downright scared. A drunken riot in the streets was one thing—a chance to free Nikias of Plataea from jail and smash some heads. But the prospect of a very real journey, of leaving behind their families and friends for war with the Spartans—a journey that would begin this very night . . . well, that was a shock for many of them.

Nikias was about to speak when somebody pushed through the throng and came out into the light. It was Aristophanes, looking frightened but determined. Nikias was surprised to see him still there. He thought that he had slunk off to report to Kleon's whisperers a while ago.

"You seem scared," said Phoenix with a challenging tone. "Are you ready to prove yourself? Because you look like you might shit your tunic."

Aristophanes smiled wryly. "I'll admit I'm scared," he replied in a resounding voice—the trained voice of an actor. "But I'm ready to join you. And if I shit anywhere it will be down a Spartan goat-raper's throat."

The crowd burst into hearty laughter and more young men stepped forward, shouting, "I'll come! I'm ready!" Soon the air was filled with their cries—hundreds of voices raised in exultation.

"To the Piraeus District!" shouted Phoenix. "To the ships!"

As Nikias and Phoenix led the group down the path from the temple, Nikias turned and saw several young men skulk off into the darkness. But the vast majority of the Athenians were still with them. By the time the mob got to the southernmost gate of the citadel—the gate that led to the Long Walls—they were in a raucous frenzy again, and the guards on duty at the exit, fearing for their lives, simply stepped aside and let them enter. The throng's noble song about democracy had degenerated into rambunctious and obscene doggerel based on Aristophanes's humorous words to Phoenix:

"*Spartans! Spartans! Rapers of goats!*
We'll shit down their bloody throats!"

Nikias and Phoenix walked side by side along the creek that ran the length of the Long Walls to Piraeus, six miles away. The moon was just beginning to rise over the mountains to the east, casting the world in a glow the color of old silver coins.

"Do you really want to leave Athens, defy the men in power?" asked Nikias. "You might not ever be able to come back."

"With Perikles dead," said Phoenix stoically, "there is nothing here for me now. I need this expedition as much as these young men."

"I've heard of Phormion," said Nikias. "He's the one who led the Athenians to victory in the battle during the siege of Potidaea, isn't he?"

"Yes. He's a great man," replied Phoenix. "The best tactician on the sea. But he needs our help. The Spartans and Korinthians can send eighty or more ships to fight him. Phormion was Perikles's man, just like me, and Kleon wants him to fail so that he can shard him and send him into exile and replace him with one of his own ball-lickers. And so the ships sit in the boat sheds, as useless as—"

"Tits on a bull?" offered Nikias.

"Precisely, Cousin," replied Phoenix, smiling for the first time.

They were approaching the Plataean camp—Nikias could see the shapes of their makeshift homes in the moonlight. A figure stood in the pathway. As Nikias got closer he could see that it was Leo, holding a large leather bag. Nikias broke from the Athenians and jogged up to him.

"Welcome back," said Leo.

"I wondered where you were," said Nikias.

"Phoenix told me to stay here at the camp in case things went awry." He handed Nikias the heavy bag and it made a jingling sound of coins.

"What's this?"

"I've collected money from everyone in the Plataean camp," said Leo. "To help pay for the expedition."

Nikias took the bag and nodded thoughtfully. The Plataeans had given up money that would have been used to pay their way in Athens—for food, clothing, and medicine. But they knew how important it was to bring help back to their citadel.

"How many of our men are at the port?" asked Nikias.

"Two hundred or so," said Leo. "Most of the cavalry. And many recently widowed Plataeans who hope to banish their grief in Spartan blood."

"You can't come with us," said Nikias flatly.

"I reckoned you'd say that."

"You have to go back to Mount Parnes," said Nikias. "Tell them what has happened here—tell them that we're going back to Plataea with help."

"I know," said Leo. "I leave at dawn."

"Take Photine with you," said Nikias, "but don't ride her. She'll throw you. Tell Phile she can have her. Phile will be able to manage her well enough."

The throng of Athenians had caught up to him and were filing past. He felt Phoenix tugging on his sleeve. Nikias kissed Leo on the cheek.

"Good-bye, brother," said Leo, wiping his tears.

"Peace, brother," replied Nikias. Then he looked straight into Leo's eyes and said, "Look out for my girls. Treat them as your own."

"I will."

"And don't look so glum," said Nikias over his shoulder. "We'll meet again."

"Either here or in the other world," replied Leo softly.

TEN

No one tried to thwart the mob as it entered the streets of Piraeus, for it had swelled to nearly three hundred strong. The young men passed through the gates into the port city and made their way down to the docks. Phoenix divided them into equal groups and distributed them amongst the five triremes, where five hundred men already stood next to their respective ships, waiting to drag them off the shore and into the water. Phoenix made sure that each ship had an equal number of Plataeans and Athenian youths, as well as veteran oarsmen. Phoenix was captain of one of the ships—the *Argo*—with three trusted veterans taking charge of the others: the *Democracy*, the *Spartan Killer*, and the *Aphrodite*.

The fifth ship—the one Phoenix told Nikias to join—sat a little apart from the others. Nikias gazed at the sleek vessel with its fiendish ram and sinister eyes made of shining marble on the curving prow. The boat was "well planked," as Phoenix would say. Standing on the beach under the prow was Diokles and, next to him, a towering figure with broad shoulders. Another man, skinny and bent, scratching at his scraggly beard, paced nearby.

"Are you ready to put your life in Poseidon's hand?" Chusor asked as Nikias approached. His tone was gruff yet good-natured, as if he wanted to say, "Years have passed, but nothing is different between us. We are still the best of friends."

Nikias smiled and held out his hand and Chusor gripped it. "I am if you're willing to take me on your ship."

Chusor smiled broadly, showing his big white teeth, and Nikias noticed how gaunt his friend now looked. Gone was the strapping giant. His cheeks were sunken and his eyes seemed to have retreated into his skull. All his ribs showed and his pectorals had withered.

"I survived the sickness," said Chusor, reading his concerned look. "Only just. And I'm ready to leave this cursed place. I'll take my chances on the sea."

"Hello, Ezekiel," said Nikias, turning to the fidgeting man.

"Good to see you again," said the doctor. "It seems like a lifetime ago that you were in Athens."

"Are you coming with us?"

"Chusor and Diokles have persuaded me to come along for the first leg of the delightful journey," replied Ezekiel sourly.

"I'm glad there will be a doctor on board," said Nikias. "I fear I suffer from seasickness."

"Oh, I have a remedy for that," said Ezekiel with a wave of his hand. He climbed up the nearest landing ladder, evidently on a mission to search through his collection of medicines.

There was a festival atmosphere on the beach. The young Athenians were inflamed—excited to be going on an adventure, to be thumbing their noses at Kleon and his rule—and talked boisterously about what the journey might entail. The Plataean warriors were also anxious to be heading out. They wanted to get back to their citadel—a place they had abandoned only so they could help deliver their women and children safely to Athens. Now they were happy to be going home to help defend their beloved city, whatever the risks.

Several of the Athenians called out, "When do we go? What's keeping us?"

Chusor said to Nikias in a low voice, "Look at these Athenian lads. They have no idea what's in store for them."

"It's in their blood," said Nikias.

"Adventure on the sea?" asked Chusor. "Or the breaking of rules?"

"It's all one and the same to us Greeks," replied Nikias.

Chusor raised his eyebrows. "We'll see how many of them want to keep going once we've made it to Serifos. Or how many of them die along the way. I fear the sickness will break out amongst the men who have yet to be infected. But we can't stay here. This miasma will come whether we're on the waves or on land. I fear all of Athens might perish before this evil has gone away."

"What's on Serifos?" Nikias asked.

"A secluded cove to the south where we can take on water and buy food from the willing locals," came the reply. "Also," he went on, peering into the bay to the south as if he were scanning across the vast sea into the future, "that way we can avoid Korinthian shipping lanes in the Saronik Gulf. And we can train the crew along the way and leave the worst of them on one of the Athenian-held islands."

Nikias stared long and hard into Chusor's eyes. "And your daughter,

Melitta?" He paused and swallowed hard. "I could not find her or Helena in the citadel."

Chusor nodded. "I took her far away. And Helena as well. I cannot tell you where. For their own safety, in case you are ever captured by the enemy."

Nikias felt a wave of relief and he sighed. "I knew you would get them out of Athens," he said, his face breaking into a wide smile. "Of course you can't tell me where they are. Just so long as I know that they're safe."

A cry came from down the beach. For a split second Nikias thought that Kleon had sent an army to Piraeus from the citadel to stop the ships from leaving. But he realized that it was Phoenix's voice shouting out a command. Nikias turned and watched as the crew of his cousin's trireme lifted the ship a few inches off the rocky beach and eased it into the water. The veteran sailors climbed swiftly on board and seized the oars while the novices clambered over the sides and landing ladders.

"Nicely done," said Chusor. "Even with half a crew of lubbers."

Chusor quickly assigned each man standing near the *Spear of Thetis* a number from one to three—that being the deck on which they would sit. He did his best to divide his veteran oarsmen amongst the young Athenians and Plataeans and told them to toss their belongings on board before the ship was put into the water. Pulling a twenty-foot-long oar was tricky work and needed steady oarsmen at intervals to keep the rhythm and set an example for the others. Some of his mariners protested when they were assigned to the lowest deck. But Chusor cajoled them with promises of extra pay and that seemed to satisfy them for the time being.

It was easy enough to get the *Spear of Thetis* into the water, for that was merely an exercise in brute strength. With guidance from Chusor and Diokles, the mixed crew of young Athenians, Plataean warriors, and veteran oarsmen managed to shove the craft into the harbor and climb on board. Nikias, up to his waist in water, looked about foolishly, wondering what to do. The boat was already drifting slowly away from the beach, guided by a few veteran oarsmen who had quickly taken their places and were dipping their oars into the water. But the landing ladders were thick with men trying to get on board. He started following the boat, wading through the water, and was quickly up to his breast. He began swimming along with many others.

"Wait!" shouted frantic voices. "We're not on the ship!"

Just then Chusor cried out from the prow, "Hold!" and the oarsmen reversed their motion and the ship came to a stop on the calm water. The men in the water laughed and swam the short distance to the ship, relieved that they weren't being left behind.

Nikias let everyone get on board, then climbed the landing ladder at the prow. As soon as he got to the top part of the ship—the open battle deck—Diokles took him by the arm and led him over to the highest tier of seats: the deck that cantilevered over the side of the ship.

"You sit behind me," Diokles said. "You do what I do. You are strong. You will catch on fast."

Nikias sat on the hard wooden seat and gripped the smooth wood shaft of the oar, moving the pole on the tholepin and testing the rope oarlock, which had been greased with tallow. The smell of the tallow and the other men's sweat made his stomach churn. The boat was filled with the din of voices—veterans giving instructions to the men near at hand. Nikias wished he wasn't soaking wet. His arse was already itching on the seat.

"Don't dig too deep with the blade," said Diokles. "And don't strain too hard. Think of it like a long arm and a hand pushing the water."

Nikias tried to do as he was told. The first couple of times he pulled on the oar the blade skimmed the water. Then he overcompensated and pushed the paddle in too far. But soon enough all of the oarsmen, given a rhythm to row by the drummer, were causing the big ship to move. Guided by the man at the tiller—who sat on his navigator's chair on the roof of the vessel—the *Spear* headed across the cove toward the seawall that guarded the inner harbors. Nikias realized, with a pang of regret, that Konon had not shown up at the shore. He wished his friend had been able to come on board. But a one-armed man wouldn't be much use on a trireme.

Rowing was easier work than Nikias had thought it would be. It actually felt good to stretch his back and torso, to feel his arms and chest stirring the sea with the oar. He was happy that his old shoulder injury, earned in a fall from Photine, had fully healed. It would have been impossible to do this kind of work with a bad shoulder. He concentrated on Diokles's ludicrously muscled back. The Helot turned around and smiled at him.

"Good, good," he said approvingly.

Nikias glanced over his shoulder in the direction they were going. Even though he couldn't see the moon high in the sky, he could see it shimmering on the choppy water. "What about the chain across the entrance to the seawall?" he asked. "How are we going to get through that?"

"Phoenix pay off guards," said Diokles. "Chain gone now."

Nikias was about to ask how much coin his cousin had had to pay to convince the guards on the seawall to let five triremes slip out of the harbor, when Ezekiel appeared at his side and shoved something into his mouth.

"Hey!"

"Ginger root," said the doctor. "Don't chew. Suck on it."

"Ginger?" said Nikias. "That's what my wife takes for menstrual cramps."

"Smart woman," replied Ezekiel. He squatted down on the deck next to Nikias and watched him with his hooded eyes. Nikias noticed that he was fingering something hanging around his neck by a leather cord. It was a gold signet ring.

"You still have the ring, I see," said Nikias, pulling on the oar, trying to keep time with Diokles. He wondered if the scrawny doctor had ever rowed, but thought it unlikely. The man was all brains and no body.

"It's a valuable thing that you gave to me on that night," said Ezekiel in a voice pitched for Nikias's ears alone. "Worth far more than the gold. The signet seal is a passport in Persian lands. I don't know why you parted with it so freely."

"The man who owned it was my family's enemy," explained Nikias. "He murdered my mother and was responsible for the sneak attack on Plataea."

They came to the gap in the seawall and, sure enough, the chain that was usually stretched from tower to tower was nowhere in sight. The fleet of ships quickly passed from the closed harbor and into the choppy water of the Saronik Gulf. A horn sounded from one of the towers—a call to Poseidon that Athenian ships were on their way into his realm. The young Athenians on board whooped with excitement. Nikias felt the ship turn. The beat of the oar drummer grew slightly faster.

"What was his name?" Ezekiel asked after a time.

Nikias turned and looked at the doctor. He had been concentrating so hard on rowing that he had forgotten the doctor was still there.

"Eurymakus is his name—a Persian-trained Theban assassin," said Nikias. "He tried to kill me with a poisoned blade in a battle at the gates of Plataea, and I turned the tainted blade against him, grazing his hand with the point. He chopped off his own arm to keep the poison from spreading into his torso and then escaped in the chaos of the battle. I don't know why I took the ring from his severed limb, or even why I brought it with me to Athens. But after I met you, and after you told me the secret of the thing, well, I had no more use for it." He thought back to the night that Ezekiel had pried off the ring's precious stone to reveal the name inscribed beneath: a name that held great import to Eurymakus, a follower of the Persian god Ahura Mazda, for it was the name of his *fravashi*—his guardian angel in the Persian tongue—a precious name that was supposed to be known only to the owner of the ring.

"After I left Athens," continued Nikias, "I was captured in the city-state of Tanagra by Eurymakus and a Plataean traitor. They kept me in an undercroft and . . . and they tortured me." He paused and pulled hard on the oar, the beats of the oar drummer echoing in his brain.

"And how did you escape?" asked Ezekiel, eyes wide with suspense.

"They were just about to kill me," said Nikias, staring with glazed eyes at the back of Diokles's dark head. "But I shouted out the name of the *fravashi*—Dana. Eurymakus could not hide his astonishment."

"If he had killed you," said Ezekiel, nodding his head and giving a feral smile, "then you would have been able to call his guardian angel to your shade, and she would no longer protect Eurymakus in *this* world *or* the next. After he died he would never be able to cross the great void and enter his heaven—his spirit would become a tormented ghost."

"A ridiculous notion," said Nikias, "but the magic of the name worked."

"You Greeks believe many things that I find absurd," replied Ezekiel.

"So you told me once before," said Nikias.

"What happened next?"

"Eurymakus took me to the Spartans and gave me to them."

"And where did he go after that?"

"I heard him tell the Spartans that he was going to go back to Persia to help procure gold to finance their war against Athens. And then I was traded for a Spartan prisoner that my grandfather had captured—a man worth far more than my life," Nikias added with chagrin.

"From what Chusor has told me about you," said Ezekiel, "I find *that* hard to believe. Anyway, he told me that I should give you back the ring. So here I am." He started to take off the cord from around his neck but Nikias stopped him with a shake of his head.

"A gift once given is never to be taken back," said Nikias. "Besides, the thing is poison to me."

Ezekiel glanced about with a hunted look, as if Chusor might be spying on him right now. But Chusor was nowhere to be seen, and the doctor put the ring back under his tunic and patted it.

"So be it."

"You saved my life with the knowledge of the ring that you imparted to me," said Nikias. "Someday I hope to repay the debt."

Ezekiel stood up and touched Nikias on the shoulder. "I'm certain that you will have many opportunities on this voyage to repay that debt," he said with a gloomy look, then walked aft down the aisle and disappeared into the cabin.

ELEVEN

By the time the sun began to rise three hours later, the ships were already twenty miles from Athens, surrounded on all sides by the dark and open sea.

And Nikias was so tired he could barely think. His body was drenched with sweat and his back, thighs, and shoulders burned. His forearms bulged ludicrously, as if they had grown in size from his first labor as an oarsman. Many of the new members of the crew had become seasick and puked up their guts on this first leg of the journey. Some had fainted, out of exhaustion, and now lay unconscious, slumped by their benches.

Nikias had not been sick the entire time, and for that he was grateful. But he knew that his body was reaching the end of its limit. He wondered why Chusor was pushing them so hard, and he started to grow churlish and snapped at the lad whose job it was to bring water to the men and ladle it into their mouths.

Finally a pipe sounded and the drumming stopped. The veteran oarsmen immediately brought in their oars and stowed them. Nikias, in a daze, pulled his oar off the tholepin and dragged it through the oarlock. His hands were frozen into claws and he couldn't make his fingers spread apart.

He looked around at the men nearby. He saw two or three hardy Plataean warriors—cavalrymen who were tremendously fit—slumped over their oars and gasping for air. Diokles, however, turned round, smiled at Nikias, and stretched his back like a cat.

"Good row," said the Helot.

Nikias stared out the gap in the side of the outrigger deck and saw two of the other triremes in the convoy on that side of the boat—close enough to spit at—bobbing on the waves.

"We made good distance," Diokles said.

"Where are the other two ships?" Nikias asked.

"On the other side," said Diokles. "We're all together. The captains made sure that nobody got left behind."

"A northwesterly wind has come up strong," said Chusor, who had suddenly appeared at Nikias's side. "We're going to set up sail."

"Thank the wind gods," said Nikias.

He leaned against the side of the boat and watched in a stupor as the veterans of the *Spear* went to work hefting the two masts from the hold. The rigging, stowed in various places beneath the benches, was dug out and run up along with the sails. It took no more than a quarter of an hour to accomplish this complicated task. During this process Chusor went to various parts of the ship, giving instructions or helping out. When it was all done he came back to where Nikias was sitting and said, "Follow me."

He led Nikias into his little cabin and shut the door. Chusor pointed at the small bed and said, "You can lie down if you wish. My helmsman is one of the best on the sea, and he is steering us straight for Serifos. You can rest easy for a while."

Nikias stared at the bed with longing but thought it would be undignified to lie down. "Why did we have to break our backs on this first run?" he asked with undisguised ill temper.

"We spotted some Korinthians," said Chusor. "We were in no shape with these lubberly crews to try and take them on. I didn't announce their presence because I didn't want anyone to panic."

"Well, I feel like an idiot now," said Nikias, sitting down heavily on a little chair and putting his face in his hands. He couldn't believe how tired he felt, but he was grateful that they hadn't been attacked. His thoughts started to drift. He imagined that he was back in his room at the farm in Plataea. He thought he could hear his mother and grandmother singing in the distance. A hand touched his back and he started.

"Eh? What?" said Nikias, getting awkwardly to his feet.

"You fell asleep," said Chusor. He was standing next to a small table with some kind of map spread out on it and held down with little bronze statues at the corners. Nikias had seen something like it once in Perikles's chambers. He leaned over it and stared. At first it was all meaningless shapes, but then the distinct outlines of islands and shorelines materialized before his eyes and his jaw dropped.

"It's a map of Greece and more," said Nikias. "Zeus's balls . . . It's the whole world! From a bird's-eye view!"

"From a *god's*-eye view," said Chusor proudly.

Nikias stared at the map in awe. "Libya, Persia . . . Tartessus to the west! Sky-thia. And look at all of the islands. Are there truly that many?" Nikias added with amazement. "Hundreds of them!"

"Most of the Greek colonies are shown," said Chusor. "Your people have hopped all over the world, colonizing it like frogs on a pond."

"Where did you get this map? I've never seen the like."

"A year ago," said Chusor, "we took the ship to Miletus in Ionia. A merchant there owed me some money. A great heap of gold, in fact. But he couldn't pay his debt. So he offered me a book in return. A copy of *Sailing Around the World*."

"I've never heard of it," said Nikias.

"I had," said Chusor. "And I had been searching for a copy for many years. I forgave the merchant his debt in exchange for that tome—more than the cost of this ship, mind you. But it was well worth it. The book is a wealth of infor-mation and had several maps that I have pieced together. And I have supple-mented Hekataeus's earlier work with my own findings. Whenever we pass shorelines, I take careful reference points and . . ." Chusor paused, realizing that Nikias was not paying attention. His finger was moving across the map from Athens to Plataea, then down to Korinth.

"What is this symbol marked at the Isthmus of Korinth?" asked Nikias.

"That is the Dialkos," said Chusor.

Nikias had heard of the three-mile-long overland track that the Korinthians used to roll ships from the Aegean Sea to the Gulf of Korinth. "I wish we could go that way," he said. "We'd be home in a few days."

"The Korinthians would have us all in chains the instant we set foot on their territory."

"So which way do we go to get to Naupaktos and Phormion's fleet?"

"Phoenix and I spoke at length about this the other day," said Chusor. "It's difficult because the entire Peloponnese is under Spartan control. There are no safe landings and the coastlines and bays are teeming with the enemy. And we can't go across the open ocean for days at a time. That would be suicide. Our plan, then, is to make our way to the western coast of Krete. From there the journey becomes treacherous. We must sail at night while this good weather holds and the moon is out. There are many small islands and barren coves in Messenia and the western Peloponnese. Once we get to the Athenian island of Zakynthos, we will be relatively safe and close to the entrance to the Gulf of Korinth and the fortress of Naupaktos, where Phormion keeps his fleet. Then we can consolidate all of the warriors—Athenian and Plataean—who will be going on to the port of Kreusis."

"How long will it take to get to Naupaktos?" asked Nikias, his head swimming with everything that Chusor had said along with all of the names written on the map. There were so many cities and islands that he had never heard of. The world seemed very big compared to little Plataea—nothing more than a tiny dot amongst the vast world represented by this chart.

"Three months if we're lucky," said Chusor.

Nikias wondered if Plataea would be able to hold out for that long. Chusor seemed to read his pensive look and said, "Don't worry. Your grandfather won't let the Spartans into the city. You'll arrive in time."

"I wonder if Kallisto is still alive," said Nikias. "She went into labor the night we left the citadel. She was supposed to come with us but she had to stay. I didn't even know that she had been forced to stay."

"That was the gods sparing her from the miasma in Athens," said Chusor.

"You think?" asked Nikias. "Sometimes I wonder if the gods are even watching."

"They are there," said Chusor with a black look. "But most of the time they're laughing at us."

The wind held strong and pushed the triremes across the dark blue sea under a sapphire-blue sky, the prows of the five ships pushing up great walls of pure white foam. Nikias stood at the prow behind the latticed spray guards next to Diokles, his face wet with mist. There was not a cloud in the sky. It felt as if they were held in the palm of a god, carried across Poseidon's watery realm.

He gazed from ship to ship, marveling at how smoothly everything had gone since they had left Athens. The triremes were still grouped together, their sails swelled taut, racing across the waves. They made Nikias think of a herd of some kind of magical sea creatures, with their painted prow eyes, snout-like rams peeking out above the cutwater, and upswept wooden stern pieces carved to resemble fish tails. He glanced back and saw Chusor standing aft by the helmsman. The old navigator sat as rigid as a statue, his gnarled arms reaching out to clutch either handle of the steering tillers, his white beard pushed forward like a miniature sail, his keen eyes staring straight ahead, hawk-like and unwavering.

Nikias looked to the right and saw Phoenix's ship. His cousin was standing by the mast, waving at him. He smiled and shouted something but Nikias couldn't hear him over the wind. He cupped a hand to his ear to show that he needed to shout louder, but Phoenix made a dismissive gesture as if to say, "It's not important."

"Phoenix say, 'We go very fast!'" said Diokles.

"I reckoned as much," said Nikias, and thought, "Nothing can stop us. Nothing can stop us from getting back to Plataea."

"Look," said Diokles, pointing at the prow of the ship. "Sea wolves."

Nikias squinted at the white foam. All of a sudden the sleek gray shapes of dolphins appeared from the lather, leaping and playing, racing the ship, the fins on their arched backs cutting through the boiling water like axe blades.

"A good sign," said Diokles, slapping Nikias on the back.

"Do you know the story of how Apollo turned himself into a dolphin?" asked Nikias.

"No. Tell me," said Diokles.

"Many years ago Apollo came to the temple of Delphi," began Nikias. "Back then there was a great serpent—a python—that terrorized the land."

"Where is Delphi?" asked Diokles. "Is it an island?"

"No. It's northwest of Plataea. On the side of a steep hill overlooking a valley of olive trees that lead to a bay. You can ride to Delphi in three days from Plataea. I've been several times with my grandfather to hear the oracles. Anyway, the snake was enormous and—"

"Bigger than a horse?" broke in Diokles.

"Oh, much bigger. As big as a pine tree."

"How did Apollo kill the giant snake?" Diokles said, his guileless face alive with wonder.

"He shot it!" said Nikias. "With his darts."

"I would have used a forge hammer," offered Diokles.

"Anyway," continued Nikias, "Mother Earth became angry with Apollo because the python was her son."

"Many women bear snakes for sons," put in Diokles.

"Too true," said Nikias. "So, to make up for this, he served a king in Thessaly as a goatherd for eight years."

"Boring," muttered Diokles.

"My story?" asked Nikias, with a surprised laugh.

"No! Watching goats all day. I used to have to do that when I was a slave in Sparta. I like the sea much better. No goats."

Nikias smiled inwardly at the childlike Diokles. There was not a malicious bone in the man's body. He had forgotten how much he liked the Helot.

"So what happened?" asked Diokles.

"When Apollo had served his time, he turned himself into a dolphin and bore priests from his temple in Krete upon his back, bringing them all the way to Delphi."

"That would hurt," said Diokles.

"If you were a dolphin?" asked Nikias.

"If you were a Kretan priest," said Diokles. "Imagine one of those fins sticking up your arse!"

TWELVE

By late afternoon the friendly wind at their back was still blowing hard and the convoy was within sight of the barren-looking island of Serifos. The *Spear of Thetis* took the lead and guided the other ships to the mouth of a bay on the northeast tip of the island—a crescent-shaped inlet with steep hills sloping up on either side. Running nearly to the beach was a swath of olive trees that snaked up a little valley to the top of a hill.

"Stow the masts!" called out Chusor.

With the same efficient grace with which the veteran mariners had put up the masts and rigging, they took it all down in a blur of activity. After the masts, sail, and all of the gear were stowed away, the men were told to get back to the benches. Even though Nikias had been resting for several hours, his body still ached from toes to neck as he sat down and eased his oar into the tholepin.

They didn't have to pull hard, however, for soon they were gliding into the gentle waves of the protected cove. They ran the ship onto the sandy beach, and then the whistle piped.

"Landing ladders," called out Diokles.

Veterans grabbed the landing ladders and locked them into place, and Nikias scrambled over the side with the others, standing next to the ship in waist-deep water. The men put their shoulders to the hull and lifted the trireme the short distance to the shore and set it down on the beach, where it listed to one side like a beached whale.

Nikias looked at the empty cove. There wasn't a person or dwelling in sight. By the look of the abundant plant life all around, he reckoned there must be a spring nearby. He shaded his eyes and peered at the top of the hill above the cove where there stood a single enormous and ancient olive tree. He saw a movement there—the figure of a small man standing up suddenly. He squinted and saw that it was a goatherd wearing a woven straw hat. And it wasn't a man but a slender lad.

Nikias turned to see if Chusor had spotted this sentinel. The captain of the *Spear* was staring straight up at the boy, holding a piece of burnished copper, which he turned this way and that to catch the light, flashing a signal. When Nikias looked back toward the hill, the goatherd was no longer there.

"Who was that up there?" Nikias asked as he walked over to Chusor.

Chusor hid the piece of copper in his palm. "Just an islander," he said abruptly. "I must have words with my crew. Perhaps you could take some men and round up wood for cooking fires. We'll have food in a few hours or so." He then called all of his veteran oarsmen together and led them off to some rocks on the left side of the beach—a crowd of the marauders, along with Diokles and Ezekiel.

Another ship from the convoy appeared in the cove and was quickly beached alongside the *Spear*. It was Phoenix's vessel and bore a one-armed sailor who leapt from the top of a landing ladder and ran triumphantly toward Nikias.

"Konon!" shouted Nikias, running up and embracing his friend. "You made it!"

"Just barely," said Konon. "They almost didn't let me on board—they said a one-armed oarsman was about as useful as a three-legged horse. But Phoenix saw me and let me come. I banged the oar drum the entire way."

"Well, I'm glad that you're here," said Nikias. The other three ships appeared at the mouth of the cove. Soon the beach would be crowded with ships and men.

"Just think!" exclaimed Konon. "This is the island where the baby Perseus and his mother washed up in the chest! This might be the very cove where the old fisherman found them!"

"These islands are all full of tales *and* fishermen," Nikias said under his breath.

Nikias rounded up some Plataeans and young Athenians and went to work gathering wood near the beach while keeping an eye on Chusor and the marauders. He couldn't hear what Chusor was saying to his crew but he could see that he spoke urgently and emphatically. Most of the men were nodding obediently at his words, but some scowled and complained. These were quickly set upon by their brethren with angry words and a few fists.

"What are they on about?" asked Konon.

"I don't know," said Nikias.

At a command from Chusor, twenty of the mariners broke off from the group and scrambled onto the *Spear*. They came down minutes later armed with spears and swords and headed into the grove, where they vanished into the dense trees.

Nikias took upon himself the task of making fires. Somehow the ship's flint had managed to go missing, so Nikias made flames using a bow drill. Soon there were several bonfires roaring on the beach, with nearly thousand men crowded around them. Some lay about resting while others swam in the water, cleaning themselves, or explored the olive grove that stood inland. A few came back reporting that they had found a well and men went off with empty amphoras to bring back a supply of freshwater. A few men, wandering off together in pairs, sought out privacy behind the rocks or in the woods for quick relief of their pent-up desires.

Nikias looked up at the hillside above the cove and saw a score of men standing at attention with spears. Curiously, they were facing the cove, as if to guard the hillside from any man who might make an attempt to journey inland. Why had Chusor set his men to guard the hill? And why had he flashed that signal to the young goatherd when they'd first arrived on the beach? He couldn't see Chusor anywhere. He did spot a group of his mariners milling about the *Spear* with sullen looks, speaking to each other in low voices. They were watched over by Diokles and some other members of the marauders' crew. One of them went up to Diokles and said something to him, pointing at the hillside, and the Helot knocked the man down—a brutal blow that made the mariner's knees wobble, then he slumped to the beach like a sack of wheat. Diokles pointed at the other men in the group threateningly and they backed off, dragging their companion to the shade cast by the ship.

Nikias saw Ezekiel and jogged over to him. "What's going on?" Nikias asked. "Why are some of Chusor's crew acting mutinous?"

Ezekiel looked crafty and shrugged. "They want to go raiding in the countryside, I suppose. Chusor won't allow it. We need the locals on our side."

Nikias glanced over at the group of six or seven mariners sitting in the shade of the boat, tending to the man whom Diokles had flattened. They did not look like bloodthirsty men bent on raiding and pillaging. Rather, they appeared depressed and surly—as though they had been struck to the heart by some grievous blow.

"Some men just won't listen to reason," said Ezekiel, and wandered off.

Several hours passed. Nikias bathed in the sea and then lay down naked on the sand and dozed, enjoying the cool evening air.

"Well, Cousin," said Phoenix, coming back from a tryst with a smile on his face, "this was much better than our last time at sea together."

"I'm astonished at the difference," said Nikias, rolling over. "I didn't feed the fishes once."

"I'm wondering how we're going to feed all of these men," said Phoenix, peering about with his crease-eyed mariner's squint.

"I was wondering the same thing," said Nikias. "We can't live on hard olives."

"Chusor told me not to worry," said Phoenix. "But all of our ships are empty. There were no spare provisions to be found in Athens."

"There's wheat on board the *Spear*," said Nikias. "Hundreds of bags in the hold. Enough to make bread for several weeks."

"Mariners need *meat*," said Phoenix. "I told Chusor that we should send raiding parties into the interior of the island, but he said the locals are warlike and will kill anyone who ventures onto their land, so I and the other captains have agreed to keep all our mariners here at the cove. But the men aren't going to remain docile if their bellies are groaning."

"Where's Aristophanes?" asked Nikias. "I saw him board your ship at Piraeus."

"What, the young comedian?" said Phoenix disdainfully. "He jumped ship before we even left the Piraeus harbor. He took one look at the bottom deck and buggered off like a hare."

Nikias shook his head and muttered, "Actors and playwrights."

"Hey, there's Chusor now," said Phoenix, pointing.

Nikias looked up. Chusor stood on the top of the hill above the cove by the spearmen, talking to the young goatherd to whom he had earlier flashed the message. The lad was perhaps fourteen years of age. It was hard to tell because the broad-brimmed woven hat hid his features. The two stood several paces apart, and when the goatherd stepped toward Chusor with his hand raised as if to touch him, Chusor backed suddenly away and held up his palm, causing the goatherd to stop. Nikias realized that Chusor didn't want to get close to this young man. He was evidently afraid that he might be carrying the Athenian sickness about him like a dark cloud.

Chusor spoke vehemently to the goatherd and the teenager nodded his head submissively and turned his face toward the beach, seeming to look straight at Nikias for a moment from under the shadow of the hat. For some reason Nikias felt an inexplicable sense of expectancy. Who was this young man? He thought of the story of Apollo that he had told to Diokles—this goatherd could have stepped from that tale. The youth turned abruptly and headed over the top of the hill, disappearing from sight down the other side on his long, slender legs.

Chusor ambled down the slope toward the cove until he was within earshot of the beach, then cupped his hands to his mouth and called out in his booming voice, "I need fifty men! Come now! And bring knives!"

"What's he up to?" asked Phoenix.

"I don't know," replied Nikias.

Nikias, Phoenix, and fifty or so men made their way through the olive grove and up a little cleft, then emerged onto the slope. They clambered up the rocks toward the hilltop above. When they crested it, they were met with a curious sight: Chusor, standing patiently and holding a cow by the lead, surrounded by scores of docile goats. Five shepherds—the ones who had obviously brought the animals—were already a quarter of a mile away, walking on a white footpath etched into the arid ground that led toward the center of the island.

"Dinner!" shouted Phoenix joyfully, scooping up a black goat.

"I didn't want the shepherds near us," said Chusor, "in case we have brought the evil miasma with us. They have agreed to bring us animals each day that we linger here. We'll have to set up racks on the beach to smoke some meat for the next leg of the voyage. Any supplies that we need can be ordered from the village, but we'll have to pay in silver."

"Excellent," said Phoenix. "I like this island."

"We'll slaughter the animals up here," said Chusor, "then sacrifice the cow to Poseidon down on the beach tonight."

"A feast!" shouted a young Athenian.

"This voyage gets better and better," said another.

Nikias picked up one of the goats and held it in his arms. He stared at the goatherds and the slender lad with the straw hat—now just a tiny figure. The young man stopped for a moment and looked back. Inexplicably Nikias's heart beat faster, matching the throbbing heartbeat of the frightened goat he held in his arms.

THIRTEEN

The sacrifice did not keep the sickness away. The savory smoke from the choicest parts of the cow—the most tender meat and thickest fat to please the gods—wafted skyward, but it did nothing to appease their apparent wrath. That night the miasma came to the camp on the beach like a ravenous beast that moves on silent paws. The victims were all men who had been lucky enough to avoid getting sick in Athens. Here, in this bright and beautiful cove, their luck ended. By next morning fifty men had fallen ill and five had died.

Days went by in a ruthless tedium of sickness, death, and manual labor. Trees had to be cut down for firewood to burn the corpses of the men who kept breathing their lives into the dust. More goats—brought by the shepherds to replenish the stock—needed to be slaughtered for food, for the living had to be fed even while the putrid dead piled up. Freshwater was gathered from the well that sat far from the beach. All the while Chusor's guard of mariners stood on the hillside like ominous statues staring down at the cove, a line of stalwart defenders.

One morning Nikias awoke to find the bodies of two marauders hanging from the biggest olive tree nearest the beach. "They tried to sneak past the guards," said Diokles.

"And Chusor hanged them?" Nikias asked, shocked at this harsh justice.

"Chusor did not want to hang them," said Diokles. "The men did that themselves. They know what is at stake if the sickness spreads to the island."

Nikias had never heard of marauders acting with such benevolence for their fellow humans, but he did not press Diokles. He had fallen into a dark gloom that neither the pure blue water of the cove nor the bright sun, nor even Konon's cheery disposition could dispel. He realized that Chusor had brought them to this isolated place to let the sickness run its course. They could not risk getting sick at sea. But how long would they have to stay here, watching their crews be whittled down? So many men had died that one of the ships would have to be left here; there weren't enough men to man all five triremes any more.

Every so often he would see the goatherd with the big straw hat standing on the top of the hill, seemingly searching him out amongst the crowd of men on the beach. At first he thought he was imagining this, but after several times he felt that he could not be mistaken. For some reason the goatherd was looking for him, and this made him uneasy.

After another three days—a week after they had arrived on Serifos—the evil miasma seemed to have run its course. No new cases of the sickness were reported, and virtually everyone who remained standing had either already survived a bout with the illness—as Nikias and Chusor had—or seemed to be miraculously immune, like Konon and Phoenix.

Phoenix and the other captains started taking men out onto the sea and training them at the complicated oar maneuvers of galley fighting. It was hard work, but Nikias was thankful to be doing something other than gathering wood for pyres or skinning goats. The young Athenians and Plataeans caught on fast, and after a week of training the four ships could come together on choppy water, aft to aft in a defensive "star" position, then burst out at full speed to ram an enemy. For this exercise they put the *Democracy*—the least seaworthy of the five ships that had set out from Athens—at anchor in the middle of the bay and took turns ramming it. The ship, its hull breached, slowly filled with more and more water after each successful ramming. Soon the *Democracy* was swamped and floated in the bay like a corpse.

Nikias enjoyed ramming another ship. It was a powerful sensation to feel the trireme jump forward, each oarsman working as one, and slam at full speed into the hull. It was the same sensation he got when punching an opponent in the jaw. Chusor said that fighting at sea was merely pankration with ships, which Nikias thought was an apt description.

Another week went by and still the sickness did not come back, but the westerly wind continued to blow hard, making it impossible for them to leave the cove: they would have had to fight the wind all the way to their next destination. But the mariners grew strong on goat meat and bread baked from the *Spear*'s supply of wheat. And the oldest mariners, including Chusor's ancient helmsman, said that a friendly wind would soon return, and then they could head on their way to the next stop on their intended route—the tiny isle of Agios, which lay south of the Spartan-held island of Kythera.

Toward dusk a little boat came into the cove and headed toward the beach. Nikias was eating the evening meal with Chusor, Diokles, Konon, and Ezekiel near one of the cooking fires—roasting chunks of goat and wild onions on sticks.

"Who's this?" asked Konon.

"Fisherman, most likely," said Nikias.

"Thank Poseidon! Maybe he'll have some squid. It would be a nice change from goat."

"It's not a fisherman," said Diokles, breaking into a broad grin as the boat cruised up to the beach and its only occupant leapt from the craft and pulled it onto the shore.

Chusor started laughing. "No, it's not a fisherman."

"Too bad," said Konon with a sigh.

"Never thought I'd see *him* again," said Ezekiel.

The short man looked around the camp and, spotting Chusor and the others waving at him, marched up to the fire, squinting at them with his narrow eyes. He had smooth skin and a wispy beard—the only hair on his face. It was difficult for Nikias to determine his age, but he sensed a great strength and intelligence—and a hint of menace—from the wiry little man.

"Let me introduce my ship's exhorter," Chusor said to Nikias. "This is Ji. He comes from a land far to the east—beyond even the country of Indika."

Ji bowed slightly to Nikias, who nodded back and said, "Peace."

"Where have you been?" asked Diokles.

"I got . . . lost," said Ji cryptically. "I did not touch ground for a week after leaving Athens. Korinthian ships everywhere. I had to hide out on Kythnos for a while." He sat on the beach cross-legged and, taking a skewer of goat meat from Ezekiel, blew on it a few times before shoving a large piece in his mouth. "I haven't eaten in many days," he said, chewing hard.

"I thought perhaps you had gone back to your own land," said Chusor.

"Too far," said Ji. "Too dangerous. I'll take my chances with you lot."

Ji ate and ate and offered little in conversation, but Nikias could tell that Chusor and the others were glad to see him. Later that night, with the setting of the sun, the wind changed to the northeast, as if Ji—the foreigner from the East—had brought the new wind with him. Nikias and Konon went off to the niche in some rocks where they had made their resting place. He lay on his back staring at the stars, wondering what the day's journey would bring.

But Nikias awoke in the middle of the night with a start. He looked around in the moonlight at the sleeping form of Konon, wondering what had woken him up. His friend lay on his stomach, snoring loudly. Nikias noticed, with surprise, that one of his own sandals was on his chest and he picked it up, staring at it in confusion. Then another sandal dropped from above and landed on his stomach and he jumped to his feet. Standing on the rocks above was the figure of the goatherd with the big straw hat, face hidden by the dark shadow cast by the brim. The stranger held a finger to his lips and gestured for Nikias to put on his sandals and follow.

Nikias, compelled by some mysterious fascination, slipped on his footwear and caught up to the goatherd, who had already moved off into the woods. The young man stepped silently, picking his way quickly along the trail. What did this stranger want of him? And why was he foolishly following him without question? There was something strange about this lad. He seemed different than when Nikias had seen him standing on top of the hill. He appeared taller now. And Nikias didn't remember him having such comely hips that swayed fetchingly as he walked.

He felt as though he were in a strange dream from which he could not break free. The goatherd led him off the main trail and onto a path that wended through the olive trees on the right side of the slope. They made their way over a rocky area and then up to a ridgeline. They walked for twenty minutes or so, the light of the moon guiding their way on a switchback trail until they came to a little plateau. Here stood a small temple made of marble, with a tiled roof. The goatherd went inside and Nikias followed. They were all alone here in this place, far from the camp and out of sight of the sentries on the hilltop. Nikias asked with a trembling voice, "Who are you?"

"Do you not know?"

The skin of Nikias's neck and cheeks tingled with excitement. The figure who stood before him was no lad—it was a woman in disguise. "Helena," he said, amazed.

She took off the straw hat to reveal her exquisite face. Her eyes shone in the bright light of the moon that poured through the temple columns, and she smiled hesitantly. She unloosed her hair that was bound at the back of her head, and her curly and untidy locks fell about her neck, touching her shoulders like fingers.

"I always liked dressing up," she said.

Nikias stood with his mouth agape. Now he understood why Chusor had acted so strangely when they first landed here, why the marauders had been so diligent about keeping everyone at the cove in isolation. Serifos was their own home. They had been terrified of infecting their loved ones who lived on the other side of the island. And Chusor had kept the knowledge of Helena's existence here a secret for the very same reason—so that Nikias would not seek her out.

Helena took a step toward him but he backed away, even though every fiber of his body was screaming at him to take her in his arms. "No!" he said emphatically, holding up his palms. "Stay where you are. You can't come near me."

"But my sister told me that the miasma was gone from the camp," she said. "There are no new illnesses."

"How does your sister know that?"

"She comes to the camp every day. The goatherd whose clothes and hat I'm wearing now—the youth with short hair."

Nikias understood. Helena's half sister—the slip of a girl he had met in Athens years ago—was the "lad" he'd seen talking to Chusor. She'd grown several inches in that time and had cut her long hair so that she now resembled a boy.

"Chusor's daughter," said Nikias. The wind had started to pick up and Nikias thought that he heard something on the wind. The sound of a cry or a horn. He strained to listen but heard nothing more.

"Chusor disguised us as boys, you see," said Helena. "To get us out of Athens. My hair was shorn just like Melitta's is now. I let it grow back, but Melitta has chosen to keep hers that way. She was always a trickster, and she has grown wild on this island." She took a step forward but Nikias held up his hand again.

"The *gods* are tricksters," he said. "We can't take the risk of being together. This sickness turns the mightiest man into a corpse in hours. I could be carrying the miasma on me now, like an invisible cloak." He thought of the hanged men—slain by their fellow marauders simply for trying to go back home to see their families. He, Nikias, was risking the same punishment merely by talking to Helena now.

"Don't be foolish."

"I'm not being foolish. I've helped burn the dead! Hundreds of men. Tens of thousands have already died in Athens. Many of my own people too. Now I must go!"

Helena's face fell and she sank to her knees, letting forth a stricken groan. "I've come nearly every day to the hilltop merely to catch a glimpse of you. And now you are to leave tomorrow and . . . and I might never see you again. I'll die if that happens. I'll die." She wiped the tears that coursed down her cheeks. "I already thought I had lost you once before. Not a day has gone by that I haven't thought of you."

"I have to go back," said Nikias in a panic. In battle or a pankration bout he was calm and keen witted. Now he felt like he was drowning. He couldn't think straight. "I can't stay here with you."

"We don't have to touch," said Helena. "Just sit for a while. I beg you. We can talk. Surely the sickness can't leap from you like a poisoned dart shot from a bow."

Nikias could not tear his eyes from her face. His desire to hold her was so strong, it was making him queasy—as if he were in a boat on a stormy sea. He felt weak and stupid. He sat down heavily on the ground and nodded. "Yes. We can talk for a while."

Helena wiped the tears from her face again and smiled. "Do I look very different from when we met in Athens?" she asked shyly. "I have been in the sun these years, working in the fields. I fear I've become dark and homely."

She did indeed look different from the hetaerae he had known and made love to in Athens. Back then she had been dressed in the finest clothes. Her skin had been painted and her hair intricately arranged. But now she resembled a dusky goddess—Persephone come to life and returned from the underworld to bring hope to the world again. "You're even more beautiful than I remembered," he said with sincerity.

His words brought a faint smile to her lips. "When Chusor came to help my sister and me escape from Athens, he told us everything that had happened to you on your journey home."

"I thought of you often," he said. "When I was tortured by the enemy, your face came to me in my fevered dreams—it was the only thought that kept me from losing my mind."

"Chusor said that you suffered greatly," said Helena. "That you almost died." She glanced at his hand with the missing finger, and then at the left side of his face with his scars and slightly squinting eye. "He told me that as soon as you awoke from your delirium, you told him about us. And then Chusor came to Athens—three weeks after you had departed the city, just like you promised he would. There is a little stronghold on the top of the mountain in the center of the island. That is where we live. There are watchtowers on the four corners of the island that keep a lookout for raiders. Life is very different here than in Athens, but I am no longer one of Kleon's puppets. I am free now. I am free to be with whomever I want," she added, giving him a significant look.

Nikias dropped his head. "Then Chusor has not told you everything."

"I don't know what you mean?" she replied uneasily, obviously sensing the gravity of his tone.

"When I returned to the Oxlands I married a woman—a woman who was bearing my child. She was pregnant before I met you. We've known each other our entire lives."

Helena's mouth opened to speak, but then she stopped herself. She stood up very slowly and smoothed her tunic.

"I—" began Nikias, but she cut him short.

"What is her name?" The question was not spoken in anger—rather in a tone of morbid curiosity.

"Kallisto."

"Pretty name. And the child?"

"Twins," said Nikias. "And another in the womb when I was forced to leave Plataea."

"Blessed woman," Helena said.

He got to his feet and faced her. The world disappeared. All that Nikias saw was Helena—her bright eyes, her long neck, her high cheekbones, her haughty nose. The very air seemed to throb with her breath from her full and parted lips. The ground beneath his feet seemed to be connected to hers.

Without a word she pulled off her tunic, standing naked before him. Here was the bold hetaera he remembered from Athens—regal, beauteous, splendid, shimmering silver in the moonlight as though she were made of marble. He stared hungrily at her full breasts, then down to the dark patch between her thighs and the curves of her shapely hips. She touched herself, stroking her breast with one hand, reaching between her thighs with the other.

Nikias felt himself swelling and forced himself to turn away. "Why are you tempting me like this?" he asked. "Gods! This is torture."

"Are you just going to stand there? Won't you come to me?" she asked.

"I can't."

"I would risk dying to be with you now. I would risk the deaths of others as well," she added, embittered.

Her words terrified him. He didn't know what to say.

"Touch yourself, if you won't touch me," she commanded. "Let me see your beautiful body. Let me feast upon you with my eyes. I want to see what you won't give me."

He could not help himself. He obeyed, taking off his tunic and standing before her. Then he took himself in his trembling hand and started stroking, gazing hungrily at her loins, her breasts, her face. She did the same while her gaze passed all over his body. Her hand started working furiously between her legs while the other stroked a swelling nipple.

Suddenly their eyes locked.

"I'm inside you now," Nikias said.

"So deep," she replied. "Oh, gods!"

"Helena—"

It did not take long. Their knees buckled at the same time and they bowed together on the temple floor like suppliants before the altar, gasping, reeling from the power of their desire—a palpable force that seemed to fill the temple like the heat from a forge fire.

"What was that sound?" Nikias asked suddenly, breaking the silence. The wind had shifted and carried on it he heard the distinct sound of a blaring horn—the same sound that he thought he had heard before . . . a quarter of an hour ago now?

"What's going on?" asked Helena.

"Something's wrong at the camp!" said Nikias, standing up and throwing on his tunic. He heard the sound again. Were the ships under attack? He dashed out of the temple and looked around. He saw a path going up the hill from behind the temple.

"Where does that path lead?" he asked.

"Up the ridgeline. Back to the stronghold."

"How far?"

"Three miles from here."

"Can you run?"

"Yes, but—"

"Go back there now," he commanded. "Don't follow me. Go and don't look back!"

She dropped her head.

"I love you, Helena," he said. "Always remember that."

He sprinted down the rocky path from the temple, back down toward the cove.

FOURTEEN

---·---

Nikias bounded from the olive grove and onto the beach. He stopped short, looking about the camp with astonishment. The cooking fires kindled for breakfast still burned. Goats waiting to be slaughtered stood bleating in their pens. The makeshift hovels that the men had fashioned over the last two weeks sat silent in the dawn.

But there was no sign of anyone else onshore. The ships and all the mariners were gone.

He peered at the empty cove. The four triremes were nowhere in sight. All that was left was the swamped hulk of the *Democracy*—a black mass floating in the dark water like the corpse of a giant beast.

He walked to the water's edge and stood there with his hands on his hips. "What's happened?" he asked aloud, conscious of how stupid he sounded talking to himself. "Where did they go?"

A goat bleated in response.

Nikias forced himself to think logically. Why had the ships departed without him? He thought back to the first time he had heard the horn faintly on the wind and how he dismissed it as fancy. That was over twenty minutes ago. The mariners had been trying to signal to him to come back to the beach, but he didn't hear them. For some reason they had to ship out. But why? There was no sign of a sea battle or sneak attack on the camp. No corpses floating on the water or lying on the beach.

Perhaps the lookouts on the hills had seen enemy sails in the moonlight coming toward the island and they went out to meet them in battle so that they would not get bottled up and trapped in the cove. He ran to the right—to the end of the beach—and scrambled up the rocks, trying to get to a higher place so that he could look out onto the sea. When he got to the ridge he stared to the west, in the direction that the fleet would have gone on the next leg of the journey. But there were no ships in sight. He looked to the right, in the direction of the rising sun.

"There you are!" he exclaimed, for he had caught sight of the convoy, the sun-bleached oars of the four proud ships gleaming in the rosy light of dawn. But why were they heading southeast.

"*Where are you going?*" he yelled. "*Come back!*"

"They're going to a cove on the eastern side of the island!" came a breathless voice from behind.

Nikias whirled. Konon was coming up the slope from the beach, clawing his way up the rocks.

"Konon! Thank the gods!"

"I've been looking everywhere for you!" said Konon, smiling with relief as he got to Nikias. "I told them I wouldn't go without you, so they left me behind." He held out Nikias's sword. "Here. I kept this safe for you."

"Why did they leave?" asked Nikias as he took the proffered sword, quickly slipping it over his shoulder and strapping it tightly to his back.

"A rider came with news that an army of Korinthians has invaded the island."

"How many?" asked Nikias.

"A thousand or more—they landed in coves all over the south side of the island, burning the villages and capturing women and children. It turns out that the mariners on Chusor's ship have a stronghold in the center of this island on the top of the mountain."

"I know," said Nikias. "All of their families dwell there. That's why they didn't want anyone leaving the cove. They didn't want to infect everyone who lives there."

"Everyone who *did* dwell there," said Konon. "The rider told us they abandoned the place and fled to a cove on the eastern side. They knew they couldn't hold their fort against an army of Korinthians—not with most of their men on Chusor's ship. They're waiting to either be rescued by our triremes or captured by the Korinthians."

Nikias turned and started walking fast up the hill, away from the water. He felt as if he had been kicked in the gut. He had ordered Helena to go back to the stronghold—across an island crawling with the enemy. He had most likely sent her to her doom when all that she had wanted was to be with him. The thought of her captured and raped—forced to be another man's thrall for the rest of her life or sold to the brothels of Korinth—made him sick.

"I'm an idiot!" he said, shaking his head in disbelief.

"That's what Phoenix said," replied Konon. "He called me one as well when I said I was staying behind. Hey, where are you going?"

"Follow me!" shouted Nikias over his shoulder as he took off running along the hillside. After half a mile he came to a spot where he could look down on the little plateau with the temple—the place where Helena had taken him. He came to a stop, calling out her name frantically. But she did not answer and there was no sign of her anywhere. He found the path—the one he had told her to follow—and took off again.

"Where are you going now?" asked Konon, trying to keep up with him.

"To the stronghold!"

"But that's where the Korinthians will be!"

Nikias didn't speak. It was hard going. The way was steep. But he did not slow down and left Konon behind. After he crested another hill, the mountain-top in the center of the island came into view, a mile away. In the dim light of dawn he could see the gray stones of the fortress walls and a thin trail of smoke issuing from the stronghold—a black and twisting plume.

The Korinthians were already there. They had sacked the place.

"Look what I found," said Konon.

Nikias stopped and looked back. Konon was running toward him carrying something in his hand—a straw goatherd's hat.

"Where did you find that?" Nikias asked, his heart leaping into his throat.

"Just over there, off the trail."

"Take me to the spot!"

Konon led him back to the place. Nikias saw many footprints and signs of a struggle. Warriors had been here. At least ten. And they had captured Helena. He could see the direction they had gone and marks where the butts of their spears had dragged in the dust. They couldn't be far away. Only a quarter of an hour or so had passed since he had left Helena at the temple.

He followed the trail, running low and hunched over like a dog on the scent of its prey. When he was certain of the direction the Korinthians were going—to the southeast—he took off at a sprint. Nikias was a fast runner: he could run the two-and-a-half-mile circumference of Plataea in a quarter of the time it took an hour water clock to spill its time—while wearing a bronze breastplate. Now his sandaled feet flew over the barren ground. He glanced back. Konon wasn't keeping up with him. But it didn't matter. He would face the enemy alone.

He went on, going out of his mind with frustration and fear. Would he find her in time?

Minutes passed but they seemed like hours. Then he saw a light flicker near a grove of trees up ahead. Torches. As he got closer he made out the shapes of men standing in a semicircle. Ten or eleven. Korinthians wearing leather armor and bearing short spears. Through the spaces in their ranks he caught a fleeting glimpse of a naked woman on her hands and knees, raped simultaneously from the front and behind, her breasts jerking wildly from the men's brutal thrusts. Was it Helena? He couldn't tell.

All he knew was that the enemy had foolishly stopped to take pleasure in their prizes. Their lust had gotten the better of them. They were not looking behind them. They had posted no sentries. Four or five children as well as another woman and a teenager lay nearby, all of them bound at their hands and ankles, facedown and gagged. He saw a baby crawling toward the circle of men—the Korinthians hadn't bothered to tie the infant. One of the Korinthians shoved the baby aside roughly with his foot and the little creature was quiet for an instant before sucking in its breath and letting forth an enraged howl. The man who had kicked the infant raised his sword, ready to quiet the baby for eternity.

Nikias burned with outrage.

He pulled his sword from the sheath as he sprang onto a large rock and leapt the last few feet to the enemy. The double-edged blade of Apollo gleamed in the dawn as if with an inner light. The Korinthian with the raised sword brought his arm down to slay the baby, but suddenly his arm was no longer attached to his shoulder and Nikias plowed straight past him and into the other enemy warriors at full speed, cutting off the heads of two men standing side by side with the same fell stroke, then lunging forward with a backslash—the Korinthian thrusting into the woman's mouth gasped and toppled over with a severed spine.

Before the other astonished Korinthians could draw their weapons, Nikias blinded the other rapist, raking him across the eyes with the tip of his sword, then rolled onto the ground and swept out with the bloody blade, hacking off a warrior's legs at the knees. He was like a whirling scythe of death, reaping men instead of wheat.

"Stop!" was all that one of the Korinthians managed to say.

Nikias jumped to his feet and parried a sword blow aimed at his guts. He kicked the man in the testicles, and sliced off his jaw with an uppercut from the fattest part of the blade, screaming like a madman and striking out with the flat of his foot, breaking another's knee. Then he plunged the sword into the warrior's abdomen.

He stood in front of the naked woman sprawled face-first on the ground, guarding her from the remaining three warriors who were still unhurt. Nikias's breath came in ragged gasps—an animal sound emanating from the back of his throat.

The three Korinthian spearmen backed away and pointed their javelins at Nikias, spreading out to surround him in a circle. The man Nikias had blinded was crawling on his hands and knees within the circle. Then he stopped and drew forth a dagger, stabbing at the air in futility. The Korinthian with the missing arm slumped to the ground, clutching his spurting stump, and looked about him in a daze, saying, "My arm! Where is it?"

"I told you to post a guard!" spat one of the spearmen to the other.

"Kill him!" bellowed the one-handed man, seizing his severed hand.

"Where is he?" asked the blinded man, spitting out the blood that had trickled into his mouth.

The Korinthian spearman nearest to Nikias pulled back his weapon, but before he could thrust it forward, his forehead exploded in a spray of blood and he pitched forward, dead.

The other two spearmen snapped their heads around. The man to Nikias's left pitched backward as though kicked by an unseen fist and lay stunned on the ground. Nikias didn't hesitate. He leapt on the last man standing, bringing his sword down upon his neck, cleaving his head and shoulder from his torso with a mighty stroke. Blood sprayed from the wound like a wave breaking on a rock—a red plume of gore.

Konon jogged up warily, his sling hanging lose at one side. He held the thong to his mouth, spat a lead pellet into the strap, swung it twice, and let fly at the one-armed Korinthian who was running away. The pellet slammed into the enemy's skull and he fell headlong on the stones.

The blinded man had gotten to his feet and was now slashing at the air with his dagger.

"Where are you?" he said with rage.

Nikias strode over to him and slashed him across the belly, and the Korinthian dropped to his knees, spilling his guts into the dust.

"All dead?" asked Konon.

Nikias grunted.

The woman who had been raped scrambled over to her baby and clutched it to her breast, trembling and gibbering violently. The woman was not Helena.

Nikias ran to the prisoners and turned over the other woman—a grandmother in her fifties. He turned over another and saw a teenaged girl's face surrounded by a mop of short hair. She bled from a cut to her cheek and one of her eyes was nearly swollen shut. He pulled the gag from her mouth.

"Nikias!" she cried, tears pouring from his eyes.

Nikias drew in his breath. "Melitta!"

"You know this one?" asked Konon.

"She's Helena's sister," said Nikias, slicing through the girl's bonds. "The girl you met in Athens. Her hair's been cut. Unbind the others," he commanded. "Quickly."

"They have her," said Melitta, her teeth chattering as Nikias helped her to stand. "I c-came to look for her when I got word of the K-Korinthians. I knew she had come to you. She told me. I said she was foolish."

"I sent her back to the stronghold," said Nikias.

"They caught her near the temple," said Melitta. "At the top of the hill. That's where I was waiting for her. They b-bound her like a goat and carried her off as a prize. I tried to stop them. I had your sword—the one you left in Athens. But they knocked me down and took the sword from me. The Korinthians divided us up and that's how we got separated." She stared at all of the corpses of the enemy warriors with a bewildered expression.

"Where is she?" asked Nikias. "Where did they take your sister?"

"To a ship," said Melitta. "A cove called the Double Axe." Her eyes grew hard and she bent over and snatched a sword from the dead hand of the Korinthian Nikias had blinded, then gutted. Then she kicked him in the side of the head and spat upon on the warrior's corpse. "A curse upon your shade!" she screamed, then handed Nikias the sword. "This is your blade."

Nikias saw the familiar pommel with the boxing Minotaur—his grandfather's old sword, which Nikias had been forced to leave in an armory outside the gates of Athens two and a half years ago upon entering the city. He had been handed a metal disk as a token by the keeper of the armory, and later gave this token to Melitta and Helena as a pledge that he wouldn't leave the citadel without helping them to escape. But he was forced to leave Athens by sea, abandoning both of them *and* his grandfather's sword.

"You keep it," he said. "The sword is yours now."

She nodded solemnly and slipped it into the scabbard on her belt. Nikias and Konon quickly cut the bonds of the other captives, and Konon helped find the dress of the woman who had been raped, covering her trembling body with it.

"Do you know where this cove is?" Nikias asked Melitta. "The Double Axe?"

"Yes," she replied.

"Can you run?" Nikias said.

"Like the wind," she replied.

"Follow us to the cove," Nikias said to the freed Serifans. "Follow us as quickly as you can."

And then he and Konon took off after Melitta, who was already sprinting ahead across the rocky ground.

FIFTEEN

———◆———

"We have to turn back! Make sail and run for the open sea!!"

Chusor could barely hear Phoenix shouting across the space between their two ships as the *Spear* and the *Argo*—cutting through the waves side by side and a stone's throw apart—fought with their sweeping oars against the strong wind, a growing gale that threatened to push them against the rocky eastern shore of Serifos an arrow's flight to their right. The *Spartan Killer* and the *Aphrodite* had fallen behind them by several ship lengths.

"There's too many of them!" shouted Phoenix.

Chusor, standing all alone on the small railed deck at the prow of the *Spear*, didn't need the Athenian captain to state the obvious—he could see for himself the eight Korinthian triremes heading for them on a collision course from the opposite direction, only a quarter of a mile away. The enemy ships had come into view as the *Spear* and the *Argo* rounded a headland. The ships coming at them were heavy Korinthian triremes—far bulkier than their Athenian-made counterparts. And they stood like a wall of death between Chusor and the cove called the Double Axe where the inhabitants of the stronghold had fled—two small coves separated by a narrow isthmus leading to a triangle-shaped promontory. He could just make out the promontory in the distance behind the Korinthian ships.

But Phoenix was right. They were coming too fast. The Korinthians were sailing with the wind and under oar power as well, which meant they were making at least twenty knots—four times the *Spear*'s speed right now moving under oars alone and into the wind. If a Korinthian ship collided with the *Spear*, it would be like a man on horseback riding at full speed into an unarmored hoplite. The destructive force would be devastating.

But there was no way that Chusor was turning back now. He had to get to the cove or die trying.

"Did you hear me?" yelled Phoenix. "This is suicide!"

"We can't outrun them!" Chusor called out. "They've got the wind at their backs! They'd be on us before we turned round! Better to face them head-on! Fall in behind me! I told you before—I have a plan!"

Chusor wiped the sweat dripping from his forehead and said a silent prayer. He thought of his daughter Melitta. She must be at the cove now, waiting for him to come to her rescue, along with the wives and children of half the oarsmen on this ship. The marauder crew members of the *Spear*, just like Chusor, had no choice. Turning and running from the Korinthians now would mean losing a treasure they could never regain. Death was preferable to living a life knowing that their loved ones had been captured and turned into slaves. Fortunately the Plataean and Athenian rowers who made up half the crew were all on the lower decks and had no idea what was coming. Otherwise they might have jumped from their seats and flung themselves into the ocean in despair.

He glanced back at the helmsman at the other end of the battle deck. Agrios was shielded on either side by wooden screens that Chusor had fitted into place before they departed the camp. This temporary shield was another of Chusor's inventions: protection for the steersman against enemy arrows. If a helmsman was killed in a fight—something Chusor had seen several times in sea battles—a trireme would suddenly and disastrously lose its brain, like a horse without a rider. The old man was leaning to one side, fighting with the rudder against the powerful swells, but his face was rigid . . . stoical. Earlier that morning, back at the camp, Agrios had sniffed the air and told Chusor that a proper gale was coming. He could feel it in his bones, he said. Chusor didn't believe him at the time, but now he was starting to think the old man was right, for the wind was howling and the waves were capped with foam. Beyond the approaching ships he could see a mass of gray clouds—and far out to sea, a swath of dark rain.

"Diokles!" barked Chusor, looking down into a small open hatch in the floor of the prow deck. The reek of naptha—the distilled resin of pine pitch—emanated from the opening. He had been taught to make the highly flammable chemical by Naxos of Syrakuse—a master inventor and a genius in the craft of war. But Naxos had dabbled too much in the incendiary arts, and was burned alive before Chusor's eyes after an experiment went awry.

"Here!" said Diokles as his head popped up through the hatch. He handed Chusor the end of a black tube capped with a brass funnel, then disappeared below. Chusor clamped the tube to the swiveling frame of the prow's bolt shooter, the other end snaking back into the hatch.

"Did you check for leaks coming out of the container?" Chusor called down into the chamber below.

"There was one, but I sealed it up tight with pitch," came Ezekiel's voice.

"Then get up here—now! I need you. And bring the pandoras."

"Coming!" Ezekiel pulled himself up through the hatch bearing a heavy leather bag. He set it down at Chusor's feet, then leaned against the ear timbers—the square wooden shields that protected the prow—peeking over the top and staring with horror at the approaching enemy ships.

"Remember, Diokles," said Chusor, calling down the hatch, "when I say, 'Go,' you pump with all your might and don't stop."

Diokles nodded vigorously and fit his feet into the straps of the big floor bellows mounted in front of the bronze container, then grabbed two rings in the ceiling, ready to move up and down with his powerful legs to work the double-action pump.

"Your tunic is soaked with naptha," said Chusor, turning his attention to Ezekiel.

"Some leaked out and I sopped it up," said Ezekiel.

"Take off your clothes or else you'll go up in flames."

Ezekiel's eyes grew wide. He quickly tore off his clothes and stood there naked, his scrawny body a stark contrast to Chusor's hulking torso.

"Are you drunk?" asked Chusor.

"Hardly," replied Ezekiel, hiding his purple-stained teeth with his hand as he spoke.

Chusor turned and peered down the gangway, where Ji was calling out encouragement to the men and upbraiding those who were slacking off. Thank the gods he had returned to the ship.

"Ji!" he yelled. "Come stand by the ladder now!" He needed the exhorter to be within earshot of him to relay orders to the oarsmen—they would never be able to hear his voice in the cramped space of the ship, where sound was deadened by so many bodies. Ji came quickly to the base of the ladder and stood, his right ear cocked toward him.

Chusor went to work in the little prow deck arranging his supplies: a bow and quiver of arrows that had been dipped in pine resin, flint and knife, some pine pitch torches, and a bronze container with a flat bottom and a pouring spout that was plugged with waxed cork. There was a big iron pot riveted to one corner—it was as black as the pitch that the mariners melted in it and used for sealing the hull. The pot was also useful for setting flaming arrows on fire. Archers could stand in this protected area at the prow and dip their darts into the pot before shooting them at enemy ships. Chusor tore the cap off the amphora and poured a clear and foul-smelling liquid into the pot.

He reached for the leather bag that Ezekiel had brought up and opened it, taking out a score of little jars that had been wrapped in straw and capped with papyrus and beeswax plugs. Each jar was marked with a red *P*. They contained a combination of volatile chemicals, including gypsum and crystals made from bat guano. When these ingredients were set alight, they created a sticking fire that burned through wood and flesh alike, and no water could douse the flames. Chusor called them "pandoras," and he had used them in Plataea to help immolate the Theban invaders on the night of the sneak attack.

"They're getting closer," said Ezekiel urgently.

Chusor stood up and looked over the prow. The Korinthian ships had formed up into two lines of four. The ships in the lead would be on the *Spear* in minutes. He shot a quick look aft: Phoenix's ship had fallen back and was following in the *Spear*'s wake, and the *Spartan Killer* and the *Aphrodite* were well behind the *Argo*.

He ducked back down and shielded the iron cauldron with his body, making a windbreak from the gust that played about on the deck of the prow. Then he struck a piece of firestone with a knife, sending a shower of sparks into the pot. The naptha caught fire instantly and a blue flame leapt from the pot, singing the hairs of his chest. He stepped back and handed Ezekiel one of the unlit torches.

"I'll be right back," Chusor said, and before the startled Ezekiel could reply he jumped out of the prow and onto the battle deck, sprinting the hundred feet to the helmsman.

"Steer straight between the two lines of ships!" Chusor commanded.

Agrios nodded grimly, never taking his eyes from the approaching ships.

"If one of them tries to ram us head-on, steer away from it," continued Chusor. "You hear me? Don't meet the ramming ship head-on. We must not become locked ram to ram. I can't shoot the liquid until we're upwind of them, otherwise it will blow back on us, setting the *Spear* on fire."

"I understand, damn you!" growled Agrios. "Now get back to your station!"

Chusor dashed back to the prow, nearly falling into the open space of the galley in the middle of the deck, and took his position at the bolt shooter with its snakelike hanging tube strapped to the top.

"What is going on?" asked Ezekiel, his teeth chattering. "What am I supposed to do with this?" he asked, holding up the unlit torch.

Chusor grabbed it from him and dipped it into the burning pot. The torch flamed to life and he handed it back to Ezekiel. "The instant the tube starts spitting naptha, you hold the torch to the funnel tip. Then you must jump back or else you will be burned to a crisp."

Ezekiel stared from the burning torch to the tube. "I'm a doctor, not a sheep-stuffing firemonger!"

"There's no such thing as a firemonger," replied Chusor. "Now grab a pandora." Ezekiel hesitated and Chusor bellowed, "Pick it up!"

Ezekiel reached for one of the clay pots with a trembling hand, gripping it by the handle.

"Don't drop it!"

"Yes. And what else?"

"After I set a ship on fire, throw the pandoras at the hull. But you must throw them hard so they break. It's quite simple, really. A child could do it."

"Oh, yes, simple," sneered Ezekiel.

The Korinthians were almost on them now. He could see the enemy warriors on the battle decks quite clearly—archers and spearmen in full armor. If those warriors managed to board the *Spear*, they would slaughter his men as though they were defenseless children.

"That's it! That's it! Put your backs into it!" he heard Ji calling out.

He shot a look at the helmsman. The old man's muscular arms were trembling, but he held the rudder handles firm. The other ships—the *Argo*, the *Spartan Killer*, and the *Aphrodite*—were still in line behind the *Spear*.

An arrow whistled past Ezekiel's head and he let forth a startled scream.

Chusor turned and peered forward, squinting into the driving wind at the Korinthian triremes. The two lead ships started to converge on the *Spear*. An arrow flew at Chusor—for a split second he saw it frozen before his eyes. He didn't have time to flinch, let alone duck. The tip grazed his cheek and slammed into the balustrade behind him.

"Gods! What are those?" Chusor asked out loud, for he had suddenly noticed something strange about the two lead Korinthian ships. They each had high double rams jutting from either side of their upper prows—long beams capped with bronze that stuck forward like the tusks of a boar. He had heard rumor of this Korinthian innovation: "boar teeth," they were said to be called. The Korinthians weren't going to meet them head-on, ram to ram. Instead they were bent on destroying the *Spear*'s outrigger deck—killing the stool rowers and thus disabling the boat's best oarsmen, then moving on to the next ship in line. The ships would all be sitting ducks after falling victim to that sort of maneuver.

One of the lead Korinthian ships—the one on the left—broke away from the other like a hunting dog anxious to be first upon the prey.

"Abandon the stool decks!" Chusor screamed at Ji. "Get the men to the gang-way!"

"Leave your oars!" Ji shouted instantly, pulling men off their seats and shov-ing them into the gangway. "Now!"

The ship was almost on them—coming at them as fast as a charging horse. "Pump! Diokles, pump!"

A moment later the Korinthian trireme hit the *Spear*, its upper ram plowing through the timbers of the outrigger deck on the *Spear*'s left side like a giant's fist.

The first ten seats of the outrigger deck, now empty of oarsmen, exploded in a shower of splinters.

Agrios turned the *Spear* hard to the right and the Korinthian's ram came clear of the trireme before it could rip apart the entire outrigger. The two vessels were so close together now that the warriors crowding the top of the Korin-thian ship could have leapt with ease onto the *Spear*'s battle deck, but the Ko-rinthian vessel was moving too fast to make this feat possible—it would have been like jumping safely from one moving war chariot to another. The triremes passed, hull to hull, and in a few seconds the Korinthian's stern was even with the *Spear*'s prow. An archer standing near the Korinthian's helmsman, barely ten feet away, aimed his arrow at Chusor's head and pulled back the string—

Suddenly a clear liquid spewed forth from the tube attached to the bolt shooter, and Chusor sprayed the surprised archer, helmsman, and four armored warriors with the poisonous mist. The archer, blinded, sent his arrow flying over Chusor's head. Chusor directed the stream of naptha along the hull, dousing the oarsmen at the back of the boat. As the Korinthian ship cruised past, Chu-sor directed the stream onto the waves, screaming, "Give me fire!"

The stunned doctor hesitated, then lurched forward and thrust the torch against the tube. Fire exploded from the nozzle, billowing out and singing the beard from Ezekiel's face, and he fell backward. But a stream of fire erupted from the hose all the way down to the sea. The water itself roared to life—the strange fire burning on the top of the waves as though it were enchanted by a god. A trail of fire meandered quickly across the sea and up the side of the Ko-rinthian ship, setting rowers on fire and traveling in a blazing line to ignite the men on the upper deck who had been sprayed. They caught fire like pine-pitch torches. The Korinthian helmsman burst into flames and leapt from his seat, flinging himself into the water.

Chusor watched in awe. It had only taken a few seconds for the fire to race across the water once the naptha had been lit. The Korinthian ship was already spinning out of control. But in the heat of the battle he had forgotten about the other Korinthian ship that was next in line.

A sound of splintered wood exploded in Chusor's ears and the *Spear* shook. He turned to the right. The second Korinthian trireme had run into them with its top ram, driving into the *Spear*'s other outrigger deck. The ships were now locked together like two wrestlers. The host of armored Korinthian hoplites, kneeling on the battle deck, made ready to leap across to the *Spear*.

But Chusor turned the flame-spitting tube in their direction, dousing the warriors with liquid fire. The flames roiled over them in a cloud of orange-and-black death. The warriors shrieked as the skin melted from their faces and hands.

"Throw the pandoras!" shouted Chusor.

Ezekiel flung one of the pots and it burst apart on the enemy deck. A red flame roared halfway up the height of the mast, catching the flaxen sail on fire.

The next two Korinthian ships in line, evidently scared off by the sight of the burning ships, veered suddenly away from the *Spear* like spooked horses. But Chusor was able to spray one of them as it passed close by, setting the deck, rigging, sails, and helmsman on fire. Without a man at the rudder the ship went out of control, heading straight for the rocky shore.

Suddenly the fire from the tube went out. The bronze container of naptha had run dry.

"Refill the container!" Chusor shouted below. There were two more amphoras filled with naptha, but they had to be poured into the bronze container.

"I'm working on it!" Diokles shouted back.

The ship attached to the *Spear* burned like a massive floating bonfire, and with every pandora that Ezekiel threw at the deck and hull the flames roared higher.

Chusor glanced down at the ruined stool deck. Ji and four men were already at work hacking off the Korinthian's upper tusk ram where it was lodged in the framework, holding them fast to the burning vessel. The roaring fire on the enemy ship licked at the *Spear*'s side planks.

"Hurry, Ji!" Chusor yelled as he sent an arrow flying into the face of a Korinthian warrior who was leaning out of the Korinthian's outrigger deck, plunging his spear at Ji and the others.

The axes of Ji and his men flew, and soon the enemy ram came free and splashed into the sea. The *Spear*'s mariners pushed off from Korinthian trireme, using their oars to shove their ship away from the doomed vessel, even as enemy warriors leapt to the *Spear* for safety and were beaten back by the mariners with their bare fists or hewed with axes and pushed over the side. They sank like stones in their armor, burning even as they plunged into the depths from this uncanny fire that an ocean of water would not quench.

SIXTEEN

Nikias, Konon, and Melitta stood on the bald hillside above the coast, struck dumb by the awesome spectacle of the sea battle taking place before their eyes in the light of dawn.

They had caught sight of the two lines of ships below, heading for each other from opposite directions on an inevitable path to destruction. Nikias had plainly made out the figures of Chusor and Ezekiel standing on the prow of the trireme, with the three other ships in a staggered line behind. When the first Korinthian vessel slammed into the outrigger deck of the *Spear*, it took a split second for the cracking sound of splintered wood to carry across the water to Nikias's ears, and Melitta fell to her knees and cried out in fear, "Father!"

What happened next—the dreamlike chaos of a sea battle watched from afar—played out so fast that it made Nikias's head swim: fire arcing through the air, another ship colliding with the *Spear* that was quickly torched, a third ship set on fire, and burning men leaping to their deaths in the churning waves.

Only a few minutes had gone by, but already three of the mighty Korinthian triremes were fiery wrecks. Two more had collided with each other in their panic to avoid the *Spear* and its terrible flame-throwing weapon, and were now sailing out of control toward the rocky shore, the ram of one ship lodged in the twin rudders of the other like a dog with its nose in another dog's arse.

"Gods! Look!" said Konon, just as the *Argo* and a Korinthian ship met prow to prow.

Crack!

The noise carried up the hillside like the sound of two mountain sheep ramming horns, and the stern of each ship seemed to rise up for an instant from the force of the meeting. Or was that a trick of Nikias's imagination? Mariners from the *Argo* swarmed over the prow and onto the enemy ship but were met by a force of equal numbers.

The *Spear*, despite its partially ruined outrigger decks on both sides, had somehow managed to get itself back under oar power. It headed straight at the two Korinthian triremes that were locked together ram to rudder. When it was within twenty feet the arc of fire roared to life again and Chusor moved the spray back and forth relentlessly, like a cruel and unforgiving god of fire, punishing the Korinthians, turning their ships to burning hulks, burning its mariners alive as though they were twigs cast into the coals of an ore furnace.

"Look!" said Konon, pointing to where the last two Korinthian ships had turned out to sea and were fleeing the battle. "They're running!"

Nikias stared back at the battle. The *Aphrodite* and the *Democracy* had finally caught up with the *Argo*. They came to a drifting stop along either side of the Korinthian trireme that the *Argo* had rammed and its men leapt to the battle deck of the enemy vessel to join their brothers in the slaughter.

"Come down to the water!" said Melitta with excitement. "My father is heading to the cove to pick up our people."

The *Spear* had disengaged from the battle. Its fire had gone out and it was moving toward the triangular promontory in the distance. The battle was won. Hundreds of the enemy had been burned alive, along with five of their ships. One Korinthian trireme was captured and two others were already far away, fleeing to the west. Chusor's genius had saved them all. But where was Helena?

Nikias pulled himself away from the sight of the burning ships and followed Melitta—she had bolted over the ridgeline in the direction of the cove.

"Come on!" he called to Konon as he ran, for the Athenian had not moved, evidently hypnotized by the sea battle.

"Eh?"

"Let's go!" said Nikias.

They ran for another quarter of a mile, chasing after the long-legged and deer-like Melitta, who outpaced them both. Suddenly she came to a stop on the edge of a cliff.

"No!" she screamed.

Nikias sprinted up to her and stared down at a rocky point jutting into the heaving sea. This jagged headland was shaped like an inverted triangle, or a primitive two-sided axe head wedged into the shore, creating two protected coves on either side. The narrower and deeper inlet on the left was deserted. But the bigger bay on the right had a wide, crescent-shaped beach that was strewn with corpses, and a black Korinthian trireme—alive with activity—sat in the calm, shallow water just offshore. A battle had been fought here—a brief and bloody battle in which one side had been completely overwhelmed and vanquished. The men and women had fled from the stronghold to the Double Axe cove, only to find the enemy already waiting for them. The men were slain, but the women and children were kept alive and now Korinthian warriors were frantically handing up this human chattel to mariners on the outrigger deck, who pulled them roughly aboard, tossing them into the hold like sacks of wheat.

A cry ripped from Nikias's throat as he caught sight of Helena. She was kicking and screaming, pulled aboard by two mariners—one holding her under each arm. They dragged her onto the deck and pummeled her until she stopped moving.

Their prizes stowed, the Korinthian warriors scrambled up the landing ladders. Almost immediately the ship's oars swept back and forth as one, and the trireme cruised away from the shore, moving swiftly toward the promontory that protected the twin coves while Melitta shrieked with outrage at the top of her lungs, "Come back! Come back!"

The Korinthians had already stepped their masts, and as soon as they were around the triangle-shaped promontory, Nikias knew, they would raise sails and catch the powerful wind. And then they would sail off with their human cargo, and Nikias would never see Helena again.

"What do we do?" asked Konon in despair.

Nikias looked to the left. He could see the *Spear* moving toward the promontory from the opposite direction, straining against the wind a quarter of a mile away, the waves breaking against the prow and exploding so high that the battle deck was covered with water. The Korinthian trireme was already rounding the little headland. The two sails unfurled and the trireme leapt forward and sailed straight out to the open sea.

"What do we do?" repeated Konon.

Nikias, frustration boiling up inside him, screamed in rage, "I don't know!" Every second counted. They couldn't wait for the *Spear* to make it to the cove. The wind was so strong now, it might take them a quarter of an hour or more to get here. If the Korinthian trireme was lost from sight, they would never find the ship.

"Here! Help me!" shouted Melitta. She had run down to the cove on the left-hand side of the isthmus—the side nearest the *Spear*—and was trying to push a little beached fishing boat into the water.

Nikias scrambled down the rocks and over to the boat, shoving it off the shore with a mighty heave. Melitta sprang into the craft and he jumped in beside her. The boat bobbed precariously. The girl went to work stepping the mast and sorting out the sail and rigging as though she'd done it a hundred times before.

"Chusor—my father—taught me to sail," she said.

Konon came running up, plunging into the water, and stopped short when Nikias held up his hand.

"You have to stay," said Nikias. "There's not enough room in this boat. We have to get to the *Spear* before that Korinthian ship is out of sight."

Konon looked crestfallen but he replied, "I understand."

Melitta dropped the sail and the boat sprang forward like a colt.

Nikias looked back over his shoulder and said, "Go back to the camp and wait, Konon! Find anybody else left alive from the stronghold! We'll come back for you!"

"Luck be with you!" called Konon, looking very forlorn.

The fishing boat raced out of the cove with Melitta holding on to the tiller with one hand and the sail rope with the other, propelled by the ever-increasing wind. Nikias could see the Korinthian ship heading north—it was already well past the *Spear*. The enemy trireme's battle deck was crowded with men. Nikias could tell they were staring in wonder at the burning ships of their fleet. He saw a man signaling to the helmsman and the ship turned sharply away from the shore. The Korinthians were not going to make an effort to rescue any of their men. They were running.

Melitta guided the fishing boat straight at the *Spear*, and when they got close enough to hail the ship, Nikias cupped his hands to his mouth and called out, "Chusor! Chusor!" But no one was at the prow. The trireme, its upper decks smashed in on either side, plowed on into the waves like a wounded and insensate beast.

"They can't hear us!" shouted Melitta.

She turned the fishing boat straight into the path of the *Spear* as if to ram it.

"What are you doing?" Nikias yelled. "They'll run us down! They can't see us!"

"I know what I'm doing!" she shouted back.

The trireme was almost on them when she pushed the rudder hard to the right and the fishing boat careened to the left, nearly dumping Nikias into the water. He clung to the side of the boat as it drove into the banks of oars, then it slammed straight into the side of the *Spear*. The fishing boat flipped over and something struck Nikias on the back of the head. He went under the water—the bitter cold water. His eyes were filled with stars. He reached up with both hands, grabbing blindly, and came to the surface gasping for air, clutching something thin and hard, like a wooden arm.

"Hey! It's Nikias! Hanging on my oar!" It was a Plataean voice calling with astonishment from the middle deck.

Confusion. Cold water. A rush of sounds. Hands seizing hold of him, pulling him from the sea and onto the ruined outrigger deck as all of the paddles ceased and the trireme slowed.

"By Zeus's bloated balls, what are you playing at?"

It was Chusor, staring down at him, face twisted in wrath. But his features were all blurry, and there was a mighty ringing in Nikias's ears. He tried to lift his head and a blinding pain flashed in his brain.

"Melitta?" gasped Nikias. "Where is she?"

"Melitta?" replied Chusor, confused.

"She was in the boat," said Nikias, struggling to get to his feet, but his knees buckled and he dropped back to the deck. Then he swooned and the world turned gray and strange. "The ship—" he said, but his mouth stopped working and the deck and Chusor seemed to tilt slowly to one side. He felt nothing when he hit the deck, and he closed his eyes. . . .

He was on Photine, riding across the Kithaerons, chasing a boar as big as a bull. As the boar ran, it shat out gold darics with a sound that went *apop*! The darics turned into Spartan warriors who smiled at him and begged him to stop, for apparently they wanted to be friends. He tried to cut off their heads as he rode past, but his sword had turned into a thistle stalk that bounced off their helms. The boar finally morphed into Eurymakus the Theban, who knocked Nikias from his horse with a wave of his hand. Nikias fell to the ground and was surrounded by snakes.

"The name of my angel dies with you," said Euryamakus. "And now I must wrap your head in linens."

And then everything was peaceful and calm.

SEVENTEEN

———————◆———————

When Nikias awoke he was lying on his back on the outrigger deck with Ezekiel leaning over him, wrapping something around his head. He could hear the rowers chanting rhythmically, an old oarsman song that mimicked the sound of the blade striking the water:

"Apop, apop, apop, apop!"

He could sense that the *Spear* was moving fast. Much faster than it could under oars alone.

"The girl!" said Nikias.

"She's safe," said Ezekiel. "They found her clinging to the bottom of the fishing boat where it was pinned against the hull of the *Spear*. She's unharmed."

Nikias struggled to a sitting position, peering down the gangway. The light hurt his eyes and he squinted. He could see masts rising from the floor of the hull and the spider's work of the rigging. They were under sail.

"How long was I out?"

"Two hours. This is the second time I've changed your bandage. Your head bleeds profusely. Good veins."

"Where's Chusor?"

"At the prow. But you shouldn't move. You've sustained a proper skull rattle. Your pupils are still wide-open. You had a nasty gash on the back of your head. Lost a lot of blood. I sewed it up but still it leaks and—"

"I'm fine," said Nikias, who had suffered more concussions than he could count on his fingers and toes. He tried to get up but he was too dizzy. He leaned over and vomited unexpectedly, spraying the men below.

"Hey, watch it!" one of them called up angrily.

"Help me to the prow," said Nikias, touching his linen-wrapped head.

Ezekiel helped him get to the little deck at the front of the ship where Chusor stood as still as a statue, hands gripping the rail, staring into the distance, his frowning and lined face resembling a graven god of the sea. Nikias squinted in the same direction and saw the Korinthian ship no more than half a mile ahead.

"Zeus," he said under his breath, a quiet prayer of thanks.

He glanced behind him, down the length of the ship to where the helmsman sat. The island of Serifos was long gone and the sky between them was roiling with dark and dangerous-looking clouds. The sea had turned from blue to dirty gray.

"Will we catch the Korinthian ship?" asked Nikias. He wondered what Helena was thinking now. She had no idea that the *Spear* was behind her. Were the Korinthians already raping her in the filthy hold?

"We will catch them," said Chusor. "The *Spear*'s crew is breaking their backs to save their kin. And the Plataean and Athenian rowers on this crew lust for more enemy blood. Besides, we carry three sails to their two."

Nikias had never heard of a trireme putting up three sails. He looked behind him again and noticed there was a smaller sail in front of the mainmast. Another of Chusor's innovations, no doubt.

An hour went by and during that time the wind continued to howl, the sails were stretched taut, and ever so slowly the space between the Korinthian ship and the *Spear* grew less. Nikias could see men at the back of the ship, staring at the *Spear* and pointing, as if they were debating what to do about the approaching ship.

"They can't turn and face us on this rough sea," said Chusor. "If they get sideways to the waves they might capsize. That's what they're talking about."

After a while the Korinthians started throwing things overboard—amphoras, barrels, and sacks that were no doubt filled with booty pillaged from the island stronghold.

"Will the storm catch us?"

"Yes. And soon."

They were silent. The sound of the wind roared in their ears along with the ceaseless "*Apop, apop, apop*" chant of the crew and the endless drone of the pipe and Ji's encouraging voice:

"Those are your women! Those are your children! Fight for them now!"

After a long silence Chusor said, "Melitta told me that you saved her from the Korinthians." He turned and looked at Nikias—his dark brown eyes were welled up with tears. "I owe you a great debt, Nikias. A *great* debt."

"We are friends," said Nikias. "There is no debt between us. I love you like a brother."

"And I you."

"Where is Melitta?"

"In my cabin," said Chusor. "She's exhausted. A brave girl."

"And clever," said Nikias. "Like her father."

Chusor smiled wryly. "Let us hope she has better *judgment* than her father."

"We all make mistakes," said Nikias.

"I have made more than most men," said Chusor. "And I have much blood on my hands. I killed hundreds of men today. Burned them alive."

"You did it to protect Melitta," said Nikias.

"How many men must we slay to protect the ones we love?" Chusor asked.

Nikias had no reply to this question. He knew that he would kill ten thousand men or more to protect his wife, daughters, and sister. His head and neck ached and he had to steady himself against the rail.

"You should go below," said Chusor.

Nikias didn't budge.

"So be it."

Chusor went to work on the bolt shooter, turning the wood crank that pulled back the powerful bowstring. His arms bulged as he worked the big wooden crank. The skeins that pulled back the taut string, Diokles had told Nikias on the journey from Athens, were woven with hair from the women of Serifos— much stronger than any rope. Chusor locked the string into place with a hook, then reached down and took hold of a three-foot-long bronze dart as thick as a child's arm and an arrowhead three times the size of the head of a battle spear. At the butt end of the projectile was an eyelet, as on a needle, and through this Chusor stuck a length of rope and tied it off.

"What is that for?" asked Nikias.

"We're going to catch ourselves a ship," said Chusor. "And then pull it in like a fish on a hook."

"And then?"

"We fight to the death. It will be a terrible battle, for we are evenly matched in numbers. We'll have to storm the enemy ship and fight them on the decks."

"Do you have any pandoras?"

"We cannot risk burning the enemy ship. The women and children—"

"Of course."

They got closer and closer. It started to rain and lightning flashed behind them, followed by a peal of thunder. Chusor called down to Ji and announced that soon they would be in range of the Korinthian ship. "When I fire the bolt, send me fifty men to pull the line!" he shouted down the gangway. Ji nodded and went back to exhorting the men. Nikias saw Diokles glance back over his shoulder. The Helot looked nervous but he kept pulling hard on his oar.

"What are they doing?" hissed Chusor.

Nikias turned and looked at the Korinthian ship. The warriors on the battle deck were throwing things off into the swelling waves—things that were moving.

"Gods, no!" blurted Nikias as he saw a little screaming boy hurled overboard, followed by a shrieking woman.

"They're jettisoning the prisoners!" Chusor shouted to Ji, and the exhorter relayed this message to the crew.

Bodies flew into the water, one after the other—fifty or more. Some sunk straight into the churning waves and did not come back up. But others shot to the surface, flailing desperately, their heads bobbing above the waves. Soon there were a hundred or more in the water, floating quickly toward the *Spear*. Nikias's heart pounded. For a split second he saw a young woman's face bobbing past, mouth open in silent terror, and he reacted without thinking—he jumped to the rail and dove in the water. The instant he came up he started swimming hard.

"Helena!" he cried, taking in a mouthful of water. "Helena!"

The *Spear* raced past. He looked back and saw something shoot from its prow—the bolt trailing its line of rope. It hit the Korinthian ship's rudder with a thud.

Nikias saw a little girl floating toward him, desperately trying to stay afloat. He reached out and grabbed her by the hair and pulled her to him.

He looked around in a frenzy. He saw mariners leaping from the *Spear* while men on the upper deck hurled objects into the sea: pieces of wood, boxes, extra spars and beams—anything for the people in the water to cling to.

Nikias saw a young woman's face fifty feet away—she went under. He hugged the little girl to him and kicked over to the drowning woman.

"Helena!" he cried.

He grabbed the woman around the waist and held her tight, swimming on his back with the girl clutched to one side and the woman to the other. The woman turned her wild eyes to him and he realized that she wasn't Helena.

"My baby!" the woman howled, clawing at his face to let her free. "Where's my baby!"

"Stop!" shouted Nikias. "You'll kill us all!"

But she would not listen. She scratched his cheek, drawing blood, and he took in a great gulp of water when a wave hit him in the side of the face. He let the woman go, otherwise she would have pulled him under, and she took one last look at him with her crazed eyes before disappearing under the sea.

Nikias held the little girl's head above the water and swam with one arm, trying to move in the direction of the *Spear*. In the troughs of the waves he could see mariners and other women and children who had been cast from the Korinthian ship.

"Come together!" shouted one of the marauder crew members. He was holding on to a spar with one hand and a half-drowned woman with the other. "Come together!" he repeated, his deep voice rising above the waves.

Nikias grabbed onto the spar and placed the little girl's hands on it. "Hold on!" he commanded. "Don't let go!" Then he swam off to help a mariner who was pulling two grown women through the water toward the spar.

Time lost all meaning. The world became nothing more than tossing waves and a thunderous sky and shivering bodies clinging to the spar. Nikias searched the water relentlessly, leaving the spar to seek out survivors, sometimes returning with a woman or a child who had somehow stayed alive on the rough waves. But many of the women and children could not swim, and so the sea was littered with the dead. The last one he found alive was a black-haired boy, stuck to an amphora like a limpet. The amphora's mouth was still sealed with its wax plug, otherwise the jar would have sunk like a stone.

By the time Nikias had utterly exhausted himself, there were twenty or so woman and children clinging to the spar and five or six mariners. As the waves rose and dipped, Nikias caught sight of other clusters of survivors, but sometimes, after a big wave came, they would vanish, pulled down to Poseidon's realm.

In the distance he saw a fire burning on the water. Whether it was the *Spear* or the Korinthian trireme, he could not tell. The lips of the people around him were turning blue. They wouldn't last for much longer in this frigid water. This sea was colder than the hands of Thanatos, the god of death.

No one spoke. No one had the energy. And what was there to say?

Erratic images flitted through Nikias's tired brain. He saw Kallisto and his daughters playing in the yard of the farm. He saw Helena dressed in her goatherd's clothes. He remembered the strange vision of the boar shitting gold darics and then turning into Eurymakus the Theban. And the eclipse. And the dead fox in the field that his grandfather had found. And the snake that swallowed the baby owl. And so many other mysterious signs. He wondered what it all meant. Any of it. Were they messages from the gods or just happenings? What did life mean?

A saying kept rolling over and over in his mind: "If only humans could be a scourge to the gods like they are to us." Who had said that? Where had he heard that before?

Somebody uttered a sigh next to him. He turned and saw the boy he'd found clinging to the amphora close his eyes then slip under the water as though he were falling into a soft bed. But Nikias grabbed him by the tunic and hauled him to the surface. "Wake up!" he yelled, and the boy's lids fluttered open.

Up and down on the sea they went—a sea that had turned as dark as the sky above. Nikias had faced death before, but it had never been so tedious. He realized how parched his mouth felt. How he couldn't feel his feet anymore. It seemed as if he had always been clinging to this spar—and would cling to it forever.

In a mist of rain he saw the *Spear* coming toward them, appearing out of nowhere as if in a dream. Its sails were down and only half the oars were at work, stirring the sea feebly. The old marauder with the deep voice—the one who had first called the others over to the spar—cried out, "Look!" and let forth a wild laugh.

The ship was real. And Chusor was at the prow, scanning the water like a hawk. When he saw them he pointed and shouted, "There!"

The *Spear* fought against a powerful wind, but the survivors clinging to the spar were moving with the current, and soon they bumped against the prow. Mariners reached down and hauled them on board. Nikias was the last one to leave the sea. They had to carry him to the gangway, for his legs would not move and his teeth chattered so hard they sounded like bone dice in a clay cup. He sat huddled with the others in the narrow hold, staring into space. Lightning flashed directly overhead, and a hard rain came, beating on the cloth covers that had been put up to keep the rain out of the open gangway. He drifted in and out of consciousness.

Then he saw two strong legs standing in front of him.

"You are the luckiest bastard I have ever known," said a raspy voice.

Nikias looked up. There stood Chusor, covered in blood, a wicked slash across his left pectoral, another across the right side of his cheek from eye to earlobe. One of his arms was badly burned and the skin was blistered and blackened. But he was smiling out of the side of his mouth.

"Wha—what happened?" Nikias stammered.

"We won," said Chusor, his voice obviously hoarse from screaming orders—from screaming in battle. "We burned the Korinthian hoplites and archers off their battle deck, then stormed the ship in the flames. We found more women and children in their hold. Our men fought like animals. It was a thing to see. The Plataeans and Athenians gave no quarter. Many died. Once we had killed all of the enemy—down to the last man—we left their ship to burn. We've been searching the sea for hours since then. Two men died at the oars from exhaustion. But the others wouldn't give up. You seem to be the last of the survivors," he added. "A third of our rowers are either dead in battle or drowned searching for their kin. We saved a hundred or so of the women and children. Now the storm is on us. And it might kill us all anyway."

Nikias closed his eyes and felt the huge up-and-down lift of a swell. He tried to speak, but his emotions had robbed him of his voice. "And Helena?" he finally forced himself to ask, fearing the answer.

When he opened his eyes Chusor was gone, but Helena was kneeling before him. Her face was bloodied and bruised. But she was alive and her eyes were filled with an inextinguishable light. He laughed with joy—a choking laugh that quickly turned into a sob. He tried to lift his arms to hold her but they were so heavy and numb, he could not make them work. He slumped into her and she embraced him.

"Chusor told me that you leapt into the sea for me," she said, her voice full of awe, full of love.

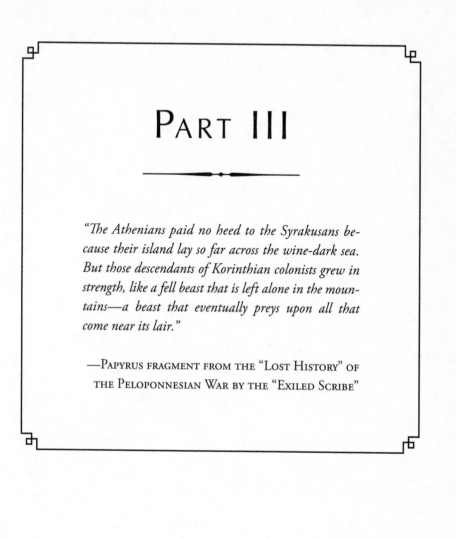

PART III

"*The Athenians paid no heed to the Syrakusans because their island lay so far across the wine-dark sea. But those descendants of Korinthian colonists grew in strength, like a fell beast that is left alone in the mountains—a beast that eventually preys upon all that come near its lair.*"

—Papyrus fragment from the "Lost History" of the Peloponnesian War by the "Exiled Scribe"

ONE

———◆———

Kolax's new master, Andros the Korinthian, had given him free rein to wander anywhere in the citadel of Syrakuse, just so long as he came back to the house where they were staying before nightfall. Then, during the evening meal, Andros would pester him with all kinds of annoying questions, asking him about the most seemingly insignificant details of the things that he had seen and overheard in the agora, or by the sacred fountain of Arethusa, or at the wharves of Ortygia—the little isle connected by a narrow stone bridge to the main island of Sicily and the place called the New City.

Kolax had decided to play along with Andros, biding his time and humoring the man until they went back to Greece and he could make his escape from the devious spy. It wasn't that he didn't like the man. He had many good qualities for a Korinthian: he was kind and knew how to make a good joke, he spoke fluent Skythian, he let Kolax drink as much uncut wine as he wanted and gave him silver coins to spend as he pleased, and he'd never once tried to rape his arse. And besides all that, Andros had saved him from those cistern-arsed Dog Raiders who were going to skin and roast him alive.

But Kolax felt as though he were repaying his life debt to Andros by being slowly bored to death. First he'd been forced to ride all the way from the Dog Raider camp in Megaria to Korinth clinging to Andros's back like a toddler. Then, before Kolax had had time to even take a crap or plan his escape back to Plataea, they boarded a trireme that took them on the spectacularly dull journey across the Gulf of Korinth, stopping each night at Korinthian forts and shabby little villages all along the way, then continued on across the mind-numbingly tedious sea to the island of Sicily—a trip that took fourteen days or more, for Kolax lost count in his apathy. They were over four hundred sea miles from Athens, whatever that meant. Kolax knew that it was a long, long way.

Along the journey Andros had forced Kolax to start wearing stupid Greek clothes, and made him do lessons every day, like sea navigation, and reading, and numbers, and even practicing Kolax's pronunciation of Greek words until he thought his lips might fall off.

"You're a quick learner, Kolax," Andros said to him once in Skythian. "But you need to learn patience. The secret to life is ataraxia—and that means equanimity. You must be evenly balanced like this ship, or else you will flip over and spill your cargo."

Kolax laughed at this bit of advice. He repeated the words that he had told Andros when they'd first met in Athens years ago: "My papa taught me the Three Skills of the Skythians—riding, shooting, and the counting of our gold . . . and that is all a man really needs to know."

Kolax had told Andros everything about his own history: how he had been captured by an enemy tribe and sold into slavery. How he had been purchased by Chusor the smith and helped the Plataeans defeat the Thebans on the night of the sneak attack. And how he had gone to Athens with Nikias, hoping to find his father, who had enlisted with the Athenians when Kolax was a small boy. That was where Kolax had first met Andros.

It was a strange tale, and one that Andros said was worthy of a book.

Now, walking across the busy bridge that led from the isle citadel of Ortygia to the mainland district for the twentieth time in as many days, Kolax wondered, for the thousandth time, if his papa and the other Skythians were still alive. Andros had told him that the fortress of the Three Heads had been seized by the Spartans, but no Skythians had been captured there. Had his people abandoned the stronghold and gone to Plataea? Or were they hiding somewhere in the Kithaeron Mountains? Kolax had heard there was a famous soothsayer living here in Syrakuse. Perhaps the soothsayer could tell him if his father was still alive.

The soothsayer lived with the man everyone called the Tyrant—a powerful oligarch named General Pantares who controlled Syrakuse and made war on other city-states with a ruthless fervor. Pantares was the man whom Andros had come on this long journey to see, but the spy had been kept waiting for weeks, and Kolax was amused to see Andros's precious ataraxia—his equanimity—slowly erode, to be replaced by a seething petulance. Kolax had discovered that Andros was a man of high standing . . . a dangerous man, to be treated with respect and fear. But Pantares ruled Syrakuse like one of the tyrants of old, obsessed with making his city-state the strongest in the land, and guided by a belief that Apollo—whose sacred shrine was said to stand on the exact spot where that god's mother had given birth to his twin sister, Artemis—watched over Pantares above all other Greeks.

Kolax had been to the temple of Apollo on Ortygia several times since they had been on the island. And he thought it looked just like every other temple he had ever seen in Greece: columns, carvings, droning priests, a statue . . . boring as shit.

Kolax crossed the bridge and stopped by a shield maker's storefront, staring at himself in the burnished surface of an unpainted shield, shaking his head with disgust at the lanky lad staring back at him. He felt so silly with his cropped hair—which Andros had forced him to dye black as soon as they arrived in Syrakuse—and this ridiculous short tunic and frilly sandals. At least Andros had given him a knife to wear on his belt, otherwise he would have felt utterly enfeebled. If his cousin Griffix could see him now, he would laugh his head off.

"—stuff the Spartans! They can't tell us what to do. And neither can the bloody Korinthians. Syrakuse rules Syrakuse as we have for centuries—"

"The Tyrant rules Syrakuse, you mean—"

"Pantares is a strong leader for dangerous times. He doesn't have to buy my vote. Our city-state may have been founded by the Korinthians, but that doesn't mean we have to bend over and grab our heels for them every time they . . .'"

Kolax listened with half an ear to the two men in the shield shop speaking with heated voices. Everywhere in the city men were talking about the Spartans and Korinthians and whether or not to side with them in the war with the Athenians. Most of the citizens of Syrakuse, Kolax knew from his conversations with Andros, were more interested in trading and making money than waging war. And they had their own enemies to deal with—rebellious city-states on the island of Sicily and Karthaginian pirates on the seas, not to mention the warlike Tyrsenians, who inhabited a place called Italia to the north. Nobody in Syrakuse wanted to send ships across the sea to fight against Athens. It seemed like a preposterous notion to the islanders to go all that way for a war. Disaster was the only thing that could come of an expedition so far from home.

Kolax yawned loudly and wandered to a pottery shop next door, perusing the plates, bowls, and vases displayed on the shelves. Most of them had naughty scenes that made Kolax laugh, especially one showing a satyr with an erection that was so huge, it took four slaves to help support the thing. He wished that Mula were here so that they could laugh about the picture together. He became sad, wondering if Mula had made it down the mountain that day they bolted from the cave. The boy was fast, and he had had a good head start.

He picked up a little olive oil container bearing a picture of an enormous griffin harnessed to a chariot and driver. The griffin was Kolax's family symbol, and his father had tattooed a snarling griffin on Kolax's upper back when he was a child. This container was an excellent piece of work, in the Skythian lad's opinion. The artist had drawn the griffin's eagle face with a fierce eye and muscular wings. And the charioteer was leaning forward over the top of the cart, his mouth open and his brow frowning as if he were shouting at the huge beast to hurry up.

He traced a finger over the letters written above the charioteer's head. "Dionysus," he read aloud. Phile would be surprised at how fast he could read now. Andros's shipboard lessons had taught him much. He could even write fluently now. He would make her a poem telling her how much he enjoyed her shapely hips and generous breasts. Merely thinking about her body made him feel odd. He looked down and realized that his tunic had started to rise up like a tent from his growing hard-on. Stupid Greek clothes! Skythian pants of leather were so much better.

"Hey!" said an angry female voice. "Put that down, you filthy boy!" An old veiled woman hustled over to him and snatched the container from his hand. "These aren't for fondling," she added, glancing at his puffed-up tunic with an offended look.

Kolax snatched the container back from her. "I've got coins in my purse, old harpy," he said, and was pleased with her look of surprise when he pulled out a Syrakusan coin and held it before her rheumy eyes, pinched between his thumb and forefinger. "I'll take this one and this other one too," he said, picking up the plate with the picture of the satyr with the giant prick. "I want them packed in a box, protected with straw," he said. "Pack them well, for I'm going to be making a sea voyage off of this dog's bunghole of an island, and not soon enough for my liking," he added under his breath.

To kill some time while the old woman packed up his purchase, Kolax ambled over to the big quarry near the new theatre, half a mile from the shops. The stones from the gigantic quarry pit had been used to construct the theatre and many other buildings in Syrakuse, or so a pesky guide had blathered to him the first time he wandered over this way. The guide also told him that there were more than three thousand men living in the pits right now—foreigners captured by the Syrakusans, pirates, criminals, and enemies of General Pantares.

When Kolax got to the path near the quarry, he spotted the guide—an oily little man with a haughty face—attempting to entice two Korinthian mariners on a guided tour of the area. They were rowers whom Kolax recognized from the *Bane of Attika*—Andros's trireme, a ship that was sitting in a boat shed on the isle of Ortygia. They'd been marooned in Syrakuse just like Kolax.

"Don't pay that goat-stuffing ape anything!" yelled Kolax to the mariners. "I'll show you all about the pit for free."

The guide gave Kolax a dark look and the mariners told the Syrakusan to shove off. The seething guide slunk off to the shade of an olive tree as the mariners walked over to Kolax, who led them to the rim of the quarry, standing precariously close to the edge, for the Skythian lad had no fear of heights. He looked down upon the pit, scored with countless chasms and chutes so that the quarrymen could get at the best limestone deep below the surface. Here and there he saw the tiny bodies of the men walking about or cutting stone below. They looked like ants from up here.

"How far down is that?" asked one of the mariners in awe.

"Over a hundred feet," said Kolax. "They have to lower the new prisoners down on that crane over there. The Syrakusan soldiers can't risk going into the pits. The men would kill them. They're led by somebody called the Quarry Lord, a Karthaginian pirate who kills men with a stone club and drinks their blood."

"Gods, the place is enormous," said the other mariner.

"I wish we could stick all of the Athenians down there and let them rot," said the first mariner.

"See that huge crevice in the rock across the way?" asked Kolax. "The enormous thing in the wall of the quarry that looks like a woman's gash? That's the Ear of Dionysus, a great cave inside the quarry. They say that if you stand on the ground above the Ear in a special listening place, you can hear everything that's said in the cavern below—even the faintest whisper. Andros told me that General Pantares comes to the listening place every night and puts his ear to it so that he can hear if any of his enemies down in the quarry are talking about him."

The Korinthian mariners looked at him dubiously. "Why would Pantares care what they're saying?" one of them asked. "They're in the pit. They'll never get out."

"I don't know," said Kolax, shrugging and turning slightly scarlet. "Hey, smell the corpses?" he asked, brightening, for the wind had just shifted in their direction and was whipping up the sheer side of the quarry. "The prisoners heap their dead below us here and let them rot. Some people say they eat the choicest parts of the corpses first," he added with macabre glee.

The mariners paled and turned away from the quarry. They had no desire to linger near such a loathsome place and headed off to a brothel they had heard about. They asked Kolax if he wanted to join them, but Kolax had never been with a woman and told them he was saving his sacred seed for his future wife and thought to himself, "Hopefully, Nikias's lovely sister."

He walked around the perimeter of the quarry to the west side where there was a walled-off area, hurling stones into the quarry as he went. He came to a ten-foot-high wall that surrounded a section of the ground next to the quarry's sheer edge. In the wall was a portal guarded by armed men who stood glowering on either side. Over this wall, Andros had told Kolax, was the listening place for the Ear of Dionysus. Kolax wanted more than anything to sneak over the wall and have a listen at the Ear. Andros would be impressed if he managed to pull that off.

The door in the wall suddenly opened and a pretty young woman dressed in sable exited, accompanied by two sinister-looking bodyguards. These men had dark skin, black curling hair, slanted eyes, and slightly upturned noses. Although they had long beards, their upper lips were shaved. And the strange bronze helms that they wore, thought Kolax, were the stupidest things that he had ever seen. They were small and round and poorly made, lacking any cheek or nose guards. It looked like they were wearing shit pots on their heads!

The woman stared at the ground as she walked, arms crossed on her chest. Her face was pensive and agitated. Kolax thought her very pretty and stepped aside from the little path to make way for her and her scowling bodyguards, who glared at Kolax as though they might slay him merely for looking at the woman. Obviously she was someone important—a wealthy man's wife or a rich man's concubine.

As she walked past Kolax she gave him the merest glance, but then she stopped all at once and turned back, looking directly into his eyes with her keen gaze—eyes like daggers.

"A Skythian dressed as a Greek," she said in a cold voice. "Tell me who you are or my men will cut off your tongue and hurl you into the Prison Pits."

TWO

———————◆———————

Kolax tried not to show his surprise. He returned the gaze of the strange woman. He didn't like being threatened by anyone, but for some reason he wasn't afraid of this creature, even though she had somehow guessed that he was a Skythian. She fascinated him, like a beautiful grass viper: menacing and alluring. Her bodyguards were dangerous enough, that was true. But he knew he could bolt right now and leave them all in the dust. He was fast and her men were heavy and wearing leather armor. But he didn't feel like running. It would be undignified. And so he remained silent.

"Who are you?" she repeated, fingering a gold ring on her right hand, twisting it round and round with the fingers of her other hand.

"Nobody," replied Kolax, meeting her gaze. "I'm just visiting this place."

She took a step toward him and looked him up and down from head to toe—until Kolax started to grow uncomfortable.

"I was only joking," she said all of a sudden, her face breaking into an impish smile. "About cutting off your tongue."

Kolax laughed. "What about throwing me into the pit?"

She ignored his question. "Tell me your name," she demanded.

"I am my master's servant," he said.

"And who is your master?"

"Andros the Korinthian."

"Oh, *him*," she said with a disdainful sniff, and chewed on her lower lip.

But Kolax asked, "How did you know that I'm Skythian?"

"You speak with a Skythian accent," she said. "But I knew where you came from before you had spoken to me. The shape of your face and nose. The color of your eyes. Your hair has been dyed. If I could see the hair under that tunic, I'm sure it would be a different color," she added with a lewd smile. "And finally, you stand bow-legged, as one who has spent more time on a horse's back than on his own two feet."

Kolax grinned. He was impressed. "You should become a soothsayer. You speak the truth. Can you see my father? Can you tell me where he is?"

She stared at him with an almost puzzled look, then reached out a hand and touched his cheek. He flinched at her touch, for her fingertips were cold, like those of a corpse.

"Who are you?" she repeated again, but this time her voice was low and urgent, as if she knew that Kolax was hiding something from her that was terribly important and it was imperative that he told her immediately.

Now that Kolax had stared at the woman for a while, her face started to change before his eyes. At first she had appeared wholly feminine, but now there seemed to be something masculine about her features that was showing through her skin, as though there were a man's bones underneath her flesh. He noticed the slight bulge at the top of her throat—

"A eunuch," blurted a voice in his head. In Skythia only the prettiest slave boys were selected for this horrifying change: they were tied down and had their balls crushed between two ingots of iron. Kolax and his friends had watched this alteration once, sneaking into a tent where it was taking place. He was fascinated by the boy's screams, for a Skythian eunuch was created without first taking opium or hemp—the men who made the eunuchs believed that the excruciating pain of having their gonads crushed sent a beneficial juice flowing through their organs.

He suddenly remembered something that Leo had told him back in Plataea—a story about a mysterious eunuch who had come to the citadel during the time that Kolax went to Athens with Nikias. Leo said that the eunuch was a friend of Chusor—that he was beauteous and forbidding and that Leo did not trust him. This eunuch was famous in Syrakuse, where he had spent much of his life. Could this be the same man? Kolax wasn't foolish enough to tell this stranger that he was a friend of Chusor, however. He had learned from Andros over the last month never to trust anyone with a secret. Especially not in this treacherous place—a city that was swarming with Spartan and Korinthian spies and the agents of General Pantares.

"I told you before," Kolax said, lowering his eyes submissively. "I am my master Andros's servant. And I must return to him now." He bowed and walked quickly away, and was relieved when the eunuch did not call his men to seize him. He glanced over his shoulders and saw him standing there, watching Kolax with a dark look on his pretty face.

When Kolax got back to the path near the southern edge of the quarry, he spotted the oily-looking guide lurking underneath an olive tree. The man now held a stout stick in one hand, and when he caught sight of Kolax he loped over to him, his face screwed up with fury, brandishing the stick in a threatening manner that made Kolax snicker.

"You!" said the guide. "I'll teach you a lesson!"

Kolax dodged the man's wild blow with a quick and fluid dart to the side, then kicked his legs out from under him. An instant later Kolax was kneeling on the man's chest with his dagger to his scrawny throat.

"Tour guide or assassin?" asked Kolax with a laugh.

The man's eyes bulged with terror as he stared at the gleaming dagger. "Apologies," he said meekly.

Kolax took out a silver drachma from his purse and said, "Open your mouth." The guide obeyed and Kolax stuck the drachma into his maw. "Now swallow." The man did as he was told. "Consider that a payment. The first of many, perhaps. Now tell me all that you know about the eunuch who was visiting the listening place behind the wall."

Walking back from the ceramic shop with his box under one arm, Kolax mused on the nature of fate. In Skythia, a chance meeting was called "a collision of arrows"—like two arrows, shot from different men's bows, meeting head-to-head in midair. The Syrakusan guide had told him that the eunuch was named Barka, and that was indeed the name of the eunuch that Leo had told him about in Plataea. Kolax wondered why the gods had brought him together with that sinister yet alluring man. The guide had also told him that Barka came to the listening place nearly every day, but he did not know why or under whose orders. Whatever the case, Kolax considered, this Barka was dangerous and should be avoided.

He returned to the house that he shared with Andros—an unremarkable little place on a narrow and twisting street near the harbor—and went directly into the kitchen, ordering the woman who cooked for them to make him something to eat. Andros returned while he was in the middle of his meal of bean soup and freshwater eels. The Korinthian was in a foul mood, the likes of which Kolax had rarely seen.

"What's wrong, master?" he asked.

"Word has come to me from a messenger ship," said Andros, sitting down and pouring himself some wine, "that one of our expeditions to root out some pirates on Serifos ended in disaster nearly a month ago."

"What happened?"

"Six triremes and their crews were lost."

"That's over twelve hundred men," said Kolax.

"Your multiplication has improved," said Andros with a mirthless smile.

"Thank you," replied Kolax.

"You don't understand sarcasm, do you, Kolax?"

"Master?"

"Twelve hundred men, and I will take the blame for their ineptitude," muttered Andros. He caught sight of the box on the floor at Kolax's feet and asked suspiciously, "What's this?"

"Nothing," said Kolax.

"A box of nothing?" Andros snatched it up and pried off the top. His dark look faded as he took out the plate embellished with the satyr. "A souvenir of Syrakuse?"

"For a friend," said Kolax.

Andros put the plate back in the box and interrogated him on what he had learned that day. Kolax told him about the conversation that he had overheard at the shield shop, and how he had taken the two mariners from the *Bane of Attika* on a tour of the rim of the quarry. But he said nothing about Barka the eunuch, nor did he say that he had recruited his own agent in the oily guide.

Andros had his secrets and Kolax had his own.

THREE

───────◆───────

Another two dreary weeks went by, and every few days Kolax went to the quarry and met with the guide, learning from him the schedule that Barka the eunuch kept on his visits to the listening place above the Ear of Dionysus. But Kolax was careful never to run into Barka again.

One afternoon, when Kolax had just returned from roaming the city, his master burst through the front door calling out, "Kolax! Put on your best tunic! We're going to a symposium!"

Andros was in a gay mood, for the symposium was at the palace of General Pantares. Kolax reluctantly put on a frilly tunic, a golden belt, and some fancy sandals, then walked alongside Andros through the winding streets to the best part of the citadel.

"You are my eyes and ears, young Kolax," Andros said. "Make yourself one with the walls and find me some diamonds."

"Diamonds" were what Andros called any bit of information that he believed to be valuable. So far Kolax had failed to deliver any of these illusionary gems.

"Yes, master," he said with a sigh. "I'll do my best."

The house of General Pantares was an enormous place, built of imported marble. Standing out front was a troop of armed guards—serious-looking men of the same race as the eunuch's bodyguards, with long chin beards and slightly upturned noses. They patted Kolax and Andros down, searching for hidden weapons.

When Kolax and Andros entered the front courtyard, they heard energetic harp music playing from within. Slaves came and led them to footbaths and removed their sandals, coating their feet in scented oils.

"Disgusting smell," said Kolax.

"Rose water," said Andros with a smile. "Would you prefer they bathed your feet in horse sweat?"

"That would be a joy," said Kolax. "And from what tribe are those pig's-arse-ugly guards out front?"

"Tyrsenians in the employ of Pantares," said Andros. "He has his own little army of them in the citadel. They're his police force, like the Athenians have your Skythian brethren. The Tyrsenians used to rule all of Italia, but they were defeated by the Syrakusans soon after the last Persian War. So they must earn their coins under Greek masters now."

"We Skythians don't have to serve anyone," said Kolax testily. "The Athenians pay well. When they stop paying, we move on."

"Would Skythian archers enlist with Korinthians like me?"

"We Skythians don't care which city's stamp a coin bears. The sweet jingling sound that they make in our pocket is exactly the same, be they Athenian owls or the winged horses of Korinth."

Andros laughed. "You are quite the pragmatist, young Kolax."

Kolax smiled. He was lying, of course. Neither he nor any of his Bindi kindred would serve the Korinthians. Maybe those Nuri dogs would lick the arses of the men of Korinth. But not Kolax and his tribe. Unless, of course, the pay was good. But Korinthians were notoriously tightfisted. And dishonest. At least, that's what his kinsman Skunxa had always told him. But Kolax didn't say what he was thinking. He had learned to honey his words and become a pragmatist under Andros's tutelage . . . even though he wasn't quite sure what being a pragmatist meant.

After scent had been applied to their hair, they were allowed to enter the big inner courtyard where the symposium was taking place. The harp music was louder here, but Kolax could not see where the musician was standing. There were fifty or so men and a few hetaerae milling about, along with some bejeweled lads with painted eyes. Everyone was drinking and talking so that the space was filled with the din of their voices and laughter. The walls around the courtyard, at first glance, were lined with the shapes of dark statues. But then Kolax realized that they were armed Tyrsenian warriors, watching the crowd with squinting eyes.

He looked up and saw that the harpist was sitting above them, suspended over the guests on a swing. Kolax scoffed. What a ridiculous profession. The only thing stupider and more useless than a musician, in his opinion, was an actor. Could not a man make his own music with voice or drum? Could not a man tell his own stories?

At the far wall was a large throne-like chair where a man sat dressed in a rich robe, his fingers adorned with rings that scintillated in the light. His bearded visage was stern and humorless. His dark eyes scanned the room from face to face, like a hawk deciding which mouse to swoop down on. There was a coiled menace in the big man who, to Kolax, looked like a pankrator who had given up his training and gone to seed, yet retained the killer instinct of one who has faced men down in the arena or in battle and beaten them soundly. He reminded Kolax of an evil and coldhearted version of the kindly Plataean Arkon Menesarkus—only with three double chins. In his hand this man held an object like a small head or a ball of gold.

"There sits Pantares," said Andros out of the side of his mouth. "None of your pert Skythian ways with him, mind you. He'll cut off your head and shove it up my arse. I've seen him slay men in here for sport. And ever since his beloved daughter died he's been as cruel as a Persian satrap."

"I'll keep out of the way," said Kolax.

When a slave approached with a tray filled with wine cups, Kolax grabbed one and slunk off toward the chamber where the slaves had washed their feet. He spotted some stairs leading to the balcony and ran up them, spilling his wine all over his tunic. He cursed and went to the balcony, leaning over it. This was a better place to watch what was going on than in the crowded courtyard below. After a while he saw Andros approach Pantares deferentially and the two spoke for a bit—rather, Andros spoke while Pantares listened and occasionally frowned or nodded ever so slightly, always fingering the golden object in his lap. After a time Pantares evidently grew frustrated with this interview and abruptly waved Andros away. Kolax could plainly see the look of dissatisfaction on his master's face.

The evening wore on and Kolax grew more and more weary, but he drank four more cups of wine, which took the edge off things. Some men got up and read poems about the glorious history of Syrakuse and the island of Ortygia, and a bard sang a tedious song about Apollo's seemingly endless attributes. Kolax thought he might slit his wrists from the dullness of it all. A party in Skythia meant dicing, drinking, and feats of strength. And sometimes even a bloody duel to the death. This sort of Greek festivity was worse than being skinned alive.

"You do not look very happy," said a purring voice at Kolax's side.

He turned and saw the brown feline face of Barka the eunuch smiling up at him. The short, slender creature with the face of a lovely teenaged girl put one of his cold hands on Kolax's arm and looked deep into his eyes.

"I-I'm enjoying myself," stuttered Kolax, caught completely off guard. "What are you doing here?" He could smell the eunuch's perfume emanating from his luxurious pile of hair and it was intoxicating, like wine mingled with orange blossoms.

"I live here," replied Barka, smiling impishly. "I am the soothsayer of Pantares. Didn't your greasy little spy the quarry guide tell you?"

"M-my what?" said Kolax, surprised that Barka knew of the man.

Barka's hand wandered down to his thigh, then slowly reached under his tunic. Kolax became very still, his heart racing.

"And I know who you are," Barka said, wrapping his cold fingers around Kolax's swelling member. "Shall I tell you your story? I've heard it all from my friends Chusor and Diokles." He kept stroking Kolax as he talked and gave him an impish and seductive smile. "We sailed together for a long time after we departed Plataea. The sea is a very dull place, as you might have discovered. We spent a lot of time talking about what had happened in that citadel. The Theban sneak attack. Your bravery. They thought you very brave, did you know that? Eh, *Kolax*? I can't imagine how you came to be here now in Syrakuse, with that Korinthian Andros. The tale must be fascinating. I long to hear it."

Barka put another hand on Kolax's chest and toyed with his nipple. Kolax's heart pounded in his ears. He felt a wild tingling up and down his spine that spread to his loins. Barka rose up on his toes and kissed Kolax full on the mouth—the eunuch's lips were warm, unlike his cold fingers. Kolax's voice caught in his throat as his hips bucked wildly, as though he had lost control of his body. Barka aimed him toward the wall of the balcony as he let forth a scream of ecstasy that was swallowed inside Barka's mouth.

The eunuch grinned and raised his eyebrows. "So fast, *Kolax*," he said, repeating the lad's name with smug satisfaction. "And you shoot your arrows so far!"

Kolax slumped to his knees in a combination of euphoria and humiliation.

"Clean yourself off," said Barka, taking a scarf from around his neck and tossing it to him.

All at once the crowd below in the courtyard stopped talking, for Pantares had stood up—the first time he had moved all evening—and was smiling nefariously at the partygoers.

"I have a surprise for all of you tonight," said Pantares in his deep voice—a threatening voice that made even the prospect of a surprise sound terrifying. "I had a visitor today. A mariner, he called himself"—this spoken with disdain—"who has been on a long and dangerous journey, or so he told me, across the sea. And he came to me bearing a relic of Apollo: a magnificent golden head that was fashioned long ago. This trader attempted to sell the valuable thing to me—or, rather, to trade it for food and supplies for his ship—knowing of my devotion to that god and his temple in our citadel. The thing that he brought to me I deem priceless—an object that I reckon has great magical power. An object that Barka, my soothsayer, told me years ago would come into my possession. The god himself has brought it to me and I will ensconce it in the treasury of the Temple of Apollo, to benefit all the citizens of Syrakuse!"

He lifted up his right arm to reveal the thing he had been cradling in his hands all night long—a smiling head of Apollo, gleaming of gold.

The partygoers clapped and cheered Pantares and wished him a long and happy life. And Pantares smiled back at them wickedly. "Now," he said, "let us meet this mariner and his servant. Bring them forth!" he said, snapping his fingers.

The doors to the courtyard flew open, slamming against the walls on either side. Kolax peered over the rail and saw a small troop of Tyrsenians enter leading two naked men, pulling them by chains attached to slave collars around the prisoners' necks. Kolax couldn't make out their faces from this angle, but he could see that one of the men was short and stocky, with black hair; the other, tall and blond. Both were muscled but overly lean, without an iota of fat on their bodies, like starved galley slaves. These wretched mariners had obviously been beaten by Pantares's henchmen, for their torsos and faces were covered with bruises and blood, and their arms were shackled to wooden stocks that they bore on their broad shoulders. Kolax wondered at the foolhardy nature of these mariners—these doomed traders—to try and deal with someone as notorious as Pantares. They must have been desperate.

As the Tyrsenians stepped aside and brought the prisoners to a stop in front of Pantares, the two bound men looked up. It was Barka who gasped first.

"No," said the eunuch in a barely audible whisper, digging into Kolax's arm with his sharp fingernails. "My Diokles—"

Then Kolax sucked in his breath, for he, too, recognized the Helot. And even though the other prisoner's face was tanned dark and lined from many days at sea—and his hair and beard longer than when Kolax had last seen him, and bleached almost white from the sun—he recognized his old friend at once, and the blood in his veins went cold.

"Is that blond mariner Nikias of Plataea?" Barka asked, in a sharp and urgent whisper. "You must tell me now, so that I can try to save his life!"

Kolax had become a mute. He could not speak. He nodded dumbly and Barka said, "Do not interfere. Whatever happens, you must not interfere. Do you understand me, Kolax? Trust me."

Kolax nodded again and the eunuch rushed away from his side, vanishing down the stairs.

FOUR

Nikias stared blankly at the floor of the courtyard, watching his sweat and blood dripping from his chin to the marble floor. He could hear Pantares speaking to the crowd, but the hateful man's words were distant and muted by the pounding of his own heartbeat in his ears. He was dizzy from the beating he had taken from the Tyrsenian guards, but he'd suffered much worse. No, it was the hunger that made him stupid and weak. He hadn't eaten more than a few bites of dried fish in the last eight days. Bad luck had brought them to Syrakuse. Bad luck and ill winds. "A desperate throw of the dice," Chusor had said. "But one we must risk."

It had been almost two months since the battle off Serifos and the mad chase of the Korinthian ship—with its cargo of captured women and children—that followed. After Nikias and the others had been rescued from the sea, the *Spear of Thetis* had been caught in the mother of storms. The gale pushed the boat southwestward, day after day, tossing them on the ocean like a child's toy, and it was a miracle they had survived that seemingly never-ending rage of wind and rain. Those days were a miserable memory—a fevered dream of seasickness, hunger, thirst . . . a constant bailing of the hold, and an unremitting terror that the ship would get broadsided and flipped, spilling all of them into the cold and merciless sea. More than two hundred people had been crammed into the cramped and suffocating hold, many injured or burned, and all in a state of profound exhaustion.

Nikias thought about Phoenix and the other ships. He reckoned that his cousin, a canny mariner, had taken the small fleet back to the safety of the harbor on Serifos after spotting the storm coming their way. At least, he prayed that was what had happened. The thought of those other three ships—the last hope of Plataea—scattered or sunk by the storm was too much to bear.

One morning, after most of them had given up hope, they awoke to a calm sea and a nearly cloudless sky. It was the fourth day after the storm. They had been blown hundreds of miles from Serifos, but they had survived the wrath of Poseidon and Oceanus. The wind, still blowing from the northeast, prevented them from sailing back in the direction of Greece. And they no longer had enough rowers to operate the trireme. There were no more provisions. The food and water had all been thrown overboard in an effort to make the ship lighter when they chased after the Korinthian ship.

Chusor knew which land lay to the south of their present position—Libya. It was a dangerous region, he told them, vast and forbidding. Its cities were ruled by the Phoenicians—enemies of the Greeks—and these seafaring people also controlled the waterways along the entire coast, from Egypt to the east to the Pillars of Herakles to the west. But they had no choice. They had to find water within the next day, so they set the masts and sails and journeyed on, drinking the rainwater that had collected in the filthy bilge to quench the terrible thirst that afflicted everyone on board.

After another day they spotted land: an endless coastline of yellow beaches and scattered palm trees—a hot, dry land where the wind blew off the desert like the heat from a forge fire. They beached the ship on a deserted shore, and everyone got off the vessel and stood on shaky legs after nearly a week at sea. Chusor immediately set out with a band of twenty armed men to look for a river or a well. A child and an old woman had already perished from thirst in the last several hours.

While they were gone, Nikias and Ji took stock of the numbers. There were only one hundred and thirty-two rowers still alive from the ship's original complement of one hundred and eighty that had set out from the Piraeus. Nearly fifty oarsmen were dead, thus rendering the trireme inoperable as a galley. Some of these rowers had died in battle with the Korinthian ships, but most of the casualties had resulted when the mariners of Serifos jumped overboard, like Nikias, in a frenzied attempt to save their loved ones whom the Korinthians had tossed into the sea. Nikias was grateful that of the forty-five Plataeans who joined the ship in Athens, only two had died.

A little more than a hundred women and children had been rescued from the Korinthians. Three times that number had set out from the stronghold of Serifos to the Double Axe cove on that ill-omened day. Many of these survivors were now ill from lack of water or wasted from seasickness. Melitta was the exception. She one of the toughest girls Nikias had ever known, and seemed perfectly healthy and full of energy. Her sister, Helena, however, had been in abject misery for most of the days of the storm: she was very pale and had black circles under her eyes.

Their stay on that Libyan beach was short-lived. Chusor and the others came running back to the boat, shouting for everyone to get the *Spear* into the sea. He and the men who had gone looking for water had stumbled upon a band of nomads—scores of warriors with skin the color of wet clay and black braided beards. These wild men chased them to the beach, but came up short when they saw the number of people huddled by the boat. The nomads shot at them with arrows, harassing them until they got the trireme back in the water.

They headed west with the wind, the exhausted rowers straining at the oars, limping along like a wounded beast until they left the hostile nomads far behind. And then their luck changed. Chusor spotted a dead whale stranded in the shallow water of a lagoon, and they brought the *Spear* into the cove. The whale had not yet started to bloat—it hadn't been dead long. It was a gift, Chusor said, from Poseidon. The crew went to work cutting into the thick fat and carving it up for meat. They made fires with driftwood and the dry shrubs and grasses that grew near the beach, and feasted on the flesh of that enormous beast.

They found a spring close to the lagoon, and for the next week they stayed in that place, living off the flesh of the whale and making what repairs they could to the ship. Once the whale had been stripped of its meat, Chusor set men to work fashioning bows from the rib bones, for they had very few bows onboard the *Spear* and the warlike nomads, he said, were a forewarning of worse to come. The women cut off their long hair—hair that went past their buttocks—so that the strands could be woven into strings for the bows.

Most everyone regained their health, including Helena, which was a great relief to Nikias. They spent most of the time working together, collecting fuel for the fires or gathering mussels along the rocks near the lagoon. When they chanced to find themselves all alone, they made love under the sun—an uncontrolled and savage kind of lovemaking that left them craving almost immediately for more.

One day Nikias went farther inland, about half a mile from the cove, and discovered something horrible: a destroyed village of mud huts where the villagers had all been executed. He brought Chusor and some others back to the evil place. All of the dark-skinned people, including the smallest children, had been hanged in a cruel manner—their necks pinioned between pieces of wood affixed to a pole. Most of the villagers' feet were inches above the ground, and they had most likely died straining desperately to touch the earth, slowly choking to death under the blistering sun. Chusor told them that this was the work of Karthaginians—this sort of gallows was their cruel mode of execution. He had no idea why the impoverished villagers had been wiped out, but the Karthaginians, he said, were a strange and oftentimes vicious people. Nikias and the others spent the day taking down the corpses and burying them.

They spent two weeks or more in this lagoon, but eventually they ran out of food and had to move on. Chusor's goal was to head west for as long as they could until they came near the great port of Karthago. From here, Chusor explained, they would be able to see the island of Sicily and the Greek colonies in Italia—lands and cities that were allies of Athens. They could hop along the coast all the way back to Naupaktos—the fortress where the Athenian admiral Phormion had gone with his fleet—in the Gulf of Korinth.

Nikias thought of his cousin. If Phoenix had steered the *Argo*, the *Spartan Killer*, and the *Aphrodite* toward Naupaktos after the great storm had ended, and they had not met with disaster along the way up the coast of the Peloponnese, the small fleet would already be halfway to the Athenian port by now. He said a silent prayer to Poseidon to protect his cousin's journey. Right now, he mused sadly, the *Spear* wasn't likely to get to Naupaktos for months . . . if ever.

Because the ship could not operate properly without all of the oars in the water, the hardiest women took up rowing. They were strong and did not complain, though the labor was backbreaking and they were unused to it. Nikias's seat was directly behind Helena's, and he gave her encouragement throughout the day, marveling at the beauty of her neck and back, his mind wandering in a daze of lust mingled with exhaustion. Whenever they beached the ship at night, the two would sleep in each other's arms, oblivious to the world around them.

Another three weeks went by—the *Spear* hugging the coast by day and resting on sandy beaches by night. They encountered another aggressive tribe of nomads, but they were able to hold them off with their makeshift whalebone bows and drive them away. After that, the few natives they did encounter along the way wanted nothing more than to trade for goods. The women gave up what little jewelry they had to buy goat meat or fish or containers for water, and the men traded their daggers for the same. But it was hard to keep more than two hundred people fed. Rowing all day was hungry work, and everyone's bellies rumbled.

One morning, after pushing off from a lagoon, they came upon a trireme as it rounded a headland. It was a warship from Karthago, most likely out patrolling for pirates, and the *Spear* had surprise and the tactical advantage with its nose pointed directly at the ship's hull. Chusor didn't hesitate. He gave the helmsman the order to steer straight into the side of the Karthaginian, and shouted at Ji to order the oarsmen, "Move quick!" The *Spear* cut through the water like a porpoise and the ram pierced deep into the enemy ship's hull. The *Spear*'s main-mast snapped off in the middle and slammed onto the enemy deck, doing great damage.

Two of the *Spear*'s veterans immediately rushed to the hold and yanked the huge wooden pins holding the ram to the ship, and Chusor gave the order, "Back oars!" The *Spear* pulled away from the Karthaginian ship with its great ram stuck into the ship's side like a spearhead. Water rushed into the enemy boat's hull. It was already starting to swamp and would not be able to follow them. But now the *Spear* was without its mainmast and its ram.

From his seat on the outrigger deck Nikias saw the Karthaginian captain on the prow of his ship shouting angrily in Phoenician at Chusor, who was calling back to the enemy in the same language, laughing and making an obscene gesture. But Chusor stopped laughing when the Karthaginians started shooting flaming arrows at the *Spear*—parting shots fired from the powerful bolt shooter. The sails of the two other masts caught fire and had to be cut down and thrown overboard.

Chusor said they could not go along the coast anymore. They were too close to Karthago. So they headed out to the open sea. They were two hundred miles, by Chusor's estimate, from the island of Sicily. And they would have to row the entire way without benefit of sails.

Another storm came, and they were buffeted about for several days, and the mariners cursed the malicious nature of the sea and winds that seemed to be trying to drown them. The ship sprang a leak and became swamped. When the weather finally cleared, they rowed and rowed, the ship moving slowly because the hold was filled with water. Days went by in a miserable muddle of rowing or bailing. They seemed stuck in one spot, never moving.

Finally, a week after they had attacked the Karthaginian ship, they came at last to the southern shore of Sicily and dragged the ship onto an isolated beach. The *Spear* was in need of substantial repairs that only a shipyard of Syrakuse could provide, but that would be costly. A good mainmast and sails alone were wildly expensive—far more than the bit of silver that Chusor had on hand. Besides that, they needed food and supplies—enough to last all the way to Naupaktos.

Chusor asked Nikias to come into his cabin. He opened a secret compartment and showed him a golden carving—an ancient head of Apollo that had been hidden inside. Nikias held the well-crafted object and stared at the enigmatic face.

"There is a man in Syrakuse," said Chusor, "named General Pantares. He is a wealthy man who owns the biggest shipyard in the citadel. He collects things.

Objects and people alike. He will pay far more than the value of this relic, than the mere weight of it in gold. I would take it to him myself to sell, but he knows me and hates me. When I was a young man I bedded his daughter." He shrugged and rolled his eyes as if to say, "I was a young idiot."

"I will go to this man," said Nikias. "What's the worst that could happen? He refuses to buy it or steals it from me? We have no choice. We must repair the ship or else we'll be stuck here on a beach with a boat full of starving women and children, prey for pirates and thieves and slavers."

"You don't know Pantares," said Chusor. "He's a beast. A barbarian masquerading as a Greek. It's a gamble."

"We have no choice," said Nikias. "And I'm lucky at dice."

"A *desperate* throw of the dice," Chusor had said. "But one we must risk. Remember this: my old shipmate Barka the eunuch, whom I've told you about over the years, may be living in the house of Pantares once more. If you need help, go to him."

It was decided that Diokles and Ji, who knew their way around Syrakuse but were unknown to Pantares, would accompany Nikias. They set out in the evening for the citadel, which lay fifteen miles or so from the beach. When they crossed the land bridge to the isle of Ortygia, Ji said that he would wait for them by the bridge, just in case something went wrong. Unarmed and dressed in their filthy tunics, Nikias and Diokles found the house of Pantares and begged an audience. They were first scrutinized by the general's scornful housekeeper, who interviewed them, took a long look at the object, then told them to wait in the slaves' quarters.

Three hours later they were brought before Pantares, who was surrounded by his guard of Tyrsenians. Nikias told a tale about finding the relic in Ionia in the ruins of a temple that had been destroyed by the Persians. The general held the head in his hands and stared at it with a detached look that Nikias knew was a mask. Pantares coveted the thing. That much was obvious. But he didn't seem interested in the origins of the relic. He wanted to know where Nikias's ship was located and how many men were on his crew. When Nikias balked at answering these questions, the general simply smiled and ordered his men to seize him and Diokles.

"You took a great risk coming to me with this thing," said Pantares. "Only Apollo can make men act so recklessly, and I thank him for it."

The Tyrsenians dragged Nikias and Diokles away, beat them savagely, then left them to bleed in a storeroom. They came back in the evening and yoked them to the wood beams, then led them into the courtyard.

Now, standing in front of the general, surrounded by his partygoers, Nikias felt his heart grow cold with hate and rage. The blood dripping from his nose had made a little pool in front of his feet. His shoulders ached from the heavy timber across his back. "A prideful man always thinks himself invincible," he thought. "And that's when he's weakest." He glanced up. Pantares stood only a few feet away, jabbering on and gloating as he held up the head of Apollo in triumph for all to see.

"—so I took it from these thieves—these cutthroats who so brazenly came into my house," Pantares was crowing. "Look at them now. They won't tell me where their ship is harbored, or if they have any more relics—pilfered, no doubt, from sacred temples."

Nikias breathed slowly, getting ready for what he knew would be his final act in this world. All he had to do was whip his torso around, turning the timber across his shoulders into a powerful weapon. One blow from the heavy thing to the side of Pantares's head would kill him. Of course, the Tyrsenians would be on him and Diokles in a second. But Nikias was ready to die, as long as it was on his own terms.

"Now, tell us your real name?" he heard Pantares say. The general was smiling at him, peering into his face with a gloating look. "Before I cut out your tongue? Eh? What's your name?"

"Death," said Nikias. But as he started to twist his body around for the killing blow, someone leapt forward and seized hold of his right arm and pulled him off balance, then kicked out his legs from under him. He looked up at a familiar face leering down at him. It took a moment for Nikias to remember exactly where he'd seen this man. Then it hit him: he was the Korinthian he'd met on the plains outside of Attika when he'd gone to trick the Spartans.

"*I* know this one's name," said Andros, turning to Pantares with a jubilant smile playing across his face. "He's Nikias of Plataea, and I claim him as my prisoner under the authority of Arkidamos, king of Sparta."

FIVE

Pantares took a step back and glared ferociously at Andros. "Who are you, Andros, to make a claim on my prisoner?" he spat.

His Tyrsenian guards edged forward, hands on the hilts of their swords, but Pantares held them back with an upraised hand. The guests in the courtyard crowded around in a semicircle, watching this strange scene playing out before their eyes with a combination of shock and titillation—as though they were witnessing a play in a theatre.

"I'm an emissary of the king," said Andros. "This Plataean is an important prisoner. At this moment, fifty thousand men surround the citadel where his grandfather is the Arkon. Nikias is a wily Oxlander. He's already deceived the Spartans twice: starting a forest fire on Mount Kithaeron and leading his people to safety in Athens, then tricking the king into thinking that he was infected with the sickness that is plaguing our enemy. I don't know how he came to be in Syrakuse, but my guess is that he has something to do with a small fleet of Korinthian ships that were destroyed on the island of Serifos."

"This Nikias seems to be a miraculous young fellow," said Pantares with a curl of his upper lip. "And yet I knew that he was a deceiver from the moment I laid eyes on him. And here he is, bound on the floor at my feet, as helpless as that other Plataean the Spartans foisted upon my house—that young man I watched over while they played his father Nauklydes like a fish on a line. And yet Demetrios of the Oxlands is long dead, and he, too, was one of your 'wily Oxlanders'—and Demetrios was far more clever than this fool here."

Nikias, sprawled on the floor, choked back his grief. All these years he had kept the faint hope alive that his best friend had somehow escaped the net that the Spartans had laid for him in Syrakuse. But here was final proof that he was dead. He tried to get up but two Tyrsenians grabbed him by either arm and flung him on his back, pinning him there.

"I need this man," said Andros. "I need to take him back to the Oxlands—to Arkidamos."

"Perhaps I'll let you have him when I'm done with him," said Pantares.

"He's no good to me if he's been ruined," said Andros. "We have our own ways of getting information out of men. I need him whole."

Pantares walked slowly up to Andros and put his face inches from his. "You can't have him," he said in a low voice.

But Andros did not flinch or back away. "Then you will not find the Spartans as agreeable after this. In fact, you may find them antagonistic."

"You think I care about the Red Cloaks?" asked Pantares. "Would they dare attack mighty Syrakuse with their puny fleet? I don't think so." He held out his hand toward one of his guards. "Sword," he said.

A guard stepped forward and bowed slightly before placing a sword in his hand.

"What are you doing?" asked Andros.

"I'm going to cut off this Nikias's right hand," said Pantares. "And then if he doesn't tell me where his ship is beached, I'm going to cut off other things."

"Stop!" said Andros, reaching out a hand to grasp Pantares's arm.

Pantares's face went slack for the briefest moment, and then his sword swept through the air and Andros's head tumbled from his shoulders, landing next to Nikias with a heavy thud. The Korinthian's neck erupted in a fountain of blood as his headless body sagged and fell, dousing the partygoers standing near with gore. Men and women screamed and fled from the courtyard, and Nikias stared at the dead face of Andros—frozen in a look of incredulity—his lids twitching ever so slightly above his dead eyes.

"Clear them all out!" Pantares ordered, and the Tyrsenians started pushing the partygoers from the courtyard.

Pantares stood over Nikias, holding the sword tip to his cheek. Andros's blood trickled down the blade to the point where it dripped into the corner of Nikias's mouth. Nikias spat out the blood but remained still. He looked up at the balcony and saw someone standing there in the shadows—a lad with dark hair and a pale face—staring back at him with mute horror.

"Now," said Pantares with a sigh after all of the partygoers had departed the room, leaving only Diokles and the guards. "Let me ask you one more time, Nikias of Plataea: Where is the ship that brought you to Sicily? I have had my men make a sweep of the entire harbor while you have been my prisoners, but there have been no new arrivals for several days, and none of the ships are carrying Athenians or Plataeans. So, tell me where they are. Upon which shore? Which of my enemies is giving you safe harbor?" He moved the tip of the sword to Nikias's groin and started to press.

"He won't tell you," said a soft female voice.

A slender and beguiling woman slid, catlike, up to Pantares's side.

"I saw you standing in the balcony this whole time, Barka," said Pantares. Addressing Nikias, he said, "My soothsayer has taken an interest in you."

So this was Barka! The eunuch walked over to the kneeling Diokles and put a finger under his chin, lifting his face to his own. Diokles was smiling, but tears coursed down his cheek.

"Hello, Diokles," said Barka.

Diokles smiled sadly. "My Lylit," he replied in the softest voice.

"You know this Helot?" asked Pantares.

"He was my servant," said Barka. "He ran away after I had him beaten." He patted him on the head. "Sullen thing, he is. Wicked little dog."

Nikias knew that the eunuch's words were a lie. Chusor and Leo had both told Nikias that Barka and Diokles had been the best of friends. "Lylit" was the Helot's pet name that he used for the eunuch. Why didn't this Barka tell Pantares that he and Diokles had been shipmates? That they were friends? Why did he not try to at least save him?

Barka glided over to Nikias, kneeling with his back to Pantares, staring hard into his eyes. When the eunuch spoke it was in the faintest of whispers—for Nikias's ears alone. "The Ear of Dionysus. Tell him that I listen at zenith." Then Barka stood and faced Pantares.

"What did you see in his eyes?" Pantares asked.

"I saw fear," said Barka. "But he will not reveal the whereabouts of his ship. He'll die first to protect his friends. But it is no matter. The head of Apollo is all that he had in his possession."

"Are you certain, Barka?" Pantares asked.

"Have I ever been wrong about anything?" asked Barka. "Did I not name all of the conspirators who secretly opposed your rising power?"

"Yes," said Pantares, staring at the golden head clutched in his hand. "And you told me that this object would come to me from the sea—a symbol of my ascendency."

"Now," said Barka, "you must listen to me. This Plataean must not be killed."

"What am I to do with him?"

"You must make him a quarryman," said Barka with a cold laugh. "I foresee a time when he will be useful to us. Do you remember me telling you that a nine-fingered man would bring you the gift?" He pointed at Nikias's missing finger on his right hand and Pantares gasped. "And that he would be invaluable to you?"

"So you did," said Pantares, stroking his beard pensively. "And the other? This Helot? Shall I have him killed?"

"He is my property," said Barka. "Throw him in the quarry until he's learned to be submissive."

"So be it," said Pantares.

As the Tyrsenians dragged Nikias out of the courtyard he looked up at the balcony and saw the young man in the shadows making the pankrator sign—a fist slamming into a palm. And then the lad vanished from sight.

SIX

The Tyrsenians locked Nikias and Diokles in a chamber for an hour or so, then returned abruptly, pulling them from the house and leading them through the streets of Syrakuse by chains. Almost immediately a crowd formed up behind them, taunting the prisoners, for the people knew where they were headed.

Nikias had been playing over and over again in his mind the strange, nightmarish scene in the courtyard. Andros the Korinthian—an emissary of King Arkidamos—slain for merely putting his hand on Pantares's arm. Barka saving them from certain death, but sending them off to the notorious quarry—the Prison Pits—a place, it was said, from which no one had ever escaped. And how had Barka known that "a nine-fingered man" would bring the golden head? And who was the lad up in the balcony who made the pankration sign? How did he know the symbol that he and his grandfather shared? And what of the strange whispered words of Barka: "The Ear of Dionysus. Tell him I listen at zenith." What did they mean? Perhaps nothing. The eunuch was most likely mad.

A bucket of filth hit him in the face, blinding him for a few seconds. He spit out the human waste and piss and saw a laughing teenager holding an empty pot and dancing while the crowd laughed and clapped.

Nikias cursed himself for being so foolish as to walk into General Pantares's house like a stupid insect flying straight into a cone-spider's web. He grit his teeth, wincing in pain from the wood digging into his shoulders, ignoring the crowds' jeers. Up ahead he saw the bridge that led from Ortygia to the mainland part of the citadel. He could see Ji standing by the bridge entrance. The exhorter's face was inscrutable as he watched Nikias approach, but he slid his hand to the handle of his sword as if to say, "Call on me and I will help." There were ten Tyrsenian guards. Helping Nikias would be suicide. He shook his head ever so slightly to let Ji know not to interfere, and the little man nodded his head with the merest hint of a gesture.

When they arrived at the quarry, the guards led Nikias to a wooden contraption at the edge of the great pit. It was a crane, like the ones used for stacking the sections of marble columns, attached to a scaffolding that went from the top of the quarry all the way to the floor nearly a hundred feet below. The men who operated the winch removed Nikias's wrists from the post shackles, and they laughed as Nikias's arms remained stiff and frozen in the position in which they had been locked for the last five hours, like outstretched wings.

"Another Ikarus, ready to fly away from the pits," sneered one of the crane operators.

"I hope you like getting your arse drilled," said one of the others. "Because it's going to be as wide-open as this pit when they're done with you down there."

"The Quarry Lord will have his fun with this one."

"Oh, yes! The Quarry Lord will have his fun."

Nikias looked over the edge into the deep pit that was scored with huge shafts, boreholes, and caverns that had been dug over the centuries. There were enormous columns of limestone that had been left standing in places, as well as vast arches and caves that seemed to delve deep into the walls. It was an eerie place, like nothing he'd ever seen before—a disordered landscape that looked as though it had been carved and scooped out by deranged Titans, a maze to hide the Minotaur and other beasts.

The workers fit him into a leather harness attached to a rope that was connected to the crane, then pushed him off the edge. Nikias hung in midair, kicking his legs instinctively, and peered down at the ground so far below. His stomach immediately felt as though it had leapt toward his throat like a frightened cat. The men turned a big crank and the crane lowered him down, down along the wall of the quarry, and he saw the little niches and score marks in the flat limestone where the first stones had been cut from the pit centuries before.

Suddenly his feet hit the floor of the quarry and he looked around in fear, expecting to be attacked by the prisoners all at once. But the space nearby was empty of men. In fact, he didn't see anyone at all. He slowly took off the harness and the instant he was free of it the thing shot toward the top of the wall.

Where were all of the prisoners hiding? Where was everyone? He bent down and cupped a handful of powdery limestone dust—the ground was thick with the stuff—and rubbed it on his face, cleansing himself as best he could of the shit and urine that had been flung at him.

Diokles hit the quarry floor with thump and a cloud of dust. Nikias helped get him out of the harness. The Helot's face was streaked with tears. "My little Lylit betrayed me," he said in a high voice, like a stricken toddler.

A figure suddenly emerged from the dark entrance of a small cave nearby and jogged over to them. As he got closer Nikias could see that the man was short and slender, with a sparse beard and one eye. Above the missing eye's socket was a deep indentation on his forehead. He had obviously suffered a serious blow to the head that had caved in his skull and wrecked his eye, and now his brow resembled a dented helm.

"Hello," said the man with a friendly smile that showed his prominent rabbit-like incisors. "My name's Thersites. Welcome to our home. What's your name?"

Nikias was taken aback by the man's good-natured introduction and replied, "My name is Nikias of Plataea. And this is my friend Diokles."

"Wait here," said Thersites, "and I'll be right back. I must make my report, and scratch my arse, for I forgot to do that this morning. Rituals, you know." He ran back into the cave from which he had come.

"Just let me do the talking," Nikias said to Diokles.

The Helot stood with his shoulders slumped, staring at his feet. "I have nothing to say," he replied morosely as hot tears continued to gush from the corners of his dark brown eyes. "I am dead in my heart."

Nikias put his hand on the short man's brawny neck and gave him a little squeeze. But Diokles shook himself away from Nikias's hand—the petulant gesture of a child who feels sad and scorned. Nikias left him alone to stew in his misery.

Men started to emerge from various niches and cave entrances around the perimeter of the quarry. Their numbers quickly swelled. Most were naked and many carried work tools—chisels and hammers. Nikias's heart started beating faster and he forced himself to be calm. He wasn't going to be gang-raped. He would die before that happened.

The quarrymen surrounded him in a big circle and stared at him silently. They were savage-looking men—tanned brown from the relentless sun, scarred, and muscled. Most had bushy beards and wild, unkempt hair. They scowled at him, staring him down, waiting for him to break. But he stood with his arms crossed on his chest, staring back at them, from one man to the next.

Thersites pushed his way through the crowd and took Nikias by the hand. "Come, this way!" he said jovially. "We're going to have fun today! It's a festival day, no? It's a blue-sky, cool-breeze day, yes?"

Nikias let himself be led by the little man, and the circle of quarrymen parted to let them through. He looked back over his shoulder and saw Diokles, docile and dejected, pushed along by the others.

Thersites led Nikias through the warren of archways to a big open area. Across the way was an enormous gash in the side of the quarry wall that went from the floor nearly to the top. Standing far back in the shadows he could see the figure of a statue with a smiling face.

"Stay where you are," said Thersites in a low voice. "Let the Quarry Lord have a look at you. Don't fart. Or smirk."

Nikias followed Thersites's eyes to the statue in the cave. As Thersites approached it, the "statue" moved and Nikias realized that it was a man wearing a crudely carved stone mask, his skin covered with gray stone dust. Nikias glanced over his shoulder. A thousand or so prisoners had made a wall of men behind him and Diokles.

"Nikias of Plataea!" shouted the naked man in the cave all of a sudden, and his voice—spoken with the grating accent of a Karthaginian—echoed in the chamber and seemed to hover in the air, repeating and shifting, slurring and morphing before the sound spilled out into the quarry and dissipated. The effect was eerie and sent a chill up Nikias's spine.

Nikias looked at Thersites and asked, "What do I say?"

"Do not speak unless spoken to," said Thersites. "That's proper manners. At least where I come from. On the moon," he added, pointing to the sky.

"Hammers or chisels?" asked the Quarry Lord, and his words repeated the same weird echoing pattern, seemingly flying around the cave like birds or insects.

Nikias turned to Thersites. "What's he talking about?"

"You get to choose the weapons for you and your opponent to fight with," said Thersites with a broad smile. "Hammers or chisels. Every time a new man comes into the quarry, a shade must depart. It's been the Quarry Lord's law since he took over. Keeps the population down," he added with a nervous laugh.

Nikias's heart sank. He realized that he was going to have to fight one of these men. And kill him. His shoulders slumped and he looked toward the blue sky, shaking his head. He felt too weak to fight now. Thersites, shuffling and bouncing with excitement, was nodding his head and grinning—a look that said, "Isn't this fun?"—and Nikias realized that the man was utterly insane.

"Can I have something to eat and a rest first?" Nikias said. Stuff these quarrymen and their little game. They could all go to Hades.

Thersites choked on his spit and gave Nikias a terrified look, then backed away from him. "This isn't a joke," he said. "The fight is to the death. You know? When they pull your shade from your body and kick dirt on your face."

"I didn't think it was a joke," said Nikias. "But I'm tired and hungry. If I'm going to die, I'd like to do it on a full belly."

The prisoners within earshot of Nikias started to grumble. They had never before heard such impudence! "He wants a meal and a nap!" one man shouted, and the others started to bark out insults. But their noise was cut short by a weird sound that erupted from the cave—the sound of mirthful laughter.

"Your Quarry King thought it was funny," Nikias said.

"Quarry *Lord*," corrected Thersites. "Remember our manners, lad. This isn't the Antipodes, where men's feet are on their heads and their mouths are in their arses."

After the laughter had died down, the Quarry Lord said in a firm voice, "You may rest while the Helot goes first."

Nikias glanced at Diokles. The Helot smiled at him dolefully and said, "I'm ready, Nik. I'll fight." He made a little gesture over his heart.

But Nikias knew that Diokles had no intention of fighting. The Helot was steeling himself for death. He had no will to live. He was going to let himself be hammered to a pulp by one of these men. . . .

"Hammers or chisels?" the Quarry Lord asked again.

"Fists!" called out Nikias, his face turning scarlet with rage. He turned to the men staring at him. "Why not fists?" he repeated. "Who will fight me, eh? Who has the balls? I'll tear the throat out of any one of you. Have any of you ever met an Oxlander? Come on! I'll fight your best man without any weapon at all! With my hands and feet alone! And I fight for the Helot. So bring on your best!"

Thersites let forth a snort of laughter. "Two at once? Without weapons? That's never been done before! Wonderful!"

The quarrymen grumbled and fidgeted. They had been insulted by this newcomer. How dare he taunt them!

"So be it," said the Quarry Lord. "Two at once. The Plataean fights for his friend and he must fight as a pankrator—no weapons for him. But my quarrymen will be armed. Take the Helot to the honeycombs. If the Oxlander dies, kill his friend."

Men came forward and grabbed Diokles, pulling him back into the crowd, where he disappeared from sight.

"Nice knowing you," said Thersites to Nikias, and scurried back to take his place amongst the prisoners in the circle.

A strapping man, his torso cut with muscles—hardened by years of pounding rock—pushed his way through the crowd and into the makeshift arena. He bore a huge hammer in one hand, and his black-bearded face was somber, his eyes as hard as stones. He outweighed Nikias. From the opposite side came a shorter and younger man with a rippled body and light brown hair and beard. He carried a chisel and his narrow, wolfish face was set in an eager grimace.

"I'm going to turn your head to pulp," said the one with the hammer.

"I'll blind him first," said the one with the chisel.

"Shut up and die," replied Nikias.

The chisel wielder charged first, swinging his weapon with all his might, but Nikias was too quick—too agile. He lunged sideways, grabbing the man by the other arm as he stumbled past, yanking it from the socket and sweeping his legs out from under him with a practiced motion. The prisoner landed on his back and Nikias lunged forward, grasping the prisoner's hand bearing the chisel with his own callused oar grippers, driving the weapon into the prisoner's left eye—deep into his brain.

Nikias stepped back from the twitching prisoner, watching him bleed his life into the dust. Then he turned his snarling face to the others. "Next," he said under his breath.

The quarrymen looked at him openmouthed.

"Evidently you've never seen someone die that quickly," said Nikias, and spat on the ground.

The other fighter circled around Nikias warily, deftly tossing the hammer from hand to hand. Nikias could tell by his stance that this one had had some pankration training. And he was trying to mesmerize him with his hammer trick.

"Dancing around me all day isn't going to help," goaded Nikias, provoking his opponent as he'd been taught by his grandfather. A man could be defeated with words before the fight had even begun. "Do they eat the dead in this stinking place?" he asked. "Which of your friends will feast on your tender prick tonight?"

The quarryman's eyes narrowed. Suddenly he flung the hammer at Nikias's head—a skillful throw that would have found its mark if Nikias hadn't been ready for it. He ducked and the heavy tool smashed into a man behind him with the sound of cracking bones.

In the next instant the big quarryman rushed Nikias and they slammed together like two triremes prow-to-prow, grappling with their arms outstretched, legs far apart. The man was strong and Nikias felt his feet sliding on the slick quarry surface. He realized with alarm that he'd forgotten to take off his slick sandals. He was losing ground to the bigger man.

"I'm going to start with your arse," said the quarryman in a hoarse whisper. "Very tender meat."

Nikias was sliding fast now, losing his balance. The man was about to flip him over. "Fall on your own terms!" he heard his grandfather's voice shout in his head.

He flung himself backward, pulling the man on top of him, and pushed up with his feet using every ounce of strength in his lower body. For a second the surprised fighter was suspended above him, supported by Nikias's powerful legs, then he flew over the top of Nikias and landed hard on his back.

Nikias was on top of him like a snake on a rat, coiling his arms around the man's neck and putting him into the Morpheus hold, clamping down on the sides of his throat with his biceps, pulling him close to his body so that they looked like two rowers on an oar bench—chest-to-spine. The quarryman thrashed and kicked, and Nikias squeezed even harder, leaning back his head to avoid the man's clawing hands. It took a minute for his opponent to pass out, and once he was limp Nikias snapped his neck with a vicious twist so that the man's head was practically reversed on his torso.

Nikias staggered away from the corpse and wiped the sweat and dirt from his face, glaring at the wall of prisoners, who stared back, dumbstruck and enraged. They looked like they were going to rush him.

Then Nikias heard a startling sound—the battle cry of "Eleu-eleu!" bursting from the cave. The sound reverberated against the stones and pierced his bones in the same way it had, years ago, when he'd snuck into the pankration championship at the Olympiads to watch his grandfather fight Damos the Theban, and the crowd of forty thousand had sung the Greek war chant.

The Quarry Lord stepped from the shadows of the cave and into the light of the open pit, marching toward Nikias with long, swinging strides. The prisoners took up the cry and the noise of it was so loud that it made Nikias's ears ring.

Now Nikias could see how big the Quarry Lord was—how tall and menacing. He carried a heavy war club carved from a single piece of rock, and his body was like the statue of a god graven in stone. He stopped a few paces from Nikias, staring at him from behind the sinister mask. Nikias faced the taller man, bracing himself to fight again.

"Coward," said Nikias above the din. "Going to fight me with that club? With a mask on? Show me your face so I can see who I'm going to kill."

But the Quarry Lord did not reply. He just stood there regarding Nikias with his head cocked slightly to the side, as if he were staring at something peculiar. Then he held up his hand for the prisoners to stop chanting and they ceased at once. After a long silence the club slipped from the Quarry Lord's hand, hitting the hard ground with a thud, and he pulled off his mask to reveal an austere yet amiable face—a striking face that wore a mysterious half smile like the enigmatic grin on an ancient kouros statue.

Nikias stepped back as if he'd been shoved by unseen hands, mouth agape, blinking rapidly.

"My old friend," said the Quarry Lord, now speaking with his true accent: a thick Plataean cadence. "The gods have a curious sense of humor, do they not?"

"Demetrios?" Nikias asked in awe.

And then the prisoners of the quarry watched in wonder as these two fierce men—their brutal chief and this violent newcomer—grabbed each other in a rowdy embrace, arms locked together like wrestlers at the start of a bout, howling and laughing, pushing each other back and forth in a riotous dance of friendship.

SEVEN

When Kolax first realized that the two prisoners standing below in the courtyard at General Pantares's house were Nikias and Diokles, he was unable to comprehend what he was looking at. It didn't make sense that they would be here
in Syrakuse together. The last time he'd seen Nikias was atop Mount Kithaeron
on the night they set the great fire. And Diokles departed Plataea soon after the
sneak attack thirty moons ago. How had the two come together so far from
Greece and in such odd circumstances?

At first he thought that what he was seeing was some kind of illusion, like a
stomach speaker's conjuring trick. He watched the scene taking place before his
eyes as though he were stuck in a strange dream or a hemp-induced vision. When
Pantares suddenly beheaded Andros, Kolax saw it happen very slowly—as if time
had turned as slow as honey. He didn't even move or cry out. He just stood blinking with dumb fascination. And when Barka the eunuch stepped forward, con-
demning Nikias and Diokles to the Prison Pits, Kolax felt his guts go slack.

Pantares's men didn't remove Nikias and Diokles from the house right away
but took them to a room and locked them inside. Kolax, baffled about what to
do next, ran back to Andros's house, which stood close by, and retrieved a small
purse of gems, gold coins, and pearls that his late master had hidden under a
floorboard—treasure used to bribe Syrakusan officials and magistrates. Kolax
didn't know what he would do with the precious things. Bribe one of Pantares's
Tyrsenian guards, perhaps? That seemed unlikely. They'd cut off his head and
take the treasure.

He tied the heavy pouch around his neck and stuffed it down his tunic, then
sprinted back to Pantares's house, hiding in the alley across the lane. If he'd

learned one thing from Andros, it was patience. Andros used to tell him a story about a tortoise and a hare having a race. In this stupid tale the slow tortoise won, simply because the idiot hare kept stopping to eat and rest. "Slow and sensible always wins the race," Andros liked to say. So Kolax hunkered down and tried to calm his mind. But he didn't have to wait long. The guards soon exited the house leading Nikias and Diokles, yanking on chains tied to metal collars around their necks as if they were beasts.

Kolax shadowed Nikias, Diokles, and the Tyrsenians through the streets of Ortygia as they made their way toward the New City in the direction of the quarry. As a crowd of jeering men and boys fell in behind the group, Kolax blended into the throng. The Skythian seethed with indignation at the way Nikias was abused by the townsmen, but he kept his temper under control . . . until a teenager threw a bucket of filth into his friend's face, and then a red rage caught fire in his veins. He quickly slipped from the crowd and found the lad with the bucket, who was laughing with his gaggle of friends. Kolax seized the bucket from the surprised boy, punched him in the gut, and jammed the bucket over his head before dashing back into the crowd.

When the throng got to the land bridge to the mainland, Kolax immediately noticed a foreign-looking man with squinting eyes loitering off to the side, watching Nikias pass with a queer expression. Being a foreigner in the Greek lands, Kolax was always aware of others who, like himself, stuck out from a crowd. And Kolax's eyes, trained by Andros to instantly pick out little details, noticed that this foreigner bore two swords on his belt. One of these was a curved scabbard—the kind of blade used by Phoenician pirates. But the other weapon was a short Greek leaf-bladed sword with a simple bronze pommel with the words "Of Plataea" scored onto the pommel's circle with deep, bold lines. Kolax had seen this ancient sword many times over the last two and a half years, and he knew who had crafted the pommel and handle: Chusor the smith.

But Kolax had made a blunder—the foreigner had seen his eyes lingering on the sword pommel, and now their gazes met for the briefest moment before the man bolted. Kolax was forced to make a decision: follow Nikias and Diokles to the quarry or follow the stranger. He chose the latter. There was nothing that he could do for Nikias and Diokles now. And he had to find out how this man had come to bear Nikias's sword. Kolax followed the foreigner as fast as he could, chasing him through the narrow streets of the New City, across the agora, and all the way to a marble road marker pointing toward the coast.

But the foreigner was fast. Kolax didn't think a man who was so small and old could be so swift. But Kolax had never been a very swift runner. He was a horseman, not a gods-forsaken distance runner! He got a sharp stitch in his side—a pain that felt like a knife in his lung—but he kept running. The foreigner was a quarter of a mile ahead of him now and Kolax's brain screamed for answers. Who was this man? Why did he have Nikias's sword? And why had he been waiting by the land bridge?

Kolax pumped his arms harder as the roadway headed up a hill. He lost sight of the foreigner and cursed himself for being so slow. He jogged along for another mile, doggedly refusing to give up. He was already out in the countryside, surrounded by olive trees. He felt as though he were running in a nightmare. "I'm on Sicily," he said to himself with vexation. "Andros is dead. Nikias is in the quarry. I'm alone chasing a foreigner down a road to the great sky god Papaeus knows where. This is madness!"

He stopped and bent over with his hands on his knees, gasping for air. His throat burned and he felt as though he might be sick. He touched the bag of precious things under his tunic. He might be able to use the money to bribe the guards at the quarry to let Nikias out. And if that didn't work he could buy a great length of rope and lower himself down. But first he would kill the eunuch who had convinced Pantares to put Nikias in that horrible place. He could sneak into the palace and slit Barka's throat in the dead of the night.

He flinched. He'd heard footsteps behind him—the gentlest sound of leather sandals scraping on pebbles. He turned around slowly and saw the foreigner he'd been chasing was now standing directly behind him, Nikias's sword raised to cut him down, and his eyes cold and steady. Kolax froze. He could tell by the way this man held himself that he was a master swordsman.

"You know this sword?" the foreigner asked.

Kolax nodded, trying to catch his breath, not daring to make a move.

"Who made the pommel and handle?"

"Chusor the smith," Kolax replied. "In Plataea. My name is Kolax of the Bindi tribe."

The foreigner's demeanor did not change. His murderer's eyes continued to bore into Kolax. "Chusor has told me of this Skythian lad who was good with a bow. A boy with *red* hair and a tattoo on his back."

"That's me," said Kolax. "I dyed my hair. Or rather, the man who captured me dyed it." He paused and asked with annoyance, "And Chusor told you that I was 'good' with a bow? Not 'great'?"

"Prove you are Kolax," said the foreigner. "Show me the tattoo. Turn around very slowly."

Kolax did as he was told, though he hated turning his back on the stranger. He lifted his tunic to reveal the tattoo of the griffin that had been inked across his skin. "You see," he said. "The griffin is eating an Arimaspian—a one-eyed giant from the north. My father—" He stopped mid-sentence as the foreigner ran past him, sheathing his sword as he went. "Hey! Where are you going?"

"Follow me, Kolax," said the foreigner, glancing back over his shoulder. "It's thirteen miles to the ship."

As they ran the stranger introduced himself as Ji, but he said little more on their run. When Kolax tried to tell him about the events at Pantares's house, Ji stopped him, saying, "Save your breath. No use repeating this story twice. You'll have to tell it to the others when we get to the ship."

After another three miles or so Kolax had to stop and throw up from over-exerting himself. But after being sick he got his second wind and the two flew down the road, racing the setting sun. They saw very few people along the way: a farmer pulling an oxcart and some women carrying water back from a well with amphoras balanced on their heads. Kolax became lulled by the seemingly endless sound of his feet slapping on the road and the noise of his own strained breathing in his ears.

They were heading down a slope toward the water, six miles in the distance, when Ji grabbed Kolax by the tunic and pulled him off to the side of the road-way as six riders crested the hill behind them, galloping past. But the riders did not go far. Evidently they'd seen Kolax and Ji, for they came to a stop up ahead, wheeled around, and headed back toward them. They were Syrakusan cavalry wearing light plate armor and bronze helms. They carried short javelins that glinted menacingly.

"Nowhere to run," said Kolax, looking around at the barren hillside on which they stood. "Give me your bow."

Ji quickly handed the weapon to Kolax, who gripped it and grimaced. "It's a left-handed bow!" he exclaimed with displeasure.

"I'm left-handed," replied Ji.

Kolax snatched a fistful of arrows from Ji's quiver as the riders trotted up and surrounded them. The horsemen glared down at Kolax and Ji, their sweat-ing horses pawing the ground and snorting. They were fine-looking horses, con-sidered Kolax, though very fidgety.

"What's your business on this road?" asked the lead rider, frowning at them from the shadows of his helm.

"That is our business," said Ji.

"Where do you come from?"

"Again, that is our concern."

The lead rider sniffed and, turning slowly to the man next to him, said, "Kill them."

One of the riders thrust his spear at Ji, but the little man dodged the blow like a snake, grabbing the spear pole and yanking the rider off his mount.

Kolax dropped down and somersaulted under the lead rider's horse, cutting the animal across the forelock with an arrowhead. The horse spooked and reared—and Kolax, now lying on his back on the road, sent an arrow flying through the underside of the chin of the lead rider.

A havoc of screaming horses and shouting men. Riders leaping to the ground. Ji whirling and darting through the armored riders with a murderous grace, both of his swords cutting through the air, hacking through limbs, disemboweling men.

Kolax shot two more riders at close range—one through the mouth, the other in the groin. Ji finished one off with Nikias's sword, cutting through his neck so cleanly that the head didn't pop off until the body hit the ground.

Only one rider was left alive and he leapt back on his mount and charged up the hill, back toward Syrakuse. Ji threw a knife at him and missed. Kolax knelt down and steadied himself, closing his right eye and sighting with his left. The bowstring thumped and the arrow struck the rider in his lower back, piercing his leather armor. The man slumped and fell to the rocky ground. The horse kept running.

The two stood for a few seconds staring in silence at the sudden and terrible carnage that they had wrought on the road—a path now cluttered with the dead and running red with blood. The horses had scattered and were galloping in different directions across the hillside.

"These warriors came from Syrakuse," said Kolax. "They must have been heading for the shore—looking for the ship that brought Nikias and Diokles."

Ji nodded but did not speak, and Kolax handed him back his bow.

"Good weapon," Kolax said. "You should see what I can do with a right-handed bow."

Ji smiled slightly and slung the weapon over his shoulder. "Help me get the bodies off the road."

They lifted the corpses one by one and dragged them behind some rocks. Kolax hurriedly went through all of their belongings—a thing, he realized, that Andros the spy would have done. He took the lead rider's leather satchel and slung it over his shoulder, and also the dead man's sword.

"Not far now," said Ji.

They left the road and headed overland, straight toward the water, then found a narrow goat path that led down to the shore. Kolax could hear the waves pounding on the rocks to the right. After a few minutes they emerged onto a hidden beach, and there, in the light of the setting sun, Kolax saw a ship and hundreds of people huddled around campfires. Ji led him through the camp to a fire closest to the vessel. Kolax saw Chusor standing next to a young woman and a skinny short-haired girl with the prettiest dark eyes that he had ever seen.

"What happened?" said Chusor when he caught sight of Ji. "Where are they? Who's this?"

"It's me," said Kolax, smiling shyly. "I was captured by a Korinthian. He dyed my hair."

Chusor was confounded. He stared back and forth from Ji to Kolax, his mouth agape.

"It's your friend Kolax," said Ji. "Good fighter. Just like you said."

Chusor reached out and grabbed Kolax by the arm, pulling him toward the fire and looking him up and down in the flickering light with an expression of out-and-out bafflement. Then he lifted Kolax's tunic and stared at the griffin tattoo on his back, muttering in astonishment.

"I've a story to tell," said Kolax, casting a quick glance at the girl with the short hair. She was staring back at him warily, her slender arms crossed on her chest.

Chusor said, "Indeed. Start with why Nikias and Diokles aren't with you."

EIGHT

"I had to let you fight. The prisoners would not have respected you if I had stepped in to save an old friend, and there would have been strife. I made the rules that we live by, and even though I am the Quarry Lord, I am beholden to my men as well. But you passed the first test of the Prison Pits. And watching you fight like that made me proud to be a Plataean again."

Nikias was sitting next to Demetrios on a stone bed carved into the wall of a small cave. They had come to this chamber—Demetrios's private abode—to talk out of earshot of the other prisoners. They leaned against each other, shoulder to shoulder, enjoying the easy accord that only the best of friends share—even ones who have been separated for many years. They had known each other since they had been toddlers and had been closer than kin, for although they had always shared a brotherly rivalry, they had never been jealous of one another. Each had only wanted the other to thrive and had pushed him to be the best, whether it was at the gymnasium or riding or practicing in the phalanx drills. Nikias knew that Demetrios felt guilty that he had stood by and watched him fight two men to the death. He could hear it in his voice. But he also knew that his old friend had spoken the truth: there was nothing that he could have done.

"I have fought many men to the death since we last met," said Nikias.

"And so have I," said Demetrios gravely. "It is the only way I stayed alive—the skills that your grandfather and my noble father and the others back home taught me. I am a sword forged in Plataea. Nothing could bend me or break me. Not even this place. And besides," he added with a harsh laugh, "I knew that you would win."

Nikias had felt an intense surge of panic at the mention of Demetrios's father. How was he going to break it to his friend that his own father had been the traitor who let the Thebans into the citadel on the night of the sneak attack? The news would break him. It seemed cruel. No, it would be vicious to reveal the horror of what Nauklydes had done. "How—how did you survive here?" he asked, his voice catching in his throat.

"I will not tell my tale until I have word of home and my father and sister," said Demetrios. "And how you came to this place. Speak, Nikias. Although seeing you has filled my heart with joy, it comes with a frost—a terror of what has happened in Plataea. For nothing good could have sent you all the way to this cursed island. Speak, before I lose my mind."

"It is all bad news," said Nikias soberly. "There is nothing good." He took Demetrios's hand and clasped it between his own. "Your father and sister are dead. Murdered by Thebans."

Demetrios's eyes welled with tears. "Speak," he said.

He told Demetrios the long and sorrowful tale of the sneak attack on Plataea and the subsequent events, omitting everything of the culpability of Demetrios's father, crafting a tale in which Nauklydes died at the battle in front of the Gates of Pausanius—a valiant death in defense of the citadel. He could not bring himself to say the truth: that Nauklydes had fallen as low as a citizen could go in his efforts to make a secret pact with the Spartans, place himself in power, and assure Demetrios's safety. And that he had perished in misery and shame, executed by his fellow citizens.

Nikias then recounted the rest of his tale—about his disastrous journey to Athens and the even more ill-starred return home. And then, two and a half years later, the fire on the mountain and the evacuation of Plataea. He told him of the contagion in Athens, and the journey to Serifos with his cousin Phoenix, and finally about the long and strange sea journey that had brought him to Syrakuse and into the clutches of Pantares. When he was done talking, Demetrios put his head on Nikias's shoulder and wept quietly. Nikias wrapped his arm around his friend's shoulder and spoke comforting words, but his mind was racing, going back over everything that he had told Demetrios, wondering if he had slipped up somewhere in his retelling of the tale. Demetrios was a clever and cunning man who had always been difficult to trick, and Nikias had never lied to him before because his friend could invariably see through a ruse.

"I'm so happy that I could hear this story from you," said Demetrios at last. "Someone that I trust with my life. For now I know that the hateful things that Pantares told me before he cast me into this place to rot were lies."

"What did he tell you?" asked Nikias.

"That my father had made an alliance with the Spartans," said Demetrios. "That he was planning to overthrow the old Arkon and seize control of Plataea. He said that my father had sent me here to Syrakuse to keep me safe until all was done. Pantares, the gloating old satyr, told me that the Spartans had whisperers who had been studying the letters that I had been sending home to my father, and that they could mimic my writing and my mind so well that once I was in the quarry they would continue sending him missives as if from my hand."

"He did get those letters," said Nikias. "I went to call on him and your sister a few months before the sneak attack. He read one of them to me. You said—or rather, the whisperer who wrote the letter said—that you'd lost fifty drachmas gambling. Your father was furious."

"Was he?" asked Demetrios with a faint smile. "He should have known better. I never lose at dice. I'm lucky."

Nikias thought about the complex web of deceit that had been woven to keep Nauklydes mollified in Plataea—to make him think that his son was still safe, while all along Demetrios had been a prisoner in the quarry. "Who is this Barka?" he asked suddenly. "Why did he give me that strange message about 'the Ear of Dionysus?' "

Demetrios stood up and stared out the cave entrance. Some men were standing guard there, making sure that nobody disturbed the Quarry Lord. Demetrios caught the eye of one of them and waved them away with the merest gesture and they disappeared from sight. But Nikias sensed that they were still nearby. It did not surprise Nikias that his friend had risen to become the leader of this group. Back home, he had been the young man whom everyone flocked to—even the older men of Plataea, many of whom had been in love with him. For Demetrios was not only unnaturally handsome, with his keen gray eyes and black hair, but he was also physically powerful. It was his magnetism, however, that made him such a force to be reckoned with. When people met him they were instantly attracted to him and wanted to be his friend . . . or more. So it was only natural that he would be tossed into a pit of criminals and killers and, expected to die, instead rise to the top of the heap.

"Barka was my lover," Demetrios said at length. "When I first arrived here in Syrakuse four years ago, the eunuch was living with the Tyrant. I was attracted to the creature immediately—you know how I am with the delicate and pretty boys. They're my weakness. My heart might be Plataean, but my prick is all Spartan. Well, when I arrived here four years ago I was like one of those idiots in a comedy who gets off the boat with their eyes as big as plates. I had been to

Athens, of course, but Syrakuse is different. It looks and smells like a place from a tale. And I was smitten from the start. Arkadios, my father's old Lydian slave—do you remember him? Wheezy old sheep-stuffer—"

"Yes, of course," said Nikias, imitating the old man's noisy breathing.

"Well, he kept warning me to keep out of trouble," continued Demetrios with a laugh. "'Don't step in bilgewater and your feet won't stink,' he'd always tell me. He had a bad feeling from the start that things were amiss here. But I dove in headfirst. Pantares was a very affable host at the beginning. He taught me how to dress. And how to speak the local lingo, so that I didn't sound like a country dweller. He even introduced me to all of his wealthy friends—the men who really control this cracked clay pot of a democracy. I bedded more rich sons than a Persian satrap." He crossed his arms on his chest, gritted his teeth, and stretched his neck, jutting forth his chin—a familiar and ugly gesture that Nikias had seen him make countless times—a look that meant that he was fuming.

"I was tutored by all the best teachers," he went on, relaxing his neck and sighing. "I even learned to play the harp after that first year, if you can believe it. You'd be amazed. I kept saying, 'My friend Nikias can play like Orpheus. He tried to teach me but it didn't stick.' But I guess it helps when your teacher is your lover." He gave Nikias an arch look, then went on. "Barka the eunuch and I kept making eyes at each other, and finally, one night, he came to my room and told me that he loved me and that he'd die without me. The sex that followed was transforming, my friend. There is no other word for it. This little creature seemed to know how to satisfy every one of my desires. He knew just the right words to utter. It was as if he were inside my head."

"They say he's a soothsayer," said Nikias.

"Not just a soothsayer," replied Demetrios. "He can see into the future. That's no lie. But he can also see into men's hearts. And he gazed into mine. Pantares bought him when he was very young from a Karthaginian slaver. Pantares is the one who made Barka a eunuch. The Tyrant is afraid of his creation, but the general is also in awe of him. Pantares allowed Barka to go off for months at a time on the crew of some marauder ship. But the eunuch would always come back from his adventures with important information about what was going on in the world that Pantares could use to strengthen his base of power. He was Pantares's spy, you see? And perhaps the spy of other men. Maybe even the Spartans."

Nikias suddenly flashed on a hazy memory. After Eurymakus had captured and tortured him, the Theban assassin took him to the Spartans who were encamped outside of Plataea and traded Nikias to General Draco. Nikias had been in a nightmarish stupor at the time, suffering from a concussion and a high fever. He remembered someone coming to him in the tent and whispering in his ear. Someone who told him that he was a friend of Demetrios. That must have been Barka! It made perfect sense: Barka had been in Plataea, visiting Chusor at the time. The eunuch could have snuck out of the citadel and made his way to the Spartan camp. Perhaps the Spartans were the ones responsible for Barka coming to Plataea in the first place. They needed a spy on the inside of the citadel, and they used Barka's love for Demetrios as leverage. Perhaps they promised to help free Demetrios from the Prison Pits if Barka helped bring Plataea to its knees. But he decided to keep this information to himself.

"I called Barka 'Hyakinthos,'" continued Demetrios. "A pretty girl's name. To flatter and please him. I gave him my mother's ring—you know, the one with Pegasos carved on it. We used to go to this little shrine on the outskirts of the town—a temple of Artemis. I took him there and put flowers in his hair and told him that we were married." He paused and shook his head. "I'm surprised that Barka has come back to Pantares's house searching for me. After what I did to him. After I left him to die."

"What do you mean?" asked Nikias.

Demetrios glanced at Nikias and chewed on the sides of his cheeks for a bit before saying, "A year after my arrival Arkadios died suddenly. It was very strange. He was an old man but in perfect health. But he got very ill one night and was dead the next morning. I know now that he had been poisoned. That night Barka came to me in hysterics. He told me that some Lakonian merchants—men who had been staying under Pantares's roof for several months—were responsible for Arkadios's death. And that they'd killed him because he'd overheard one of them talking about me. Barka said that these men were Spartan spies and that they had been sent to order Pantares to lock me up. I thought that Barka was out of his mind. I asked him why the Spartans would have any interest in me. And he told me that my father was a tool of the Spartans—that he was planning to betray Plataea." He stopped and bared his teeth. "Well, you can imagine how I reacted. I grabbed Barka around the throat and threatened to kill him for saying such a thing. But he told me that Pantares had given him this information during their love play. He said that even if my father wasn't a traitor, that Pantares was in league with the Spartans and that I was in danger. He said he'd seen a Spartan skytale. Do you know what this is?"

"A length of cloth," said Nikias. "You wrap it around a dowel of a particular thickness and write out a message. The person who receives the skytale must have a dowel of the same thickness or the message is meaningless."

Demetrios nodded. "So Barka begged me to come away with him. He was so distraught that I agreed to his plan: to head north on foot from Syrakuse, then hire a fishing boat to cross the narrow sea to Italia. From there we'd hire mules and trek overland across Greater Greece to the city-state of Kroton where Barka's marauder friends would take us to the Gulf of Korinth and thence to Plataea. So we fled. He had a small fortune in darics sewn into the hem of his gown. Now, how had he come by those? I never asked.

"When we got to the Strait of Messina we realized that we were being followed by cavalry—Pantares's Tyrsenians. There wasn't enough time to hire a boat. But it's only two miles across the strait to Italia—Skylla on one side and Kharybdis on the other. So I jumped in and started swimming for my life. Barka followed me but he wasn't a strong swimmer. There are strange currents there, and a whirlpool—just like in Homer's tale. Barka got caught up in the pull and . . ." Demetrios stopped and shrugged. "I swam over and he clung to me, thinking I was going to save him. But I tore off his dress with the gold coins and pushed him away, swimming to the opposite shore. I had brought nothing with me, you see, for I had nothing of any worth except some rings given to me by admirers. And that was not going to be enough to get me back home. I left the poor creature screaming as he was pulled away on the current, screaming madly. I made it to the shore. You know how strong I am in the water—I could even outswim you, Nik." He stared silently at the floor for a time, shaking his head.

"So what happened?"

"They tracked me down five days later," said Demetrios. "They brought me back here and put me in the quarry. Barka wasn't here. I assumed that he was dead. But now I know he'd gotten away while I had been captured. That's irony for you."

Nikias shook his head sadly. He realized that if Demetrios had escaped from Pantares's clutches, even if it had taken him a year to get back to Plataea, he still would have arrived before the Theban sneak attack. Nauklydes would have known that the Spartans had no intention of keeping their word, and Nauklydes would have called off his alliance with Eurymakus the Theban and Draco the Spartan. None of the terrible chain of events would have happened.

"You must tell me, friend," said Demetrios, "how Penelope, my sister, died. And do not lie to me, for I will know."

Nikias's mind leapt back to the night of the sneak attack. He'd been moving stealthily around the citadel's dark lanes, evading the army of Theban warriors who were occupying the streets and walls. He'd heard screams coming from Nauklydes's house and went to the undercroft, where he discovered a nightmare scene: Nauklydes bound and gagged by Thebans who had raped and beheaded Penelope, his daughter. The three warriors who had done this evil thing were savagely raping one of Nauklydes's young slave girls, and Nikias destroyed them all in a blind rage. . . .

But he could not bring himself to tell this part of the tale.

He stood up and put both hands on Demetrios's shoulders and looked into his eyes. "She died very quickly. In her sleep. And I performed her burial service myself after your father was slain." The first part was a lie, of course. But the story of Penelope's burial was the truth, and Nikias's voice carried with it the conviction of this important and sacred deed. Demetrios smiled faintly and kissed him on the cheek.

"You are my brother," he said. "And my father's burial? Who performed that?"

"My—my grandfather, of course," said Nikias, picturing Nauklydes's ruined body dumped from a cart in the no-man's-land between Plataea and Thebes. Left to rot like a dead dog for his traitorous act.

For a moment Nikias thought that he saw a shadow pass across Demetrios's face. But then he nodded and said, "Of course. It is only proper that Menesarkus should bury his former shield man. My father told me once that he'd had a vision in his youth that Menesarkus would stand over him as he breathed out his last breath."

Nikias pictured his grandfather standing in front of Nauklydes in the agora after all of the stones had been thrown and Nauklydes's face was obliterated: his lower jaw completely gone, his left eye turned to pulp, his nose smashed, his head caved in . . . and yet he clung to life, wheezing through one nostril. Menesarkus stood over him, hour after hour, until Nauklydes finally died. Nikias's grandfather had loved Nauklydes like a son, and his betrayal broke his heart.

"My grandfather was there when he died," said Nikias, in plain truth.

Demetrios looked at Nikias curiously. "But I thought that you said your grandfather had been taken prisoner by the Spartans when my father was killed at the battle at the gates."

"Eh?" said Nikias, his heart racing with the realization he had been caught in a lie.

"You told me," said Demetrios, with a glint in his eye, "that when the Thebans attacked your farmhouse and set it on fire, Menesarkus took the women to the roof. They were able to escape before the flames consumed the house, but Menesarkus had to jump into the chimney to save himself. And that's where he was still trapped when the Spartan prince Arkilokus found him the next day and took him back to the Spartan camp. They kept him there for two days. That would mean that Menesarkus could not have been at the battle where my father died—the morning after the sneak attack."

"I meant that my grandfather was there when your father was *buried*," said Nikias briskly. "I misspoke." But he silently cursed himself for blundering this part of the tale.

Demetrios regarded him with a piercing look, then cocked his head to one side. "All that matters is that my father was given a proper burial," he said. "I had a terrible dream—about the time of the sneak attack, I now reckon—in which my father's bloody shade came to me and told me that his corpse was unburied."

"Strange," said Nikias, and crossed his arms to hide the bumps that had appeared on the skin of his forearms. "I had a dream about you," he added quickly. "When Eurymakus was torturing me. I dreamt that you had brought me to the golden fleece. It kept me from losing my mind. I felt as though we were connected somehow. As though you were truly there. Then Eurymakus told me that you had been killed and the thought nearly drove me mad."

"And yet here I am," said Demetrios. "I'm harder to kill than a cockroach. Or *you*, it would seem," he added with a laugh.

NINE

"Come now," said Demetrios cheerfully. "I'll take you on a tour of my domain." He strode out of the cave and Nikias followed. Demetrios's retinue—a score of scowling men—fell in behind as Demetrios wended his way through the labyrinth of carved paths, like eerie alleys in some strange underground city. Men were hard at work in various places, cutting limestone blocks and dragging them to the hoists, and the air was filled with the constant, cacophonous noise of their labor: pounding and scraping . . . the spectacularly slow harvesting of stone.

Despite the fact that he had been reunited with his old friend, Nikias was depressed. He had hated lying to Demetrios, and recounting the events of the preceding years had weighed heavily on his soul. He thought of Kallisto and his daughters with worry and sorrow . . . and when a vision of Helena appeared before his eyes, he felt a stab of profound guilt.

"How did you become the Quarry Lord?" Nikias asked as they walked.

"I killed the old Quarry Lord," said Demetrios. "I challenged him on my first day. It wasn't hard. I'd been trained in the pankration by the great Menesarkus of Plataea, after all."

Nikias glanced at Demetrios. He thought that he'd detected a hint of scorn when Demetrios said his grandfather's name. Or had he just imagined it?

"I reckoned I could last for a couple of months with the poor rations they were giving us," continued Demetrios, "and then someone from the Upside who was stronger would come in and slay me in my turn. So I concocted a plan." He spoke in a loud voice—as though to say to his men, "We have no secrets between us."

Nikias looked around at the gang prisoners. Most stared at Demetrios with respect, while a few frowned at Nikias with suspicion. "What kind of plan?" he asked.

"I told the prisoners that we must refuse to cut stone until they upped our rations," said Demetrios. "I told them that we might all starve to death, didn't I?"

The men muttered and smiled.

"And things went hard for the first month," said Demetrios. "Many *did* starve, but we held out. It's all economics, my friend," he said, slapping Nikias on the back. "The war between the Spartans and Athenians is all about resources. Nothing more. Oh, men on the Upside like Perikles and the Spartan kings might blather on about the glories of war and the oaths and the gods and all of that rubbish. But we in the Pit know the truth. Half of the men here were the enemies of Pantares—merchants and mariners who defied the oligarchs of Syrakuse and lost. But those same rich and powerful men finally gave up and promised us more rations. We get the wheat, meat, and wine, and they get their precious limestone. As long as they keep building, we eat. We live another day. We live to get revenge."

They had come to a stop by a wall pockmarked with many deep orifices. It reminded Nikias of a dead tree that had been riddled with holes from a woodpecker, only these dark openings were about as broad as a man's shoulders.

"Welcome to the honeycombs," said Demetrios.

Nikias realized that men's feet protruded from the holes. Prisoners had been stuffed into these narrow man-made fissures face-first . . . crammed so tightly that there wasn't enough room to budge an inch from side to side, tighter than a tomb. He shuddered as the memory of the secret tunnel in Plataea came rushing back to him. The tunnel had collapsed around him, dousing his lantern, and he had been stuck for a time, buried underground in the darkest place he had ever know. And it terrified him.

The reek of human waste wafted from the holes.

"Why are they in there?" Nikias asked, his voice barely above a whisper.

"They are being punished," said Demetrios. "They are lawbreakers. Men who steal from their brother quarrymen, or refuse to work."

All at once Nikias remembered that Diokles had been taken to the honeycombs before Nikias had fought the two quarrymen to the death. The Helot had already been in here for, what? Five or six hours? Stewing in his own shit and urine. Barely able to breathe in the stultifying space. "Where is my friend?" he asked, running to the wall and searching for the Helot's dark feet. He found them and put his hand on one of Diokles's heels and a muffled cry came from within the hole. He grabbed Diokles's ankles and started to drag him out, but someone bulled into him, knocking him down. Demetrios stood over him, smiling dangerously.

"What are you doing, Nik?" Demetrios asked in a toneless voice.

"You can't keep him in there—he'll go mad!" said Nikias, springing to his feet.

"It's the law of the quarry," said Demetrios. "Your friend didn't want to fight and you had to kill for him. I spared his life but he must be punished for indolence. If you try to pull him out again, my men will slay you both."

Nikias tore his eyes away from Demetrios's chilling gaze and stared at the men in his entourage, who were glaring back, ready to attack. He looked back at Demetrios. Gone was the best friend from his youth—standing before him was the Quarry Lord, and he expected to be obeyed.

"How long must he stay like that?" Nikias asked.

"We'll give him a few days to ponder his misdeed," said Demetrios.

"He's a skilled digger," said Nikias. "He was a slave in a Spartan ore mine. He escaped during an earthquake. He could be of use to you."

"We'll come back to him in a few days," came Demetrios's icy reply.

Nikias realized there was nothing that he could do, and although he burned with fury, he had learned to mask his anger in the last couple of years. He'd learned to wait and bide his time. He forced himself to smile and said, "You're the Quarry Lord. You rule here."

"The *law* rules here," said Demetrios sternly. "Not Demetrios." Then his dark look faded and he smiled good-naturedly. He gestured at one of the holes and said, "Let's see how our old friend the Admiral is doing." Two of his men went to a hole near the floor of the quarry, grabbed a man by the ankles, and dragged him out. He was as stiff as a piece of wood pulled from a lumber pile. They rolled him onto his back and Nikias recoiled at the sight. The man was emaciated, his hair lank. He was covered with his own filth and stank horribly, and his legs and torso were covered with sores. His eyes stared vacantly into nothing and his body trembled and twitched. He had been a stately-looking man once, Nikias supposed, but his face was gaunt and haunted, the eyes sunk into his skull. He could not tell if he was young or old.

"This one was an unfortunate Syrakusan admiral who lost a sea battle with some Karthaginians," said Demetrios. "His fellow citizens put him on trial and he was found guilty of negligence. They sent him here, and he did all right at first. He won his fight handily and so earned the right—like you—to live, and he set to work pounding stone like a good man. But word came to me from my whisperers that the Admiral was trying to undermine my authority. Called me a tyrant behind my back."

Demetrios squatted by the Admiral and looked him up and down, shaking his head sadly. "Now look at him."

"How long has he been in there?" asked Nikias, aghast.

"Three weeks at least," said Demetrios. "A little too long, I think. I forgot about him. Now I think he's overcooked. We'll be sure to remember your friend the Helot, though."

Nikias stared in horror at his friend—at the callous way he was talking about this human being—a man who had once been an admiral, a skilled seaman and a leader . . . a man who was now crushed and ruined. Nothing more than a shell. He had seen something in Demetrios's face and manner just then that reminded him of someone else—a man who had tried to take control of Plataea and who had stood in front of its citizens in the Assembly Hall, full of self-importance and hubris, and acting very much like a tyrant. That man had been Nauklydes, Demetrios's own father.

"Take the Admiral to the infirmary," said Demetrios brusquely. "Give him some water."

The quarrymen who'd pulled him from the hole easily lifted up the Admiral's skinny body and carried him away. Demetrios put his hand on Nikias's back and said jovially, "Come on. I've got something to show you."

Nikias followed Demetrios in a daze. When they stopped he looked up and saw they were standing outside of the great gash in the side of the quarry—the Ear of Dionysus.

"Stay outside," Demetrios commanded his entourage, then he led Nikias into the cool dark cave that was lit by a few oil lamps sitting on the floor and in wall niches. Once they were deep inside Demetrios whispered, "Remember the Cave of Nymphs?" And his voice seemed to fly and hiss around the chamber like a living thing, twisting and flapping and hanging in the air overhead.

"Of course," said Nikias, and his words joined Demetrios's, bouncing and echoing above. Nikias thought of the Cave of Nymphs—the place where he and Kallisto had first made love. It seemed so long ago now. Like something that had happened to another man in a different life. A character in a bard's song. That cave was very different from this expansive place. The Cave of Nymphs was small and welcoming . . . a place of refuge and secrecy. "We used to hunt the Minotaur in there when we were boys," said Nikias, and the word "Minotaur" morphed into a beast-like growl.

"The Tyrant has a place above where he listens," said Demetrios in the bar-est whisper, and his words seemed to soar upward to the top of the cave. "He can hear everything we say." He grinned and put a finger to his lips, then sucked in his breath and shouted in his loudest voice. "Hello, Pantares, you greasy goat-stuffing pimple on a satyr's prick!"

Nikias stopped his ears with his hands and grimaced as Demetrios's voice reverberated like a storm throughout the cave. Demetrios picked up a lamp and gestured for Nikias to follow him through a fissure in the rock and passed down a narrow corridor. They walked in silence for some distance until they came to a wall of stone. At the bottom of this wall was a small opening that led into a dark horizontal shaft. They were now far from the Ear of Dionysus—probably a hundred feet away, straight into the heart of the mass of limestone. When Demetrios spoke his voice was muffled.

"Interesting that Barka told you to tell me that he listens at the Ear at noontime every day. That may come in very useful."

"Useful for what?" asked Nikias. He was growing agitated in this confined space. He didn't know why Demetrios had brought him here and he was loath to ask, for he realized that he was now afraid of his friend. He had thought that there had been a cord that had connected them all of these years—like a golden rope crafted by a god. But now he realized that that notion was an illusion. Demetrios was not the same person that he had once been. Or perhaps he was *exactly* the same person, only amplified by what had happened to him here in Syrakuse. His soul had become twisted, like the sound of his voice flying about in the Ear of Dionysus.

"Do you believe in the gods anymore?" asked Demetrios. "After all that has happened to you? Your mother and all of our friends murdered by Thebans. And you—shipwrecked and tortured and mutilated by the enemy? And now you're here, cut off from your wife and children—an exile from your land. You don't even know if Kallisto and your baby are alive."

"I want to believe in Zeus and Apollo and all of the others," said Nikias. "It's all that I know."

"But isn't belief in the *self* enough?" asked Demetrios. "Do you know yourself, Nikias? Do you truly know who you are?"

"I think so."

"Who are you, then?"

"A Plataean. A father. A husband."

"Is that all?"

Nikias frowned. "Isn't that enough?"

"Men made up the gods," said Demetrios. "Tales to scare children. If I blow out this lamp and we are plunged into darkness, who made it so?" He puffed out his cheeks and exhaled. The flame vanished and an inky blackness surrounded them like a cloak of death.

Nikias tried not to panic, but the utter lack of light was unnerving. He felt as if he was floating.

"Did a god make it dark?" asked Demetrios. "No. It was me. Nothing more than my air. And if I am wise enough to have brought flint and a knife to start another spark, who would be responsible for that? Did a god put that thought into my head? Was it Prometheus? The fire bringer? No, Nikias."

Nikias saw a shower of sparks erupt in the darkness. In the flash of light made by the sparks he saw that Demetrios was now on his knees in front of the lamp. Another spray of sparks and the lamp's wick flamed to life again.

"*I* am Prometheus," said Demetrios. "*You* are Apollo. Or Ares, or whatever god you choose to be. Humans came up with things like fire and the building of temples all on our own. The gods are dead, because they were never alive. They're the ashes of men's dreams."

What Demetrios was saying wasn't new to Nikias. He had heard overeducated men say things like this before, at symposiums or standing on boxes in the agora. But it was the manner in which his friend was saying the words that was so startling—with absolute conviction and without emotion. Demetrios had always been very pious. But now the gods were nothing to him. In his mind they didn't exist. And that was shocking.

"The moment that I was lowered down into the quarry," continued Demetrios, leaning against the wall and staring at the light of the lamp, "I knew that I would one day escape. I knew that there would be no god in a machine to rescue me, like at the ending of some stupid play. I knew that I would have to be the one to come up with a plan. For I have always believed that I am the master of my own fate, and not some toothless old hags who live in a dream world."

"So?" asked Nikias, somewhat petulantly. "What have you done since you've been here other than make up laws and torture your fellow prisoners?"

Demetrios smiled. "And that's why I love you, Nik. You were never afraid of me. Everyone has always been afraid of me, my entire life. Even my own father. For he could see my potential and it scared him. He knew that I would rise above anything that he had ever done. But you . . . you always saw yourself as my equal, and I loved you for it. Great things are coming in this war with the Spartans and Athenians. The chance to make names for ourselves. The opportunity to become legends."

Nikias couldn't believe how unhinged Demetrios sounded. How full of self-love, even in this wretched state. "Don't go kissing your own reflection in a pond," he said. "You might end up drowning."

Demetrios laughed, evidently amused by the appalled look on Nikias's face. "You think I'm touched," he said. "I may be a little mad, I'll admit. But I am a genius. Behold." He gestured at the opening.

"What am I looking at?" asked Nikias. "Another Honeycomb hole? Are you going to put me in this one?" He was starting to grow angry. The confined space was stifling. He suddenly hated Demetrios and wanted to throttle him.

"Listen," said Demetrios. "They're coming."

Nikias put his head to the shaft and listened. At first he heard nothing, but then came the faintest sound of voices, the shuffling of feet, and the scraping of stones. After a while a man appeared crawling on hands and knees, dragging a wineskin filled with rocks and dirt. When he saw Demetrios standing outside the shaft entrance, he smiled and saluted him, then stood up and hefted the bag over his shoulder.

"The ground is becoming moist, Quarry Lord," said the digger. "Just like you said it would. We're getting close to the swamp."

"Excellent," said Demetrios.

Nikias stood in silence and watched as half a dozen more men came out bearing wineskins full of debris. They were covered with dust, their hair matted with sweat.

"They have to work in small groups now," said Demetrios. "It takes a long time to get to the end of the shaft. It's almost half a mile long, and only the most stalwart diggers can handle the confined space."

"What's the shaft for?" asked Nikias.

"What's it for?" asked Demetrios. "What do you think I've been doing these last three years? Lording around this quarry like a crackpot tyrant? Pounding rocks so the Syrakusans can build themselves another public latrine? No. I've been putting this mighty army to work for me. A few feet every day, year after year. Like a ceaselessly pounding wave that slowly eats away a shore. My ancestors—like yours, Nikias—were leaders and heroes. We were born to lead."

"Where does it go?" asked Nikias, though he reckoned he knew the answer as soon as he'd asked the question, and he couldn't help but smile at the sheer audacity of what Demetrios had done.

"To freedom, of course!" Demetrios turned and headed back up the corridor in the direction of the Ear of Dionysus. "You lucky sheep-stuffer," he said over his shoulder. "We'll be out of here in a month, on our way to Naupaktos to join your cousin Phoenix and the others. And together we'll make our way back to the Oxlands and save our citadel from the enemy."

TEN

It was just after sunrise and Chusor walked the battle deck of the *Spear of Thetis* with a mingled feeling of pride and relief. Over the last four weeks almost all of the repairs to the ship had been made, thanks to the small fortune in treasure that Kolax had brought with him, and the ship was beautiful and seaworthy once again.

How strange that a dead Korinthian spy's gold and jewels had saved them from disaster!

The ship was now fitted with a new mainmast and fine hemp sails. The outrigger decks that had been partially wrecked in the battle off Serifos had been completely repaired, and a new bronze-covered ram had been made and fitted into the prow. Chusor had even found a source of naptha and had renewed their stockpile of the precious stuff for his fire-spewing weapon. Most important, the crew and women and children—who had been on the verge of starvation—had been eating well all this time. Nobody was sick, which made Ezekiel happy and allowed the doctor to spend his days basking like a tortoise on whatever shore the ship was beached.

There were many city-states on the island of Sicily that were bitter enemies of Syrakuse—men who had followed the rebel Syrakusan Doketios years ago, and were still craving freedom. And so the *Spear*, bearing precious gems as its passport, had been able to find havens all along the coast of the vast island, as well as buy these much-needed supplies. Kolax had brought so much wealth with him that they had been able to purchase a sleek black sixty-oared ship to hold their excess crew members. They named her the *Briseis* after the bewitching princess that Akilles had captured during the Trojan War. Now that the women of Serifos were proficient rowers, they could operate both ships with mixed male and female crews. Kolax started calling the women the *Oiorpatas*, which meant "Man-killers" in Skythian. In the Greek tongue the word was "Amazon"—a name the women proudly bore, though they joked that they weren't about to hack off one of their breasts like those famous female warriors of Sarmatia.

The two vessels had made nearly a complete circle around Sicily over the last cycle of the moon, going first west, then east, somehow managing to avoid the many Syrakusan triremes that were on the prowl in the shipping lanes. They were now beached on a little barren cove ten miles north of Syrakuse, and the crew was spread out on the sand, sitting around multiple fires, eating their morning meal.

All was well. . . .

But how long would their good fortune last? And what had made Chusor steer the ship so close to Syrakuse? At least, that was what many of the crew had been muttering.

The answer was simple: he knew that Barka had saved Nikias and Kolax from certain death that day in the courtyard. Based on what Kolax had said about the events that had unfolded, Pantares had been in a murdering mood and would have slain Nikias and Diokles, mingling their blood with the Korinthian spy's, if Barka had not stepped in and convinced the Tyrant to send them to the quarries. Now that the ship was repaired—now that they weren't like a crippled man drowning in the sea—Chusor could risk trying to get more information from the eunuch—to find out if Nikias and Diokles yet lived. The only way to do that was to send someone back into the city and make contact with him.

He looked over the side of the boat to where Kolax was practicing archery with Melitta. The two had grown close over the last month. The Skythian boy obviously adored his daughter, doting on her like a lovesick fool, and Chusor had been loath to discover that Melitta had begun to return his affections. The thought of his only beloved child marrying a barbarian—especially one as dangerous and brutish as Kolax—was repulsive. The two fourteen-year-olds were laughing about something now, and Melitta was slapping Kolax playfully. Kolax pretended to trip and fall, begging her to spare his life as she stood over him brandishing her bow. Chusor had never seen Kolax so frolicsome, nor could he recall Melitta taking even the slightest interest in any boy.

"I am ready to depart," said a voice at Chusor's side.

He turned and stared vacantly at Ji. "Good," he said. "Be careful. And watch out that Kolax doesn't do anything stupid."

"The boy can take care of himself," said Ji.

Melitta was on top of Kolax now, pinning him with her knees and tickling him mercilessly. Kolax's pale face grew red and he screamed with laughter.

Chusor wondered if it was even worth the risk to send Ji and Kolax on this mission. What hope was there to rescue Nikias and Diokles from the horrible Prison Pits? Chusor knew what the place was like firsthand. Years ago he had lived in Syrakuse—an apprentice of the famous siege master Naxos. General Pantares, hearing a rumor that Chusor had meddled with his daughter, had him locked in a beehive cell to punish him and break his spirit. Chusor spent a week crammed into one of those narrow stone tubes. He was saved only because Naxos paid a great sum for his release. Afterward Pantares's men tried to slay Chusor in the streets of Ortygia; he escaped through a sewer tunnel into the bay, where he crawled on board Zana's old ship and hid in the hold.

He watched Ji climb down the ladder and onto the beach. Then the assassin strode over to the barbarian and told him to get up—that it was time to go. Kolax got to his feet and started to follow Ji up the beach, but Melitta ran after them, stopping the Skythian lad and kissing him on the cheek. Kolax smiled and ruffled her hair affectionately.

"Gods spare me," said Chusor under his breath.

He made his way down the ladder to the lower deck and opened the door to the cabin. Helena sat on the bed with her back to the wall, a bucket on her lap, looking very pale. The room smelled of vomit. Ezekiel sat by her side, taking her pulse. He handed the bucket to Chusor and said, "Dump this in the sea, if you will."

"Is she all right?" Chusor asked, taking the bucket.

"Fine, fine," said Ezekiel. "As I've already told you, strong babies make the mother sick."

Helena looked at Chusor and smiled wanly. "Nikias is coming back to us," she said. "I told you that I saw him in my dream. He wore a red cloak. . . ."

Chusor nodded and left the cabin, shutting the door behind him. He climbed down one of the landing ladders to the beach and walked to the water, dumping the bucket in the lapping waves, then washed it until the stink was gone. He thought of Helena, pregnant with Nikias's child, and shook his head sadly. Even amidst such strife the human body creates new life. It seemed idiotic—almost contrary to nature. He thought of Helena's strange dream, too—a vision that she had had two days ago as they'd passed Mount Aetna. She'd seen Nikias standing beneath the volcano, and fire raining down upon him, but the fire did not burn him. And he wore a red cloak like a Spartan.

The sound of angry voices stirred him from his musings. He tossed the bucket on the beach and sprinted around the prow, where he found a large crowd of men facing each other—Plataean rowers on one side, Serifans on the other.

"It's suicide!" a rower of Serifos was saying. "We're too close to Syrakuse. I know this shore. We're lucky we haven't been spotted yet."

"We're going to rescue Nikias," replied a Plataean rower. "That's why we're here."

"Insanity—"

"You can't rescue a prisoner from the quarries!"

"What's going on?" Chusor asked, pushing his way into the center of the men.

Agrios stepped forward and said, "My Serifan brothers wish to depart immediately for Naupaktos. The Plataeans want to stay until there is word of their young friend."

Chusor looked around at the angry faces on either side. He could sense that a brawl might break out at any moment. "We wait for Ji and Kolax to return," he said. "We give them two days."

"You're an idiot, Chusor!" said one of the more pugnacious of the Serifan rowers. He took a threatening step toward Chusor, but an instant later he was hit in the face with a bucket of water and he spluttered as he wiped the stinging seawater from his eyes, "Stupid girl!"

Chusor whirled and saw Melitta standing there holding a dripping bucket, a dark scowl on her pretty face. "Nikias saved my life on Serifos," she said, throwing down the bucket at the rower's feet. "If it hadn't been for him, many of us would be dead." She turned and pointed at Agrios. "Let's let him decide."

Chusor grimaced. Even though he was the captain of the *Spear*, the Serifans would heed whatever Agrios said. If the old man were to tell them they must depart Sicily now, there would be a riot if Chusor tried to thwart this course. So he held his tongue and waited for the man to speak.

"This is what I have to say," said Agrios. "On the day that the Korinthians threw our women and children into the sea, young Nikias jumped in to save them. He found my only grandson clinging to an amphora, near dead, and swam him over to a spar and held him there until we came and pulled them from the sea. My only heir is alive because of Nikias, so if you want someone to steer your ship, you'll wait here with me for two days longer. Then we go."

The crowd quickly dispersed and Chusor and Melitta were left alone. His daughter looked at him contritely.

"I didn't know what else to do," she said.

"Take this back to your sister," said Chusor, picking up the bucket and handing it to her.

She nodded demurely. "Yes, Father."

"And thank you," he said. "You're a clever girl."

She smiled and skipped toward the landing ladder.

ELEVEN

"Hyakinthos, if you still love me, kill Pantares. . . ."

Barka lay with his head crammed between silk pillows. He was in Pantares's bed. It was morning. He had to get up. But he couldn't make himself move. All that he could hear was Demetrios's voice echoing in his brain—a voice distorted by the weird acoustics of the Ear of Dionysus.

"K-k-kill Pantaressss-aresssss-aressss. . . ."

The eunuch sat up abruptly and looked at the bed. Pantares had gotten up early that morning but Barka could still see the impression in the bed made by the corpulent general's body. He could have killed Pantares last night when they were making love. Or at any time that he had been asleep during the last week since Demetrios had made his request. It would be so easy. Barka wore a bejeweled ring on his left hand. The ring had a hinged top. All he had to do was wedge one of his fingernails under the jewel and push it open to reveal a poisoned needle. It was a deadly toxin—nightshade, foxglove, and oleander. One scratch and Pantares's heart would soon stop beating.

Why hadn't he done so, then? Barka wasn't afraid of killing. He had poisoned men before for less important things than a lover's request. But he was afraid of what would happen *afterward*. How would he escape from the citadel? And why was Demetrios asking him to put himself in such danger? How would they be reunited?

He shifted on his bed. He could hear the general's household slaves chattering in the hallway outside his bedchamber. He wanted to scream at them to shut up, but he couldn't make himself speak. He felt sick.

"Kill . . ."

It had been twenty-eight days since Demetrios had first spoken to him through the Ear of Dionysus. What a glorious moment that had been! It had occurred two days after Nikias and Diokles were consigned to the quarry. Barka went to listen at the Ear at zenith as he always did, hoping against hope to hear his lover's voice. At first he heard the familiar voice of the Quarry Lord, speaking with his harsh Karthaginian accent. But then the voice changed suddenly into Demetrios's—a soft whisper like a hand on silk that sent a shiver up his spine. The Quarry Lord and Demetrios were one and the same. Oh, strong and clever youth!

"My friend Nikias claims that you are the listener," he had said. "Give me a token so that I know you are my Hyakinthos and not a trick."

At the sound of the pet name Demetrios had given him, Barka had felt his heart skip a beat. He dropped his ring down the chute and into the cave. It was the ring that Demetrios had given him on their "wedding day," bearing a carving of Pegasos.

"I know this ring," Demetrios had said. "And only Hyakinthos, my true love, would know the importance of it."

Demetrios had then begged Barka's forgiveness for leaving him in the sea. He said he'd panicked. That he'd been a coward. That he'd never forgiven himself. Barka wept at these words and wanted to shout to him that he was forgiven, but he could not let Pantares's men hear him conversing with someone in the cave below. The Tyrant would become suspicious. So all that Barka could do was listen and weep with joy.

The next time Demetrios spoke to him, a few days later, Barka dropped a note down the hole. In the message he had written that he still loved Demetrios and forgave him everything. He had signed the missive, "Still your slave." Their magical correspondence continued for several weeks, then stopped abruptly, sending Barka into a state of near hysteria. But then, ten days ago, Demetrios's voice whispered to him the message: "Hyakinthos, if you still love me, kill Pantares." And then he had added something cryptic: "Persephone will arise at our shrine on the next black moon."

He knew that Demetrios had to be mysterious in case somebody else was listening. But it didn't make sense. "Our shrine" . . . Barka knew what that meant: the Shrine of Artemis, where Demetrios had given him the Pegasos ring. But what did the young maiden Persephone—the goddess stolen by Hades and taken to the underworld—have to do with anything? Demetrios did not speak to him again after that. A wretched week passed without the sound of his dear voice. There would be no moon in two days' time.

"You!" shouted Barka as a slave peeked her head in the door. "Where is your master?"

"Away," replied the slave fearfully. "I have brought you clean water for your basin." The slave quickly did her duties. When she was done, Barka told her to get out and she scurried from the chamber.

The eunuch got up and went to a basin and washed his face. Then he put on a dress and pinned up his hair. He slipped into his sandals and went down the stairs where his two scowling guards were waiting for him. How Barka hated those two!

He ignored them and swept out the door and they fell in behind him. Barka didn't know where he was going. It was too early to go to the Ear and listen. So he headed for the Old Market. When he turned a corner he caught sight of a lad peering at him from the shadows of a wine shop across the street. It was Kolax! He hadn't seen the Skythian since the day at Pantares's on the balcony.

One of the guards grabbed Barka by the arm and turned him in the opposite direction—toward the dike that connected Ortygia to the mainland.

"The general wants to see you at the theatre," said the guard, squeezing Barka's slender arm.

"You're hurting me!" hissed Barka, and pulled his arm away from the guard.

The Tyrsenians fell in on either side of Barka, leading him on a silent march across the land bridge and into the New City. Barka kept casting surreptitious glances behind him to see if Kolax was following, but he didn't see the barbarian again. When they got near the path that led to the quarry, Barka was shocked to see phalanxes of armored soldiers moving in that direction.

"What's going on?" Barka asked with trepidation.

But the guards were silent. They made him turn left and headed toward the Theatre of Dionysus. There were men at work toting stone for the new marble seats that Barka knew Pantares had purchased for the magistrates of Syrakuse. And when Barka entered the theatre he saw the Tyrant sitting on a great marble throne-like chair that had been placed there for him—the seat of honor for the chief of the oligarchs to watch the plays that he paid to be performed. Six of his Tyrsenian bodyguards stood nearby.

"I have written to Euripides of Athens," Pantares said as Barka approached. "I had the letter delivered to a cave on the island of Salamis, where he lives. Imagine living in a cave? Ludicrous."

"Why have you written to a playwright?" asked Barka.

"Inviting him to come to Syrakuse, of course," said Pantares. "To write a play about the lad Bellerophon who blasphemed against the gods and tried to fly to Mount Olympus. It was always my favorite tale—a young and overweening man, full of hubris, defying the gods. I want a great crane built that will fly horse and rider over the audience. It will be spectacular."

Barka trembled, thinking of the carved ring that he had dropped into the Ear of Dionysus. Bellerophon's horse was Pegasos—the same image carved on Demetrios's ring. Did Pantares know that he had been communicating with Demetrios? But the general's sagging eyes betrayed nothing but lassitude.

"Why are the warriors amassing near the quarry?" Barka asked.

"I have decided to root out this man called the Quarry Lord," said Pantares. "I'm going to burn all of the prisoners out of their caves with oil and naptha, slay them to the man, and stock the place with skilled stonecutters from Italia. What does my soothsayer think of this plan?"

Barka blanched and tried not to show any emotion. "It seems strange to kill prisoners who work for free."

"Free? I have to feed them," said Pantares. "They don't live off the air." He stared at Barka and his eyes became cold and hard. "What do you hear when you go to the Ear of Dionysus, Barka my love?"

"Nothing," said Barka. "I've told you. Just the ravings of a mad man. The Quarry Lord—"

Pantares stood up suddenly and smiled at Barka, and the eunuch stopped speaking. "Ah, Barka," said Pantares, with a sly smile. "We both know who the Quarry Lord is. Your lover Demetrios. The one I should have killed long ago, when I first had the chance. But I wanted him to suffer and be humiliated before he died, and that was a mistake, for that young man proved himself to be as wily as Odysseus."

A distant din carried on the wind just then—the sound of men shouting, the clash of weapons . . . and screams. The noise came from the direction of the quarry.

Barka stood very still, but he couldn't control the shudders that kept coursing through his body. Pantares was sending an army into the quarry to kill Demetrios. He looked around the theatre but the entrances were blocked by the Tyrsenians.

"Don't try to run," said Pantares, evidently catching sight of Barka's glances. "There's no way that you can warn him. It's too late. The quarrymen will not be able to fight against armored men. It amazes me that two bumpkins from Plataea—a place that I have never been and never wish to see—have caused me so much annoyance."

Barka threw himself at Pantares's feet, clinging to them. "Please, don't kill Demetrios. He's just a foolish lad. He never did you any harm."

"He stole you from me!" snapped Pantares. "When I have his corpse I'm going to stick you in a beehive cell with it, face-to-face like sweet lovers, and you can kiss his dead lips until the flesh rots! You stinking tool of the Spartans! Don't deny it. I know that you have spied on me for the Red Cloaks." He put one foot on the top of Barka's head and ground his face into the stone floor, as Barka grasped desperately at Pantares's heel.

"Ah! What have you done?" asked Pantares in surprise, dancing away and holding his foot. "What did you poke into my foot?"

Barka looked up with a cold smile, blood pouring from his nose. He got slowly to a sitting position and laughed—a laugh filled with hatred and mockery. He showed Pantares the poison ring, then held the deadly needle close to his own neck.

"What have you done?" repeated Pantares, and stumbled back to his marble chair, collapsing onto it, his face white. "My heart!" he cried, holding a hand to his breast. "It aches!"

The Tyrsenians came forward and looked at Pantares with mute curiosity.

"Your master is having a seizure of the heart," said Barka. "You should call for a doctor."

"Kill . . . Barka," Pantares wheezed with his dying breath, then went very still and his eyes rolled up toward the blue sky.

The Tyrsenians surrounded Barka, eyeing the small man as if he were a dangerous snake. But Barka made no movement. He was ready to die. But by his own hand. He exhaled slowly, summoning the courage to plunge the needle into his vein, when something strange happened—the Tyrsenians started falling—struck with arrows—spurting blood. Then there was a whirl of bodies and swords—a weird and frantic windstorm of blood and iron. Barka squeezed his eyes shut, shrinking back, and when he opened them a few seconds later—after the sound of violence had stopped—he saw Ji and Kolax staring down at him. They were spattered with blood and breathing hard, but they seemed to be unscathed.

"Barka," said Ji. "Put your poison ring away."

Barka closed the cap on the ring with trembling fingers and allowed Kolax to help him to his feet. The orchestra of the theatre was covered with gore and bodies—like at the end of a tragedy. And the corpse of Pantares sat with his palms together, as if he had died clapping.

"Do you know anything about Nikias?" Kolax asked. "Tell us, quickly!"

Barka swooned, but Kolax and Ji caught him. Then the eunuch had a strange vision—the ground near the Shrine of Artemis collapsing and hands reaching from the ground. It was so obvious. How could he have not understood the message?

"There's a tunnel," said Barka in a constricted voice. "A tunnel. They're going to escape. The egress. I know where it lies."

TWELVE

———◆———

Nikias gripped a stone club with two hands, swinging back and forth at a Syrakusan shield painted with the symbol of the triskeles—three bent legs connected at the center. He focused his fury on the image, pounding relentlessly until the armored warrior bearing the shield let it droop, exposing the crown of his head.

Boom!

His blow spun the enemy hoplite's helm halfway around, snapping his neck. The Syrakusan had taken a wrong turn in the labyrinth of the quarry and been cut off from his comrades. Nikias had leapt from a small cave entrance, surprising him. And now the warrior's life was bleeding into the gray limestone dust at Nikias's feet.

Nikias pounced on the corpse, stripping the man of helm, shield, and sword. There was no time to take the hoplite's armor, and it would only slow him down in the escape tunnel—the place that he had to get to before the seemingly endless stream of Syrakusan hoplites managed to seal off the entrance. He put on the helm, strapped the shield to his arm, and gripped the sword, running down the narrow passageway to an open space near the place below the cranes.

Everywhere naptha fires burned and prisoners fought for their lives in the grottos, arches, and narrow passageways of the quarry. The Syrakusan attack had not caught the quarrymen off guard—the foolish warriors had taken a long time to descend to the quarry on the cranes, guarded by archers from above. And they were overconfident in their armor. The prisoners had been secreting weapons for years—chisels attached to poles with animal sinews, iron hammers, slings made from hides, and stone clubs cut from the limestone itself. And the quarrymen knew every twist and turn of their prison—a maze that could not be mapped from above.

Demetrios had been preparing for a day like this. But he had been dismayed that it had come so close to the completion of the escape tunnel. The best diggers were sent into the passageway to attempt to break through the last few feet of the tunnel, while the rest fought the Syrakusans and defended the entrance to the Ear of Dionysus. They even hastily erected a low wall in front of the cave, guarded by peltasts.

Nikias ran past the honeycombs. Diokles had long since been freed from the wretched cells, and had shown his worth as a digger—he was in the escape tunnel right now. But Nikias stopped at the sight of two feet wriggling frantically. He grabbed the ankles and pulled hard, dragging a body from the stone tube. It was Thersites—the crazy little man he'd met when he was lowered into the quarry on that first day. Thersites had been accused of stealing someone's meat ration the day before and had been punished. He lay on the ground, twitching and blinking.

"What's going on?" he asked, smiling in his lunatic way.

"Syrakusan hoplites, in the quarry," said Nikias.

"A festival of some sort?" asked Thersites.

"Follow me," said Nikias.

He crept through a nearby archway where a score of prisoners lay dead and burned on the ground. The place reeked of naptha and charred flesh.

"A sacrifice," said Thersites. "The Karthaginians slay their firstborn sons, you know?"

Nikias picked up a dead man's club and handed it to Thersites.

"What's this for?" Thersites asked.

"To slay men."

"Oh, I can do that," replied Thersites. "I fought with the rebel Doketios!" he added proudly. He swung the club, barely missing Nikias's head.

"Give me that!" said Nikias angrily. He snatched the club from him and threw it on the ground. Thersites's face fell and his eyes welled up with tears. Nikias handed him the shield and dagger, saying, "Here, take these."

"Where are we going?" asked Thersites.

"We have to get back to the Ear."

"I know a better way," said Thersites, for just then a mass of Syrakusan hoplites came into view from around the corner of a wall. Thersites darted out the way they had come and led Nikias through a narrow opening cut in the outer wall of the quarry. They entered a dark passageway that Nikias had never been in before.

"Are you sure you know where this goes?" Nikias asked. Ever since he had escaped from the secret tunnel under Plataea, he had developed a profound fear of cramped spaces. Here his shoulders touched each side of the passage, and there were places where he had to turn sideways to squeeze through. He shuddered at the thought of Thersites coming to a dead end and having to turn around in this tight space. Nikias wanted to tear off the helm, but he couldn't move his hands up high enough to grasp it, and he started to feel as though he might suffocate.

"Thersites!" he cried.

"Follow!" said Thersites cheerfully. "Almost there. The last earthquake made this passage. It's tight up here. As tight as a sheep's cunny, if you know what I mean," he added with a lascivious tone, and made a crude sound with his lips.

Finally Nikias started to see an orange glow up ahead, and soon enough they emerged into a cave that Nikias recognized as one of the places that contained a huge cistern—a chamber that was only a spear's throw from the Ear of Dionysus.

He went to the mouth of the cave and peered out to the left. A naptha fire raged at the entrance to the Ear. The Syrakusans had tried to burn out the quarrymen from their hiding place behind the limestone barricade. But the fire only created another impediment to the cave, forcing the Syrakusans to back up into the open space, where they had formed up a phalanx with their shields making a protective wall.

The area in front of the barricade was littered with dead prisoners and Syrakusans. Through the flames Nikias could see Demetrios wearing the stone mask and wielding a sling. He flung a pellet through the flames, straight into the helm of an enemy warrior in the phalanx—a killing shot that sent the man tumbling backward.

"Lovely aim," said Thersites, who was now crouched by his side.

Many more stones flew from the cave, slamming into the Syrakusans, and they were forced to move even farther back.

Nikias looked to the right and saw prisoners cut off from the Ear like himself, fighting the Syrakusans in ones and twos. But they were quickly being overwhelmed by the armored hoplites. The enemy had them outnumbered now. Nikias wondered if Diokles and the others had broken through the final section of tunnel yet.

"We have to get into the Ear," said Nikias.

Two Syrakusans stepped from the phalanx and hurled clay pots at the barricade. They burst into flames and the fire roared halfway up the height of the gash—almost fifty feet into the air.

"That will prove difficult now," said Thersites, slipping into the shadows of the cave.

Nikias cursed and tried to think of what to do with armored Syrakusans on one side and a wall of flames on the other.

"Have a bath!" called out Thersites.

Nikias heard a splash. Thersites had jumped into one of the cisterns and submerged himself in the tank. He came up spitting water and laughing.

"What are you doing, you sheep-stuffing madman?"

"Making myself wet so I don't burn when we run through the fire," replied Thersites. "I was a mariner before coming on vacation here. I know all about Poseidon's piss!"

Nikias smiled. "You mad genius!" he said, and plunged into the tank beside him. He took off the helm and soaked his head, then got out and put the helm back on.

"Quick, now!" shouted Thersites.

They bolted from the cave, screaming as they ran. A warrior tried to step in front of Nikias to block their way, but Nikias struck him down with a brutal blow and leapt into the flames. His skin sizzled as he plunged through the orange fire, and he ran blindly, slamming into the wall outside the cave and nearly knocking himself out. He reached up, grabbing onto the top of the wall, heaving himself up and over. The crudely built wall crumbled under his weight and he fell onto the floor of the cave, covered in debris, with flames rolling across him like a wave of fire.

"Nikias!"

Demetrios was on him, striking his body with an animal hide to put out the flames that clung to his body.

Nikias got to his feet and tore off the helm. His arms and thighs had been singed, but other than that he was unharmed. Thersites had not fared as well—his eyebrows and beard had been burned off his face, but the scraggly hair on the top of his head remained.

There were only twenty or so quarrymen left in the cave, and Demetrios ordered them all to head for the passage that led to the escape tunnel.

"Is the tunnel open?" Nikias shouted above the roar of the fire, and his voice echoed strangely.

"I don't know," answered Demetrios. "We might all become trapped in the tunnel, but we have to risk it. Come on!"

The remaining quarrymen ducked into the passage and disappeared. Thersites went behind them, leaving Demetrios and Nikias. Nikias cast aside his weapons and they entered the narrow corridor, which was lit by oil lamps.

"Help me push these rocks," said Demetrios after they had ducked under the low archway. Nikias saw that big stones had been stacked on either side.

They pushed on them and they tumbled down, cutting off the passage from the Ear of Dionysus completely. This should buy them some time before the enemy burrowed through and discovered their secret escape path.

Nikias followed Demetrios down the dimly lit corridor to the low place where the escape tunnel began. But Demetrios stopped in front of it, blocking Nikias's way. He turned suddenly and held out his sword at arm's length, pointing it at Nikias's chest.

"What are you doing?" Nikias asked, unnerved by the strange look in Demetrios's eyes.

"Something doesn't add up," said Demetrios quietly. "About what you told me. About my father."

Nikias dropped his head. He should have known this was coming. Demetrios had been questioning him over the last few weeks, asking about the events of the sneak attack on Plataea over and over again. Asking about the tiniest details, like an armor maker going over an old breastplate, looking for cracks in the bronze, or places where the metal had grown thin.

"I've told you everything," said Nikias.

"And now I want the *truth*," replied Demetrios, and held the tip of the blade an inch from Nikias's heart. "I'll run the point of this blade through your heart, Nikias, I swear to Zeus I will."

Nikias backed up against the wall of rubble. He could hear the muffled shouts of warriors on the other side. They had stormed the Ear. It would only be a matter of time before they started clearing the rubble away from this passageway.

He looked past Demetrios to the black entrance of the escape tunnel. There was no way to get past him in this narrow space. No way to fight him.

THIRTEEN

"This is madness!" said Nikias. "We have to move!"

Demetrios studied him with hooded eyes. "Do you remember when we were boys," he said, "and we snuck into Thebes, just to have a look around?"

"Your stupid idea," said Nikias.

Demetrios nodded. "But we learned a lot about the enemy. And I killed my first man. When we were making our way back home, we made a solemn vow never to betray one another."

"I haven't betrayed you," pleaded Nikias.

"Lying is betrayal," said Demetrios. "You said that you saved my father in the undercroft of our house on the night of the sneak attack. Where they made him watch my sister getting raped. Where they cut off his fingers to get his signet ring."

"That was true," said Nikias. "I swear on the gods it was true."

"I believe you," said Demetrios. "But there are other things that don't hold water. Your story . . . you made small mistakes in the retelling. Crucial mistakes about the order of events. I have a mind for details, as you know. And the biggest mistake was the first time you told me the tale—the part about your grandfather being at my father's side after he died in the battle at the gates—"

"A slip of the tongue," cut in Nikias.

"A slip of the *heart*!" shouted Demetrios insanely, his voice twisted with wrath.

Nikias could hear the Syrakusans directly behind him now. They were starting to pull the rocks away.

"I told you what I did because I love you," said Nikias calmly. "Because you are my brother."

"Brothers don't lie!"

Nikias grabbed the flat of the blade in one hand and pulled it suddenly toward his heart, piercing his skin. "You want to kill me?" he shouted. "Then be done with it! I would rather die then tell you the truth! I would rather die than break your heart!" The tears poured from his eyes and he turned away from Demetrios's startled face. He let his bleeding hand go from the sword.

"Speak," said Demetrios. "I must know. Please. My friend." He dropped the sword and it clattered on the stone floor.

Nikias sagged to the floor, his head drooping on his neck. There was nothing he could do. He had to tell Demetrios the truth, once and for all. "Your father was the traitor," he said. "He made an alliance with Draco the Spartan and Eurymakus the Theban. He was given Persian gold. He signed a secret treaty. He opened the gates of Plataea to the enemy but they betrayed him. That's when I found him. They had raped and killed your sister in front of him to torment him. They had cut off his finger to take his ring as a prize. I saved him, thinking that he was just another victim of the sneak attack. But later, after the Thebans were defeated, an Athenian whisperer who had been spying in Plataea told me that your father was the traitor. The Persian gold and the treaty with the Spartans—signed in his own hand—all came to light in a trial that was led by my grandfather. Your family's own steward, Phakas, gave testimony against your father. And later your father, filled with remorse, admitted what he had done. The Assembly convicted him of treason."

Nikias lifted his head and stared at Demetrios. His friend's face had gone white.

"What reason did he give?" Demetrios asked, in a voice full of outrage and shame. "What reason did my father give for this most heinous crime?"

"Because he thought he was the man to lead Plataea," said Nikias. "He wanted us to break our oath with the Athenians and join the Spartans. He did not believe that the Athenians could beat the Spartans in a prolonged war, and he feared that Plataea would be crushed by our alliance with Athens. Before he was executed he told my grandfather that he did everything to save you from the Spartans. He had had a vision before he sent you here to Syrakuse—a vision that Plataea would be obliterated and that you would be enslaved."

"Irony is the bitterest poison," said Demetrios flatly. "And how was he executed?"

"A tunic of stones," said Nikias.

Demetrios closed his eyes and swallowed hard. "And his body?"

"Cast outside the borders of Plataea."

Demetrios let forth a stricken groan and fell to his knees. He started retching and was sick on the floor. "Kill me now," he said, coughing and choking on his vomit.

Nikias leapt to his feet and grabbed Demetrios's sword, then turned and plunged it through a hole in the rubble wall where a Syrakusan's face had appeared, skewering the man through the eye.

"Into the tunnel!" Nikias shouted. "Into the tunnel!" He thrust the sword into the gap again. "Demetrios!" he bellowed. But his friend did not move.

Nikias cast aside the sword and grabbed Demetrios by his right arm, dragging him to the low entrance of the escape tunnel and pushing him in. "Crawl!" shouted Nikias. "Crawl or you'll trap me! They're coming!"

This seemed to rouse Demetrios from his stupor, for he started inching along on hands and knees. The light cast from lamps in the outer passage was growing dim. Soon they were moving along in total darkness and the sounds of the enemy became muffled. The air was stifling and hot and Nikias had to fight with all of his strength of will to keep from panicking and screaming. His heart pounded in his ears. Sweat poured into his eyes. Every so often he would reach out and touch Demetrios's heels just to make certain he was still moving, for he was terrified that his friend would come to a stop in the tunnel, and there was not enough space anywhere along the way to push past him. And what if Diokles and the others hadn't managed to create an opening? Eventually he and Demetrios would come to a place where the prisoners were crammed together in the tunnel, and then they would be trapped in this dark and horrible place. The floor was slick with urine and feces in some places where frightened men had relieved themselves. The gods themselves couldn't have thought of a worse punishment. He fought against an animal fear.

Time became meaningless. All was darkness and terror. He wondered if the Syrakusans had sent somebody into the tunnel after them. Was a warrior directly behind him now, ready to spear him in his exposed backside? That would be an ignoble way to die—a spear up the arse. But he couldn't hear anyone behind him. The Syrakusans probably thought that this tunnel was a dead end. Or they would try to smoke them out.

After what seemed like hours Nikias saw a glow up ahead and let forth a sigh of relief, thinking that it was daylight. But it was just a guttering lamp that one of the prisoners had left in the passageway.

"How far have we gone, Demetrios?" Nikias gasped.

"Don't know," Demetrios replied. "Keep moving."

They plunged into darkness again, and after a while Nikias started seeing things. He saw faces: his grandparents, his mother, his sister, and Kallisto. He saw a vision of his daughters, but Helena was holding them, not their mother. And then he saw Leo and Kolax, and old Saeed dancing around a fire at the lagoon in Lydia. He imagined that he was riding on Photine, but she threw him and he landed on top of Eurymakus, who embraced him with his one arm and turned into a huge fox.

"You're talking to yourself," said Demetrios. "Shut up."

Nikias started weeping and kept crawling—squirming forever down this evil shaft. When would it ever end? Would they see light again? He started moving faster, but all at once he collided with Demetrios.

"Why have you stopped?" Nikias asked desperately.

"Someone in front of me," replied Demetrios. "They must not have been able to break an opening. Perhaps they dug the wrong way at the end. It's easy to do."

Nikias sucked in his breath and let out an agonized howl. He lay flat on the floor of the passage and contorted as his body was wracked with sobs. He felt something on his head and shuddered. It was Demetrios's hand in his hair. His friend reached back to stroke him on the head like a father with a crying toddler.

"I'm sorry," Nikias said. "I'm so sorry."

"You have nothing to be sorry for," said Demetrios, in a voice that was also choked with tears.

Another few minutes went by—minutes that might as well have been days. Then a voice in front of Demetrios shouted in joy, "They're moving again! I smell fresh air!"

"They're moving again!" said Demetrios to Nikias. "Did you hear? Come on!"

The tunnel started to slope up and became narrower. They wormed their way up it. They squirmed and fought until the skin on their knees was raw. And then, up ahead, Nikias saw a blurry glow—sunlight! The passage here went sharply upward, and by the time they got to the opening they could barely move, they were so exhausted. Many hands pulled Demetrios into the open air, and a great cheer went up from the men outside the shaft. And then more hands reached for Nikias and dragged him to freedom.

"Thank the gods," Diokles said as he helped Nikias sit down with his back against a stone. "I thought you were dead."

"You did it," said Nikias, squinting in the brilliant light. He saw trees. And seagulls circling overhead. "You broke through."

"Hard ground," said Diokles. "And harder still with a tunnel full of men behind taking all the air. We took a chance and went straight up."

Nikias peered at his surroundings. They were in a forest on a rocky slope.

Several hundred of the prisoners stood or squatted nearby. Many were gasping for air, while others who had had time to recover stood as sentinels, waiting for the Syrakusans to arrive. But there was no sign of them as yet. He saw Thersites lying on the ground, kissing the earth as though it were a lover.

"Where are you going? Quarry Lord!"

Nikias looked up and saw Demetrios staggering away from the group. Several of the quarrymen tried to follow him, but he pushed them away.

"Leave me be!" shouted Demetrios.

Nikias got up and followed him down the slope and over a hill. On the other side was a grove of olive trees and an old shrine. A figure stood there, looking around expectantly—what appeared to be a slender young woman. When she saw Demetrios she let forth a cry and held a hand to her cheek, then ran to him and leapt into his arms, and Demetrios uttered the name "Barka."

"Nikias!" yelled a voice from the woods. He looked up and saw a blur rushing toward him and was practically knocked on his back from the wild embrace that followed.

"Kolax?" asked Nikias in amazement. He stared at him closer and was astonished to see the Skythian's face under the mop of dark hair with its red roots. "How . . . ?"

"Such a long tale!" said Kolax. "And we've got miles for me to tell it to you. I'm so glad that you escaped."

Ji loped up to them and said, "Come, Nikias. We must get back to the ships. They will leave without us."

"Demetrios!" Nikias called out to where his friend and the eunuch stood together. "Come, we have to go! We can't stay here!"

They went back to the tunnel egress and rounded up all of the surviving quarrymen—five hundred strong—then headed northeast over the hills, dog-trotting through the fields, for every one of the men in the company was exhausted. But they saw no sign of the Syrakusans, and made fast time. Kolax stayed glued to Nikias's side and talked the whole way, telling him about his adventures after they had become separated on Mount Kithaeron. Nikias was glad to have the barbarian with him, for his talking kept his mind off the pain of the burns he'd suffered on his arms and legs. He wondered how badly he would have fared if he and Thersites had not plunged themselves into the cisterns. He saw Thersites running at the front of the pack of men. He glanced back now and then, smiling and nodding at Nikias in his simple way.

They stopped several times to take water and rest, but Demetrios drove them on at a relentless pace. The quarrymen did whatever he said. By the time they got to the cove where the *Spear* and the *Briseis* were beached, Nikias could hardly move his legs, and his mind was numb with the sound of Kolax's voice. The ships were still there, and from the top of the ridge that overlooked the beach Nikias could see Chusor and Helena standing near the prow of the *Spear* like sentinels. Kolax took off down the steep bank like a dog and ran to Melitta, who stood by the lapping waves. He tackled her and they fell into the sea, laughing uproariously.

"There's the *Spear*," said Nikias to Demetrios. "I've been thinking about this. We can ferry some of your quarrymen over to Italia and then come back and get the rest. The ships can't take everyone at once."

"I'm staying here," said Demetrios adamantly. He was standing next to Barka, who had both of his arms wrapped around his waist, as though to hold Demetrios fast to his side. "I'm staying with my men. There are many city-states on this island that will give us refuge, enemies of Syrakuse looking for strong warriors. And now that Pantares is dead, things will change on this island."

"But you have to come home," said Nikias.

"I don't have a home," said Demetrios. "My father made sure of that. I'm a citizen of nowhere. I have to make a new place for myself. A new name. With Hyakinthos at my side. May Poseidon guide your ships to Naupaktos, and thence to Plataea."

Nikias didn't argue with him. He knew there was nothing that he could say. If Demetrios came back to Plataea, he would be scorned and possibly murdered by the citizens left alive in the citadel . . . if any *were* left alive. He went up to his friend and hugged him, and Demetrios stood limp with his arms at his sides. "I love you, my brother," Nikias said, and squeezed him tighter. "I will always love you."

Demetrios suddenly wrapped his arms around Nikias and put his mouth close to his ear. "Find my father's bones, Nik, and bury them, will you? I would do the same for you if our stories were changed."

Nikias nodded.

He made his way down to the *Spear* and Helena ran to him across the beach. He took her in his arms and she covered his face with kisses.

"The gods smile upon me this day," she said, her face streaming with tears.

The men of the *Spear* gave food, water, and weapons to the quarrymen. And then the small army, led by their general, Demetrios, left the cove and headed overland in the direction of the smoldering volcano, Mount Aetna. Nikias saw Chusor and Barka exchange a final word. Then Barka went to Diokles and kissed him. The Helot smiled as if to say, "All is forgiven." And then the eunuch was gone, smiling and running toward Demetrios like a carefree girl heading off on a lark.

Nikias helped put the *Spear* in the water, then went to the prow and stood next to Chusor, Melitta, and Helena. Ji's voice carried from below deck, exhorting the men at their labors.

Nikias saw Thersites standing amongst the mariners assigned to unfurl the sails, skillfully helping the crew members with the ropes. He was the only quarryman who had decided to leave Demetrios and remain with the ship. Thersites was insane, Nikias knew, but he hadn't lied about being a mariner—he fit right in on the trireme.

"Do your arms hurt?" Helena asked.

Ezekiel had covered Nikias's burns with a healing unguent and had given him some opium for the pain. Now he felt as though he were drifting in the clouds.

"I feel fine," he replied.

"I didn't think . . . I'd ever see you again," whispered Helena.

He noticed that she held both hands over her womb as if to suppress a stomachache, but she showed no signs of being ill. In fact, she looked exceptionally beauteous. And then he realized all of a sudden that she was pregnant and glowing from being with child.

"There's the new moon," said Melitta, pointing at a sliver of moon rising in the gloaming. Kolax stood by her side, gazing at her lovingly. Nikias noticed she brushed Kolax's palm with her littlest finger and he winked at her. Nikias looked to see if Chusor had seen this exchange, but he was staring out to sea as if trying to read the pattern of the waves.

"And look at Apollo's chariot," said Kolax, pointing at the setting sun, which had turned the clouds the sacrificial hues of wine and blood.

The beauty of the sun's descent was not lost on Nikias. He stared in awe. When he had been in the tunnel, crawling like a worm, he had thought he would never see the sky or sun or anything beautiful ever again.

"This is how Theseus must have felt when he came out of the Labyrinth," Nikias thought. "When he got on board his ship and headed home."

He became aware that Helena was staring at him intently, and he kissed her on the forehead. But even as his lips touched her skin, he thought of Kallisto and the euphoria of the opium vanished and a bitter taste filled his mouth.

FOURTEEN

It took several weeks for Nikias's burns to heal, and so he was excused from taking his turn at the oars. He spent the days shadowing Chusor, learning how to navigate as well as rig the sails.

Thersites tried to be helpful as well, but half of what the man said was gibberish. Nikias had to watch him tie a knot or set a sail rope rather than listen to him, otherwise his instructions wouldn't make sense. Ezekiel told Nikias that the part of the brain that controlled speech must have been damaged by the blow Thersites had suffered long ago. "It's as if his tongue is a chariot connected to wild dogs instead of obedient horses." The doctor was fascinated by Thersites and would sit with him for long spells, asking him questions and writing down notes.

For several hours each day Nikias and Chusor locked themselves in the little cabin and Chusor taught him everything that he had learned from Naxos of Syrakuse concerning siegecraft. He drew meticulous diagrams for making bolt shooters like the ones mounted to the *Spear*, and wall-mounted cranes that could hook siege towers and flip them over. He explained in exacting detail how to manufacture the parts and assemble these machines so that Nikias would be able to guide the craftsmen who had been left behind in the citadel. Chusor also made a diagram of Plataea showing a counterwall around it, and speculated on how the Persian known as the City-Killer might try to breach the walls.

"There's three ways into Plataea," Chusor said. "Straight through the wall, over, and under. And we're going to study all three."

Scaling ladders, tunnels, counter-tunnels, defending against earthen ramps, rams and their construction, the ingredients and measurements for the sticking fire . . . all of these were hammered into Nikias's head until he thought his brain would burst. He started to dream about catapults and the tunnels that Chusor had dug—and meticulously mapped—beneath the streets of Plataea. Nikias's dreams of these tunnels were dark and terrifying, and often he woke gasping for air and crying out.

For some reason Chusor told Nikias to keep from cutting his hair, which had grown very long over the last several months. When Nikias asked him why, Chusor said mysteriously, "It might come in useful. Leave it be."

Every night they beached the ship in a deserted cove along the coast of Italia, and sometimes Nikias and Helena found the opportunity to sneak off and make love in private. But they never talked about what would happen when they reached the port of Kreusis. Nikias knew that he would have to leave Helena with the ship—abandon his pregnant lover and return to his wife. During this strange, uneventful, and nearly languid journey—for the weather was fine and calm and warm—he started to feel as though he were a shade, a mere vapor existing between two worlds. There was the present, in which he was a useless member of a ship's crew, making love with a woman who was not his wife. And there was the future—citizen of a city under siege, living with a wife whom he had betrayed. Part of him wanted the voyage to never end. The other half could not wait to arrive home to help defend the citadel.

But would Phoenix and the others be in Naupaktos once the *Spear* and the *Briseis* finally got there? Or had they perished on the sea? Or been captured by the enemy? And even if he was reunited with his cousin and the young volunteers who had set out from Athens, would Plataea still be standing once they arrived at the gates of the citadel? He tried not to think about all of these nagging questions. He was grateful when he could finally return to rowing. Ten minutes after sitting down on a bench and pulling at an oar, his mind drifted into a state of blissful oblivion. It was as if he had tasted the waters of Lethe—that river in Hades that, once sipped, made a soul forget its life on earth. All that he could see was the back of the rower in front of him, or the shining sea glimpsed through the oar hole. The only sounds were the drums, the squeak of the oar locks, and the splash of the waves against the hull.

Nikias had never seen Kolax so happy. He and Melitta spent their days climbing the masts like monkeys, or chattering endlessly together along with a small band of Serifan youths who were around their own age—the laughter of children often filled the ship and the crew was tolerant of their many mischievous ways, such as when someone greased the bottom deckers' seats overnight, or pissed in the water bucket. Chusor was the exception. He threatened to throw

Kolax overboard on several occasions—he was the obvious ringleader—but Helena told Nikias that Melitta was the main culprit. The girl had always had a wicked sense of humor.

Kolax started to tie his hair in a topknot again, and the black dye was beginning to wear off to reveal his bright red mane. Nikias had not seen much of the young man over the last several years because he had been living with Osyrus and the other Skythians in the fortress of the Three Heads. He realized that Kolax had changed greatly. He was much taller than when they had first met—nearly as tall as Nikias—and he had morphed from a lean boy into a muscular young man.

"Melitta thinks Kolax is very handsome," Helena said to Nikias one night when they lay naked on a beach, entwined like snakes under the bright stars. "Though she would never say as much. I see the way she looks at him. She is going to be heartbroken when he leaves the ship at Kreusis."

"She's not the only one," Nikias replied softly. But Helena made no reply. Instead she put his hand on her belly and asked him what she wanted him to name the child if he was a boy.

"Apollo," he said. He thought of the sword that Chusor had found in the ancient tomb beneath Plataea. He was glad that he had given it to Ji for safekeeping before he went into the house of Pantares. It would have been a terrible blow to lose that heirloom. He wore it always, except when he was pulling at an oar or making love with Helena. But even then the sword was always within arm's reach. He felt that the sword had a magical property—that the blade had to be brought back into the citadel. Only then would Plataea be safe.

The next day they came to the great port city of Kroton, "the most famous athlete factory in the world," as his grandfather used to tell him. The *Spear* and the *Briseis* were two of several hundred ships in the bustling harbor and no one paid them any heed, and they felt safe in this powerful, independent Greek city-state; they were now far from Syrakuse and beyond the grasp of those people. Even so, the women and children were kept either on board or on the beach near the two ships, for fear that evil mariners called "shell pluckers" might kidnap them. Greater Greece was a dangerous place.

Chusor headed off into the marketplace with Ezekiel on what he said was an errand of great importance, and sent Nikias, Kolax, and forty other men to round up provisions and water. Melitta was furious that she had been left behind, but Kolax promised to bring her back a souvenir. Helena was angry, too, for she had wanted to visit the famous Temple of Hera. But Chusor said that it was too risky—the walls of Kroton were twelve miles in circumference, and it would be too easy to lose someone in so vast a place. Diokles, having received instructions from Chusor to guard Helena and Melitta with his life, stayed very close to the two women—a stern and silent watchman.

Nikias had never seen so many imposing people in one city—both men and women, young and old. Everywhere he looked, it was like strolling through a citadel of the gods. After purchasing everything that the ships needed, he sent the men back to the harbor loaded with goods. Then he and Kolax made a quick trip to the gymnasium, for Nikias had always wanted to see the famed spot where Milo of Kroton—the greatest wrestler in the history of the Olympiads—had been trained. He was impressed with the pankrators he saw practicing there.

On the way back to the ships he passed the Temple of Hera, where Nikias paused at a stall selling votive statues of the goddess. He picked up one of the figures and stared at it. The thing was made of bronze with glass eyes, and its gaze seemed to follow him no matter which way he turned his head. He picked out two of them: one for Helena and the other for Kallisto. Nikias realized the ludicrousness of what he was doing—buying the same trinkets for his wife *and* lover. But he bought them anyway, and the stall keeper wrapped them in straw and put them in a leather pouch.

"Do you think Melitta would like this?" Kolax asked. He was at the next stall over—a place filled with potters' wares—holding up a cup painted with a scene of an Amazon battle: warrior women slaying Greeks.

"Yes," said Nikias without compunction. "For that girl has the heart of an Amazon."

Kolax grinned. "Doesn't she?" he said reverently. "In Skythia we'd call her a 'pole breaker.' Highly sought after as a wife. My father will like her. Oh! I forgot to tell you!" he said, seizing hold of Nikias's arm and nearly causing him to drop his statues. "Barka had a vision of my father. He is safe! He and the others are hiding in the mountains northwest of Plataea. On the road to Delphi. Near a broken tower."

Nikias could see just such a tower in his mind's eye. It lay on that road leading to the sacred city of the seers, and he had ridden past it several times on his way to Delphi. But he couldn't help but scoff. "That's a very specific vision," he commented wryly. "Seers and soothsayers are usually more vague."

"Chusor told me that Barka is never wrong." Kolax smiled happily. "The eunuch also told me that you would have a son!"

Nikias said nothing. He didn't want to "stir shit in Kolax's wine," as the Skythian saying went. The young man seemed so hopeful. "Let him believe in magic," he thought. "Like I used to do."

When they got back to the harbor, they met Chusor and Ezekiel returning from their foray into the citadel. Chusor carried two huge rolls of red cloth on either shoulder, and he was followed by a troop of shopkeepers, each bearing a roll of the same crimson fabric. The doctor was so weighted down with baskets of herbs and other medicines that his thin torso bent under the load.

"What's the red cloth for?" asked Kolax.

"Perhaps it's the solution to a riddle," said Chusor cryptically.

"Are you going to trade it?"

"This is the same cloth the Spartans buy," said Ezekiel. "Indeed, it has great value in Lakonia and other parts."

"They don't need to hear about the cloth, Ezekiel," said Chusor with an edge to his voice, and headed toward the beach.

So this was Chusor's "important" errand? Nikias was nettled by Chusor's evident desire to fill the already stuffed holds of the ships with goods that he might trade with the enemy. But he held his tongue and said nothing. Chusor was a great mystery to him sometimes.

After eight days they came to the Kretan colony of Hydros, situated at the long end of a narrow peninsula of Italia. Here they loaded the ship with freshwater, for they were going to head to open sea in the direction of the Greek island called the Scythe—a place that had been settled by Korinthians hundreds of years ago but which had remained neutral during the war. The Korkyrans—the city-state that controlled the Scythe—had grown angry with Korinth over the rule of a shared colony to the north. At least, that's what Phoenix had told him in one of their conversations on Serifos.

To get to the Scythe, the *Spear* had to cross a hundred miles of open sea, and it would take at least a day and a half to do so. And neither Chusor nor any of the Serifan sailors had ever been this far north before. The weather was perfect, however, with no sign of storms or rough waves. But they had to be on the lookout for Korinthian and Spartan triremes. Chusor ordered Kolax to climb to the top of the mainmast and keep a lookout all day. He thought that he had finally figured out how to separate his beloved daughter from the wild barbarian, at least for a few hours. But Melitta climbed the tall pole and clung to it next to Kolax, refusing to come down when her father ordered her to do so, and Chusor finally gave up and went to the prow, glaring at the sea.

They made the crossing in good time and did not catch sight of any ships. At night, with a full moon and a favorable wind, the two ships stayed on course, with Chusor and Agrios navigating by the stars, and by afternoon of the next day they spotted the western coast of the Scythe—a green and mountainous island covered with trees. They beached the ship and were about to go in search of a well to replenish their water, when Kolax spotted a man sitting on the rocks fifty feet above.

"Who are you?" the stranger shouted down at them.

"Friends of Athens," called back Nikias.

"Be more specific," came the man's reply.

Nikias turned to Chusor and the others standing near him. "I'll go up and talk to him. Maybe he can tell us where there's a spring. I don't want to scare him off, though; everyone else stay here."

He slowly climbed up the rocks to the little ledge where the man sat under the shade of a gnarled cypress. As he got close he could see that this islander was in his early thirties—a bear of a man with a dark black beard and a wide, friendly face. He wore a simple tunic with an old leather belt and a battered scabbard. And on his lap was an ornate and well-crafted tortoiseshell kithara. He smiled at Nikias when he got to the ledge, but didn't bother to get up.

"Hello," he said. "Name's Argus of Korkyra. Who might you be?"

"Nikias of Plataea."

"You're a long way from home!" Argus replied with a curious and unexpected enthusiasm. "I've always wanted to go to Plataea. See the famous battlefield where the Persians were mowed like barley."

"You wouldn't want to go there now," said Nikias. "It's under siege."

"So I've heard," said Argus, his face turning serious. "Spartans. News came to the citadel of Korkyra"—here he made a vague gesture behind him at the dark forest, as if the city lay somewhere in that direction—"a few weeks ago when the Athenians arrived."

"Athenians?" Nikias asked.

"Some of Phormion's ships," said Argus. "Trying to get us to help them in their fight against the Korinthians and their blockade at the mouth of the Gulf of Korinth. The Athenians have gone now. Back south."

"Did your people agree to help?"

"No," said Argus, shaking his head sadly. "We remain neutral. At least for now. And word is that there's a huge fleet of Korinthian triremes headed to Naupaktos to destroy Phormion. That's why they were so desperate for help."

"Weren't you afraid that we might be raiders when you saw our ship come to shore?" Nikias asked. "Why didn't you run away?"

"What would raiders want with me?" asked Argus. "Steal my harp?"

This man was either a simpleton or fearless, mused Nikias. He didn't look like an idiot, though. There was the light of intelligence in his eye. Nikias said, "To take you as a slave, of course."

"I'd like to see you try," said Argus with a hearty laugh. He got up slowly, and although he stood a little shorter than Nikias, he was twice as broad—the widest man whom Nikias had ever laid eyes on. "You've heard the stories about this island, no? We cut the cocks off raiders and send them on their way. This island isn't called the Scythe for nothing."

"I don't want to fight you," said Nikias, holding up his hands and grinning. "It would be like fighting Atlas. Or Milo of Kroton."

"Of course you wouldn't!" exclaimed Argus, throwing back his head and laughing. "I don't care how good a pankrator you are. You'd never take me. I've got a skull of bronze—fists don't work against it. And I'm too heavy for you. My neck's thick as well. I'm hard to choke. I trained in Kroton, by the way. There was a great-grandson of Milo who taught at the gymnasium, and he said that I outweighed the old man in his prime. I was supposed to represent our city for the games next year."

"There won't be any games for us Plataeans," said Nikias.

"Cheer up!" said Argus merrily. "The Olympic officials will order a sacred truce to the war! You'll be able to fight next year. We'll go to Olympus together, eh?"

"How did you know I was a pankrator?" Nikias asked.

"I can see the signs," said Argus. "Your scarred knuckles, your misshapen ears, your bent nose. You're either a very good pankrator or a poor one, by the look of all your marks and dents." He held Nikias's gaze for a long time. Then he shook his head somberly. "No. You're a good fighter, all right. And you've seen many men to their graves. Now"—he slapped Nikias on the shoulder and started clambering down the rocks toward the beach, careful not to harm the kithara as he went—"your people will need water. I'll take them to a hidden well over yonder. I can get you fresh meat, too—there's a village nearby. Your people must be hungry after crossing over from Italia. That's a long pull."

"How did you know we came from Italia?" Nikias asked, following him down.

"I watched you for the last two hours, making your way toward the island. Unless you rose up out of the sea, you've come from Italia—most likely, the port of Hydros in Kalabria."

"We have silver," said Nikias. "To pay for your help."

The harp banged against a rock, making a weird, dejected noise, and Argus stopped his descent. His face went slack and he blinked rapidly, as if waking from a dream—as if the sound of the harp had stirred him from a happy sleep. "I'm a dead man if I stay here. They broke my brother's neck, you see? He did nothing wrong! The girl . . . she was in love with him . . ." He trailed off into silence then shrugged. "And so I slew them all." The air was filled with the sound of crying gulls and the noises of the men and women of the *Spear* on the beach.

"Nikias!" called Chusor impatiently. "What are you doing?"

Nikias waved back. "I'm coming!"

"Listen, Nikias of Plataea," said Argus, becoming very serious, "I've been a mariner since I was a lad. I know the sea and all of the islands and currents from here to Naupaktos—that's where you're headed, I take it? To join up with Phormion?"

Nikias nodded. "And then to Plataea."

"I'll come with you to Plataea," said Argus, nodding vigorously. "Who would pass up the opportunity to fight the Spartans? Only the dullest sort of coward, eh? I'd rather die in battle instead of swinging from a rope. Let me come along," he pleaded. "Like I said, I'm an oarsman by trade. I can earn my keep on the ship. And I can man a wall well enough once we get to Plataea. How do you propose to get into the citadel, by the way, if they've built a counterwall?"

Nikias was taken aback by this question. Getting into Plataea was something that he and Chusor had not even discussed. If the Spartans had built a counterwall, they would have to storm this barricade, get over it, and make a break for the walls. How could Chusor have neglected to talk about such an important and basic thing?

"We'll have to bull our way through," said Nikias.

"'Bull our way through,'" repeated Argus, smiling. "Like the famous Bull of Plataea—you've heard of him, right? Menesarkus the champion? The one who killed the Theban at the Olympiads with the Morpheus hold?"

Nikias said, "Yes. Menesarkus and his hold are well known to me."

"We'll smash our way in!"

Nikias knew that it was foolish to trust a stranger whom he'd just met—to let this man on board the *Spear*. But he felt in his gut that Argus was being honest with him. His brother must have been murdered and then he had committed some heinous act of revenge for which he would have to pay, most likely with his life. He had probably been hiding out on this side of the island, trying to figure out what to do. The gods, for some reason, had brought them together on this shore. Only time would tell for what reason. And only an idiot would pass up the opportunity to bring such an obvious fighting man along—especially one who was willing to help smash his way into a city under siege.

"So?"

"I'll ask them to take you on board," said Nikias. "We could use some music."

Argus sighed. "It was my dear little brother's kithara," he said ruefully. "I can't even play the stinking thing."

FIFTEEN

The fair wind and weather held. The *Spear* and the *Briseis* made a fast journey on this last leg, guided by the cheerful Argus, who had been welcomed aboard somewhat warily at first but had instantly fit right in with the crew, impressing all of the mariners with his strength and knowledge. Even Chusor thought that the man was a rare find, and pressed him for information about this region and its islands, gleaning from him everything that he could.

Two days after leaving the Scythe, they beached the ship on Ithaka, the island where Odysseus himself had been born and raised, and they made a great sacrifice to Zeus after purchasing ten cows from the islanders with the last of Kolax's treasure. For tomorrow they would have to pull across an open stretch of water where they would be exposed to enemy ships. But if Zeus blessed them, they would reach the mouth of the Gulf of Korinth near the end of the day, and lie safe in the harbor of Naupaktos with the Athenian fleet by sunset.

After the meat was cooked and shared amongst the over three hundred men, women, and children of the two ships, Nikias and the Plataean mariners performed the Oxlander harvest dance. It was a dance that every Plataean boy learned as soon as he could stand; it taught him the fundamental stance and movements of a phalanx warrior, to the rhythm of drums and the trill of pipes. The watchers clapped as they danced and shouted out their war cry of "Freedom, sweet freedom!" By the time they were done, many of the dancers, like Nikias, were crying, for the dance and the music had brought back the memory of their beloved citadel and everything that they stood to lose if Plataea fell to the Spartans.

Later, when everyone was tipsy on wine—except for the unlucky men who'd drawn lots to stand guard—Helena borrowed Argus's kithara and played "The

Shield of Akilles" while Nikias sang. He had learned the song from Linos the bard, and he sang it in his clear, deep voice. Helena was a superior musician who made the lyre's catgut sing. Together, in music and voice, they painted a picture of that famous shield that seemed to hang in the air over the bonfire—a shield that bore images of the world and even the heavens hammered into its shining face: the constellations and the sun and moon, weddings and murders, shepherds and marauders, a city at peace and one under siege, war and festivals, lions and bulls, men and women, friends and enemies. Many shining eyes watched their performance in front of that roaring fire, and when they were done there was a profound moment of silence, filled only by the ceaselessly crashing waves, until the crowd burst into applause and cheers.

Nikias and Helena found a place on the beach and wrapped themselves in a blanket. They made love in silence, and said nothing afterward, and Helena fell into a fitful sleep while Nikias contemplated how odd it was that in his short and strange life he had seen and lived so many of the very things depicted on the shield of Akilles. "The shield stands for civilization," Linos had told him once. "That is obvious. But there's something more. There's a secret in that shield that we bards spend our entire lives trying to decipher." Nikias asked the old man if he had discovered that secret, but Linos merely smiled and raised his eyebrows slightly as if to say, "If I have discovered the secret, I will never tell."

In the morning they boarded the ships and Nikias took one of the first turns at the oar benches. It was another calm and sunny day, with a slight wind at their backs, and the two ships cut across the sea side by side like a whale swimming with a porpoise. Four hours into his stretch Nikias heard shouting. A few minutes later a mariner came and relieved him and told him that Chusor wanted to see him on the battle deck. Nikias walked quickly down the gangway and paused at the closed door to the little cabin, where he could hear Helena retching. Then he went up the ladder onto the battle deck and looked around quickly—they were in the middle of a wide gulf that he knew to be the Gulf of Patros, with land on either side. On the port side a tall heap of a mountain rose from the earth, the peaks clinging to a few white clouds. Chusor stood near Agrios, staring in that direction.

"What is it?" asked Nikias as he went over to him.

"Look," said Chusor despondently. "Our luck has run out."

Nikias saw the shapes of triremes on the waves perhaps half a mile away. Scores of them. So many that he could not count them. His heart dropped to his knees.

"How many?" he asked.

"Kolax up in the mast counts sixty-two," replied Chusor. "And he has keener eyes than me."

"I didn't know he could count that high," said Nikias under his breath. "And you think they're enemy ships?"

"I have no doubt," said Chusor. "They were waiting on a beach over there under Mount Arakynthos. When the ships saw us they put into the water. Perhaps they were planning a sneak attack on Naupaktos today and they're afraid we'll warn the Athenians. Whatever the case, they're coming for us."

"What about the fire machine?"

"We have to face them head-on to use that device. There's too many of them. We might be able to set a few of them on fire, but they'll swarm us. Our only hope is to get to Naupaktos. The Athenian fortress lies on the other side of that place up ahead where the gulf narrows. But we're still twenty miles away."

Nikias looked at the sails. Both were starting to go slack. The wind was dying. And the ship was too laden with people and provisions to outpace ships with rested oarsmen. "We'll have to throw everything overboard," he said.

"That will give us some time," said Chusor. "I think we should tell the *Briseis* to make a run for it. They're faster than us."

"Yes," said Nikias. Argus and Thersites were on the little single-decker now, along with thirty or so Plataeans and a small number of Serifan women and children. Nearly a hundred people in all, including the Serifan rowers. "It will be good if some of us get away." But he cursed under his breath. They had come so far. They had almost made it to the safety of the Athenian fortress.

Chusor turned and faced Nikias, but he would not look him in the eye. "I did something wrong," he said, staring at the deck, his dark and striking face dripping with sweat, his jaw trembling slightly. "I came to Plataea years ago seeking a treasure. I found it beneath the city while you were in Athens. I stole the gold and precious things, and used the wealth to buy this ship."

So many mysteries concerning Chusor and his activities had been answered for Nikias in that simple admission. But rather than anger toward his old friend, he felt only relief. "That's all?" he asked. "I thought by the look on your face that you'd killed someone."

"Then—"

"I don't care," cut in Nikias. "It doesn't mean anything."

Chusor looked into his eyes. "You have a heart that's as big as this ship, Nikias. You and I should have been friends in a time of peace."

"It would have been lovely, would it not?" said Nikias. "To have lived in the peaceful city shown on Akilles's shield."

"Not many people, it seems, have that lucky fate."

Nikias nodded. "Promise me . . ." he began, but his voice became ensnared in his throat and it took a great effort to speak. "Promise me that you won't let Helena and our unborn child be taken alive."

"The same for my daughter," Chusor whispered. "Don't let her become a Korinthian thrall."

They clasped hands firmly.

"We can outrun them, can't we, Father?"

Nikias turned and saw Melitta and Helena standing behind them. Helena clutched the little statue of Hera in both hands. Her face was white as she stared into the distance at the fast-approaching ships.

"Of course," said Chusor, with a forced laugh. "We just need to lighten our load."

They threw everything overboard that was not joined to the ship: water, food, armor, and shields. Even the spare mast and extra sails were jettisoned. The rowers, knowing that the enemy was coming quickly, broke their backs at the oars and the ship surged ahead for a time. But the mariners were tired from the long haul that had brought them here from Ithaka. A few of the men and women working the oars fainted and were quickly replaced. Nikias sat at a bench for a two-hour stint, then went back up to the battle deck and found Chusor at the stern.

The Korinthians were much closer now. There were five ships out in front of the fleet, and Nikias could clearly see the marble eyes mounted to their prows and the tops of their gleaming rams cutting through the water. He looked toward the bow. There was no sign of the *Briseis*, the ship and its crew having reluctantly departed an hour ago. The single-decker must have passed through the narrow gap in the gulf that Nikias could see so tantalizingly close up ahead. To the right stood the country of Akhaia and, to the left, Aetolia. The two lands were separated by a watery gap no more than a mile across.

Something flew screaming overhead and the mainsail split. A broken yard-arm clattered to the deck. The Korinthians had started firing the bolt shooters mounted on their prows. Another projectile smashed into the curving stern, sending fragments of wood flying through the air. Nikias and Chusor were knocked back, and when they got up Nikias saw that Agrios lay slumped on his seat, a splinter of wood wedged into his neck.

Kolax jumped down from the mainmast and fit an arrow to his bow, sending it flying in the direction of the Korinthian ships.

Chusor pulled the dead helmsman from his seat and took over the tiller handles while Nikias and the other mariners on the top deck tried to clear the debris from the fallen sail. The sound of Ji's voice carried from below deck, calling upon the men and women to row for their lives. But the sound of his voice was drowned out by the screams of the enemy warriors coming from the ships closing on them. Nikias looked back and saw armored men crowding the decks of twenty triremes that were now within bowshot range. Arrows started whizzing around him and several mariners fell.

"Get back below, stupid girl!" Chusor bellowed suddenly, for Melitta had poked her head up the ladder from the gangway. She scowled and ducked back down again.

Nikias ran to the bow and looked into the distance. They were just about to enter the gap. It was only a mile from side to side here—two spits jutting out from the north and south. In the distance, a few miles to the northeast, he could see a harbor and a fortress. That was Naupaktos. They were almost there! They passed through the gap, and then Chusor was steering them for the port. But the Korinthian fleet was right behind them.

And then the ship was rocked by a huge blow and Nikias nearly tumbled over the side. A Korinthian had rammed them from behind and the *Spear* started spinning around.

"The rudders are both wrecked!" shouted Chusor, rising from Agrios's seat. He sprinted across the deck to the bow, seizing hold of the bolt shooter that had been rigged with the tube for spraying fire. "The pump!" he shouted at Nikias.

Nikias reacted as though slapped in the face and leapt down to the hold, shouting, "Onto the battle deck! Leave the oars!" Rowers jumped from the benches, abandoning their oars and grabbing their weapons. They surged up the ladders.

Nikias went into the pump room and slipped his feet into the straps on the bellows, grabbing the rings on the beams above. He could hear the fluid gush through the tube as he moved his body up and down. A few seconds later he felt an enemy trireme scrape against the side, followed by the sound of splintering oars.

Then agonized screams cried out and Nikias knew that the deadly fire was sweeping over the enemy ships. He pumped as hard as he could. "Burn!" he cried, choking on the naptha fumes. "Burn, all of you!" he raged. It only took a few minutes for the liquid to run out, and then Nikias staggered from the chamber, coming face-to-face with the women and children who now sat huddled in the hold. The women held long knives and their eyes were wide and terrified. But he saw Melitta clutching the sword that he had given her, looking defiant and unafraid.

"I'm not going to stay down here!" she said, and ran to the opposite end and scrambled up the ladder.

He called to her but she wouldn't stop. He turned and clambered up the bow ladder, sword in hand, expecting to find the battle deck strewn with bodies and the enemy storming the ship.

But what he saw when he emerged onto the crowded deck stopped him in his tracks: enemy ships burning, enemy ships rammed by black triremes, enemy ships spinning out of control with oars in disarray, and others backing up and heading back for the gap—running like dogs with their tails between their legs. And the *Spear* was all alone, separated from this chaos, drifting peacefully toward the shore.

The black ships were Athenian. That much Nikias's confused brain could understand. But he could not figure out where they had come from. Had they appeared from the air? Was he hallucinating? He saw armored men swarming from the decks of the Athenian ships onto Korinthian vessels that had been rammed—struck through the side like hoplites with spears in their guts.

"What happened?" Nikias asked of no one in particular.

"Chusor set those Korinthians on fire before they could board us," said Diokles, appearing at Nikias's side amongst the mariners standing shoulder to shoulder, "and then those Athenians came out of nowhere and rammed the others in the sides."

"The Athenian triremes were hiding on either side of the gap," said Ji, smiling widely. "Waiting like lions for the Korinthian sheep to come through. It was a trap."

The mariners watched in awe as forty or more Korinthian ships were pressed closer and closer together in a clump of confused oars and jammed rams, hemmed in on all sides by the Athenian ships, which were moving about the water with the ease of predatory beasts, forming up a perfectly coordinated circle—a ring of death around them.

"Where's Chusor?" Nikias asked.

"Rigging a new rudder," one of the mariners replied.

Nikias found Chusor and some mariners at the stern, working quickly to fit a spare rudder into place. When it was done, Chusor called out, "Back to the oars!" and took his place at the helmsman's seat. With this one smaller rudder he was able to guide the ship on an irregular but steady course toward Naupaktos, giving the battle a wide berth. Nikias, standing with Kolax at the bow, could see the *Briseis* in the distance, floating with its nose toward the sea battle like a hovering hawk that longed to pounce on a hare. But there was no point trying to enter the fray now. The two ships would only add to the confusion:

the *Spear* could barely maneuver with its temporary rudder, and half of its oars had been smashed when the Korinthian ship had come alongside; and the *Briseis* was too small to do any good.

The battle was virtually over, anyway. Some of the Athenian triremes were breaking off from the circle, towing enemy ships behind them. Half of the Korinthian ships had fled—a muddled line stretching back through the gap and into the Gulf of Patros. But many had been boarded and taken as prizes. After a while the *Spear* caught up to the *Briseis* and Nikias looked down to see Thersites on the deck.

"Excellent day for a chariot race!" Thersites called up to them happily.

"We made it to Naupaktos!" added Argus. "And we warned the Athenian fleet that the Korinthians were coming! You've never seen triremes move that fast off the beach!"

The *Spear* limped toward the harbor of Naupaktos. A mile from the port, an Athenian trireme came up fast behind them, even though it was towing a sixty-oared Korinthian dispatch vessel, and Nikias's heart soared when he saw a familiar face standing on the trireme's deck, smiling back at him across the blue waves.

"Phoenix!" Nikias shouted.

"Nice to finally see you here, Cousin!" Phoenix called back. "Took you long enough. But you always have uncanny timing!"

SIXTEEN

———————◆———————

That night, after all of the Athenian ships had returned to Naupaktos with their prizes, Phoenix came to the place where the *Spear* and the *Briseis* had been beached and found Nikias, then brought him to the house of Admiral Phormion—a place crowded with mariners and officials, all of them exultant over the stunning victory.

As Nikias entered the building a one-armed man dressed in a mariner's tunic practically knocked him over, embracing him with one strong arm and a stump.

"Nik!"

"Konon!" Nikias cried. "What are you doing here?"

Konon quickly told him about his adventures—how Phoenix had returned to the cove on Serifos and found him weeping like a child, and then a hasty description of their perilous journey north to Naupaktos. Here Konon had been reunited with his older brother, a mariner under Phormion's command. Because of his skill at writing, Konon had been made one of the admiral's scribes.

"I didn't know that you could write," said Nikias.

"I kept all of our farm's accounts," said Konon happily. "Now I'll be writing down the names of Korinthian prisoners for the next week! Ha, ha!"

Nikias was glad that his friend had found a place amongst these stalwart mariners. Phormion, their leader, had already proven himself—even before this victory—to be one of the canniest admirals that Athens had ever produced. At least, that's what Konon told him as he led Nikias to the admiral's office. The burly and affable Phormion promised to send four triremes to escort the *Spear* all the way across the Gulf of Korinth to the port of Kreusis, for the waters here, the admiral proclaimed, "teemed with the enemy like so many sharks."

The openhanded admiral, red-faced and tipsy from celebratory wine, also wrote orders for the *Spear* and the *Briseis* to be given all the supplies they needed to replenish those that had been cast overboard, as well as any timber or gear needed to outfit their ships. He then scribbled a message on a piece of papyrus and sealed it with his signet ring.

"This note is for your grandfather," he said. "We are old friends, Menesarkus and I. My grandfather and Menesarkus's father fought together at Marathon during the first Persian invasion. Did you know that, young Nikias?"

"I did," replied Nikias. "I've heard the tale many times. My great-grandfather was one of the few Plataeans who died there. My grandfather was a small boy at the time. But he got his revenge at the Battle of Plataea ten years later."

"We Athenians and Plataeans were the only two city-states to stand against the Persians at Marathon," said Phormion with sincere emotion, his eyes welling up with tears. "And we drove the invaders into the sea and made it red with their blood! Your ancestor died a heroic death. You should only be so lucky." He handed Nikias the note and added in a low voice, "But may Zeus protect you and see you returned to Plataea safely."

The *Spear* was fitted with new rudders taken from one of the captured triremes, and oars to replace the ones that had been smashed. By morning of the next day they were ready to leave, and the convoy departed the crowded harbor, which was filled with captured triremes, and headed east along the northern shore of the gulf along with the *Briseis*. Three of the ships that Phormion had sent to protect them were the same triremes that had left Athens with them more than two months ago: the *Argo*, the *Spartan Killer*, and the *Aphrodite*.

It was only after they were well under way that Chusor took Nikias aside and told him the plan that he had been formulating—the scheme to get Nikias and his men back into Plataea past the counterwall.

"The plan is mad," said Nikias after he had heard it. "But it's better than anything that I can think of."

The women of the *Spear* went to work cutting and sewing the rolls of red cloth—the same stuff that Chusor had bought in Kroton—into capes in the Lakonian style. The material, Nikias discovered, had been one of the few items not cast overboard when they were being chased by the Korinthians, for it had been stowed in the little cabin and nobody had thought to look there when they were seeking things to jettison. Helena insisted on making Nikias's robe herself, while Melitta made Kolax's.

"I never thought I'd wear a cloak of *this* color," said Kolax disparagingly after he and Nikias had tried on their capes and stood staring at themselves in the surface of a burnished shield.

"Me neither," said Nikias. He pushed his long bangs over his brow and squinted at his reflection, shifting his jaw forward a little and making a haughty expression until he saw another man's face staring back—his cousin Arkilokus the Spartan.

They met no enemy ships and, after two days of hard rowing, entered the little cove of Kreusis at sunset. The only vessels on the beach were fishing boats, and so they brought all of the triremes and the single-decker onshore. Nikias climbed down and strode through the water to the beach, then reached down and scooped up a handful of the familiar dark gray sand—little pebbles mixed with broken shells. He had ridden here hundreds of times over the years to swim. His horse, Photine, loved to roll on the sand.

The cove was situated at the end of a valley filled with olive trees and surrounded by steep hills on either side. One had to walk eight miles through the valley to get to Plataea. There was no sign of an enemy encampment here, which surprised him. He reckoned the Spartans were using the protected cove that lay south in Megarian territory, on the other side of the mountain. This spot would be too vulnerable to raids from Naupaktos.

He walked over to a limestone tower that clung to the lower part of the northern hill. It was surrounded by walls that ran straight down into the sea where there was a small protected harbor. This was an ancient and crumbling Plataean fort that had been virtually abandoned at the start of the invasion.

"Hey!" he shouted. "Is anybody up there?"

After a long silence somebody called from the tower's uppermost window, "Who's there?" It was the voice of a very old man.

"Me. Nikias."

"Nikias who?"

"Is this a joke?" Nikias asked. "Who's up there? Is that you, Adonis?" He had recognized the man's voice—an olive farmer who owned most of the land near this cove.

"Nikias the goat doctor from Thespis?" asked the old man.

"No, Nikias from Plataea!"

Nikias could hear Adonis muttering with some other men in the tower.

"Aristo's son?" asked another voice from the dark window. "Menesarkus's heir?"

"Yes, yes! Who else?" said Nikias impatiently.

"Well, I'll be arse plowed!" cried the second voice. "It's me! Baklydes!"

Eventually Nikias heard the tower's ground-level door creak open, and then a knotted rope was flung over the wall. Adonis—an aged but hale old man—climbed down, and with him came Baklydes. Nikias hadn't seen his old friend since he and Leo had been forced to abandon their injured companion in Megarian territory on the morning after they had set the fire on the mountain, and he embraced Baklydes in a bear hug. The other inhabitants of the fort crowded the wall above, peering down at them.

"How did you get here?" Nikias asked.

"Long story," said Baklydes. "I practically crawled my way here through the smoking mountains. That old Megarian hermit helped me, Zeus bless him. The citadel was already surrounded by the enemy, so I headed here."

"We haven't heard any news from Plataea in weeks," Adonis said to Nikias in a whining tone. "What's happening?"

"How should I know?" said Nikias. "I came from the sea."

"You have a story to tell," said Baklydes, looking at the ships. "We thought those were Korinthians at first, come to storm the fort. Adonis here practically soiled his tunic."

"How many men do you have here at the fort?" asked Nikias.

"It's just me and Baklydes here with my kin and slaves and the fishermen," said Adonis. "Thirty men and boys. Nobody else could be spared from Plataea—all the fighting men were called back to the citadel months ago. So what are you doing here? Did our people make it to Athens?"

Nikias quickly told them the tale of the flight to Athens, his return by sea, and about his plan to reenter Plataea. While he spoke, the men from the ships assembled on the beach. When Nikias was done talking, Adonis said, "I think you're crazy and you'll most likely all die, but it will be an exciting way to go."

"The citadel is completely surrounded by a wooden wall," said Baklydes. "The distance between the barricade and the walls of Plataea is two bowshots. And they're building a dirt ramp up against the Gates of Pausanius. I snuck up into the Kithaerons the other night and spied on them by moonlight. Thousands of Helots have been dumping dirt like a horde of insects. The ramp is nearly three-quarters of the way up—the gates are completely hidden by dirt now. In another week they'll be at wall height and they'll be able to march up this sheep-stuffing ramp and simply jump over the bastions to the other side!"

"Describe the counterwall," said Nikias.

"It's made of logs, nearly twenty feet high, and braced. There's only one entrance and that's on the southern side. The Spartans patrol the perimeter of this barricade night and day—thousands of them. You'll never get close enough to even attempt to scale their barricade, let alone make a dash for the walls of the citadel." Baklydes paused and looked down at the beach. "Not even with all of those men you brought."

Nikias looked to the northeast. Two miles away, high on another hilltop that overlooked the cove, stood the Hill Tower—a Plataean watchtower that afforded a view of both Plataea and the fort of Kreusis.

"Can you send a worded message to the Hill Tower," he asked, "and tell them to relay it to the citadel?"

"Of course," replied Adonis. "The size and position of the torches each represent a letter. But the message must be short, otherwise it can get muddled. Once we sent them a signal telling them that a Korinthian ship had been spotted in the cove and they thought we'd said—"

" 'Sword of Apollo,' " interrupted Nikias. "Send that message to the Hill Tower."

" 'Sword of Apollo,' " repeated Adonis. "And if you make it to Plataea, tell your grandfather that the fort of Kreusis stands strong. But that we're out of wine," he added grumpily.

"Let's go," said Baklydes to Nikias. He slapped Adonis on the back and said heartily, "Thanks for all the fish and beans, old man. But I'm going home."

Nikias said good-bye to Helena in the *Spear*'s cabin. He had no words, and neither did she. They held each other and kissed, and Nikias put his hand on her belly. She wept quietly, clutching the statue of Hera, moving her lips silently in prayer.

Nikias's heart felt as heavy as marble—a cold stone object sagging in his chest. He was about to leave this superb woman—a woman who was bearing his child!—on a marauder ship. She, Chusor, and the Serifans had lost their home. They had nowhere to run to. His child would be born a bastard and an exile. A citizen of nowhere.

And where was he, Nikias, going to now? Most likely to his own death at the hands of the hated Spartans in a futile attempt to rejoin a doomed citadel. Even if he made it back into Plataea, he would be forced to watch his wife and child—if the baby had even lived—starve to death as the city's supplies slowly dwindled. In the end, if the city was overrun, he would have to slay his own wife and child to prevent them from being captured and turned into slaves. He saw himself cutting Kallisto's long neck and putting his dagger through a baby's soft breast . . . and he shuddered.

He heard Helena utter the names of Hera and Zeus as she held him tighter.

He thought about what Aristophanes had said in the jail in Athens . . . about how people in that city—angered by the coming of the terrible sickness and so many pointless deaths—had stopped believing in the gods, claiming that they had never existed. Demetrios had been certain that the gods were made up, and had asked Nikias, "Isn't the belief in the self enough?"

Nikias had a disconcerting thought all of a sudden. He still believed that the gods were real. But what if they had all *died*? What if they, too, had contracted some contagion of their own and vanished like so much vapor? What if humans were all alone now? What if prayers and sacrifices were all useless? What if temples were nothing more than tombs for the *memory* of the gods?

These dark thoughts made him sick to his stomach. He left Helena weeping in the cabin. As he climbed down the landing ladder he saw Diokles and Chusor standing on the beach. "Watch out for Helena," he said, and Chusor and Diokles both nodded. He embraced them in turn, then said good-bye to Ji, Ezekiel, and the Serifan sailors. Then he put on his crimson cloak and walked up the beach where the men—all wearing red capes and helms—were milling about by the stream that ran down the valley to the cove. Kolax was amongst them, fidgeting like a restless horse.

"Did you say good-bye to Melitta?" Nikias asked. "I couldn't find her."

"She was angry," said Kolax in a hurt tone. "She wanted to come with me, the crazy girl." His voice was full of admiration, however. Melitta was Kolax's sort of crazy, and the Skythian obviously admired her for it.

Nikias gathered together the nearly one hundred Plataean warriors, and got up on a large rock so that everyone could see him. He stared into the faces of these fellow citizens, all of whom he knew by name—men he had grown up with, men he had fought with against the Thebans and the Spartans and the Megarians, men who had made the long and treacherous journey around the Peloponnese or with him by way of Lydia and Syrakuse to get here, so achingly close to home. They had already been told the plan: they would march to the end of the valley, then walk brazenly into the heart of the Spartan camp and then to the counterwall. "You'll be just like Odysseus and Diomedes sneaking into the Trojan camp," Chusor had told him.

"Brothers," Nikias said to the men, "we are eight miles from our home! But the land that we departed months ago is now occupied by a hated and treacherous enemy, and they have surrounded our beloved citadel with a wooden wall—to cut off Plataea from its allies, to starve our defenders out like trapped animals. Tonight we play Spartans with these red cloaks. . . . Tonight we risk our lives to join our kin inside the walls, to help defend against the coming onslaught. We will all die tonight if this subterfuge does not work. But I hope you die fighting the Spartans—clawing at them with your final breath, like a pankrator who refuses to raise his littlest finger, even in the face of defeat.

"Perikles told me once that the gods honor our deaths in battle more than the deaths of the Spartans, because we, as members of a democracy, have more to lose than they do. I tell you this: they don't hate us for the freedom that we share. Rather, they do not even *comprehend* it. For they are slave masters who are *themselves* the slaves of kings. But we were born and bred in freedom, and freedom will give us the strength of gods!"

The men were silent as they gazed back at him, but he knew that they had been affected by his words. Their faces had become stern and grim as he was speaking, and they now stood up straighter—full of pride. A burning light was in their eyes. He saw Argus of Korkyra grinning back at him. And Kolax beside the giant man—there was a look of feral excitement on his young face. Nikias made the pankrator sign: right hand smashing into left palm, and all of the men repeated this action. They were warriors. *He* was a warrior. Fear had been cast aside like a useless crutch or a bone stripped of meat. They were ready to kill the enemy, or die trying.

"Baklydes," said Nikias as he came down from the rock. "You walk next to me out front." He glanced at the tower and saw two torches raised up and down.

"That's the first signal," said Baklydes. "To let the Hill Tower know that a message is coming from Kreusis. If they're watching up in the tower, they will respond with two torches."

Nikias hadn't even thought that the men in the Hill Tower might not be paying attention. He counted the seconds. Twenty went by before he saw two tiny torch lights moving up and down in response.

"Good," said Baklydes. "They're ready to receive the message."

They didn't wait to see the rest of the exchange between the fort at the cove and the tower on the hill. They marched up a winding path that ran through the olive groves, heading away from the cove and up the valley. Nikias took one last glance at the tower before he entered the heart of the grove and caught a glimpse of more torches being raised and lowered. He wondered if his grandfather would get the message. Would he understand that his grandson was coming home? If he did not receive the message, or interpret the meaning correctly, this all might end in disaster beneath the very walls of Plataea. Because even if they got through the Spartan barricade, they still had to get from the top of the unfinished ramp over the walls. They might be shot down by their own Plataean kin manning the bastions, or trapped by the Spartans—hemmed in against the walls of their own citadel.

But there was no reason to contemplate this desperate gamble. The dice were rattling in the cup. Now he had to make the throw.

SEVENTEEN

———— · ————

Chusor started to panic.

Twenty minutes had passed since Nikias and his hundred warriors had departed the cove, and he could not find his daughter. At first he had looked for her on the *Spear* and the *Briseis*, but Melitta was nowhere to be found. Then he, Diokles, and several of the Serifans lit torches and went through the olive grove near the beach.

He heard Helena calling to him urgently from the ship and ran back to it. She was standing on the prow, holding a lamp and a piece of papyrus. Her face wore an expression of horror. "I found this by her bed!" she said, holding up the papyrus. "A note in Melitta's hand. She's run away. She took her sword, that Nikias gave her—"

"*Run away to where?*" asked Chusor with a stricken voice.

"To Plataea!" she cried. "To stand by Kolax!"

Chusor found Diokles in the grove and grabbed him by the shoulders. "If I don't return with Melitta, you are the captain of the *Spear*. Return to Naupaktos with the *Briseis* and the Athenian triremes."

"Where are you going?" asked Diokles.

"To find my daughter!" Chusor replied.

He ran away from the cove, heading into the dark grove. The path glowed like a long white snake. Chusor had not run in a long time and he was almost immediately short of breath. He used to be a fast runner. Before he became indolent. His lungs burned and he felt an oppressive dread—as if he were being squeezed in the fist of a Titan, as if his legs were made of lead. He uttered a growl of rage and pushed himself through the pain, pumping his arms harder.

He pulled both of his long knives from their sheaths and held them in either hand to keep the sheaths from slapping against his legs as he ran. He banished all thoughts from his mind, save one: Keep running.

Soon all that he could hear was the sound of his own harsh breathing. . . .

Prince Arkilokus lay on the pallet in his tent, arms wrapped around his young lover—a gift from the Persian siege master Darius the City-Killer. The pretty teenager's name was Jishti, and making love with him was one of the only diverting things that Arkilokus had found to do in the Oxlands. It was still some time before dawn; they had spent several hours engaged in love play, but Arkilokus was far from satiated.

He sipped a little wine and held the cup to Jishti's beardless lips. Some wine spilled and Arkilokus kissed it off his lover's mouth, causing the lad to giggle. Arkilokus knew that Jishti had been given to him by the City-Killer to spy on him—so that the Persian could know what was going on in the Spartan camp. But Arkilokus didn't care. He had no secrets to keep from the Persians. They both had the same objective: to bring Plataea to its knees.

Arkilokus's tent was set up near the barricade by the Plataean cemetery. The Persian Fort would have been a much more pleasant place to bivouac, since it was so sheltered from the damnable winds that blew crazily across the valley and up the slope; but the Plataeans had poisoned the wells there, and so they had been forced to set up the main camp on this miserable spot just west of the citadel. The City-Killer, who had arrived in the Oxlands soon after Arkilokus returned from Megaria, made his base in Thebes and rode the eight miles to Plataea every day to inspect the counterwall and the construction of the earthen ramp.

"I have half a mind to take you back to Sparta with me when all of this is done," said Arkilokus, kissing Jishti on the forehead. The teen's skin was wet and salty from his exertions. The lamplight showed a pretty, smooth face grinning back at him.

"I will go wherever you ask, my lord," said Jishti in his flawless Greek. "I will serve you in all things." He reached down and took Arkilokus in his slender hand and started to stroke him teasingly. "Night and day."

Arkilokus heard the sound of men approaching the tent—voices arguing heatedly. He pushed Jishti's hand away and listened intently.

"I tell you, he's in there, General!"

"I'll see for myself!"

Suddenly men with torches burst into the tent and ripped back the curtain surrounding the prince's pallet. Arkilokus sat up and reached for the knife that he kept close by. A burning torch was thrust toward his face and Jishti shrieked. Arkilokus recognized two of his personal bodyguards grasping the arms of a warrior wearing Megarian armor. A grizzled Spartan general named Kalkas was there, too, as well as the general's attendant.

"See! There he is!" said one of Arkilokus's bodyguards. "The prince has not left the tent all night!"

"What is this?" Arkilokus demanded imperiously. "How dare you come—"

"An imposter," cut in Kalkas, his eyes growing wide with mounting surprise. "There's an imposter in the camp." He rushed from the tent, followed by his attendant, shouting the alarm at the top of his lungs. A few seconds later the noise of salpinx war trumpets blared and were answered almost immediately on the farthest side of the counterwall, two miles away.

Arkilokus leapt up and grabbed the Megarian by the hair. "Speak! What is going on?"

"I was guarding the western picket," said the Megarian quickly, "where it blocks off the entrance to the valley that leads to Kreusis. And a man who looked like you came up the valley, leading a host of Spartans. My commander was cowed by him and let him through the picket and into the camp, but I said there was something wrong about you—about that *man*, I mean. You see, I had been near you once before up close. And the man who came to the picket seemed younger than you and he had a scar by his left eye. But my commander wouldn't believe me—said I was crazy—because the man who claimed to be you was also missing his signet ring finger from his right hand, just like you. So I ran here to tell General Kalkas!"

Arkilokus shoved the Megarian aside and grabbed his sword. "Follow me," he said to his bodyguard as he rushed from the tent.

Nikias had just stepped up to the closed gates built into the counterwall when he heard the trumpets blaring from the Spartan camp two hundred yards away. Until now everything had gone perfectly. He and his men had sauntered right through the heart of the Megarian part of the camp and up to the wooden barricade without a hindrance. It had all gone so smoothly that Nikias heard Baklydes, at one point, stifle a laugh when some sleeping Megarians leapt to their feet and bowed deferentially upon seeing the "Spartan prince" approach.

But his old friend wasn't laughing now. The ten men guarding the gates gripped their spears in both hands and turned toward the horns. "What's going on?" one of them asked. A split second later other horns started answering from all around the barricade.

Nikias pulled out his sword and bellowed, "Attack!" and cut down the guard nearest to him. The other Plataeans fell on the guards with ferocity, slaying the surprised men. But a few of them screamed for help before they died, alerting warriors in the distance.

Nikias grabbed the giant log barring the gate and started to heave desperately. Ten men, including Argus, came to his aid. They lifted the log together and tossed it aside, then pushed open the wooden gates. The walls of Plataea, black against the starlit sky, loomed ahead, a hundred and fifty yards away.

"Run!" Nikias yelled, urging the men through the gate. "Run for the ramp! The earthen ramp!"

He stared back into the darkness toward the enemy camp and saw fires kindling to life everywhere. And now disembodied torches, evidently drawn by the guards' death cries, were heading toward the gates at the barricade. The Plataeans streamed through the opening, sprinting for the earthen ramp, calling out, "Plataea!" Some were already scrambling up the mound of dirt.

Nikias glanced at the wall above the ramp. He thought he saw the shapes of ladders lowered over the sides of the walls above the ramp—or was that a trick of his mind? He waited until the last Plataean was through the barricade gate, then turned to follow. But the sound of footsteps behind made him stop and whirl around.

A huge shape came hurtling from the darkness and Nikias stepped forward to cut the man down, but stopped short his sweeping blow and stumbled forward, thrown off balance.

"Chusor! What are you doing here?"

Chusor was breathing so hard he couldn't talk. He looked around, wild-eyed, and sheathed two blood-smeared daggers. Arrows whistled from the dark and hit the wooden wall behind them. Chusor grabbed Nikias and pulled him through the opening.

They ran.

"Nikias! Nikias!" cried a voice, shrill with rage.

Nikias knew that voice screaming his name. It was Prince Arkilokus. He glanced over his shoulder and saw a horde of men pouring through the gates. Hundreds of them, clad in armor and bearing spears and torches. Arkilokus was out front, naked and holding a sword.

Nikias looked back toward the ramp—his men at the top were climbing ladders and leaping over the wall. His grandfather had gotten the message from the tower! Half of them were over and safely behind the walls when he and Chusor reached the man-made slope.

An arrow buzzed past his ear. Then something struck him in the back of the leg. He knew he'd been hit by an arrow, but all he'd felt was something hard, like the kick of an ox. But it knocked his leg out from under him just the same, and he fell face-first into the dirt.

"Help!" Chusor cried. "Help me with Nikias!"

Argus came barreling back down the earthen ramp with Baklydes at his side. They grabbed Nikias under either arm, pulled him to his feet, and started dragging him up the steep incline.

"No!" shouted Nikias. "We must hold off the Spartans so the others can get over the wall!"

Ten or so Plataeans, hearing his voice, came back down the ramp and together they made a line of red-cloaked men—a thin wall of flesh to thwart the army of Spartans running toward them like a tidal wave of iron.

Nikias twisted his torso around, reached down, and snapped off the feathered end of the arrow protruding from the back of his leg, then slammed the broken end with the flat of his palm. The arrowhead popped out the front of his thigh and Nikias screamed.

"Here!" said Chusor. He gripped the arrow below the head, yanking it out and tossing it on the ground.

The burst of pain this action caused sent a shock wave through Nikias's body—like plunging into freezing water or getting punched in the nose. Every muscle in his body was tensed, ready to deal death.

The throng of Spartans—now a thousand strong—began screaming as one. It was a bone-chilling cry that made Nikias suck in his breath. He gripped his sword, then glanced at Chusor, who took a long, deep breath like a diver coming to the surface, then calmly raised his knives. Why had his friend come back? There was no time to ask. He would never know the answer.

The Spartans were a hundred feet away when Nikias cried out, "Kallisto!"—the name of his beloved wife bursting from his lips like a prayer . . . a dead man's final word.

And as if in response, a rapid and staggered thumping sounded from the walls above—a sound akin to the beating of a hundred drums that raced the length of the bastion. The Spartans out in front of the pack fell in a broad swath, as though they were barley that had been reaped by a great invisible scythe, tripping the men behind them. A split second later another wave of arrows rained down, and many more Spartans fell.

Archers on the walls—hundreds of them! Shooting with deadly accuracy.

The Spartans had been roused from sleep. Only a few wore complete armor. None had brought shields. They fell back, surrounding their prince, forcing the raving warrior, blinded by bloodlust, to go back to the safety of the barricade.

"Nikias!" screamed Arkilokus. "Come back!"

Baklydes and Argus half carried, half dragged the wounded Nikias to the top of the ramp and hefted him up a ladder. He scaled it as fast as a wall lizard despite the arrow wound in his leg.

"Haul him over!"

Many hands grabbed Nikias and pulled him over the parapet and onto the stone walkway, heaving him out of the way to make room for the others—Argus, Baklydes, and last of all Chusor, who was calling out the name of his daughter— calling desperately as though he had lost his mind. But neither Kolax nor Melitta answered him from the crowd gathered on the wall.

Nikias lay with his back against the rough limestone for a long time, breathing hard, his brain swimming from loss of blood, his leg burning from the arrow wound. Men with torches ran to and fro along the wide parapet. The air was filled with cries, the thumping of bowstrings, and the clash of arms. He could hear his grandfather barking out orders nearby, but he couldn't see him in the darkness. And then an archer ran to Nikias and knelt by his side. A slender hand reached out and touched his face, and he knew who it was in an instant.

"We got the message from the Tower Hill and—"

"Our child?" Nikias interrupted, seizing his wife's hand.

"*He* is well," answered Kallisto.

Nikias's heart swelled. "A *boy*."

There was a slight pause—then Kallisto asked, "And . . . the girls?" Her voice was hopeful, yet full of fear.

Before he could reply, the men along the wall cried out in unison—in triumph. "The enemy has fled back to their counterwall!" shouted a voice. Once the din had died down, Nikias said, "Our daughters are safe in the Parnes Mountains," and kissed her hand.

Menesarkus appeared behind Kallisto bearing a torch. Nikias saw his grandfather's face illuminated by the blaze of light, a wide smile spreading across his leonine face as he gazed down at him.

"Welcome home, warrior of Plataea," said the Arkon. "Welcome home, Grandson."